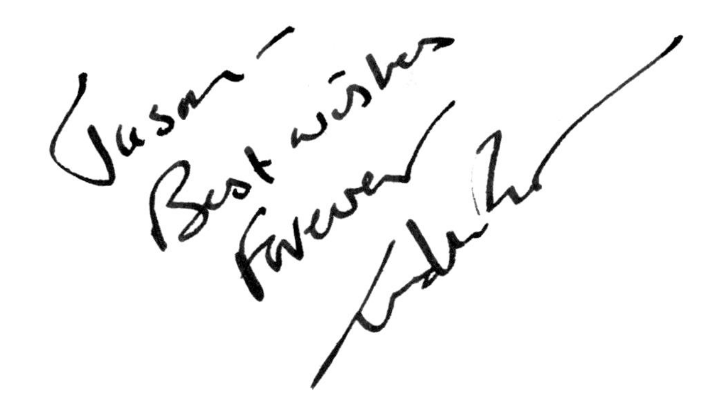

Forever Man

Forever Man

George Michael Greider

Pennycorner Press
First Edition
Gilman, Connecticut
1995

Library of Congress Catalog Card Number: 94-74974

Greider, George Michael, 1944-
Forever man / George Michael Greider. -- 1st ed.
p. cm.
ISBN 1-886559-73-2
I Title
PS3557.R4367F67 1995
813' .54 - - dc.20 94-74974
CIP

First Edition
Published by Pennycorner Press

For Frankie

with unending gratitude to Gayle,
Eric, and Nancy

In the middle of the journey of life, I found myself in a dark wood having lost the true path.

D. Alighieri

Forever Man

One

When the third attempt at second-round financing fell through, we all treated it like any of the other crises of the previous four-and-a-half years. It was critical, somehow, without being serious. Jonathan smiled his tight little horizontal smile; Carol said something affirmative that sounded flat. Then she and Jonathan went out for a run and I spent the next three hours making our dbase system sing and dance.

The next day was business as usual until the end of the day when, about five-thirty, Jonathan came to the door of my office and gave me the basic 75-watt, I'm-fond-of-you smile and said, "Can I talk to you?"

I welcomed him. He entered, closing the door.

"This is heavy," he said.

His smile reverted to the placid ministerial half-smile he will wear in his coffin. He sat down.

"The Board has decided to liquidate the company."

Well, I have had better days in Aprils past. There was, for example, one 15th when I put a wood chisel into my hand after learning that I owed the IRS a month's salary by midnight.

The corporate dismemberment was not exactly dispassionate. But, in the end, failure is an orphan and the funeral was lightly attended. In the process, several principals felt freed thereby to pronounce unilaterally on the failures of others.

I had one final Andy-and-the-Judge session with Jonathan whereat he said he was sure I would find many interesting opportunities available to me. This readily proved to be the last of the grossly unfounded assurances he gave me.

The bloom was a long way off the Massachusetts Miracle. My preliminary investigation of the "many interesting opportunities" hypothesis indicated there was slight demand for executives experienced in business failures.

The real estate market had hit the wall of greed beyond which there were no buyers. The weekend seminars at suburban Holiday Inns on investing in Boston real estate had long ago been canceled. Even the doctors and dentists were wising up.

I probably could have sold my 750-square-foot Back Bay condo and netted about two months' living expenses, provided I left town. That just seemed so damned little for what the last six years had cost me personally. I refused to leave. I refused to give up. I was determined to make a life for myself from these ashes and cinders and not run again. I had too many dead-end stories about leaving a long list of cities, and the stories did not seem to be getting better.

By late May, the air in my bank account was getting thin. I got a check for seven thousand dollars and some change at the corporation's summary execution. On my way out the door after a round robin of waivers and quit claim signings, a now erstwhile board member, either underestimating my ambitions or accurately guessing my finances, stopped me. His name was Ken Sedgwick and his banking firm, Sedgwick, Baxter was looking for a computer consultant. He remembered I was "always the one with the computer programs." It does not have to make sense if a board member says it; even directors of defunct corporations can be presumed to speak for the Deity.

∞

I called the man-in-charge at Sedgwick, Baxter, who appeared to be having a world class bad day. Six-and-a-half-seconds into my intro, he broke in yelling, "Wait a minute; this is my project! Why is a senior partner sending some hot shit outsider in on this?!? Who are you?!"

"Mr. Shell, if you'll take a deep breath, exhale slowly and listen to me, I'll tell you."

"Go," he said, "you've got 60 seconds."

So, the One-Minute Manager meets the Sixty-Minute Man. I decided to say nothing for a breath count of ten; nothing fries these pre-cardiac types like silence. By seven, he was on-line again.

"C'mon, c'mon."

"If I could guarantee to finish your project on schedule, would you give me 20 minutes of your time?" I am sure my soul shriveled down to the last one percent of its substance, but, as Faust promised, it worked.

"Tuesday, two o'clock," he said, and hung up before I could nauseate myself further.

∞

As you would figure, someone that out of control was over his head. Harry Shell was a man whose ambition had vastly exceeded his abilities. This type is a miserable bastard to work for, but to a consultant, he is USDA prime luncheon loaf.

He ranted for 15 minutes without saying anything factual or useful, but it must have made him feel better because when he ran down and stared at me, he endured my silence for almost a full 30 seconds.

"Well," he said, with no rising inflection but making it a question anyway.

"Well," I said, "you need to install an integrated, computer-based information management system here before the end of the third quarter and I can do it."

∞

He loosened up enough to actually answer my questions, in his own way. Every reply was liberally decorated with self-aggrandizements and set about with defensive explanations about how he was not responsible for getting where he was now, which was nowhere and desperate. Although it was a straight-forward project from a systems standpoint, he was in trouble with it, had an impossible (for him) deadline and was not listed on the stationery as a partner. My only question was how much of the partners' cash he had left to spend.

Because he had basically accomplished nothing trying to do it himself, I guessed the answer was: " a good deal."

I have a triangular theory relating time, money and information. In any situation, there is an inverse zero-sum relationship among them. If you are short on one, it's going to take more of the other two. He was short of time, I had the information necessary to do the job, so it was going to cost him enough money to be interesting.

In another 15 minutes, I had enough from him to adjourn to a vacant office and, amid someone's unread *Wall Street Journals*, accumulated mail and pink Ampad messages, wrote a three-page project description, a one-page project management schedule and a budget. In less than three months, I planned to spend about $300,000 of the firm's money; peanuts to them if I guessed their billings (or, as I managed to misspell it once, bilkings) correctly, but it made old Harry pale. That's how I knew I had the numbers about right.

∞

Harry surprised me by calling the next day before I had gotten too far into the funk of the unengaged to be uncivil. He asked if I could get started that afternoon. He sounded almost polite.

The next several weeks began an intense flurry of evaluating and buying some proprietary applications packages and hiring the right systems consultants to customize them and train the staff. Harry bitched about all the costs, but his whatdayacallit was on the block and I was his only hope to save his shot at partner, the house in Brookline and his ever-precarious self-respect.

We bought a package called COM+3 from a group named Teamwork Systems in San Francisco. It can communicate with virtually any software application or data base management system and is not tied to any hardware. Two local jocks had done most of the basic design work and we got them to modify input/output formats to my systems analysis of the firm's operations.

Word processing, personnel and accounting were easy, but we ran into a headache in the Trusts and Estates department. His name was Ralph; Ralph Stonington Adams Baxter... the Third. He was an ancient headache and a pompous and incompetent one.

In any organizational change there will be points of resistance and difficulty. I had anticipated little at Sedgwick, Baxter because of my Sedgwick connection and because I knew how well paid and professionally secure their people were, for the most part. Having encountered Harry I might have been more cautious, but Harry's temperament rose and fell with his perception of the status and usefulness of the person before him, which is pretty much standard operating practice in upwardly servile corporate America. So, I assumed he was only a slight anomaly. S, B had the reputation for being a Shangri-La in the hostile Himalayas of the Beantown banking profession.

The partners in the eighteenth and nineteenth centuries had invested substantial undistributed earnings and their managed trust accounts so as to create a good-sized small merchant bank and trading house with an impressive array of worldwide assets. The twentieth century partners had avoided all the available economic disasters so far. The firm had even done exceptionally well, under varying management strategies, in the bull markets of the twenties, sixties and eighties.

They had not lost any money on World War II either. A great deal of their WWII-era profits grew out of a corresponding relationship with a similar hybrid organization in Switzerland, Boehrkopf Frères, established after bargain hunting by both firms in Europe and the Far East in the thirties led them to each other.

Ralph Stonington Adams Baxter... the Third had been the vehicle of this encounter.

Shakespeare wrote that FDR line about "born to greatness....had greatness thrust upon...etc." Ralph Stonington Adams Baxter... the Third, a lifelong incompetent jerk, was propelled to something approaching a bit part in greatness for one brief shining, etc. by the simple accident of birth coupled with coincidence and a twist in U.S. banking law. This intersection was driven, although I was a long way from knowing it at the time, by a deep and frightening intrigue.

∞

Ralph was not a partner in the firm. Whatever talent his progenitors had had, and the firm's rich oral and meager written history said it was great, had been bred out by the time Ralph incorporated the name. Through a deft series of lateral arabesques, all financial and investment responsibilities had been excised from his purview. However, he ran an efficient bookkeeping operation for what appeared to be an active and substantial Trusts and Estates department.

He did so with a unique and complex card file system that was absolutely state-of-the-art in 1870 when it was designed by an MIT professor and which only Ralph Stonington Adams Baxter... the Third truly understood.

He was determined not to give up anything without a fight. He thought he knew two things that I didn't: one, that this was just another ephemeral attack on his perfect system that had withstood attempts uncounted in the past and which would be abandoned like all the rest if he just held out long enough to wreck the project (and Harry Shell's career); and two, that the card system held unique data.

I knew two things he didn't. I already had access to all the asset information from Planning and Investments, and I already had all the fund transfer and payment records from Accounting. In theory, I could already construct a new operating system for Trusts and Estates without talking to him or any of his people, but I started out trying to do it the friendly way.

Getting to my first working meeting with him was inauspiciously difficult due to an apparently unconnected variety of small vexations. It was postponed once by him, then delayed again when the building was evacuated for an afternoon because of a power failure. Next, I was called to a command performance to "report on progress" at a "Partners' Lunch". Our copy machine broke down as I was preparing for the sit-down with Ralph, leaving me with no extra copies of my presentation should he bring a staff of thousands. The unannounced staff tactic is a hoary military technique for gaining control of a meeting. Not only does the other party have unexpected reinforcements, but you lose the agenda waiting while some determinedly slow member of his gang burns enough copies. Someone raises an extraneous issue while you all sit there, then someone else changes the subject, a long-standing unresolvable argument of no relevance is raised and the papers once delivered are found to be collated backwards. In trained hands, this is almost always lethal.

But he was alone, insofar as anyone so full of himself can be alone and I took the first step into Forever.

∞

Ralph Stonington Adams Baxter... the Third had an unfortunate face. It reflected the general state of his health and intellect by being slack, pale and puffy. A small cascade of chins fell from a tight little downturned mouth. Indeed the only tension or life in his body was that tightly drawn pursing of his lips and the frantic darting of his eyes.

"Who are you?" he began, in surprisingly good voice. I guess I had expected one of Mel Blanc's voices to proceed from this character—Elmer Fudd or Porky. I had not expected the question. Was he feebleminded, an early-stage Alzheimer's?

"I'm Phillip Gardiner, Mr. Baxter. We had an appointment. About the data processing conversion? We spoke on the phone?"

I was running down and not seeing any signs of recognition. His eyes bounced from the wall behind my right ear, to my tie, to his anally rectilinear desktop, back to the wall.

"Yes, but who are you? Where did you come from? What is your background?"

"I am your three o'clock appointment. My name is Phillip Gardiner. I came from my office. What exactly about my background do you wish to know?"

"Do not get shirty with me, Mr. Gardiner. The impulse to modernize, as it is called, which is now sweeping this firm, shall not be an occasion for our opening records of the most deeply personal nature, concerning some of the oldest and best families of this Republic, to the kind of easy electronic access you are pushing. The trust placed in this firm, and in me, to manage and maintain in confidence, is not going to be modernized away. I shouldn't wonder if your family background has not prepared you for an appreciation of such trust and confidence. I understand you attended a state university."

Amazing, I thought. As a guy named Clem, with whom I worked on an assembly line one summer break, used to say, just fucking amazing.

"Mr. Baxter," I said, sitting down, uninvited, across the desk from him in the only chair in the room—a low one, as you might expect—"I understand your concern about record security and I have here an outline of the file access and security structures that we are building into the Sedgwick, Baxter systems."

His eyes were following an invisible pelota around the room, but avoided the paper I slid across the leather writing pad.

"These key and code access measures have been reviewed and approved by electronic security committees of both the American Bar Association and the American Banking Association. We would probably find that, in addition to being easier and faster and more accurate to use, this new system will actually improve security here."

"Oh, I doubt that, Mr. Gardiner. I truly do," he replied and then wagged his lower jaw up and out several times. It looked like a cross between a yoga exercise my ex-wife Jayne used to do to firm her jaw line and the way a smug three year old will taunt a vanquished opponent just before saying 'Nyah, Nyah'. I am not sure how he developed this tick, but I tentatively concluded that it was the outgrowth of several failed attempts at learning how to smile.

We went on in this vein for the rest of the hour that he evidently felt propriety, my status or his schedule required. I was in there pitching for the task at hand. He bounced around the Jai Lai court in his head, interjecting platitudes, potential problems and personally invidious comparisons of our differing perspectives, values and histories.

You can run off three and a half yards of that kind of dialogue and cut it to suit you. I have mercifully forgotten most of what we both said, but we ended with what I took as an agreement.

"If you will give me just one of your no longer active files, I will work up a demonstration of how the system will work for you and show you how secure and trustworthy it will be."

"Very well, Mr. Gardiner, we shall see."

∞

I love the summer light in Boston. I had deck rights on the building's common roof planking which was always smeared with yuppoids in the evening. But in the mornings when I would wake up before five, I could sit up there alone with my Optimus mountain stove and brew cups of the blackest tea sold on Charles Street and read whatever book or magazines I was working on until the *Globe* arrived around six. The *Globe* would usually last until the red-eye from L.A. blew over on its way into Logan just before seven. By that time, the madding crowd would be winding up downstairs and on the street, and I would be cranked and centered enough to join it.

All through a day that would start like that, sometimes for days after, and even now, the color of that aqueous yellow light shading into the lightest, sheerest silver would be with me.

Boston

At night when I walked home between seven and eight, the yellow would be back in the light, but bloodied by the injuries of the day to a high-carat gold. The extreme angle of the setting sun would strike through the buildings as it will through a forest and pick out and spotlight the most common details of the city and glorify them.

Commonwealth Avenue would seem like a movie set, overlit, over-real, on the days around the solstice when the street and the sun aligned in the evening.

I walked down Commonwealth that night, occasionally enjoying the sunlight shining through a backlit summer cotton dress, mostly on auto-pilot, planning dinner, avoiding the dog shit. As I got near my building, I saw fire trucks and flashing red lights which I hurriedly learned had converged on the building next door. This was better than having them swinging axes and emptying hoses around 224B but only just. In addition to whatever collateral damage they or the fire might be doing to the Bank of Boston's (and my) condo, there was the immediately inconvenient fact that I could not get in.

It actually looked like a semi-serious fire had hit the top floor at 224. One window and frame were broken and black with soot, with scorch marks on the stone lintel. As urban disasters go, it was not much of a spectacle and it got less interesting as time went on and the bureaucracy of public safety continued to keep us out of the building. My cat, Camille, wandered up at some point and thudded her head against my right shin.

I am always amazed to find her alive. She is an absolutely average-sized, declawed twelve-year-old female who will absolutely not tolerate any other cat nor most dogs. By this, I mean that she actively threatens or attacks every cat and most dogs she sees. When we first moved here, I thought for a while that she only did it when I was around, thinking I was an omnipotent protector, big brother, secret weapon. But then, after a couple of weeks, I saw her through the window drive something that looked like a dingo off the sidewalk and almost directly under the wheels of a furniture truck.

As I said, I am always amazed to find her alive, but she never shows a scratch.

She likes to sit on my shoulders, and as stupid as it must look, I mostly accommodate her when I'm home in order to keep work and reading surfaces free and to avoid being tripped. She was starting to bruise my ankle so I picked her up and set her on my shoulders as the people in the funny costumes milled around and the over-amped police and fire radios squawked unintelligible signals. At about the same time, I felt someone approach on my left and heard the fast little slap-click of a single lens reflex camera.

"Hi, what's your name?" a red-headed young woman in pigtails asked, like she was at a sorority mixer and going for the pledge class congeniality award.

It took me a while to turn without throwing the cat, maybe a nanosecond. It took longer to assimilate the Becky Thatcher act with the Nikon.

"Who," I said, "are you?"

"Clio Murphy, *Boston Globe*." She flashed me a business card just long enough for me to read the '*Boston Globe*' and be substantially sure that none of the other words said anything like 'Clio Murphy'.

"Phillip Gardiner."

We shook hands and she pulled out a spiral pocket notebook.

"One 'l' or two?"

"Two, but why are you writing this down?"

"For the caption."

"What caption?"

"How do you spell Gardiner?"

"What caption?"

She looked at me with the tolerant smile bright people reserve for others they temporarily outsmart.

"In the *Globe*, you know. What's your cat's name?"

"Ask her."

"C'mon, what is it really?"

The fire drill was showing no signs of letting me get into my apartment.

"If I tell you her name, you have to tell me how a Boston Irish lass got a name out of Greek mythology."

"Okay. What's her name?"

"Camille."

"How's that spelled?"

"Two 'l's' just like Phillip; now what about Clio?"

"I don't know. Mom said it was my father's idea, but they split up when I was eight."

"You never asked him? He never said?"

"No."

I shuddered, thinking of the regressions and permutations of my given and family names that twined through the dusty generations of family bibles, graveyards and my sister's expert genealogies.

With no announcement the police and fire people began reassembling their tools and toys, getting back in the cars and trucks and beginning the apparently impossible task of clearing the street. A yellow "Police Line–Keep Out" tape snapped in front of me and I could finally walk to my apartment.

"So long, Scoop," I said, "Good luck."

∞

The next morning I retracted my benevolence. On page three of the Metro section, top dead center was my stupid profile with the cat draped around it, both of us looking upward and to the left. "Phillip Gardner and his cat, Camille, watch as his apartment burns in Back Bay Tuesday night."

I sniffed the air and caught a whiff of the sharp wet smoke and ash from next door. I closed my eyes and rubbed my face. The smell went away, but the photo and caption were still there. Below it read "Photo: C. Murphy."

∞

That day at the office was predictable. Lots of sympathy and offers to help which turned to embarrassment as I repeated the facts. Ralph Stonington Adams Baxter... the Third did not deliver any files and neither took nor returned any calls.

In the afternoon, Petra called.

"How are you?" She had an intensity in her voice that I always respond to.

"I'm fine. It wasn't my apartment. The paper got it wrong. How did you find me?"

"I called Jonathan. He was working at home today. (Today and everyday, I thought.)

"He said you were consulting at S, B."

"I am."

"What else are you doing?"

I thought of things to say, all wrong.

"I don't know, not much."

"What are you reading?"

"Look," I said, "I can't do this. I can't have a normal conversation with you and just pretend we have no history. I am horrified that I thought you were the greatest thing in the world—greater than the greatest thing in the world—and then found out we couldn't manage to live together. I blew apart everyone's life, destroyed myself with Jayne, lost my house, got one dime away from the monkey ward, and then failed to make anything out of it with you. If you would like to have a deep, drunken, heartfelt encounter ending in bed or a bitter argument, I'm your man, but let's not start about books."

"You ought to talk to someone."

"I thought I was talking to you."

"I mean someone professional."

"Bartenders count?"

Medium pause.

"I am glad your apartment wasn't burned. I am sorry we can't talk without your being so painful or so glib. I am sorry we're not friends anymore."

"Me, too," I said defeated. "Thanks for calling."

"Thank you," she said, and hung up.

That was bad enough, but what had happened to my marriage and afterwards with Petra was my own doing. So, even though I didn't understand why I did what I did, they were my choices and I figured I pretty much deserved whatever proceeded from them.

Ackley's phone call was not deserved. I have always said that no one deserves an Ackley in his life and that I have done everything in my power to attempt to evade him since fate and the Headmaster's office installed us both in the same room.

He called me at the apartment that night.

"Gard-i-ner, old man, so good to find you home and one hopes uninjured."

"Ackley, you ass, where are you calling from?"

"Here in the Hub, old Li-on, here in the Hub. Harbor Towers actually. More to the point, what is your situation? Do you need a place to stay? I've called a few of the old boys and we're getting household goods together from attics and cellars to help you refurnish and one or two fellows are throwing in some money, anonymously of course, just to help until insurance and things get you back to normal. And... "

"Ackley, it wasn't my apartment. The fire was next door. The paper got it wrong."

"Oh."

"I don't need any household goods and I certainly don't want anyone's money."

"Oh, how embarrassing."

"Yes, it certainly is embarrassing to find you've

been soliciting charity for me. Now you'll have to call the alumni association back and tell them I'm not in need of handouts."

"Oh, I couldn't do that. Why don't you just take the donations and keep quiet?"

"Ackley, think for a minute. Even if I were that needy or greedy or amoral, there was no fire here, anyone dropping off rummage goods could see that. Call off your eleemosynary hordes or you'll get us both in trouble when the *Globe* prints the retraction in tomorrow's paper."

"Oh, well, I was only trying to help."

"I believe I have been asking you for nearly thirty years to stop trying to help me."

"Well, don't get pissy, old Leon." Again, he pronounced my middle name Lion, knowing I hated it.

I said nothing.

"Well, I guess I'll hang up."

"On the evidence, your best idea so far today."

"Good-bye."

"Good-bye, Ackley."

∞

I called the *Globe* and asked for the night editor and was told there was no such thing. The Metro section editor also only worked days.

"Look, what if I had some great pictures I just took at a fire in town an hour ago—who would I talk to about giving them to the *Globe*?"

"Giving them?"

"Yeah, who?"

"Just a minute."

Musical hold. I hate musical hold.

"This is Mike Mullusco, can I help you?"

"Hi. Are you the guy that would buy photos from free lancers?"

"Yeah, maybe, whatta you got?"

"Did you buy the photo of the guy with the cat that was in this morning's Metro section?"

"Who wants to know?"

"Me, I'm the guy. I want to get in touch with the photographer, Murphy. I want a print."

"The paper will sell you a print. Call back tomorrow and ask for the photo department. She doesn't own it anymore; we do."

"Wait a minute. She took other shots. I want one you didn't take. Of the cat."

"We don't give out reporters' or stringers' home numbers. Give me your name and number. I'll let her know you called. Maybe she'll get back to you."

"Look, the photo credit shows she's free-lance, so we both know she's not covered by your policy. In addition, she got the facts wrong enough that I ought to press for a retraction and if you deal with her regularly, I wouldn't be surprised if it was your business card she's flashing as a press credential. Now all I'm trying to do here is get a picture of my cat. Give me a break and I'll leave you and the paper alone."

"Hold on... it's C-L-I-O M-U-R-P-H-Y... 436-5375."

He hung up before I said thanks.

∞

I called her number, but got a machine that played a recording inviting me, in a relentlessly cheery voice, to leave a message, but then disconnected before I could.

The next day was a light replay of the day before. The clerical staff evidently reads the morning paper in the evening, so once again the sympathy flowed and the embarrassment ebbed.

Ralph Stonington Adams Baxter... the Third once again avoided me all morning. I learned that the *Globe* had little interest in nor inclination toward printing a retraction and that a print of me and the cat would cost fifteen dollars. I declined.

At least Ackley and Petra didn't call and I resisted calling her. I am always churned up for days after talking with her. It was that way before we began sleeping together and it's like that now that we have stopped. Living with her was a firestorm of emotions. And I want to see her again and talk about everything and hold her and all of the rest. The physical memories of our times together lash me, before the physicality took over, we had such an emotional kinship. We seemed to react to people and situations identically. Like a twin she was to me. And, of course, she was my wife's best friend.

Tell me who do you love.

In the afternoon, an inter-office envelope showed up with an inch-and-a-half thick folder of paper from Trusts and Estates. And I swallowed my surprise and submerged as best I could self and my memories in the minutiae of the lifelong accounts of one Mary Stebbins Clark, late of Duxbury, Mass., who shuffled off this old mortal helix in Lausanne, Switzerland a year and a half ago.

A copy of her death certificate was stapled to the inside cover of the file and the material within was in approximately reverse chronological order. At the end of the day I had learned that she was supported all her life by holdings inherited from her aunt who reared her and was her guardian. She never married and apparently divided her time between her Duxbury address and Lausanne, where she stayed in an apartment also inherited from the aunt. She must have been a shade eccentric, as she apparently never took airplanes, but made her Atlantic crossings on the few remaining dowager luxury liners. Old Ralph, etc., etc.... the Third would have, doubtless, found my prurience a further sign of my unsuitedness to be viewing these sacred documents, but

I was mostly just scanning them for type of information and implicit structure. I paid slight attention to the contents at the time. The structure was total chaos. There seemed to be no standard formats to the system. I expected annual statements of account activity, earnings from listed investments, payments to listed vendors and lenders. This was a mare's nest of receipts, letters of instruction, copies of bills, tax forms, little pieces of everything, but no order. By the time I ran out of heart for the task, it was after seven and I was finding myself simply trying to put together small patterns in the late Ms. Clark's life, merely to impose some slight sense of order—clearly a dead end.

∞

When I got home, I called Clio Murphy. She answered with a hiccup.

"Hell-op."

"Ms. Murphy, this is Phillip Gardiner. You took my picture with my cat."

She broke into a wail.

"Yooou. You called the *Globe*. You cost me the *Globe*. They dropped me." 'Me' trailed off in a more controlled wail.

"Ms. Murphy, I am terribly sorry! Please forgive me.

Dead air.

"I am very sorry. Let me buy you dinner tonight—you choose—make it expensive—make me pay. You tell me what happened and I'll try to figure out a way to make it better."

"Why did you call me?"

"I wanted to talk to you, now can I? I'll start with an apology, but you should take me up on the dinner. Besides, I might be able to help."

"Op-Kay."

"Okay?"

"Okay."

The dialogue was running down.

"Can you meet me in the Copley Plaza bar in forty-five minutes?"

"I could."

A small improvement.

"Let me apologize to you. Please. Let me try to help."

"Well..."

"Good, I'll see you then. I won't be wearing a tortoiseshell cat."

She laughed, a big improvement.

∞

The Copley Plaza bar is truly one of the western world's compensations for the slings and arrows. Huge brass cauldrons hold massive robust ferns high over age-darkened hardwood furnishings. Brass rails and brocade drapes define a space that is a specific for the quotidian.

I got there in ten minutes and chose a seat in the far corner where I could watch the length of the room.

She was right on time—a product of Catholic schools, no doubt, always doing what was asked of her even if it was short notice and inconvenient.

I was surprised when I finally recognized her though she had walked nearly halfway across the room towards me. She wore a deep green, spaghetti-strapped, silk cocktail dress that was a bit past the evening's requirements. Her auburn hair was loose and curly around pale, lightly freckled shoulders. She walked with a delicious mix of awkwardness and possession. Not unexpectedly, lust reared its lovely head.

"Ms. Murphy, thank you for coming and please accept my apologies. I didn't think you would come."

"Me either."

"You look great."

"I'm over-dressed and call me Clio."

She sat down and gave me a smile I can only call game. Her eyes were good, steady. She might be many things—unconvinced, unhappy, unsure, or too young for me—but she wasn't scared.

"For the record, I am sorry I got you in trouble with the *Globe*."

"No, I screwed up. I got the facts wrong."

She had a strong way of looking at me—deep green eyes alive with a kind of yellow or gold near the iris. I seemed to stare forever. They seemed to get bigger.

The waiter broke the moment.

"What may I get you this evening?"

No ersatz *gemütlichkeit*, pure function; he was in his thirties; neither an aspiring actor nor a marginal Emerson College student, just a good waiter. I looked at her and saw uncertainty. Well, if there is anything I am good at, it's ordering drinks.

"May we see your wine list, please; and I'd like a Jack Daniel's and soda, no ice."

"Very good, sir."

After passing fifteen thousand days, I admire being called sir. I've used the word so much in my life. It always felt like an IRA, a remote investment; it is nice to see it pay off.

I ordered her a glass of white Bordeaux while we worked on the prelims. I followed my apology by repeating my promise to make it up to her. She was skeptical, but I really did have an idea. And I was sorry.

We talked about externalities. She worked for an ad agency during the day. She had sold two other things to the *Globe*, done publicity stills for a local band I had actually heard of and had twelve photos in a Greenpeace/Clamshell Alliance Environment Exhibit. I told her of my intermittent, but long-standing involvement with photography. We agreed on dinner at Allegro's.

∞

As we were served our trendy vegetable salads, I told her my idea.

"Let's do a book of photos. I'll tell you where to find them. You take them. We both edit; I publish it. We both can sell it directly to local book stores and split the profits."

"You tell me where to find them?"

"Yep. I have an absolutely great idea for a photo book plus hoards of research to back it up. I don't have time to take the pictures, at least not all of them."

"What's the idea?"

"I'll tell you the idea because I owe you, but I want to see more of your work before I agree to go ahead."

She thought about this for awhile.

"Okay. That's fair; what's the idea?"

"Graves of interesting people, Boston's full of them. The Baby Boomers are beginning to get intimations of mortality and they'll love it. A book of gravestone photos will sell great if we can get it out by Halloween."

"Graves?"

She put down her fork.

"People will be fascinated. Mother Goose, Miles Standish, Henry David Thoreau, Mary Baker Eddy, half a dozen signers of the Declaration of Independence, dozens of fascinating lives have their ends in the dirt around Boston. One of the most beautiful cemeteries in the world is about two miles from here."

"I never thought of cemeteries being beautiful."

"You show me beautiful photos, I'll show you a beautiful cemetery."

"Deal," she said and smiled. Did I mention she had a great smile? It was a touch asymmetric like Lauren Hutton's. I liked her best in *American Gigolo* trying to pick up Richard Gere first in school girl French and then in Anglo-Saxon.

When the wine was well on its way, she came back to the idea.

"You said you had a lot of research."

"I have a huge file on where people are buried all over the world, from Jacques Brel and Paul Gauguin on Hiva Oa to Richard Henry Dana in Harvard Square."

"How long have you been collecting things like this?"

"About eight years."

"Why death?"

"Death is the most important thing in the world. Once you understand how it works, everything else is just salad dressing. Death is the main course. It's what the meal is all about. It's the naked lunch. It's not scary or frightening... it's just... it's like... it's like this computer design program I have for three dimensional objects where you can move all around the object, see it from different perspectives, change the lighting. The world looks different; an object looks different when the lighting is reversed or you see it from the back or flip it horizontal. We live in the context of unquestioned life, but the shining circumorbital fact is that we all go down.

"And we all know that. And whether we listen or not, I believe we talk to ourselves about what every event in our lives means in terms of that fact. Some people, probably most people, have this tape loop that says: 'don't think about it, don't think about it, don't think about it, don't think about it'. And so they have no perspective, and death is a constant unarticulated fear. They have no perspective. Of course, you can be overwhelmed by perspective. Too much perspective and you lose your place; everything becomes totally relative."

There was a silence that was beginning to get embarrassing when she spoke.

"You're wicked weird about this, aren't you?"

I looked again at the top of her dress. She seemed to be wearing a bandeau bra.

"I think you're right."

∞

After dinner, we stepped onto Boylston Street still firmly in perspective, my inebriation nicely balanced or neutralized by the emotions. We walked towards Back Bay Station; the night temperature was descending through the seventies while the buildings and the side-walks radiated the stored heat of the day. We looked into a few windows, inclined our heads and grinned at the colorful creatures of the street. As we got to the cab ranks at the station, I popped the question.

"Do you want to show me those beautiful photos now?"

Again, that steady, unafraid look.

"I want to think about it."

Oh, well.

"Taxi!"

She waved and a yellow cab pulled up. She gave an address I missed in Dorchester.

"You need a new answering machine," I said as she got in.

She looked back at me, "Call anyway."

Not the most romantic of good-nights, but prom-ising.

∞

The next day, I carried the reliquary of the late Ms. Clark back to Trusts and Estates where RSAB... the T was absent. I wandered into the clerical office next door, which was also lightly staffed. There were six desks scattered around a breastwork of file cabinets and room dividers. Many of the file cabinets were wooden and card-sized. I guessed they contained the last operating McBee Key-Sort system in the western world, probably installed by Professor Hollerith himself and some of his students at MIT. I looked around for the sorting needles, but perhaps they were gilded, sacred and kept in a some nineteenth century padlocked oak tabernacle of security.

A sour-looking, painfully white male sitting in the far corner pointedly ignored me, so I took the opportunity to snoop. The way to do this is keep moving as slowly as you can make look purposeful, appearing to pay only the most casual attention to things you pass. I consulted the Clark file, as if checking a name, while I read file names, office notes and publication titles in my vicinity. A round younger man with almost bare-scalp short, short, ink-black hair walked in the door behind me as I was trying to decipher the title of an article in an upside-down issue of *The International Economy.*

"Hi, I was trying to get an account record on a deceased. Somehow I got the wrong file."

"Oh? What was the name?"

I told him.

"Sure, I remember. I pulled it yesterday. It was supposed to go to... let me look... Gardiner in 1123."

I showed him the folder of miscellany.

"That's it."

"This? This is an account record?"

"Well, that is what Mr. B. told me to send... the 'C' file on Clark, Mary Stebbins, deceased."

"What's in the "A" and "B" files?"

"Oh, those are the card files. Mr. Bancroft," he nodded at the sour-looking, painfully white man who was now working twice as hard at ignoring both of us, "and Mrs. Allen maintain them."

"Respectively or alphabetically?"

"Huh?"

"Never mind. What's in them?"

"I don't know. Nobody can read them; they're all

just drawers of punch cards."

"Geoffrey, who are you talking to?" The man in back finally spoke, apparently raising a question that struck Geoffrey by surprise. I introduced myself as the addressee of the file and left, taking the 'C' file on Clark, Mary Stebbins, deceased with me.

Back at my office, I wrote RSAB a letter requesting a record of the regular activity on the Clark account for all the reasons I had vainly presented to him in person. I made several copies.

The next day I called; he was out. A few days later, he was in a meeting. I sent a copy of my letter with a note explaining the deadline situation. I called. He was out.

∞

After several weeks of this, I played my other card and wrote a MATCHUP program to merge all the bookkeeping and investment data bases. I set it up to run over a Friday night and wedged it into the mainframe schedule ahead of a few weekly chores it was already taking on. I had been plagued by ill-timed power interruptions especially on overnight runs. Because we had internal instantaneous-on emergency power, the interruptions don't do any real damage to the system, but even with the best surge and phase circuitry controls available, there will be a signal anomaly in the processor, so I make it a point to have whatever program is running during an interrupted off-hours run stopped and instruct the machine to go to the next. Otherwise, it is easy to lock up or get stuck in a DOLOOP; it is better and more productive for the overall system to have the unfortunate run remounted manually and run when I was around to monitor and troubleshoot.

Because we had been hit with the problem several times on overnight runs, I had hooked into the system a beeper that I carried whenever I had something running overnight.

It chirped as I was pouring an inch of Jack Daniel's into my rinsed-out morning tea mug. I liked mixing it with plain, cold Poland Springs sparkling water, no ice. In the mug I didn't have to look at how dark I was making them these evenings.

The beeper was sitting among the pile of stuff I had dumped out of my pockets on the kitchen table. I looked at the clock, only eight-thirty—the window, still light—and the drink. I put the Jack Daniel's mug in the refrigerator, not sure why, turned off the beeper and poured more Poland Springs into a fresh cup. It fizzed and foamed in the microwave for four minutes while I washed my face, changed my shirt, grabbed a sport coat and redistributed pocket junk. When the timer beeped, I flipped a Twinings Prince of Wales bag into the cup and carried it out to the curb. In about thirty seconds I got a cab to Post Office Square. The tea was just about drinkable when I got out and paid.

"Whaddya got there, whiskey?" the cabby asked.

"No, I left that one in the refrigerator." He looked at me blankly; it happens a lot.

∞

The security guard recognized me and did not check my ID while I signed in as Grover Cleveland.

When I got off the elevator on 11, I was surprised to see the elusive Ralph Stonington, etc., etc., stepping into a car in the opposite bank. I was surprised because 1) it was nowhere near his office and he was famous for never straying far from his small pond and 2) because it was long past quitting time for all but the most overworked acolytes, associates and junior partners and he was equally famous for not overworking. He was also most surprised to see me, but 15 generations of cold-blooded Boston breeding and fifty-plus years of gin had given him a fairly inexpressive countenance.

"M-Mister Gardiner," he barely stammered.

I had time to say "Good evening" before the doors closed.

Auf wiedersehen.

In the computer room, the file server's green screen listed the MATCHUP program in a Hold sector. I stared at the monitor for a while and thought about Ralph's being on this floor just ten minutes after I got the interrupt alarm. He did not seem bright enough to know how to tamper with either the machine or the code, but if it was a coincidence, it was a strange one.

I downloaded the MATCHUP to a diskette and then, still seeing Ralph rabbitting into the elevator, downloaded the two data bases onto other disks. Five hard-plastic three-and-a half inch disks fit into my jacket with the satisfying clatter and heft of old European casino plaques.

Another walk across Boston, especially after dark, was off the chart. I am not paranoid, but things do happen. I called Red and White from the office. They promised to send someone right away. I've been lied to before. After five or ten minutes waiting in front of the door in the wind tunnel of the street, I flagged a yellow cab. The S, B building is cantilevered or overhung by an architectural or engineering trick to give an unusually large entrance plaza (with limo drive up) while getting maximum floor space starting about eight or ten stories up. The building looks massively pregnant; on stormy days the wind at street level roars.

Back home, the whiskey was still in the cup in the refrigerator. It was about the only thing still in place. My apartment, as they say in the trade, had been tossed.

Two

If you have ever been burgled or burglarized or what ever the proper verb form, you can never forget that horrid sinking feeling as your sense of security is gutted. This was the first time I had been hit in Boston, but I was no virgin. While dialing 911, I took a quick inventory. When the recorded operator came on, I gave the details in a kind of trance. My shock was deepening as I realized what was still there: all the stereo equipment (admittedly bulky, but new and expensive-looking); the TV (probably too big for one person to carry inconspicuously)—these things made sense; but the Discman, the two Nikon's, my grandmother's sterling ice bucket were visible, although randomly redistributed. I hung up and walked through the disarray. My grandfather's watch and chain were still in the plush box in my dresser. The Denon clock radio was unplugged, laying on its side on the box spring; the mattress was on the floor. A scatter of climbing equipment was piled on the floor. Two 150-foot coils of 11-mm perlon (one red and one blue) lay underneath a small mound of stainless steel nuts and chocks and carabineers. It looked like a high tech, alpine interpretation of pasta primavera.

In fact, I could find nothing missing. If it wasn't theft, was someone here looking for something? And if they didn't steal anything, they were either stupid or wanted me to know that theft wasn't the motivation. I set the clock radio back on the night stand and plugged it back in. It began flashing: 12:00 12:00 12:00. I was fumbling with the three buttons you have to hold down simultaneously to reset the time when the police arrived.

I wished they had taken longer.

A salt and pepper set in BPD uniforms was at the door. Salt looked about twenty and was trying to grow a mustache, perhaps as a sign of maturity. It was working about as well as a set of Mouseketeer ears. His name tag said Braithwaite. Pepper wore stripes, a face as ancient as an Easter Island statue and a tag that read Coleman.

Sergeant Coleman introduced herself and fired up the clanky old routine of retail standard, urban police procedure.

When we got to the part about what was missing, I hesitated and then decided that I needed all the help I could get.

"As far as I can tell, nothing."

"Nothing? You see anybody leaving when you came in?"

"No."

"Is there a back door?"

"Yes."

"Get behind me and show me the way." She unsnapped her holster and nodded once to her partner.

Behind Sgt. Coleman's comforting substance (and revolver), I directed us to the kitchen, pausing for dramatic visits to each room and its closets on the way. The kitchen was a shambles, but unoccupied. The back door, dead bolt and steel frame were just as I had left them. I looked at the door slightly longer than the Sergeant.

"Nothing missing?"

"As far as I can tell."

Sgt. Coleman had upped the wattage in her inspection of me.

"Someone else have a key?"

"No."

"You know who did this?"

"No."

"Did you do this?"

"No! Why would I do this and then call you and tell you nothing's missing?"

"I gave up on wondering why people do things before he was born," she said, nodding toward the front of the building where Braithwaite waited, no doubt mutely admiring my disheveled home. "Now I just try to figure out who did what."

I opened my eyes wide and shrugged.

"Well, if you didn't do this and have no idea who did and nothing was taken, we're not likely to get very far. When you're putting it back together, if you do find anything missing or get any ideas, call me." She handed me a card that said her first name was Elizabeth. She collected Braithwaite and gave me a yellow NCR copy of a full page form with most of the spaces blank. They left.

I carried the form into the kitchen and stuck it to the refrigerator door with the letters "f," "u" and "k" from the Fisher-Price set I keep scattered there for just such editorial expressions. While looking for the "c", I gratefully remembered and retrieved my Jack Daniel's tea mug.

The kitchen was a lesser mess than the living or bed rooms, since there was less in it to begin with. How long had I been gone—thirty, forty minutes? This was fast work; and for what? I turned the kitchen table right side up, then a chair, and sat down to sip and think about it, but everywhere I looked was chaos; all the drawers dumped on the floor. The hollow feeling got worse. Instead of the rage that I had felt in the past for thieves, I now had only fear and confusion—Who? Why? What was the intruder after? How did he, she, it get in? Why? Who? Why?

The phone rang. The sound rattled around the kitchen. The room seemed hollow and too bright. I realized every light in the room was on.

It was Clio.

"Thank you for dinner the other night. I want to talk about the book idea."

"Okay." I truly felt like I was talking to someone in another country.

"You said you wanted to see some beautiful pictures. I don't know if they're beautiful, but I think some are pretty good."

"Okay."

"Are you not interested, sick, or just rude?"

"I'm sorry; the police just left. My place was broken into." (Not only ungrammatical, but incorrect.)

"Oh, my God, are you all right?"

"I'm a little wobbly."

"Would you like me to come over? I can bring my pictures."

"It may sound like a bit of a cliché, but the place is a mess."

"I'll help clean up. What's the address?"

I told her and hung up feeling considerably better, and then, as I looked around, came crashing back down. Who? Why?

∞

She arrived in about forty minutes with a shoulder bag and two paper sacks. In that time I had pulled the kitchen back together, but everything else was just as-is, where-is I found it. The front room probably looked the worst since all the books on the floor gave it the flavor of an incipient bonfire. I don't know why I started straightening up the kitchen first. I am certain my mother would have told me to do the front room first, especially if I were expecting company.

"Wow, really scrambled."

"Yeah, I noticed. Come on back to the kitchen; the chairs are right side up."

"Did you lose much?"

"I don't think so. There is nothing missing from the kitchen anyway. Here, let me take those."

She gave me the two paper sacks that proved to hold shortbread, strawberry and orange cream cheese and a bottle of Jadot Beaujolais Villages. I made these items more accessible. She brought a Moroccan leather folio from her shoulder bag, and unzipped it on the table.

Her pictures were, in fact, excellent.

A dirty, broken padlocked door with a grubby, fading "Kennedy for President" decal on the window; concrete sidewalk section with finger cut graffito inscribing a tribute to some three-lettered drug experience; old men leaning on parking meters; young children staring at broken bicycles or the middle distance, off camera. My favorite was a toddler in overalls pounding furiously in the dirt with a carpenter's hammer.

The technical quality was high, lots of middle to dark greys, excellent grain, a real Mary Ellen Mark, gritty feeling. I told her this and more.

"So do you want to try this book idea?" I said. "I'm game, if you are."

"You're supposed to show me the beautiful cemetery next."

"Tomorrow; we can take a picnic."

"To a cemetery?"

"In some countries, they have national party days in their cemeteries."

"Not in Boston."

"Certainly not; anyway, this one's in Cambridge."

"Not there either, I bet."

∞

We talked about the picnic and sat in the kitchen and drank the wine and I forgot about the chaos in the rest of the place until she came back from the john.

"Do you want me to help you clean up? And what happened? How did they get in? Did you say nothing is missing?"

All the peaceful normalcy and the warmth of the wine in the kitchen dropped away.

"I don't know what happened. I have not figured out how he, she, it or they got in. I haven't found anything missing. And I would love to have your help. I'll open another bottle of wine."

We started in the front room. I resettled the furniture; she did the books. We moved to the dining room, then the bath. By the time we got to the bedroom, the second bottle of wine was well on its way and we were making stupid jokes about the stuff you find behind furniture. I pretended to be an archaeologist reconstructing a lost civilization.

We got the mattress reestablished on the springs and began making the bed. The easy domesticity of making the bed together turned the corner for us. It seemed the most natural thing in the world to turn off the ginger jar lamp on the dresser and lay down together.

She was a beauty and her face changed to something eternal when I moved on top of her.

∞

I woke up at five-thirty and lay there for about fifteen minutes enjoying and securing the memories of what we had done last night and watching her sleep. She slept on her back. I can't do that; it gives me a sore back and vivid, disturbing dreams. She slept beautifully, unlined face, freckles, good cheekbones—ah, youth.

"Psst, Murphy, wake up."

I watched her face flinch, flutter, run through uncertainty, confusion, remembrance, surprise, and then, turning to face me, opening her eyes with a smile.

"Hi."

"Hello, how are you this morning?"

"Surprised to be here. What time is it?"

"Don't look. I want us to get up now and get dressed. I'll show you something even more beautiful than we planned."

I rolled out of bed, grabbed a shirt from the floor and did my best bare-bottomed exit.

∞

We drove over the bridge to Cambridge just as Dwayne Ingalls Glasscock signed on with an Aerosmith cut. I turned off the radio, my normal Saturday attitude of snotty rock and Don Drysdale dust-off driving was far away. The streets were open with few cars and even fewer walkers. The shadows were still blue-grey, as if the colors of darkness were not yet touched by the light in the sky, and lay pooled in the recesses along Mass. Ave. and down Mt. Auburn past the hospital. I turned right onto Coolidge and parked behind a commercial building on the left, past the East Gate of Mt. Auburn Cemetery.

The street was fully lit when we got out of the car and I took us over the fence where a trio of ancient birders had shown me a remarkable staircase of limbs through a pair of inter-branching trees on opposite sides. We walked through the old forested garden of shrubs arrayed in Olmstead's grandly realized plan up towards the tower and off Walnut Avenue. I showed her cigar-smoking Amy Lowell and R. Buckminster Fuller: "Call Me Trimtab." We talked about what he might have meant; I gave a brief lecture on cybernetics. We visited Longfellow and Amy's brother, J. R., and brilliant, tortured Francis Parkman.

Clio spent a thoughtful amount of time, circling the stones moving out and in, taking dozens of shots at each.

Like giving a gift, watching her discover and then enjoy the place and its spirit was a measured joy. She really loved the lake at the Mary Baker Eddy Memorial. Personally, it's not my favorite spot. I find it like reading Thomas Grey in Vietnam, overstated and unpersuasive. But she had dirt on her Levi's and too many freckles, and she was not, thank God, a brunette.

We walked toward the North Gate down Ash Avenue and I showed her the stone that read, "Blessed are they that look on graves and believe none dead" and did not allow her to see my name on the lintel of a voracious-looking red stone reliquary across the street.

When we got to the North Gate it was still locked and there was a sign that the Chapel was closed for renovations. We headed back along Spruce Avenue and I pointed out how the property values declined as we neared the Roman Catholic Cemetery. We made the loop around back to the now-open East Gate. As I headed across the parking lot toward the gate, she stopped me.

"Wait, I don't want to leave yet."

I walked back to her.

"Come back away from the gate with me. I want to ask you something."

We walked a few yards back to a modern chrome steel monument of an oversize half-open door.

"What does this place mean to you? What do you feel here?"

I looked in her eyes and saw a rapid series of pictures and ideas I had no idea how to put into words.

I said, "There is something majestic and unusual here and I am comfortable in it."

"Yes," she said and leaned against me and we leaned together against the monument and faced the sun and said nothing more.

On the way back, I did not stop to show her the

plaque on the Harvard Bridge erroneously memorializing the fictional suicide of Quentin Compson. The traffic was picking up and, besides, feeling so good, I was unwilling to tempt fate and bring up Faulkner.

∞

First thing Monday I went to work on my five disks.

The MATCHUP run gave me a relational database which I sorted into account files and then tabulated the transactions for each of the accounts. I had the machine analyze investment mix and payment histories for each account and create summaries as sample management reports. By the time I got this set up and running, the mail and the mid-morning crash of calls swept me up in the day.

I didn't have a chance to look at the printout until the end of the day. It was about an inch and a half thick, accordion-folded, continuous paper which I find maddening to deal with. Like an unstructured, slippery, self-destructive Slinky, accordion fold is willfully difficult to use without breaking unless you can open it across a great table or the floor. I put the mass in my Danish schoolkid book bag, threw that over my left shoulder and walked out onto State Street at the relatively non-workaholic hour of six-fifteen, listing slightly to port.

This time when I got home my order was undisturbed, my cat was still alive, there were no messages on the machine and no window-envelope hate-mail in the box. After the better part of a cheese sandwich and a cup of Poland Springs Tennessee Tea, I opened the printout on the old Rya rug and clipped my halogen desk lamp to the coffee table. I don't need glasses, just a bit more light these days.

The summaries indicated 33 accounts with an aggregate value over a billion dollars. This was higher than

I expected on a per-account basis. Old money tends to be diluted rather than concentrated. Sedgwick, Baxter accounts were rich enough to look like one of the aggressive young investment firms with partners' names one generation out of electoral politics and lots of greedy, ill-bred vice presidents. But the principals here were not married-up-from-the-South oil heiresses and Route 128 success stories. Most of the names were familiar parts of New England statuary, street and town nomenclature: Brainerd, Spencer, Coe, Carver, etc.; another good sample was Anglo-European: de Palfrey, Langlois, Zolle. There was a decidedly bi-continental flavor to the mix, many accounts having addresses or payees on both sides of the big pond.

In fact, as I shuffled through the superficial accounts of these lives, there was a grand pattern of coming and going in several of them, like a sea flowing and ebbing between the Eastern shore of the United States and the countries of western European and the British Isles. I imagined tides of wealth and privilege carrying loose driftage of aged, disengaged, talentless, unambitious, otherworldly, dissolute and confused beneficiaries of more money than they would ever need.

It was easy to see the facts of these files as lives. I had read of them in history—the McLeans and the Murphys. I had seen them at parties and clubs where I grew up and my father belonged. And my father's death at any time could have visited the same on me were it not for the hatred between us.

But our estrangement was permanent and complete long before I clearly understood how wealth arranges life. And by then no amount of money was worth the feelings it cost to live with him.

The wealthy I have known did youth fairly well, with a few spectacular failures; the careless immortality of the young buttressed by the divine irresponsibility of unquestioned security and power can produce great flights of existential poetry, grand gestures, disturbing friendships, and magnificent drunks followed by vague notes from distant places. They seem to be aging poorly, finishing nothing, caring for little; either determinedly inconsequential or uninventively committed to something shallow.

As a social study, I went to the clunky old Compaq that I got in my old company's property settlement, reparations and liquidation sale and began charting the lives here laid bare. About one-third were active business executives with a few Route 128 connections, but of the An Wang generation, more with lines to State Street and midtown Manhattan. There was one tenant of the Beverly Wilshire, a few addresses in Palm Beach County. The majority were New England and/or European addresses. These were the transatlantic travelers. There were 23 such accounts. I sorted them for marital status—21 were single—and for relationship to previous beneficiary—21 were collateral. Twenty-one unmarried rich people who inherited from an aunt or uncle seemed strange. Unusual, remarkable, but not impossible. What was bothering me about these people? There. A shock touched me when I saw that all 21 had inherited from a collateral relative of the same sex. At about the same age.

I opened the first file: Ashbrook, Myron Chubb. It occurred to me that at some point soon I was likely to be doing something illegal. I wondered if this were it.

Payables [ENTER] Account Info [ENTER] All lines [ENTER].

Mr. Ashbrook had a hotel address in the Fifth Arrondisement, although he could certainly afford a place in L'île de la Cité or St. Louis; perhaps he is a trust fund bohemian, maybe he likes Middle Eastern food. He traveled by Cunard earlier this year, another little curious similarity. A sailor like Ms. Clark.

Most payments were made to other banks in France and the U.S. There was a payment to an agency in Brittany. Most payments were opaque bank-to-bank transfers. Why? Why not have the efficient Sedgwick, Baxter bookkeepers pay the household credit card and merchant account bills for their service fee? Why add another layer of bankers and fees? My eyes flip-focused to my reflection on the computer screen. Should I get a glare shield... maybe an ELF radiation mask? A Frank Zappa voice laughed in my head.

Other files, more banks, more sailors. No doctors; no hospitals; no dentists, even. One bank, in particular, showed up frequently, Boehrkopf Frères, the Zurich connection I had heard about. The *Agence Privée de Bretagne* with the address of Morbihan, Basse Bretagne was a payee at the beginning of every account.

I wrote down these three questions: 1. Who were these people? Their lives had such drop-in similarities. 2. With all this subterfuge, are they hiding something? For all the personality or identity shown in their spending, they could have been each other. 3. They could be identities maintained by an intelligence service. Twenty-one solitaires more than well provided for by their myriad, mirrored uncles and aunts. It could be a money laundering pipeline. I had a return of the sense of unreality and hollowness that I got on opening the door at my place last Friday night. A fourth question: any connection? Fifth question: am I clinically paranoid?

The phone rang. I let the machine pick it up. It was someone from the Learning Annex about a course I had proposed to teach. A voice left a name and a number I was too far away to make out clearly. I felt like I had gotten off the elevator at an unfinished floor. Everything looked alien and unsettled.

What was bothering me about these people? I ran the payees by account by year. Another curious pattern emerged. Each of the current accounts began with a substantial payment to this *Agence Privée de Bretagne* somewhere I had never heard of in France. In each case, the payment was in September or March; a minority of accounts had two payments, in which case the March date was always the first.

I walked out to the kitchen and made another cup of evening tea. I went back to the front room and sat sideways on the couch with the tea on the bay windowsill. I took a sip and looked for anything interesting playing on the Street Channel, cars, wrecked and respectable, dog and power walkers, increasing darkness. I thought of another question and went back to the computer and printed a list of names and addresses while I finished the drink.

∞

The next day I called Clio and made a date to look at the proofs from Mt. Auburn. I put the box of papers from the Clark estate in a file cabinet behind my desk and waited to see if anyone called for them.

With the MATCHUP, I had integrated the system and largely finished the technical part of the job with a week to spare on the PERT chart. The remaining six weeks would be consumed by the people problems that would emerge in the training sessions and the inevitable bugs that would hide until we came on-line. While my consultants were drafting the documentation I evaded everyone by spending most of the week in the airless offices of the Secretary of State and Department of Health in the Saltonstall and McCormick buildings, finding and copying birth and death certificates.

One person at a time, I worked out the following additional information from the public records. This cadre of 21 people had all established Massachusetts residency and U.S. citizenship while still minors as dependent wards of auntie or uncle whoever. Most of thc files showed documents that had passed through, originated from or been notarized by Sedgwick, Baxter. Birth certificates were from everywhere but Massachusetts, no pattern. Their benefactors had all died overseas, either in Switzerland or in France. I had a set of addresses at birth and death and the names of the certifier where available and legible (usually not) on the certificate copies. One notable peculiarity was age at death, all the deceased were between the ages of forty and sixty, none younger, none older, more forties than fifties.

I had nothing else to show: a dead end. I went back to the MATCHUP data. If I was going any further with this I would have to start snooping directly and personally into someone's life. I have spent all my life trying to avoid or escape getting any more involved with people than absolutely necessary—particularly with those I don't know. In my experience, the less you know about people, the easier it is to get along with them. With strangers, I can even smile. The idea of poking into someone's life, especially someone about whose affairs I already knew more than I could ethically explain, was repugnant. I'm not sure when I decided to do it.

∞

I met Clio at a Mexican place down an alley off Chestnut Street. Her pictures were as good as the first ones she had shown me. She had caught the way I saw the early morning light without making it a Forest Lawn by Stephen Spielberg effort. The stones were almost incidental, legible, but quietly effaced, scarcely more than shapes, floating words, the last simplest assertion of human will and artifice.

I suggested we go to Duxbury the following Saturday. I told her that John Alden lies there, speaking for himself one final time. I did not tell her that Myron Chubb Ashbrook and the late Mary Stebbins Clark are, and were, respectively, legal residents. She requested a later departure. I told her I would settle for 8 a.m. if I could wake up the same as last Saturday. She ducked her head and then looked up at me.

"Your place or mine?" We both laughed. The dialogue gets creaky, but the song remains the same. The melody lingers on. It's still the same old story.

So we played it again, as the man did not say... at her place in Dorchester. It was a pleasant apartment on one Pleasant Street, according to the street sign outside. She had the top front floor of a flatiron building about a third of the way up a hill. There was a darkroom set up under a loft bed in the smaller bedroom and a studio of sorts intermixed with minimal clean-lined furniture in the two front rooms. The roll of seamless paper that backdropped the dining table was cerise. I had a roll of that color during my flirt with commercial photography. The morning sun on it would color the whole room outrageously.

The kitchen was standard 1930s and I knew exactly what kind of claw-footed fixtures I would find in the bath. I mixed up the yeast for homemade pizza, having lugged a nine pound stone from Back Bay. It is the indispensable secret to a good pizza. She uncorked one of the Riojas I had brought.

"Tell me about your parents. Do they both live around here?"

"Mom, my mother, lives in Lynn, where we grew up. She's the director of the town library there. My father is back in Boston for the first time in twenty years. He'll be at Harvard in the fall."

"Doing what?"

"Teaching, writing, I guess, being a professor."

"In which school?"

"Divinity."

Divinity.

"Out of town for twenty years... since...?"

"Yes, most of the time he's been at Heidelberg, you know, in Germany?"

"Yes, I know; and now the Prodigal returns, or isn't this his home?"

"Oh, yes. He went to Boston Public Latin. But he's not very prodigal; he should have been a priest, Mom said."

"Do you see him often?"

"Usually once a year, usually around the school breaks."

"When will he be here, do you know?"

"Next week, why?"

"I want to meet him."

"Why?"

"I want to ask him why he named you Clio."

∞

The rain started about six a.m., but I had felt the barometric pressure drop around five and was half awake waiting for it. By seven, we were into a solid, drenching summer rain. I sat up and pulled on last night's Levi's from where they lay folded neatly in fourths on top of my shoes and socks. Always know where your shoes are at night. I left the shoes there, picked my shirt off the doorknob and went to the kitchen. I put on water to boil in a white enamel pan with red trim and an owl eye on the bottom. I went back to the bathroom and rinsed my face eight or ten times with what passes for water in Boston taps. The windblown rain seemed to follow me from window to window as the storm whipped around the building.

On the way back to the kitchen, I grabbed the remote and punched on the cable, muting the volume. The weather channel showed a green mass obscuring the New England coast. I changed to MTV and left the volume off. The water was not boiling yet, but I got out rudimentary breakfast items, juice, cups. I watched the rain and wind. Eventually the water began to steam, then bubble; I started a cup of tea for myself and took a glass of juice in to Murphy.

She woke up reluctantly. looked outside and then, frowning, back at me.

"Let's go anyway, "I said, "maybe it'll quit." I handed her the juice.

She blinked blankly.

"Coffee or tea?"

"Coffee. There's instant in the cupboard behind the stove."

∞

We left around eight. She wore a black Gore-Tex parka and carried a covered camera bag. I vainly held up a half-broken, collapsible umbrella and stepped into a deceptively deep, cold puddle next to my car, completely soaking my right foot.

We got into the car and with so much moisture on us, the windows steamed up. We hydroplaned down 93 to the Route 3 turnoff with the defroster going full blast and water pooling in my right heel.

"I want to talk about where we are going," she said looking straight ahead.

"Duxbury?" I ventured optimistically.

"I mean us, you and me; where are we going?"

"Can't we just be going to Duxbury?"

She looked flatly at me and then back out the window at the tunnel of water we were shooting through and did not say another word.

In Duxbury, I stopped in front of a small post office called Snug Harbor and stepped into a lobby with oak paneling and counters and brass grills and combination boxes of Smithsonian quality. Presently, a face came to the window and I got directions to the library, the historical society museum and a local bookstore; only the lattermost, I learned, was open now. At the bookstore,

Murphy again stayed in the car and I soaked my other foot getting back with an historical society pamphlet, a map and the information that the library would open in 20 minutes, but the historical society would be closed all day. I drove to the library. The parking lot was empty, but there was a light on inside. I pulled into the non-handicapped spot nearest the door.

The rain slackened. I opened my window an inch and turned to tell Clio to do the same.

"Now what?" she said.

"Well, you could open your window. You could sit there. You could go over this map and orient us and find cemeteries while I go through this history. It's up to you."

"So now we're in Duxbury and you're still in charge and I'm still supposed to do what you say."

"Look," I said, "you can do what you like, but your disposition seems pretty clear. In...," I glanced at the dash clock, "...ten minutes, I'm going into the library. At that point, you can take the car and go take pictures, leave the car and go off on your own, come into the library and read the *Globe* or *Jack and the Beanstalk* in silence, or go back to Boston with the car and leave me here, but ten minutes. That's it."

At three minutes to ten by my clock, a slim, middle-aged woman in a green-checked suit opened the outside set of double doors. Neither of us had said a thing. I got tired of watching the Ralph Lauren mothers dash through the rain to the high school bake sale across the street. Clio was staring at the neon-colored soccer players huddled under a tree at the Fisher School.

"I'm leaving now," I said.

Silence.

"What are you going to do?" I asked.

"I'll see after you're gone."

∞

The Duxbury Free Library was a compact, modern package of information. Clio never came in and I was soon lost in pure runs of unassimilated data. I spent two hours scanning microfilm archives of *The Duxbury Chronicle*.

In 1959, I found, as expected, the obit for Myron Chubb Ashbrook's maternal uncle, Michael Charles Carver, and learned he was reported dead in a mountaineering accident in Wales. I began running backward in the 'Goings On' and 'Local Society' columns and found a sailing in 1956 on the *U.S.S. United States'* maiden voyage and an earlier Christmas reception for residents of the town at 'Brown Shears', Carver's home on St. George Street. He was described as well-known for his contributions to the war effort. The file ended in 1950.

I searched for Mary Stebbins Clark. There was no record of her living in Duxbury during the span of the Duxbury Free Library files of *The Duxbury Chronicle*.

Fortunately, I had encountered the reference librarian on entering and learned that there was a locked local history room which I could sign myself into. I did. I got lucky. In the first alcove off the main room to my left was a collection of local documents in manuscript form. On top of the pile was the Official Town Report of 1913: "Bring this copy with you to the meeting." Directly underneath was "Remembrances of Duxbury I Knew" by Andrew Gershon.

It began: "My first memory of Duxbury was the Centennial Celebration of 1876 when I was two. There were a lot of fireworks and explosions. My uncle lost two fingers of his right hand, but went on to become a successful butcher. His shop was on Water Street for years."

The narrative continued in that vein for 19 pages until I read: "After the war when Miss Megan Seaward Clark moved into 'Brown Shears' and opened it once again to life, we danced every night of the Summer, it seemed, to a different live orchestra." I calculated the chronology. It was the first war, i.e. the First World War, The Big One, as they told the men of my father's generation about the one before theirs; the one to end all wars.

At the end of the narrative on page 26, I found Mr. Gershon's summation: "Life becomes so complex and then it becomes so simple."

The rest of my stay in that low-ceilinged room, with the rain occasionally driving on the flat roof close overhead, I looked up Jonathan Alden and Captain Miles Standish. The latter did not seem to be much a part of the community for all the crucial times it turned to him. I checked into a piece of gossip about Priscilla who may have been no better than she had to be, but was certainly a better judge of character than Standish, at least in Longfellow's telling.

I looked up my family's entry in a four-volume History of the Commonwealth of Massachusetts published by the State Historical Society. We passed through the Commonwealth on our way up to going broke in the Mohawk Valley. I found a delightful story about an accidentally permanent sojourner from Denmark.

When I got back to the door after exploring all the nooks, I turned off the lights and locked myself out. On the steps back to the main desk, I encountered the reference librarian.

"Did you have any trouble finding things?"

"Not at all; everything was most accessible. Tell me, do you know of a house called 'Brown Shears'?"

"On St. George Street?"

"I don't know, I just read a reference to it."

"Well, yes, I know where it is."

"Do you know whose it is?"

"I believe... What are you inquiring about?"

"I was interested in a Miss Clark who owned it in the early part of this century."

"Oh, well, old Miss Clark. She wasn't here much

by the time I was growing up, but the older boys used to talk about her."

"Was she a scandal?"

"Well, she grew up in Europe. She was different from girls around here."

"More direct, would you say?"

"I wouldn't say, but you did. Do you know about her?"

She looked at me coolly. I found I was sparring with her. I found it unsettling.

"Tell me about her. What was her life? What was her story?"

"She was the niece of a spinster named Brigham. I think she was born in Europe; her parents died there and she was adopted by her aunt who was from here but lived someplace in France."

"When did she come here?"

"Oh, she arrived with a big splash, they say, in the early twenties. A lot of parties, a lot of late nights. After the Eighteenth Amendment passed, there was no shortage of Joe Kennedy's 'Canadian imports'. It was a lively scene, I hear."

"And the lady herself?"

"Oh, she was a beauty! We have a picture of her in the rotunda. She was a major donor."

She led me past the main desk to a round room of shelves directly behind.

"There," she said.

At about eye level was a bust portrait of a brunette with milky pale, young skin, dressed and made up like a woman of middle age, but with a vitality that looked decades younger. It was a jarringly ineffective, amateurish composite.

"What did she really look like?" I turned to the librarian.

"I never saw her, but those who did said this was a good likeness."

"She looks like a strong lady."

"I understand she was."

"One last thing, what is the actual street address of the house called 'Brown Shears'?"

She looked at me, again askance. After a pause, she replied, "186 St. George."

I was not surprised. It was the current legal address of Mr. Ashbrook.

The recognition must have registered on my face. The librarian continued to look at me with skepticism.

"What are you looking for?" she finally asked, proving even stern librarians can lapse into vernacular constructions.

"Just trying to make sense of how someone lived, someone different than I and from a long time ago. The house seems to be a part of it. Is there any place I can sit and write up my notes for about an hour?"

She directed me to an old stone-floored room off the rotunda. It seemed to be a medieval great hall in concept, wrought in much finer wood, stone and craftsmanship, and reduced to haute-bourgeois manor size. An obvious fireplace commanded the far end, but the proportion and grace of the space coupled with the now steady rain outside was ethereal: a Saturday matinee ideal castle keep. As one of the boys in the band said, I adore cheap sentiment.

I chose a yellowing, Queen Anne, crewel-work wing-back closer to the working radiator than the decorative fireplace, picked up my yellow letter pad and wrote:

Things I Know

I. 186 St. George Street is now owned by Myron Chubb Ashbrook, a beneficiary trustee of S, B. It was previously owned by Mary Stebbins Clark who inherited it from her 'aunt' Megan Seaward Clark; both of them were also

S, B clients. Incestuous, but not necessarily unheard of.

A. There are many things which are strikingly congruent in the lives of these 21 special people I have found. Is this another one of them?

B. Do they all pass around select properties like Boardwalk and Park Place?

C. So what?

I thought back to my earlier questions to see if I was any wiser. 1. Who are these people? Still no idea, but they seem to have a great deal in common. 2. The question that led me here: What do they have in common? Property; property exchanged through S, B. 3. Are they hiding something? Their identity? Their antecedents? Their money? 4. What and from whom are they hiding? Everyone, anyone, me? 5. Any connection to the break-in? No sense to it.

Back to I.C. above, so what? A real estate scheme? This felt stranger than a Boston real estate swindle. The identity of the people had to be the key. Back to Question One: who are or were these people?

The history predates World War Two, so Jews in flight and Nazis in hiding were out. Offspring of European royalty swept aside by the social and political reforms of the nineteenth century, the last Romanovs, Anastasia's... what, granddaughter? Much too far-fetched. Who or what would care enough about a long lost crown to make 21 grandchildren or great-grandchildren this security conscious? And why would this paranoid behavior be managed or administered through a major law firm? Delusional behavior—outside of the Nixon White House—is rarely so formally organized. There had to be a reason, and it was probably venal, doubtless had to do with money—there was certainly enough involved—and it had been going on for a while. Perhaps these people were legatees of a corrupt old fortune—pirate loot, Apache gold, slavery's rancid take. But that would all have long been laundered into Ivory Snow respectability by historical indifference.

Why the funny life stories: never married, inheritance from the same sex; in the case of Mary Stebbins Clark even the same initials? No doctors, always sailing. Were these all a species of false identity used by a spy agency? Megan Seaward Clark did not appear to have acted at all covertly, to say nothing of predating the OSS by a good three decades.

My first question, 'Who are they?' returned with more corollaries. What are they doing? Why are they doing it? And, how long have they been at this?

∞

I got uncomfortable at that point with sitting quietly in my chair. I stuffed my pad and the thermal copies I had made into my book bag and did a quick but neat job of fastening both straps, something I rarely do even on an international flight carrying cameras.

The rain was either almost stopped or stopping. Stray drops of windblown spray misted the windows; the wind seemed to be picking up. Maybe I felt a draft.

I went back to the main desk and out the door, tugging my zippers and snaps closed.

As I got to the street, it occurred to me my immediate situation was more pragmatically existential than anything mysterious or metaphysical. More to the point, I had not thought of how to meet up with Clio and my car. I walked toward the water, the wind behind me, until I crossed Washington Street and then it seemed to shift out of the north. I followed the signs to: Beach—No Parking—No Bath House. I passed the solitary grave of someone apparently once known as 'Honest Dick'. With all the cemeteries in this town, honesty must have been no more popular in his day than today. It's not a bad name to leave behind when you're dead, but I guess it never does play well to a live audience.

About a mile up the road I came in view of the point, the bay and my car. It was parked in a small lot at the foot of a low, narrow bridge; Clio was sitting in the driver's seat. As I walked closer to verify this, I remembered the jangly, schizophrenic conversations I had with reality when I was falling in whatever with Petra and destroying what was left of my marriage and other things. I would open a collection of short stories and discover myself living something by Salinger down to the dialogue, the color of her eyes and the timing of a phone call. Disc jockeys in every major East Coast market were programmed to play nostalgically apposite songs during crucial car rides. Streetlights flickered out at my passing and I found my name and my life written everywhere. Even Jung would not have believed the synchronous intersections. Coming upon Clio now made me feel back at home. Hello, universe. Hello, Phillip.

I tapped on the window. She did not look surprised; she must have seen me coming in the mirrors.

"How did you find me here?"

"Kismet. We are fated to be together. Want to go for a walk? I'd like to try to talk."

She got out and we started across the old wooden bridge to the beach. It reminded me of the one Senator Kennedy made famous, fairly broad and without side rails. I looked in the water, no Oldsmobiles.

We got to the beach and turned right. As we walked, I tried to tell her how it is with me.

"I haven't been very successful at getting along with people in my life. It seems to have gotten worse lately. In the last few years, I've really stopped seeing practically everyone but my cat."

She looked at me with sympathy.

"I don't think of myself as unfortunate. As a matter of fact, I think I always wanted to be alone. I mean, I don't think I knew it, but I think it's what I've always wanted. And now I've been able to arrange it, maybe not consciously, but that's how it's turned out."

"Are you happy like that?"

"I'm not unhappy and, sometimes, I am as happy as I get."

We walked for a while; the wind and the water spoke. I took her hand.

"I want you to know you're important to me. You are the only point of undamaged human contact I have. I am afraid of something going wrong. I am wary of everything. But I've had the only...I have relaxed...I find something special, something unique and it matters to me and...."

At this point she was kind enough to put her hand over my mouth. I took her hand again in mine and we walked toward the Gurnet Light with beige Clarks Island brooding to our right.

When we got to the high point, I retrieved from my pocket a copy I had made of a page from a local history book and read it to her.

> "This is probably the famous promontory, called by the Northmen, in their discoveries along the coast of the continent in the eleventh century, by the name Krossaness. In the spring of 1004, Thorwald, son of Eric the Red, sailing eastward in his large ship from his winter quarters at Vineland [Providence] and then northward, passed a remarkable headland [Cape Cod] inclosing a bay; and came to another, but smaller one, on the other side of the bay, covered with wood [Gurnet]. The spot so charmed Thorwald, that he exclaimed,—'This is a beautiful spot, and here I would like to fix my dwell-

> ing.' He was soon after wounded in a skirmish with the natives, and perceiving that his wound was mortal, he said to his companions: 'I now advise you to prepare for your departure as soon as possible; but me ye shall bring to the promontory, where I thought it good to dwell. It may be that it was a prophetic word which fell from my mouth, about abiding there for a season. There shall ye bury me, and plant a cross at my head, and another at my feet, and call the place Krossaness in all coming time.' The commandant was obeyed. *Antiquitates Americanae* of the Royal Society of Northern Antiquaries of Copenhagen."

She shot the rest of the roll of film in her camera as we walked back and we discussed the facts and the likelihoods. She asked great questions. I went on endlessly about Vineland theories and the Danes, eleventh century Europe, worked in the Crusades, the Knights Templar. We were back in the car in no time. She really did appear to like me; I appeared to be likable. We stayed together that night. She laughed first, then I did too, then we both did. We spent Sunday doing deliciously nothing that did not involve newsprint or food. Her new answering machine kept the world at bay, date and time stamping each potential intruder in a medium cool synthesized voice.

∞

One Monday in early August, Clio called and asked if I wanted to meet her father for dinner the following night after we looked at the contacts. We agreed to meet at my place at seven and meet him in Harvard Square at eight.

She was early and I was late, we met on the front step. She looked impatient while I apologized. I almost got a little pissed. We spoke in single words while looking at the proofs, but they were fine. She completely surprised me with a set of page layouts for the Mount Auburn, Duxbury, Lexington and Concord photos done with her employer's magazine quality scanners, processors, and printers.

"If we can keep the publication under a hundred pages, I can do the whole thing at work," she said.

"Do you have company approval?"

"I'm lightly supervised."

"That would appear to be a mistake."

She gave me the finger. I was shocked, but wrote it off to the generation gap.

We cabbed over to the Square, got out and walked past a black woman with a guitar and short dreadlocks singing a song about having a fast car. We went downstairs to any one of the infinity of basements that regularly recreate themselves as restaurants there.

Murphy *père* was a thin, grey-haired, hawk-nosed type who did not look at all like his daughter. He was enough my senior and I do not show all my mileage, so we got around any awkwardness about my being maybe closer to his age than to hers.

She and he exchanged a brief hug and a quick series of how-are-you-doing's while I worked out the moves to get us all seated.

In the first pause, I asked him, "What will you be teaching in the fall?"

"There will be a graduate seminar on John Wesley and the Church of England, another on Martin Luther and the German Separatists and I will have an undergraduate section on Animism."

"What is Animism, the worship of animals?"

"It has two shades of meaning. Edward Tyler used the word to describe his etiology of religion, the persistence of memory, the veridical appearance of dreams and other such imaginings leading to the conclusion of transpersonal or transphysical reality. Anthropologists use the term today to refer to primitive beliefs in the power or life of plants and animals. I intend to focus the course on a dialogue between the two ideas."

"Can you give me an example?"

"I can give you hundreds. Bog sacrifices. Megalithic circles. Cave paintings. Masks. Puppets. Focus on cave paintings: people have taken the image, the idea of the prey animal—the mammoth, the ungulate, whatever—and have brought it into the bowel of the earth in a lightless cavern, then put the image up, on a wall, outside themselves, inside the earth. And it is not just one man alone; others are there. Another figure is drawn; this one has spears and arrows sticking in it. Another gushes blood from his head. Are they recreating a successful hunt or praying for success on the next? Did they think their ability to imagine—to capture a sense (an essential sense) of the absent mammoth—and manipulate it gave or might give them a power, maybe an infallible power over it? And ultimately, was that not the case?"

"Sounds like you have fun with it. What do you think they were trying to do?"

"I think they were integrating by trial and error a flawed consciousness with a malign and aleatory reality. We have museums full of artifacts people created to reconcile the pictures or ideas in their heads with what was going on in their lives. Imagine the proto-sapien, an effective hunter-gatherer with little or no more than a mechanical advantage over other species. At some point, one has a dream, or is near death or fevered, or intoxicated from something he or she ate, and experiences apparent reality that is contrary to or dramatically apart from past physical experience. At that point an image life, an imaginative life begins; but it is separate from direct experience. Out of this dialogue and dialectic—because both thought and action are at work and are worked upon—consciousness, consensual reality and religion emerge."

"Julian Jaynes," I said.

"Required reading; although I think he goes rather far in his reliance on hallucinations and puts too much faith in his own knowledge of anthropology. In addition, his thesis drives him to ignore other functions and dynamics, such as tribal memory and non-oracular rituals. But he is a major influence. I first heard him on his thesis in Washington, DC in 1969."

"When you were at Georgetown, the year after you and Mom split up," Clio put in.

"You came to visit that fall."

"There was a big demonstration."

"Against the war in Vietnam. It was called the Mobilization," Professor Murphy noted.

He turned to me, "Were you there?"

"I was in Chicago that weekend. Tell me what your animism has to say about death."

"Death is a good one. The other hunter or your mate stops moving, stops making sounds, stops responding to you, begins to decay. But you can still see him in your thoughts, still remember a kill with him, still dream of living with her. Maybe like Jaynes says, his or her voice still speaks to you as a fragment of your right hemisphere. But then that all fades, too."

"It must have taken the species a while to figure out when death physically occurs."

"And nearly all the very early artifacts available are burial finds. One of my colleagues, Thomas Palmer, says that human identity proceeds from the sense of death and dates that awareness to a cave in Iraq. Sixty thousand years ago on a summer day, a Neanderthal was placed in a dug grave and his body covered with yarrow blossoms, cornflowers, hyacinths and mallows. The belief in the persistence of human physical needs was apparently very common, very widespread. We still build houses and gardens for our dead. People go to them for communication and communion, even today."

I acknowledged his reference to our Mt. Auburn outing with a nod and a smile.

"So that the essence of funerary ritual is the persistence of human needs and communion?"

"There's also transcendence. The transpersonal world of thought and symbol reconcile the voice, the presence being gone but not extinguished. Because one can still remember and have pictures of and feelings for the dead, it is difficult for even the most rational to accept a finality. Most fossil hominids are found buried with ritual and artifacts indicating belief in migration or transcendence: the children of ancient Northern Europe buried on swan's wings; dynastic Egypt's monuments to the world of the dead; the Hindu and Buddhist ideas of transmigration; Shinto, Islam, Christianity, even Judaism in the last two thousand years, all have included a belief in immortality and resurrection. It is the most common belief of man, more universal than monotheism."

"For the living know that they will die, but the dead know nothing and they have no more reward," I said.

They both looked at me. A real conversation killer.

"Ecclesiastes," I explained.

∞

That Saturday, Clio and I did Newbury Street and, when we got tired of looking at high-priced art and Models Inc. fashions, went up to Mass. Ave. to the Coop cafe/bookstore and then over to Boylston. We spent a long time in Buddenbooks while I mostly squatted on the floor in the back, petting the cat. When we came back out of the dark, woody, old, piled-high bookstore onto Boylston, I had a brief rocky disoriented adjustment to the scale of the broad sidewalk, the blaze of the bright sun. Urgent traffic rattled and banged past the eternal construction work on Pru Plaza. The Lord and Taylor signature scrawled across a brilliant white wall four or five stories tall, the glare was spectacular, blinding.

"C'mon," Clio said ahead of me, half across a stream of Saturday shoppers toward the street. "Let me show you something. I'll bet I can show you something you've never seen."

I dodged an androgynous obesity pushing a stroller with another wad of dough inside. I was entertaining politically incorrect eugenic thoughts as Clio slipped between two cars mashed tight against the curb about a foot apart.

She checked the traffic right and then, like a good urban skeptic at a one-way street, left and started toward the front of a car double-parked across the far lane. She stepped out and looked back to me over her left shoulder.

And then I saw the cab.

It was fifty, sixty yards behind her to the right accelerating up to street speed from an open garage door under the Plaza and heading on a straight line for the lane Clio took the next step into, still looking back at me.

As best I can reconstruct, I made a standing broad jump next to her, grabbed an arm and her waist and tumbled us both back to the gutter between the two parked cars. An angular part of one of them struck me sharply on my upper back. I landed on the bottom and our heads banged together sharply, loudly, brightly.

The cab went by, braying its horn in frustration and anger. I looked into her eyes as she swam back into consciousness and I began to cry.

It was a terrible thing to do to her. I remember the first time I climbed into a boxing ring. And I remember being helped off the canvas, but nothing in between. So she came to in the gutter with me crying in her arms. I was shaking.

"Phillip," she said, "are you all right?"

I kept seeing her standing there with the cab bearing down, looking back at me.

This being Boston, no one interrupted us.

We got back onto the sidewalk and with a pad of tissues from her and some brushing from both of us, we did a damage assessment; no major wounds, a few sore spots, a strong need to hold hands, a general unwillingness to say much, slight fevers, ringing ears. My shaking stopped.

We walked up Boylston to the marked crosswalk for the Prudential Center Plaza. For once, I was not completely overwhelmed by what a loathsome and ugly, dysfunctional and inhuman monument to greed it is. She led me in through a maze-like series of hallways, enclosed walks, stairs, galleries, storefronts. Flashing lights and primary-colored commercial imagery lead to construction zones with screaming, diamond-tooth saws chewing on concrete and steel, lit by bare bulbs, smelling of hydrocarbon exhaust and gypsum dust.

We came outside onto a gravel paved terrace and down a stalled escalator. Immediately across the street was a serpentine block of town houses that was a passable imitation of decent. She took us around the curve of the street until it seemed to turn into a private lane. The building on the left side of the block was an institutionally plain, dressed granite and glass. On the right the townhouse facades undulated with window bays and recessed doors in a smooth long sinusoidal series that felt safely relaxing and settled. The cars parked along the opposite curb were muted colors matching the dove grey stones on either side.

Clio's presence beside me felt like the rightest thing in the world. The act of walking down that street with her seemed somehow timeless and perfect, inevitable, final, significant and determinant. It was a physical comfort.

She appeared to be more attenuated and finely

drawn. I saw how her face would look as she got older. I saw her strength of will and intelligence and her beauty that was not youth but simply her.

"In here," she said.

She smiled short of a grin at my confusion and wonder and we entered a tall faux medieval foyer with the flags of the world's nations the only burst of color over to one side. A platoon of almost identical, thin, pale, white-haired women sat at desks in the foyer or walked through it.

"What is this place?"

She smiled again and I followed her across the hall into a smaller room where an illuminated billboard held the biblical words: "And there appeared a great wonder in heaven; a woman clothed with the sun, and the moon at her feet." Rev 12:1. In the lower right corner of the billboard was a copy of the *Christian Science Monitor*, my first clue.

But I forgot almost all of it because Clio had stepped onto a carpeted walkway with transparent side rails that transected the inside of a huge globe, 30 feet in diameter. A map of the world had been stained onto concave glass panels which were mounted on a meridianal framework into a sphere. Lit from behind, the panels were glowing to exceptionally dramatic effect. The map colors were orange and red and yellow and green; the lakes, seas and shorelines were blue; the oceans' expanse, deeper blue. All the features were as clearly labeled as a textbook in authoritatively legible Times Bold.

Stunned and amazed, I craned my neck all over looking for familiar features; the U.S. cut up like a kid's jig saw puzzle, the exotic high hipped equatorial mass of Africa with unfamiliar names like Bechuanland across the Kalihari and an odd piece on the western Tropic of Cancer called Rio de Oro. At the other end of the walkway, a dark, muted, library waited vacant and large.

"What is this place?"

As I began to speak, my voice boomed and echoed loudly, bounced and died. I ended in a whisper.

Clio ran over to the far library end of the walk and whispered.

"It's the Christian Science World Headquarters."

I heard her whisper in my ear as clearly as if she were on my shoulder. As she walked the five steps back to me, the line from Revelations "...a great wonder in heaven, a woman clothed with the sun...." reminded me and I said to her.

"I will find out where she has gone
And see her face and take her hand
And walk through long green dappled grass
And pluck till time and times are done
The silver apples of the moon
The golden apples of the sun."

And in the middle of the earth I held her very, very close.

∞

That was the last weekend I had free through Labor Day as the normal crises ran us down to the wire getting fully and reliably operational.

Somewhere in there I explained to Harry that I had been obliged to work around Trusts and Estates and one of us was going to have to talk to Ken about it. He howled like banana break at the monkey house. When he calmed down I told him that I thought I should do it alone. The play of relief and suspicion across his face was worth whatever came next.

Ken's office had no couch or conversational group of chairs, no conference table. Facing the visitor was an arte moderne pedestal desk that looked like a Frank Lloyd Wright. Two matching, uncomfortable, but striking chairs were opposite the desk. On a black enameled credenza top to the left an army of ten inch tall Chinese funerary figures marched toward the door. The two wood paneled walls right and left each held a large Oriental wood block print with multiple chop marks.

You had to pay attention to notice any of that because the other two walls were floor-to-ceiling glass. Half of Boston from the burnished aluminum Federal Building at South Station across the glittering, busy Inner Harbor to the jumble of the North End surrounded the room.

Behind the desk, Ken seemed to float above it all. He was on the phone when he waved me in speaking forcefully on points of legal strategy to someone who was either a close colleague or a deep enemy—with lawyers you never know.

Ken was a small man who filled a great deal of space with his physical energy. His free arm extended, pointed to the sky, made a fist, opened, swept through a broad arc. He winked at me.

Smiling I looked past him out the window, trying to guess which Jesus-bug might be the Logan water shuttle, which shadow the Old North Church.

"So, Phillip, how is our project?"

He had glacier blue eyes, but put a lot of warmth into his smile. He leaned back relaxed in his chair.

"There is a problem in Trusts & Estates."

"I've heard from him."

I smiled.

"What do you propose," he asked.

"You have three choices: Force Mr. Baxter to change; limp along with parallel systems until he retires which will cost significantly in error, confusion and redundancy; or fire him."

"This is not a pleasant set of choices you are offering here."

"Excuse me, sir; I am not the problem here. I am just the messenger."

"Baxter said the same."

"Oh?"

He leaned over his desk. "We hired you to solve problems not create them."

"The problem preceded me."

He leaned back. "You're right," he said. "Something has to be done."

He stared at me. His round face reminded me of a Paul Klee painting that had scared me as a child. It was titled "One Who Knows".

"I don't know," I said, "how things are done here, but traditionally the individual is offered the chance to make his own choice."

The One Who Knows face looked back at me. I shrugged. Ken nodded. I left.

∞

The dog days panted along. For the last two weeks of August, a high pressure system stalled over Bermuda, pumping heat and humidity up the Jersey coast to us. Along the way, industrial and urban chemical fractions were added. The Boston air on such nights was the warm, moist, foul exhalation of Yeats' rough beast. Each breath enervated me. I had no appetite, then diarrhea. Clio got the book layout done. She chose a printer.

By day, I taught clerks and typists the keyboard and input basics and fiddled with output fields to please management committees. The former was possible. At night when I finally got home I sat, read and drank for a half hour and frequently awoke in the chair in the awful hours.

Scientific American had an issue on Aging. The bottom line seemed to be that every human cell has a built in timekeeper. The DNA chain of each healthy cell's chromosome sheds a piece of its leading end each time it replicates, until the leading end—called the teleomere—is gone. Then the chromosome breaks down and the cell dies. After seven or eight cycles, time's up for that cell.

Lose enough cell function and the tissue and organ begins to decline.

Sometimes I think, life is just a rodeo. The trick is to ride, make it to the bell.

∞

On the Wednesday after Labor Day, at the "Partners' Lunch" I gave my report on the new system. I readily allowed Harry to strut and fret before and after from the briefing sheet I had given him three hours earlier. He was a quick study. Anyone not knowing him or anything about integrated data base management would have gotten the impression that he was right on top of this thing.

The first question was a cream puff I volleyed to Harry and while he was getting around to an answer, I relaxed enough to look around the table. I immediately noticed a stranger—a thirtyish woman I had not seen before. She was sitting next to Ken Sedgwick and looking pointedly at me. And when I looked back at her she did not turn away.

We looked directly at each other from a distance of about twenty feet for the length of time it took me to get embarrassed or thrilled or frightened and break off with a shudder and a weak smile and a serious adrenaline spike. When I glanced back sidelong, she was writing on a yellow pad and, for the rest of the meeting, she never looked my way again.

I pretended to pay attention to the round of questions which Harry now more and more confidently fielded without me, all the time keeping a surreptitious eye on her. She showed whatever she had written on the pad to Ken, who nodded, then glanced my way. I became once again intent on Harry's steeplechase around the facts. When I checked back, she and Ken were looking at the next questioner at their end of the table.

It is difficult to get a clear impression of someone

It is hard to get a clear sense of someone who is sitting down; relative stature, style of presentation and movement are much of what we take for the measure of another. She was wearing a simple dark grey almost black jacket with a square-cut collar and a pale grey, man-tailored shirt. Her hair seemed to be almost the same color as her jacket, cut moderately short and lightly permed so that it stood out framing her face in an old-fashioned marcelled look. I remember noticing how fair her skin appeared and I had an impression of a small nose and good cheekbones. It was an ordinary enough face but for her eyes, which were set perhaps a millimeter wide and which even when not looking at me seemed large, strikingly pale-colored, lively and strongly intelligent.

∞

This being a quarterly lunch, it was followed by a reception nicely done with excellent settings and service, including a beautifully detailed, large, cut-crystal punch bowl filled with glaringly discordant colored soda cans packed in ice. There were four green bottles of wine—an unusual white Chateauneuf-de-Pape—but a glass of white wine at 3:00 p.m. is amateur drinking at its worst. I got a cup of tea in a nearly transparent Rosenthal cup and was answering a question from one of the international law partners when Ken caught my eye and called me over in the totally silent and nearly invisible way only powerful old Alphas like him develop.

As I got closer, I saw the woman was standing next to him. She turned and looked at me again as intently as before while Ken introduced her with words I never heard. I felt pulled into her and confronted with nothing; it was a look of complete openness and utter reserve. She turned back to Ken and I retrieved my hand from where it seemed to hang in the air after she released it. I felt the impress of her grip remain. I knew where each of her fingers had touched my palm. I remembered the rhythm of her grasp.

A conversation already in progress turned expectantly to me.

"I'm not sure I understand," I said honestly.

"Well," said Ken, giving no indication that I was as out-of-it as I felt, "I mean to say, can computers in this country communicate with computers in Europe?"

"Oh, absolutely, but the ease and sophistication of that communication varies a great deal, particularly among smaller systems. The most common operating systems require English commands to use; European and Japanese systems are more likely to rely on operating systems that are not linguistically restricted. The system we just installed here is the most popular in Europe and number two with the Japanese. Why do you ask?"

Time, give me time; somebody else talk so I can figure out what's going on.

"Well, it seems to me," Ken continued, "if we can do all the processing you described together with our European partners, we will cut weeks out of the time it takes to send information back and forth, that would save a great deal."

"It might, but all your really crucial communication is nearly instantaneous anyway with wire fund transfers, telex, and now fax transmission."

"But those are not secure." The woman joined the conversation and glanced at me briefly as though I were a face in the crowd.

"Still, I think we all agree," Ken went on, "that where compatibility between the two offices can be arranged, the ease of communication will be improved."

It was penetrating my skull that we were talking about Boehrkopf.

"Certainly," I ventured, "and if security is an issue, information transfer in digital form permits CIA-quality encryption."

"Cannot the same computers that create the codes be used to break them?" she asked me blandly, her eyes now hooded and inexpressive. Was I having hallucinations, hot flashes, brucellosis?

"The standard practice is now a one-time code based on a large set of random numbers. In theory the experts say, and so far in practice, with proper access security it is an impenetrable system."

"Well, I think you might help us again, Phillip. Ms. Morgan has just gotten our partners' approval to establish a currency trading function for us managed out of Zurich. We would like you to make a brief review of the computer connections between the two locations with a special eye to security. We were all impressed with how thoroughly your report covered our file security in the new system here."

I had played the safe-as-houses note heavily to inoculate against any last-minute moves by Ralph. Now I began to wonder what I had bought for myself.

Ms. Morgan turned to me in a way that excluded Ken. Her face opened again and her eyes seemed as big as the world. I felt the same hollow rush from my throat to my guts.

"I will talk with my partners in Zurich. We will be in touch."

She held my eyes two seconds longer, then turned and disappeared into a hole in the crowd. I turned back to where Ken had been and found myself stepping into Harry's smarmy personal space.

"Good work, Gardiner; better than a poke in the eye!"

"Thanks, Harry."

A poke in the eye?

"By the way, who was the woman sitting beside Ken?"

"You mean the woman Ken just introduced you to and you were just talking to?"

"Yes, Harry, that woman." Churl.

"Her name is something Morgan; she's a partner at Boehrkopf," Harry said, adding nothing to my supply of information.

"One of the *frères*?"

"What... oh yeah, guess they ought to change it. Never be able to keep that name in the States, some women's group would be on them like flies on shit."

Harry was getting expansive and I needed a serious drink, a wholly incompatible set of circumstances. I told him I would be in tomorrow to go over final documents and records and good-byes.

I went directly to the elevator bank, directly to the street, and directly to the Blue Moon.

∞

On a foggy night, the Blue Moon looks like a mirage or a movie set piece: blue neon, curved front, dark windows backed with plywood; quintessentially harbor front, blue collar, whiskey bar. In the daytime, it is a raw sore of stained stone, cracked facade and rusted signage. If it looks timeless at night, in the daylight it looks like it is out of time—a hapless survivor of harder, coarser days heading the way of Scollay Square and Quincy Market, but holding onto the barrail with one work-hardened hand and calling for another round. I went in.

My eyes began to dilate; the low, blue fluorescent, ultra smoky atmosphere resolved into figures. Two to my right on the short ell of the bar in name tagged green twill work uniforms were talking over draft beers.

"Ya, I always take Opening Day. Usually get drunk by eleven, though, and sleep through the game."

I moved down the bar to a stool past the service station. The vampire behind the bar looked at me and said nothing.

"Jack Daniel's on the rocks."

He reached for the Jack Daniel's bottle on the back shelf.

"Not the Heinz 57, the real bottle."

Without turning around, he said, "Two dollars a shot."

"Make it a double."

His hand came out of a cabinet with a Jack Daniel's bottle showing considerably less wear on the label than the hardy perennial behind the bar. I laid a five dollar bill on the bar and he poured me a decent drink.

I sipped it quickly in small, greedy bites, taking in the low, foul air of the place. It exactly matched my mood. The Blue Moon was the end of a gritty era in downtown Boston. Development had sanitized everything outside of the doomed Combat Zone into fern bars, running-shoe stores and Brigham's ice cream outlets. The Chinese Merchants Association, or one of their *hui*'s, would take care of the Zone in a few years, I was sure, and the Blue Moon was way overdue for its final last call.

I started coming in after our offices moved to Russia Wharf in '83. After about 11:00 p.m. my productivity at the office or my guilt- and greed-driven need to be there fell off steeply, but I would be wired from byte-bashing and occasionally want to look at another form of life for a few minutes before burrowing into my solitary hole. There was a bare-brick and singles bar *et* grille on the street level of the office which compounded its unattractiveness by having the loudest stereo juke box in the zip code and displaying sporting events with no sound on too many TVs. So I wandered the streets on those nights looking for a place to drink where I would not run any risk of seeing anyone who knew me or my histories. The Blue Moon was a natural—the absolute antithesis of the clean, well-lighted place.

The first drink disappeared without a trace or perceptible effect. I was humming. I remembered the first time I encountered this. Returning to the tight social circle I grew up in for an evening attempt at reconciliation with my father, I drove to his country club for a dinner dance. While sitting nervously not talking to my family, I noticed the girl I was supposed to have happily-ever-aftered with across the room ignoring me and laughing loud enough so I could not do the same. I ordered a gin and tonic and then another one. By the time the orchestra started, I was on number five and as sober as when I walked in. Emotional tension has the same effect, at least on me, as tropical heat; the body burns off alcohol faster than I can drink.

I spent the rest of the afternoon trying to get ahead of the curve.

The mysterious Ms. Morgan with those predator eyes was in front of me like a dream memory. She had 'Danger' and 'Bridge Out' written all over her. And I knew I would see her again whether I thought I wanted to or not.

The emotional heat I felt standing in front of her was as real as the thermal impact at an open hearth furnace. But instead of driving me away, I was pulled in, and instead of a white hot center, I sensed an Arctic ice, just as white and just as deadly.

As I was obsessing on these feelings, the two sportsmen I passed on the way in got into a yelling match which culminated in one of them shouting, "Well, a right-wing dictatorship is better than a fucking left-wing dictatorship any day!"

I had breathing room now. When I saw Harry tomorrow, I would submit invoices that would provide enough money for another eight to ten months. I did not have to go anywhere. I did not have to do anything more for Ken or Harry or any of their tribe. On the other hand, turning down work was not the best strategy for someone with my limited options, and all the answers, or at least all the next questions about these special people seemed to lead to Europe.

I came back to Ms. Morgan; what were her given names? And Clio, I had forgotten to ask her father about the name Clio. I thought about calling him to ask and realized that the whiskey was on its way.

I had another drink.

I relived the scene where I walked into the garage at the age of three and found my lovely, lyrical grandfather dead. I saw again the body's last dirty tricks.

I had another drink.

I am sure I had another after that, but, at some point, I got sufficiently ahead of the curve to realize the value of getting closer to my bed. It was after dark. In the only Boston cab with shock absorbers, I flowed through the streets, cruising like a power boat, leaning into the curves, singing "With or Without You." The driver, as the Limeliters used to say, while not wildly enthusiastic, was tolerant.

"Sleight of hand and twist of fate, on a bed of nails she makes me wait."

At the door, I scooped Camille to my shoulders, overbalanced, and stumbled in. She bailed out and headed for the kitchen. I followed and fed her immediately to keep her from walking on my face while I slept and woke to find her doing just that and the morning sun shining in my eyes.

I did not have anything to do for four hours except wake up, get out from under the hangover as far as I could and get presentable for my final sit-down with Harry. To get my mind off the pain and stupidity and remorse, I read the *Globe* in minute detail, did the Word Jumble, which took forever—evidently a quantity of the cells I had burned up were involved with verbal skills—and watched a "Hart-to-Hart" rerun. At ten-thirty, I headed for State Street via the Gardens, the Commons, and the MTA. The last was a mistake. A warm enough day coupled with the borrowings and leavings of the night before and a defective air-conditioning system in the car

I boarded put me into the office sweaty, funky and drained.

Collecting the final corrections of the training manual I had left the previous morning, I found two typos, made a minor refinement that was probably no improvement and walked over to Harry's office. It didn't matter to me what he said, so we got along just fine.

As he was gathering up the files at the end of our discussion, his elderly secretary handed him a piece of paper. He looked at it and passed it over.

"It's a telex for you."

Three

PHILLIP L. GARDINER CONFIRMED RESERVATIONS ON SWISSAIR 16; ARRIVE ZURICH 1000 10 SEPTEMBER. YOU WILL BE MET. TICKETS FOLLOW.

When I looked up after reading it a few times, I was surprised to see Harry still there. The sub-aqueous stupidity of my hangover and our conversation had been incinerated by the imperative tone and memory of the woman who signed the telex, "Morgan."

"We have anything else?" I asked, getting up.

Harry agreed we didn't, probably shook my hand, may have said good-bye. It was a week later before it occurred to me that I might not ever have to see the poor, sorry son of a bitch again.

I went directly to the library section of the forty-second floor. The receptionist/clerk/librarian was a delightful, dark Caribbean lady with a perfect British public school accent. I had previously wondered how Boston's better bigots reacted when she showed up for an appointment; wondered if that was why she was in the library instead of the front offices.

I had returned books several times that had been pulled at my request, but I had no idea how to get things out, what was included in the library, and what might be proscribed.

"I have to meet with Boehrkopf Frères in two days. Are there any files I could review that would help me understand their history or the relationship?"

"The files on Boehrkopf Frères and the agreement are in the Partners' Archives. They must be requested by a partner in writing. Do you have such a written request?"

I thought of ironically showing her the telex. This silver bullet should tell you who I am. I touched it, folded in my pocket.

"Is there anything more accessible? I have to leave tomorrow. Is there a clipping file?"

"There has never been a clipping file on the firm; any clips go into case or individual files. But there may be something helpful in another spot. Please wait here."

She locked her desk and went through a door in a side wall that latched behind her. Information is power, to paraphrase an aphorism by Bacon that was chiseled into an Academy cornerstone I stood next to twice a day for four years. Sir Francis or Sweet Roger, whichever it was, had it that knowledge was power, but that puts too high a value on human wisdom. Maybe it was true in their day, but now knowledge won't get you nearly as much as a richly organized data base. Knowledge is personal, but information—data of value to decision making—is universally useful, and valuable. It's the difference between your good looks and your bank account; people may envy them both, but they can or will only steal the money. Knowledge is nowhere near the liquid commodity information is, and if we live in an information age, as the Rocky Mountain High Sociologists/ Priests have it, that information is also preeminently a commodity. The information behind this door would be substantially easier for someone to shop around town or the Eastern Seaboard than the wisdom of all the S, B greybeards. Like Hong Kong in Clavell's romances—everything is available; everything is for sale.

The Bajan librarian came back with two fairly large scrapbooks. I had leafed through the current 'baby book' in the main waiting room once and was disappointed if all she had was pictures of two years' crops of interns and new associates.

She put them both on the long table next to her desk and, indeed, one of them did prove to be the baby book for 1952.

"It is a bit dark in that corner so I brought them both. Here, this is the one I had in mind." She opened the second, a green-embossed leather book about eighteen inches square with braided, green-ribbon binding.

"S, B: The First Hundred Years: 1835-1935" was hand-engrossed on the title page.

"Can I borrow this?"

"You may borrow it if you sign it out," she corrected me, passing over a piece of paper which I filled out in Ralph's name, office and phone number.

"This is for a project for Mr. Baxter," I explained. "He'll return it."

It fit in my book bag, but the flap would not close over it, so it stood up like a grey billboard, about as persuasive as an "I'm not stealing this" sign. I put the scrapbook under my arm and carried it as nonchalantly as possible down the hall to the elevator bank and through the lobby to the street.

∞

On the street, the heat and humidity grabbed me like a great hand. I broke into a quick sweat in which I basted as the open-window taxi I hailed crawled through afternoon traffic to Back Bay. I told myself I was ignoring the book which I did not release.

It was around three-thirty when I got home. There

was a notice stuck in the door to call Mitchell Couriers for a delivery.

I dropped everything I was carrying on the big table and exploded out of my clothes on the way to the bathroom where I showered for about fifteen minutes; to hell with the Quabbin Reservoir. I tried to wash the Blue Moon, the T, the taxi and everything else off my skin.

As I got out, I had the inescapable opportunity virtually every bathroom in the United States affords of seeing oneself nude. I looked skinny, but not nearly as dissipated as I felt.

In an old 'Spiro T. Agnew: A Great American' T-shirt and a loose pair of Levi's, I redistributed my work clothes, retrieved the scrapbook, picked up something for my hand from the bar, and sat down at the window.

The scrapbook was a poor collection of internal ephemera: announcement cards, business cards, a report cover; the firm appeared to either ignore or avoid press coverage. In fact, in the four and half years I had watched S, B moving many large corporate and legal chips around the Financial District, neither the firm's name nor that of its partners had ever been publicized.

Here was an invitation to a reception for "...the Partners of Boehrkopf Frères" on May 18, 1934. The envelope had been addressed to Ralph. I went back through the collection looking for other personal indicia. There was an announcement from 1891 regarding the partnership of a Timothy Baxter Bourne and a calling card of one David S. Berman. Turning through the pages again toward the back, I noticed one piece of newsprint with the headline:

"Glass-Steagall Act Passes
Senator Pecora Ascendant"

It was from a *Washington Times* dated 1933. The

article quoted the Senator's aide as saying "The final legislation as passed will thoroughly protect the country from any recurrence of the unfortunate events of October 1929." The aide was none other than Ralph the Baxter. The Senator was further quoted as saying that it would in effect create marvelous new business opportunities as the securities industry reorganized. A J.P. Morgan vice-president expressed an opposite view point.

There was a photo. The Senator was reading a document Ralph appeared to have handed him. Unidentified and standing behind the men, her distinctive eyes just catching the sight of the photographer, was the woman I had met yesterday. Impossible. My mind rebelled. Maybe it was the hair style and the tailoring of her clothes. I got out the Bausch & Lomb magnifying glass from the small cardboard drawer above my compact OED set. The picture dissolved into dots. I looked again. It wasn't her.

I took a sip of the early evening tea. My alcohol-hungry cells switched on with full power vacuum and I shuddered.

For the first time that day a sense of reality came over me. It was not at all clear that I knew what I was doing and I no longer seemed to have much control over what was going on; events and my increasingly unpredictable reactions were hurling me forward.

The second sip was kinder and I began to relax. I was leaving for Europe tomorrow; I should pack.

∞

The next morning, I sent the scrapbook and the certificate copies to myself at Murphy's place; I also included the MATCHUP disks. I called her to say goodbye. I told her it was an unexpected business trip onto which I was going to graft a week of travel on the Continent. I told her I was sorry and that a package might arrive for me at her place. I told her I was sending it to her for extra safekeeping and asked her to hide it in a remote but accessible spot. When she asked what it was, I brought up the subject of my recent break-in. I promised to call her as soon as I got back.

It was bumpy. We had been so close a month ago, but I felt like I had aged several years since then.

I moved Camille to her least favorite place in the universe: a metal cage surrounded by strangers—clearly, she was a prisoner in a previous life. I left her an old red Orvis chamois shirt of mine to sleep on. She was not as understanding as Clio and obviously much less polite. She is too dignified to scratch, but no one hearing her voice as we went would have any doubts that I was a brutal bastard to be doing whatever it was to that poor cat.

I picked up my tickets on the way to Logan. I took a cab, air-conditioned this time. I was early. The plane was late.

SwissAir opened the check-in at five and told us all to convene "over there" at six for a bus to dinner. The agent said a ten o'clock departure was expected; three hours late.

The one useful thing I learned in the United States Army was how to wait. I always carry at least one dense paperback book whenever I go a place I can't walk home from anytime I want. Modern travel is tolerable only with patience and detachment. Doing three thousand to five thousand miles a week during the endless startup years taught me, too. Primarily, I learned that the difference between professional travelers and miserable, self-destructive amateurs was that professionals never take anything which happens any more personally than is strictly required to get to the destination. It is the closest I get to a Zen state. The world zips by around me, a thousand human dramas are bared, strange sights are seen, I travel on. Oo bop she bam, as the late Richard Fariña once put it.

So I picked a seat near the traffic flow, in sight of the meeting point, away from the ashtrays, in good light. I was reading a Pelican book on Middle Eastern Mythology.

At about six, people who had been standing docilely at the designated spot began to shuffle out the door whereat I could see them boarding a bus. I went out another exit and approached the uniformed woman standing next to the open bus door.

"Is there a second bus?"

She nodded to one idling behind the one whose boarding she supervised. I politely broke through the line of fellow passengers, walked down and boarded bus number two. I took the single seat behind the driver, flicked on the light, and went back to ancient Mesopotamia.

The buses took us to the Holiday Inn at the airport where a smallish ballroom had been set with a mediocre buffet. I loaded up on fruit, then went to the bar and drank soda water and read until the herd began to shuffle and moo on the front sidewalk.

We began boarding the plane about twenty after ten and took off around eleven; four hours late.

∞

I lucked out; not only was I in Business Class, but the other seat was empty, so I was as comfortable as it is possible to be on a commercial flight since PanAm took the sleeping berths off the Clipper. I've read all the Johns Hopkins' stuff about jet-lag avoidance diets, but I am not going to turn down free drinks, especially when I'm bored and uncomfortable. I spent the flight, as I always do, in a series of boozy, half-awake, half-asleep cycles. Since I don't wear a watch, I don't know how long the cycles last, probably a couple hours. Have a second drink, close eyes, dream state, head rolls, wake up, sort of, day dream, close eyes, dream state, movie-watchers laugh, wake up, sort of, order another drink, day dream....

A short time after the movie was over, I fell deeply asleep and I had a clear and vivid dream.

I was walking in a forest with a figure in a green-hooded robe or cape. Was it a woman? Was she leading me? I followed. We came out of the woods to an open plain. The moon was full and high and the air cool. We walked a distance from the woods to a tall column of stone. Around it was laid a circle of stepping stones. As I stepped on to the first stone, menace blossomed like a flame and I shrank back. The figure began to turn and face me and I woke up terrified and gasping.

Having a nightmare in the middle of a hundred or so strangers at 37,000 feet is single life at its worst. Jayne always insisted on holding hands during takeoffs and landings and I have always deeply hated sleeping alone. Trying to hide the fear and pretend the emotion was as groundless as the dream, surrounded by people to whom my death would be of no interest unless it occurred in a notable way in their presence, I tried to will my pulse rate and adrenaline level down. One huge network of human neurocircuitry must be dedicated to making each of us believe in the significance of our own unique existence. Certainly nothing in experience would support the idea. I breathed deeply and slowly, closed my eyes and looked up.

I thought about Murphy. She was young and not particularly dramatic, but she was a strong, bright person of enthusiasm, open to novelty and not without irony and humor. I heard the 'yes-but' tone of everything I was thinking. The fact of the matter is that I have never managed to make what I call love last. When I was young, the most gonadotropic and the most intellectual connections would one day wake up dead. As I got older, the reasons, the motivations, the nuances grew more complex and articulated, but the process and result were the same. My cat is the only successful relationship in my life and at least once a month I want to slug or strangle her. Doubtless, it's something genetic.

The fear receded, but I could still see the green figure turning to me and feel that awful knowing that the face I was about to confront was the worst thing I would ever see. I saw the scrub plain, the central rock a rough finger of undressed stone. Was she about to tell me something?

Once I read about an island people in the South Pacific who believed that the dream world was an important arena for human will and action. Children were taught how to dream. There were lessons to be learned from the dream experience. I guess I have always assumed it to be a dustbin for useless reactions and irrelevant associations swept up after the day's experiences. The elements are either obviously proximate and recognizable or fantastically and transparently symbolic. I remember the times I've stopped drinking, the dreams have been incessant and pointless. This one was sui generis. As I thought about what it might mean, the juke box in my head played selections from Brecht-Weill. Lenya sang, "Show me the way to the next whiskey bar....Oh moon of Allah-bahma."

Presently, the cabin attendants began raising the lights and window shades announcing that, ready or not, a new day was beginning in Zurich. Outside the sky gave irrefutable evidence that, as unlikely as it felt, the announcement was true. However, since we were so late out of Boston, we still had about half a day of flying left. I read the current *Vanity Fair—People Magazine* for the semi-literate—then a copy of *Inc.* that I picked up because I knew the company featured on the cover. I started a book about a sex-murder in suburban Philadelphia; bread and circuses, twentieth-century style.

Breakfast was actually on the verge of good and I was able to get an extra carafe of hot water so I had a good supply of tea. Just about the time I was coming fully awake from it all, two women in the group traveling in jackets of an odd shade of plum convened a seminar on soap operas in the aisle immediately behind my right ear. A shifting party of about five or six spent the next hour and more discussing story lines and characters going back over fifteen or twenty years for each of a dozen different series. It was a stunning performance. For total outright decadent banality and utterly unselfconscious pathos, you can't beat listening to Americans talk about television. One of the women had an exceptionally shrill laugh that reminded me of the only time I carried a piglet. It turns out that the right way to carry a smallish pig is by its back legs. I would ignore the seminar's nattering fairly well and then she would squeal and I would be back running across Skip's barnyard with thirty pounds of wiggling pork hanging upside down crapping on my hands.

Eventually the steward and the captain got everybody back to their seats for another meal, which I passed on save for the wine, one split each of Medoc and St. Julien. I snoozed again painfully until the engines reduced speed, indicating contact with Zurich ground control. I made a fast run to the head with a razor and toothbrush. The experience was as pleasant as the effort was effective, which is to say, not very. However, I got my shirt tucked back in and my clothes looked presentable. They seemed to be traveling better than I.

We landed about 3:30 local time. I left the sex-murder book and magazines for the turnaround crew, assembled myself and my dunnage, and plodded out the tube to the terminal. The Zurich airport resembled a Midwestern suburban shopping mall, only with luggage. As I came through the door to the arrivals lounge, a man in a black, almost military cut, uniform stepped towards me with a five-by-eight inch card displaying my last name in hand-lettered script about three inches high; underneath, in smaller gold embossing, was the Boehrkopf Frères imprint.

"*Bonjour,*" I said, determined not to let my practiced dialogue go to waste, "*Guten Tag.*"

He said, "*Tag,*" and took my luggage. I held onto the grey book bag and we walked through a bland, red carpeted lobby under a museum collection of small old planes hung above. I kept trying to look at them, but it made me dizzier and prone to bump into people; it also put me well behind the driver. I caught up to him as we came out to a Clockwork Orange concrete porte-cochère. We waited for a bright blue Hertz van with a luggage trailer to pass and then he led me to a deepwater blue Bentley, late fifties vintage, much like the Rolls of that period—identical, it was always said, except for the grille and the 'B' instead of the Lady on the radiator cap.

He let me into the back and went to stow the luggage. On the seat was an envelope addressed to me. Inside, on heavy, deckle-edged grey paper, was a handwritten note.

"Due to delayed arrival, the driver will take you to your room. He will pick you up at nine tomorrow morning. I will see you."

Ana M. Morgan

∞

After a fast run into the center of Zurich, where I got just a quick look at the river, we made two right turns and pulled into a courtyard surrounded by a yellow stone building of five or six stories with absurdly ornate pediments and cornices. In the yard was a silver Mark X Jaguar and a red 948. Hmm, tough choice. I noticed the chatty driver was waiting silently for me at the door in the front of the Bentley. He was good at being quiet; he made it a separate dimension.

Inside, a black and white marble floor blared up at rococo gilt mirrors and ornately tortured furniture,

Mad King Ludwig's idea of a welcome mat. My eyes felt gritty and too large and there were too many mirrors. I caught serial glimpses of Motormouth and me going up a wide wooden staircase past deep, muddy oils of apparently deformed and defaced persons, perverse Calvinist pride insisting their portraits be as ugly as possible.

At the top of the stairs, we turned right and the decorations settled down to a white and blue brocaded wall covering, simple cherry wainscoting and the occasional intrusion of an Empire table or wall sconce. He led me to an open room, hung the one bag in the closet on the right and put the other on the bed. Through a doorway to my left, I could see a bath; at the end of the room, another door was ajar. He pushed it open and gestured me in.

It was a largish sitting room with a fireplace at one end and, nearest the door, a table set with a smorgasbord of cold foods, several bottles of wine and *The International Herald Tribune*.

I did not hear him leave. I drank half a bottle of wine while I half unpacked, showered and changed into Levi's, wool socks and a red cotton sweater. The rest of the first bottle went during the attack on the cold cuts. I took a second bottle with me for bedside entertainment as I pretended to finish the IHT.

∞

I was back in the land of my earlier dream. I was again at the edge of the woods. The grassy plain was not clear but undulant in a cover of heather and gorse and rising to a center mass of many dark objects surmounted now by a flashing star that strobed through the colors of red, blue and green. The figure stepped forward onto the plain and turned with head bowed and covered face hidden, but held out a left hand to me. I believe I took it.

I must have come awake slowly; I had been deeply

asleep, nothing was familiar, nothing was clear. She sat on the edge of the bed on the side that I faced, lying there. She pushed my hair back across my forehead and smoothed it down. I tried to focus. She seemed to have on the same tailored outfit I had last seen in Boston.

"Are you awake?"

"Apparently."

"May I see you?"

She pulled the bedclothes back, leaving me under the sheet. I sat up, the sheet fell back to my lap. She lifted it. In the event, my penis was bent under my left leg. She reached down and unfolded it.

"You are large, aren't you?" She squeezed a response from me.

"I want to suck, kiss, how do you say?"

"Under the circumstances," I believe I said, " I say go ahead."

She did. She told me a good deal about herself without speaking again. She liked to be on top. Under the circumstances, I let her. She rode me to a tricky end, freezing at the top of a stroke just before I knew I was about to come and then, after my first spasm, pouncing and driving, to wrench from something deep in me my last source of energy and consciousness.

∞

It was full daylight when I came awake, confused and unsure of time and place. As I sat up, I had that instant of total recall the brain seems to reserve for the worst of our nighttime excesses. I shuddered, physically shook myself and looked quickly around. I was alone.

The smell of coffee led me into the sitting room where I learned the time was 7:20 a.m. A collection of juices, breakfast rolls and cold cereals now covered the side board. Who did you have to fuck to get a hot meal around here?

I felt awful. I was stiff and weak and frightened and wanted nothing more than to get back into bed, preferably any bed but the one I had left. Then I thought about Lurch showing up at nine and thought about just bolting. I could be packed and gone in ten minutes; twenty, if I took a shower and shaved.

But then what? Good-bye, Boehrkopf Frères, good-bye S, B? I could call in sick from the airport; better yet, the train station, but tell them the airport. No. I couldn't do it. I refused to act that afraid. I felt a sense of shame and embarrassment that could only be controlled if I pretended nothing last night had happened. I thought to run and remembered a line from a seventeenth century German story: *Schade, schade. Ich werde nach Hause wiedergehen.* Zurich would be another place I couldn't go again.

So, for any number of bad reasons, I stayed and made a cup of tea from my own supply with the hot water next to the collection of Swiss Miss chocolate drink packets; the banality of the counterfeit and the conceit somehow relaxed me.

And with my eyes wide open—blood-shot, but wide open—and seeing virtually nothing of what was in front of me, I took the other step into Forever.

Four

The walking cadaver knocked just after the clock began striking a discreet nine tiny tinkles of its unimaginably tiny Swiss chimes. The stodgy bourgeois furniture and the ornate Swiss decoration were getting on my nerves. There was an inbred and constipated predictability that came from centuries of monocultural identity. In the U. S. we have developed a plastic, commercial style of design and decoration based on our lowest common denominators, wiping out not only regional differences, but also showing other cultures how to merchandise themselves, witness the Swiss Miss.

I was fed up with the pretension I felt in the room and from the driver and that which I anticipated at the Boehrkopf Frères office.

The driver and I had the same conversation as the day before, but the atmosphere felt different as he followed me down the hall and the stairs. The help always know.

We took the Bentley and, in it, a series of short turns that ended next to a relatively modern granite building in a court just off the Banhoff Strasse. He escorted me to a recessed entry and pushed a button next to a well-shined brass plaque which identified the tenants as

Boehrkopf Frères. He was back to the car before the doors, with a dull clack, unlocked and I walked into a nearly featureless lobby done in the same sort of industrial strength modernity as the exterior. The floor was the kind of polished granite most popular with a certain class of mortuary stonecutters, just a shade too bright in grey. The walls were paneled in blond wood last seen as the cabinetry for a Sylvania Halo-Light console television advertised by Bud Collier on "Beat the Clock."

One of the two elevator doors opened before I got further in the inventory and critique. The car went up two floors and opened on a mostly tasteful, mostly Empire foyer with a medium-size oval Queen Anne table in the center and a matching mirror on the left wall. There were two torchiere lamps opposite and one closed door in the wall facing me. About the time I was beginning to spike serious adrenaline, thinking about who might be coming through the door, it was opened by a pleasant-faced, notably young looking man in an expensively baggy, black suit, white shirt and unfigured blue tie.

He introduced himself as Ian, said he was English, inquired about my trip and arrival, accommodations, etc. as he led me down a dark green carpeted hallway with cream-papered, undecorated walls. Unlike the starkness of the lobby, the interior felt actually peaceful especially after the riot of decoration back at the residence. We turned into a conference area about twenty by thirty feet where Ian introduced me to four men, three of whose names I forgot as quickly as I heard the next. The only name I retained was Claude-Philippe, who looked to be the oldest, but was introduced last. I was directed to sit next to him.

Claude-Philippe was somewhat tall by European standards, and certainly an inch or more above my five-ten, but not really as tall as he seemed. He had the presence and stature that military posture or aristo breeding seem to confer, so he filled more space than he took up. He had fair skin with the outlines of a distinguished skein of wrinkles, nearly white hair, thick but cut short, and strong, glacier-blue eyes. Where Ian's suit hung as precisely pressed as a uniform, his of a similar style and just slightly richer cut, had the loose, flowing grace of a second well-worn outer skin.

He spoke first.

"We are pleased you were able to visit us on this topic. Let us discuss what we hope to learn." He looked at me expectantly and relaxed further in his chair.

"I understand I am here in the employ of S, B of Boston with whom your firm has a contractual agreement; I am to advise on the most effective and secure means of transferring electronic computer files between the two firms. I need to learn how your systems work."

"Very well," he said standing up, to my surprise, and motioning me to stay seated, "these gentlemen are the administrative managers of our three directorates; Ian will see that you get anything you need. I should like to meet you around four in my office, for tea, Ian." He smiled at the two of us and left.

∞

We spent the day in their data processing facility on another floor, using a much smaller space with four terminals and an immense expanse of beige glass looking in on the heart of the beast.

Behind smoked panels, three brown and beige towers served each of the two (count 'em) Cray C-90 YP-1's. Each tower held tiers of carousels of magnetic tape which were being shuttled up and down, back and forth, feeding instructions to the CPU. There was enough horse power to predict the effect of a butterfly migration on weather systems worldwide.

One print out gave a 3-D wire frame graph plotting the age of fifty countries' governing party, the country's known cash and precious metal reserves and a K factor that was a complex reciprocal function of national debt minus a productivity deflator plus three times the GNP, or something close to that. The high values formed a short, serpentine ridge in the upper right quadrant. Ian indicated those were watch/raid currency targets.

The C-90's said nothing. The air had an ozone bite to it and it looked cold inside. With the human lights out, only the exit signs and a row of orange jewel lights on one of the file servers showed any occupation within. But the air handling units pumping heat out of the room gave the windows a resonant hum.

They were light years ahead of what I had done for S, B but I think I managed to hide the majority of my ignorance and some of my awe. The three units or directorates, as Claude-Philippe termed them, were engaged in international trade, respectively in real estate instruments, stocks, bonds and commercial paper, and currency. Each unit had a research and analysis function that was jointly managed by these three as a triumvirate. The information they spoke of analyzing was so extensive it would be the envy of a medium-size nation's secret service. They seriously intended to be able to trade intelligently in every regional market in the world.

The principals of the firm were organized in subcommittees of the governing board along these same three lines: real property; debt and equity--both corporate and public; and currency. These subcommittees were the ultimate customer for all the analyses and the source of all strategic decisions. Day-to-day trading was the responsibility of another group of three managers. Each of the principals held a portfolio of primary responsibility outside of the subcommittee format; Claude-Philippe was the principal responsible for overseeing research and analysis.

With Ian's considerate and discreet help I sorted out the three names and with only a few side conversations in French, which I could follow slightly, and German, which I could largely not, they were able to explain things to me well enough in English. The managers indicated an immense respect for Claude-Philippe's intelligence and knowledge. A cold lunch was sent in; Ian arranged for hot water and was most appreciative of my Prince of Wales cache.

I came to understand that as part of a long range plan of Claude-Philippe's, S, B was to take advantage of the recent Reaganiste relaxations in U.S. banking law and regulation to act as a subsidiary agent for BF on unspecified transactions, ideally involving direct channel connection to the system in Zurich. A satellite link was deemed the best for immediacy, accuracy and reliability. The drawback was security which could be handled by the random-number joint-substitution code I had described to Ken and Ana in Boston. But, it would clearly require a dedicated decryption device in Boston with as much horsepower as the supercomputer installation whose tape drives and cooling fans thrummed outside the glass wall. It would probably be a stretch, but I was confident such a system could be devised on this mainframe to mate with the donkey engine data base management system I had installed at S, B. But it was way beyond my ability to even pretend that I knew how to do that.

They agreed to document the encryption system's electronic parameters and give me a copy of the information on the requirements and performance of the satellite links.

∞

At just four o'clock, Ian and I went up an interior set of stairs to the top floor and into an open doorway of a conventional sitting room done in early twentieth century British Clubman style with Spy and Audubon prints. I was admiring a pair of the Audubons—a Roseate Spoonbill and a Peregrine Falcon—when Claude-Philippe entered from an adjacent room carrying a large silver tray which rattled solidly as he set it on a low table.

"Have you ever seen one of those?" he asked me pointedly, looking over half-lens reading glasses.

"Two out of three—I've never seen a Spoonbill, but the Audubons are in many museums, and the falcons are returning along our East Coast. They seem to do quite well in the taller cities; New York has several pair, Boston has two, I heard there was even a pair in Hartford."

"In Europe, the falcon is known for its range, for its wandering, but you describe it as a settled city dweller."

"They are also common along railroad, highway and utility cuts in the countryside. I used to see them when I drove around New England on business."

"So, that is more like it. And which way does the falcon find itself perceived by Americans?"

I exhaled. "The average American only knows the falcon as a professional sports franchise or as a funny looking, discontinued car model. And," I threw in for good measure, "Audubon is now an environmental action group and a bunch of wildlife sanctuaries named after a man who spent his life shooting or suffocating members of species that even in his day were declining, in order to supply the amateur interests of gentlemen naturalists. In Key West, where he was a local resident, the name is a more generally merchandisable commodity, and is probably available on T-shirts and as a sandwich."

Now what set that off?

"Come over here, Mr. Gardiner, and have a cup of Whittard Original. Ian tells me you favor dark teas."

It was delicious and I handled my side of the conversational volley better as he went on.

"I like that image of the falcon finding a newly favorable niche in your less humanly congenial urban jungles as well as in other blights on the land you called 'cuts'. Predators are good at finding new opportunities, they are most adventitious."

"Frank Norris wrote that foxes on the Plains would hunt the game flushed by the passing trains. I always wondered if this might explain the animals you see struck by cars; some irony there."

"The survival instinct can be perverse, many have fallen only through fear. Set a man to walk on a ten-foot beam, six inches off the floor, and he does it with a smile; at six stories, it's a considerably different proposition."

We wandered philosophically in and out of various trivial and weighty observations and enjoyed scones with whipped cream and strawberries. At the end of my second cup of tea, I was entirely refreshed, greatly entertained and relaxed by the conversation and Claude-Philippe's apparently sincere interest in my opinions on topics of the greatest range.

At the end, I remember we were talking about global communication and culture. I played my ragtime version of Cassandra on the theme that commercial communication led to cultural implosion or reduction to the lowest common and trivial or vulgar denominator.

"So to you, the world becomes smaller and more alike everywhere, everyday?" he asked. I nodded.

"I think," he said, "that is rather the perspective from any one person's point of view, but, overall, it is the opposite. The world remains as unlike and atomistic as ever, but people everywhere think it is all the same and that they are all alike because they get the same video and print images and commercial products. But, in fact, all these technological connections are really culling people into smaller and smaller networks of more and more specialized exchanges. This allows great freedom for those able to move outside."

As I was thinking about whether I had greater freedom, Ana entered the room. She was wearing a yellow suit with dark trim and large buttons that whistled Chanel in a hip, high Big-Noise-from-Winnetka key. On an athletic twenty-year-old girl, it would have been superb; on a woman of, what, maybe thirty-six, it was audacious. She looked stunning, world-class.

She made her way through greetings with first Claude-Philippe to whom she gave a small, wrapped and beribboned gift and then Ian. When she reached me, she seemed as relaxed and pleased to be with me as an old friend. She shook my hand vigorously and looked me in the eye. I saw nothing. Her face was relaxed, without tension. She smiled.

I think I began to see her for the first time. Her face was perhaps a bit pale, her eyes were deep. There seemed to be so much to see. It seemed to beckon like an open book, a high wall, a still pond, a long valley.

I had a rush of emotion for which I have no words. She turned away from me while I continued to stare bemusedly where she no longer was.

"So, Claude-Philippe, you have been entertaining our American with your stories?"

"Mr. Gardiner and I have been entertaining each other with our views of the world. He seems to be of the opinion that most humans give scant thought to life; the results appear to offend him."

"And you, Claude-Philippe," I found myself asking, "do you disagree with either premise or reaction?"

"Your premise is certainly true, almost no humans give much thought to life or, in any real sense, much thought to their own life. But while the effects may be offensive if one focuses on them—the merchandising of the lowest common denominator, as you put it—the resulting social order I find interesting, entertaining, unconsciously diverse and fragile. One could fairly say I find it quite rewarding."

"Yes," put in Ana from where she was now seated next to Ian and the tea, "there is not likely any equal to Claude-Philippe as a student of the human social order."

He responded with a look that indicated this was somehow an old topic between them.

"Just for a minute, let me turn to business now that Ana is here, Mr. Gardiner. This morning you described your purpose: to advise on the most effective and secure means of transferring computer files between here and Boston. Have you learned what you need to do here today, or will you need more time?"

"Your managers have agreed to give me all the documentation I will need to specify the equipment S, B will require for a completely effective and cryptographically secure channel. I am to receive that information tomorrow, at which point, I will be done here."

"You said 'completely effective,' but only 'cryptographically secure'—not completely secure?"

"Nothing is going to be able to crack the codes, but humans must select the codes, do the programming, handle the in-clear input. People will always be the weak link in any security system. They are fallible and fragile; they will get lazy and take a short cut, get drunk and brag about their job; they can be tricked, bribed, seduced, subverted, blackmailed, extorted, and tortured. Nothing involving people can ever be secure. If someone wants in badly enough, there will be a human link available. Minimize access, break up tasks, rotate assignments, use the machine to do as much of the work as possible. Eliminate all unsecured connections to the mainframe. Only input files you generate to the mainframe. Your people input gigabytes of files everyday. Any of them could contain what the hackers call a Trojan Horse which will cut them a side door in your security. Have you had a security evaluation?"

"We rather do our own security evaluation and I think we are far less vulnerable than you assume. But you raise a good point about input to the mainframe. And we will do that immediately, Ian."

Directly, Ian went to a cabinet at the back of the room and picked up a phone which he began to dial. I was impressed.

Claude-Philippe continued, "You have been most helpful and quite stimulating. Please do come to see me before you leave tomorrow. What are your plans, will you return to Boston then?"

"No, I'm going to travel for a week in France."

"And where will you go," Ian suddenly asked, prompting all of us to look at him, then all of them to turn to me.

"Brittany," I replied, "I'm not sure where, but I have never been there. Maybe I will go to Finisterre and see what the end of the Earth looks like."

There was a shade more silence than the rhythm of the conversation to that point would have predicted, certainly more than the wit deserved.

"Ms. Morgan is familiar with Brittany," Claude-Philippe observed, looking at her.

"Yes," she said, giving me all her attention and something more, the way she had in Boston, "I know the area well. What do you hope to see?"

I felt a flood of desire for her.

I looked as straight at her as I would a shooter, a wolf or a banker. It may have been the most courageous thing I did in my life.

"I want to see what it is like. I am curious about it. How do you know this place?"

"My great aunt lives there." An owl; maybe an owl could have those all-knowing, inexpressive eyes.

"Do you have a visa?" Claude-Philippe snapped my focus back to the world.

"No, I assumed I could get one readily here in Zurich."

"Ian can see to that, just give him your passport

before you leave. It will be with your papers tomorrow. In fact, I will have the papers from my managers, your visa and passport all waiting for you here in my office at 11:00 tomorrow. Let us agree to meet then. I shall look forward to it."

He rose, we followed, and, on the way to the door, Ian relieved me of my passport and Ana, with whom I found myself alone at the door said, "May we have dinner tonight? I very much want to talk with you." So cool and direct and I felt my face flush. She gave no sign of noticing anything beyond my saying yes.

"André will pick you up at eight." She smiled and closed the door.

I was not surprised to find silent André waiting for me. It was just before six when I got back to the rooms and I decided to try to get a light measure of sleep before dinner. I locked both the doors.

∞

I was waiting in the courtyard when the Bentley pulled in. Tired of walking through silent corridors behind André, I helped myself and hopped inside before he could get out to open the door.

"*Roulez*," I called through the partition, figuring he probably hated French. It was no easy job turning the Bentley around. André gave it all his attention.

We drove a few twists and turns back towards the Zurich See, then across the Quai bridge and up the hill to the Dolder Grand Hotel. I got out under the portico and, acting like I knew where I was going, walked to the lobby where an inlaid signboard showed the directions to various locations. Taped to the top left was a white sheet of glossy card stock that read "Global Monetary Project—All meetings in Bavaria Suites" in bright red and blue ink. Visiting greed heads come to conspire and cavort with the gnomes.

The *maître d'* showed me to a good-sized table for four set for two. The room was nearly full, mostly with blue or black suits. The cuts ran about even between American and European styles, but the bodies ran mostly to fat. One of the disappointing truisms of the Grand Places is that by the time people have the wealth and taste to pay the bills, time has worked its rude magic. As Andy Capp once said, "Time may be a great healer, but it's no flippin' beauty specialist."

I was rubbing the edge of the heavy table cloth and contemplating the woodwork when the *maître d'* pulled out a chair for Ana and I hopped belatedly into a half crouch. At least I didn't knock anything over.

She was back to tailored grey; a deeper, almost charcoal, fine worsted wool suit with a short stand-up collar that just met her hair which looked to have been restyled (since we parted?) to puff out from her face. The effect both softened her appearance and heightened the contrast, emphasizing her pale glowing face like a dark halo.

She sat up straight and her eyes were the green of the sea in a storm.

"We have had so little time to talk," she said with no trace of innuendo or irony. "I wanted to find out what you thought of our organization. I was particularly interested in your strong feelings about our security. Claude-Philippe says you appear to have an instinct for it."

"Maybe I have a strong eye for the way things can and will go wrong. Someone once called me the man who wouldn't take 'yes' for an answer."

"What weaknesses do you see in what we do?"

"I guess I should assume that you can truly use all the raw data that is being collected. It is such an exceptional amount for a modest-size organization to analyze. I would question the value of so much input."

"The material is not entered without analysis.

Claude-Philippe has written expert systems which evaluate, compare and integrate information from many sources."

"It still seems like too much information to support a trading organization, even one with worldwide ambitions."

"These are not ambitions. We are truly worldwide."

"Then why not rely on local agents or offices to manage regional trading? They would be closer to the real world, have many more sources of information, and be in a better position to make good, quick decisions."

"Local agents may not share our goals, perspective or insights. Experience has shown central control is required. Additionally, a strong secretariat can have many other useful support functions."

"All right, then your three enemies are rivals, hackers, and entropy. One of them will break your security. You can be smart about the enemies, guard against business antagonists, be clever about hackers, but entropy always prevails."

"I don't believe in entropy."

"Really. What about chance, probability, random error, uncertainty, bad luck, chaos, one-of-those-things, indeterminacy; because sooner or later everything breaks down."

"Not if it is constantly renewed."

"You can't keep rebuilding, redesigning your system constantly and using it at the same time. You would have chaos."

"No, I was only talking of an annual renovation, or what do you say, 'upgrade'."

Wine came and food, excellent food. She had the quality Claude-Philippe (and, I must admit, Jonathan in Boston) had of paying such focused, interested attention to what I was saying that I became readily convinced she was as fascinated with it as I. She appeared so thoughtful in her responses. I felt assured of the intelligence of my company.

The next course arrived. She changed the subject.

"How are you traveling to Finisterre?"

"The train."

"That will be a long ride. We have airplanes now in Europe you know, Mr. Gardiner. This is not a quaint museum."

"I prefer to pretend they don't exist. If I flew, I would be surrounded by people like myself back in the States traveling on business, all dressed in uniform business suits, reading the same best-sellers, the same newspapers and magazines. I would rather see the country I travel and the other people."

"Well, in that case, you would not be in Brittany for several days even if you leave tomorrow. May I suggest that we meet there over the weekend? I could show you the countryside. I think my great aunt would like to meet you."

I still felt out of my depth with her. She reached into a small, black purse and gave me a card that read:

Ana Megan Morgan
Folgoât St. Chèldré
La Forêt Basse Bretagne

"Anyone can direct you. Come at noon on Saturday. We can ride around the area and then have dinner with Aunt Vera. You should stay the night. And I have something for you."

Again from the small, black purse she drew, this time, a flat three- or four-inch square black velvet drawstring bag. She reached out and drew my right hand toward her, then placed the bag in my upraised palm, making a warm sandwich of the bag and my hand between her two.

"I want to spend more time with you," she said. "I

find you very attractive. This is something I want you to have from me."

She withdrew her hands and I opened the bag to find a piece of rudely worked ruddy metal about as big around as my little finger, C-shaped in an incomplete, flattened circle; an open oval about four inches by three inches. There were half-inch bosses at each end; other than that, it was completely plain. But the substance of it was powerful. Though not particularly heavy, the unusual, dull reddish color, the simplicity of the design and execution gave it a feeling of age, significance, worth and substance. It felt terribly valuable to me.

"This is a torc, made of bronze. It comes from the time of the Roman occupation of Gaul. It was worn as a bracelet. Sometimes one also finds neck and arm bands. This was found when we put in the swimming pool at *Folgoât*."

There was a frisson of pleasure as I realized that I held something going on 2000 years old, and it was mine.

"I do not talk very much about how I feel," she said, "but I find you very exciting. I want you to have that from me."

She looked straight at me and I was swept once again into her eyes. I saw her finally as beautiful and realized that what made her so unique all along was not that she was beautiful but that she was completely aware of, but totally unconcerned about, her beauty. I have known conventionally beautiful women on occasion—one had been an actress; the other, actually, a social worker. But they both were deeply affected by their appearance. The actress dedicated her life to her appearance to the sacrifice of everything else—humor, thought, adventure, love. The social worker was more balanced, but always, I think, uncomfortable with the attention her arresting appearance drew. Ana had such confidence, such repose as Fitzgerald wrote of Dick Diver.

I looked at the torc in my hand. I think I trembled.

I know that when she rose still holding my eyes and I got up mesmerically with her, my legs were weak.

"I have to go now," she said as she turned to go. I looked at the table and was surprised to see the meal was over.

"André will take you back," she said, facing me again. "Please come at noon on Saturday."

I nodded, smiling, flushed with pleasure and desire.

∞

André appeared the next morning at ten, as I had requested. I was wearing my traveling suit, which had been rejuvenated by an invisible staff member of the establishment.

I nodded toward my bags and stepped through the door. It worked; finally, a language he understood. André followed me down the hall with my bags. The book bag hung heavier on my right shoulder with cameras and traveling gear.

Claude-Philippe was writing something at a small escritoire when I entered. He stood up immediately and approached with that air of an eager friend.

"We have all of your papers here." He led me around to the low table about which we had tea the day before.

"Before you go, I wanted to ask what your plans are for your future."

"I'm not very sure. My future has been arriving faster than I can plan for it recently. I expect when I go back to Boston, I will look for another consulting opportunity."

"Would not you be helpful in the system installation at S, B?"

"No. Too specialized a technical task. I don't speak the language that well."

"You have a background in business, but an advanced academic degree, I believe."

"Yes."

"Your career shows some unusual transitions." He gestured to a copy of my three-and-a-half-year-old resumé that had once been part of a business plan for our late, lamentable venture.

I had to admit this was true.

"Do you enjoy travel?"

"Camus wrote in his journals that there is no pleasure in traveling, he said he looked on it as an occasion for spiritual testing. I tolerate it well enough, but I can't say I enjoy it. I do like new places, though, and the only way to get to them is by traveling."

"Yes, that's true enough. Well, the point is, you have a quality of intelligence and energy that might be quite helpful to us in our wider operations. I'd like you to give some thought to the terms on which you might offer to help with our other sources of information outside of the electronic media.

"We have a foundation here that supports academic research on contemporary topics. I am the managing director; I need someone to manage field relationships with researchers, editors, publishers. The position would be based here in Zurich at a different address." He folded my resumé in quarters and dropped it in his side coat pocket, handed me a buff, sealed A4 envelope with my name typed on a card pinned to it; shook my hand, and led me to the door.

"Call Ian to make an appointment when you will be coming back through Zurich. His card is in the envelope."

He smiled and turned back into the room; I closed the door and left.

∞

I found my luggage in the foyer; André apparently got the last laugh. On the street I hailed a cab for the quick trip down to the station, another grand temple to early twentieth century transportation gods.

I do love trains, for all the obvious reasons. I found a baggage cart, a timetable, the right line, the correct change and a seat on a bench near the gate. An hour later, I was heading west.

When I was very young and my father was away at war, my mother and I shuttled between my grandparents' homes on trains whose schedules I still remember. My favorite was the 11:45 sleeper out of Easthampton that got us into Philadelphia around five in the morning to change for the local to Chester. My mother's sister always met us on the first train into Chester Station and I could relax again after the cold winter discipline of my father's island home and run through the warm, narrow halls of my grandfather's hotel. I have no early memories of my father's father and few of his mother, and my maternal grandmother had died very young, but Michael—my mother's father—I remember as vividly as anyone I have ever known.

He played the violin and found me gifts everywhere we went and pulled coins from my nose and ears. We chased the circus calliopes. We decorated the windows and doors at every season. He had beautiful white hair and he died when I was three and a half. Two months later, my father came home and life continued downhill after that. We lived with my uncle and aunt in the big old house. Cousins and brothers arrived. We moved to a place my father designed. He had no patience for me. I had no love for him.

I remember when I first came to Europe with my father. I was a few months shy of sixteen and saw him for the first time in an environment he did not, could not control. I was totally invigorated by his frustration and impatience. The day of the Versailles excursion, I pretended to be sick and spent the day roaming Paris, enthralled that there was this entire city, country, civilization that did not know my father and did not seem to give the first damn about what he wanted or how he thought things should be done.

It is amazing I found my way back to the hotel and clearly a good thing I did not discover Montmartre and the girls on the street who made my solo return visit to Paris three years later so memorable. What would I have done at the age of fifteen armed with a vast wealth of ignorance, misinformation, fool-hardiness, testosterone and traveler's checks?

∞

As we got closer to Paris, I began questioning my plans; always a dangerous idea en route. I could stay in Paris, spend the night or the week at *Les Jardins*, laze the day away on the *Rive Gauche* among Arab students, salacious art and great coffee. I could go back to the Savannah Cafe below the Pantheon where Petra and I had eaten every night but one during the best week in my life. I could talk to Richard behind the bar; he had seen me through the arc of all my errors. Our last visit there had been as maudlin as a funeral and just as effective at reviving what it celebrated. Paris was as dead to me as old transplanted Heloise and Abelard in gaudy *Père Lachaise*.

I took a taxi direct from Austerlitz to Gare de l'Ouest, booked a compartment on a train leaving forty minutes later. When I got to the compartment, I pulled down the bed and fell asleep immediately. I seemed to be sleeping so much.

Sometime later I woke. Why was Ana so quickly into me? I thought about seeing her again; there was anxiety and hunger, like a secret sin. I pushed the thought away. I went back to the people who had propelled me here.

Staring out at the regular and occasional lights of the French countryside, I thought back to my lists in Boston, all the names and addresses, all randomly distributed around New England and Europe. And all clients of S, B. And all orphans. And all favored by their forty- to sixty-year old aunts or uncles. And never sick. And all sailors?

I had gotten as deep into S, B files as there was and there were no answers there. I had collected all the public data available in Massachusetts and there was nothing there either. By my own device, the data at Boehrkopf was secure beyond my reach. The only remaining clue I had, outside of looking one of these people up and asking outrageous questions, was the "*Agence Privée de Bretagne*" somewhere in the vicinity of Morbihan on the southwestern coast of Brittany.

My facts added up to nothing. I could speculate endlessly. Something was going on with the 21 identities, but the more I thought about it, the more likely it seemed I had tripped into a little nest of Cold Warriors, Langley spooks or maybe humint types from Meade, or who knows where; part of the black budget. S, B was unlikely to be involved in a real estate swindle, but the espionage establishment was a real good fit.

Spooks scare me. Back from Vietnam in graduate school, I was engulfed by a small swarm of CIA/NSA neophytes once and they introduced me to an interviewer. The neophytes were in full Nietzschean rut; the interviewer looked at me like I was already dead. Nothing is true; everything is permitted. Who's next?

So I was done with it and well out of it. I would throw away the disks and the certificate copies when I got back. I do not want to know.

Boehrkopf Frères with all that electronic horsepower and international ambitions was more of the same. And Claude-Philippe wanted to talk about my future.

I thought about going back to Paris from the next

stop. But I needed time away from cities and memories and days I knew how to fill without thinking.

Also I had gotten curious about Brittany when I looked up the location of *Agence Privée de Bretagne* in the London Times Atlas. It was in the province next to Finisterre which had sounded romantic, opposite Land's End in Great Britain forming the lower side of the English Channel and the upper point of the Bay of Biscay.

The Globe Travel Book Store had nothing on the area. In a *Frommer's Dollarwise Guide to Europe*, I had found that the railroad to Finisterre follows the old Roman Road, with stops along the way including one a few dozen kilometers from the village of Morbihan.

What might I find of the *Agence Privée* , etc.; an electrified fence, no trace, an offer I couldn't refuse? No, thanks.

At that point, the rhythm of the cars induced my reptile brain to begin the chorus of "The Gambler" by Kenny Rogers. I spent my remaining minutes or hours of consciousness across the Midi trying to remember the first line. I remembered, to my surprise and disgust, every other stupid word, but the first. " . . . .; on a train bound for nowhere, I met up with a Gambler, we were both too tired to sleep." Over and over, like the cavity of a lost filling your tongue can't help but find.

Mercifully, I finally slept again.

∞

The train got into Vannes about 6:00 a.m. With the necessary intricate, yogic maneuvers, I managed to be dressed and repacked and staring out the window as we slowed into the station. Travel by train seems so well-scaled and blended to each arrival, our grand mechanical conveyance easing into another grand stone cathedral to travel and commerce.

The schedule indicated the first train to Brest was

leaving in less than an hour. By determined effort, I wrestled my impedimenta to a café just opening in the station and was able to secure oatmeal, juice and coffee. I had no luck with "*aqua chaud pour le thé*" and a display of my tea bag. The further I got from Paris, the less frequently anyone pretended to understand my French.

∞

The local to Brest was full and I shared a seat with a heavy man dressed in the remains of a business suit. He had the obligatory florid complexion, bad teeth, odor of carnivore spiced with garlic and a *soupçon* of too-long-since-last-bath-or-laundry- maybe-both. Fortunately, or not, I had gotten the window seat so, although I could not escape, I did at least have something else to look at. The train ran inland crossing an occasional large river flowing south down land I knew to be breaking toward the sea. Twice I caught sight of a larger body of water.

The land itself was open, rolling; golden broom and purple heather were the dominant weeds. The various holdings were walled with a brightish limestone, and ribbons of stone in perfect repair wrapped the earth, occasionally swelling into dooryards and paddocks from which grew houses and barns of the self-same stone. I watched the beautifully smooth progress and recession of the land; then, for a while I became fascinated by the way the five telegraph lines that followed the track looked like a musical scale for a minimalist composition with occasional birds for notation.

We made many stops, after one of which I was relieved of my seatmate with *l'air du* tramp. The passenger count was down considerably when I got off at Responden. There was a *restante* counter where I left the two large bags and then walked out into the streets. It was good to be moving on my own, walking, free to be a stranger.

Many of the buildings were of the half-timbered style called Tudor in the States. The people were shorter and darker than the French of the interior. I remembered once for an obscure professional reason spending most of a week in a small town in Kansas that had grown from a small Mennonite community imported en masse from Ukraine by the Sante Fe Railroad as an agriculture base for a stockyard operation. Virtually everyone in town must have descended from four women and three men who had left Germany in 1630. The males were all round-headed and the females, all freckled. There was that same remarkable genetic sameness about these people, but they certainly had not come from Germany.

In an eighteenth century monument to someone's wealth now called Hotel de France, I got a desk clerk to conjure up and introduce me to a means of getting to Morbihan. His name was Jules, which had mythic resonance for me because of a remarkably large man of that same name, now deceased, whom I once watched throw a 350 cc Japanese motorcycle off a bridge abutment on Highway 101 north of San Francisco.

This was not Big Jules; in fact, the incarnation in front of me was smaller than I. We agreed on a price of 180 francs and, an hour later, at about four in the afternoon, I was paying Jules that amount and twenty francs more in front of the fountain in bustling, downtown Morbihan. After Jules and his Peugot left, there ceased to be any bustle. There was just me and my luggage.

I was violating one of my primary rules of travel—always know where you're going to stay the first night—but I was glad to be here, far away from everything familiar and apparently sure. There was a cafe on the southwestern side of the square and the sea breeze, I began to notice, made me feel like it would be a good idea to sit in the sun there and perhaps have a drink.

I felt even better after the second Ricard *avec* and was able to learn of a hotel around the corner. Considerably less grand than the Hotel de France, it was also full, but the manager made two phone calls and presently a dun-colored flatbed truck about 1/16 ton capacity pulled up in front and my luggage and I were directed onto the back.

In this august fashion, rather like a *grande dame* of the *ancien régime*, born on her chaise to the cathedral for her feast day, I was carried to the outskirts of town, about three quarters of a mile of low half-timbered, then brick, then stone buildings. We pulled into a cobbled courtyard past a sign that said *La Ruche d'epi* and hastened a proud but nervous flock of deep-keeled grey geese on their way. After the driver cut the engine and before my ears could recover from the rumble through town, a large wooden door opened and I was greeted as though I was expected by a woman of leathery years dressed in bright sky blue and snowy white.

"M. Gardiner, allo; welcome to *La Ruche*."

"*Merci, Madame, merci bien.*"

"*Donnez-lui vos bagages, et entrez,*" she directed; so I *donnez*-ed the baggage to *lui* and *entrez*-ed.

The wall through which we passed was the same bright stone I had occasion to admire along the way. We walked past a large, open, studded dark wood door into a stone-floored foyer with heavy, medieval-looking side chairs and a long trestle table.

"*Je suis Madame Mulon,*" she introduced herself inside. "You wish a room for how long?"

"*Une semaine, si possible?* A week, if possible."

Consulting a large fabric bound ledger on the table, she frowned.

"In one week begins hunting season and all rooms are rented. So, one week only we can have you with us."

"This is good then, one week only I will stay. *C'est bien, merci, une semaine seulement.*"

We were both pleased by our agreement and our multilingual skills. For a modest number of traveler's checks, I secured a room to which she then led me by a roundabout excursion through the dining room—small tables for two and four, totaling maybe twelve at most—the kitchen, the garden, up a spiral stone staircase in an attached building, to a long, somewhat low room with dormers and thick, heavy furniture floating in a sea of white: white walls, white ceiling, white curtains, white covers, white dust ruffle, white dresser scarf. Thick, dark beams outlined the edges of the room across the ceiling, at the corners and doors. The dark wood-polished floor was scattered with oval rag rugs of occasionally bright fabrics.

"*Cette chambre c'est le numéro huit*," she said, handing me a key ring about as large as the torc, with two keys. "*Pour la chambre*," she said and held up the modern key and "*pour la porte*," she gestured downstairs with an older skeleton-type key. Not too hard to keep that straight. *Lui* had gotten there first with my bags and departed. After Madame introduced me to my closet and my bath, I was left alone.

I had not eaten anything but train station forage since breakfast in Zurich the day before. I was creaky from the train ride and I was sobering up from the two pernods. First things first; I retrieved my traveling flask from the center of the infinitely expandable, blue Boyt bag and poured three or four ounces into the heavy rough tumbler from the bathroom, kicked off my shoes, pulled out my shirttails, and sat down in the chair. Then, before taking a drink, I got up and opened all the windows and the sea air flooded the room. I sat quietly for twenty minutes, sipping the drink and watching the shadows cross the walls and floors, and listened to the shore birds call.

By the time the drink was gone, I was extremely hungry and fully re-energized in a way I knew would not last long. Without unpacking, I flipped my shirts, slacks and suits out of the hanging bag and fanned them along the closet pole in one motion. I left the Boyt bag for later, took a fast shower, shaved, changed and was out the door in ten minutes. The small restaurant was open, but empty, and I had wild duck in watercress sauce, a spinach salad and a delightful bowl of tiny, fresh, explosively flavorful strawberries. The whole dinner flowed on a bottle of muscadet and afterwards I defied gravity by floating up the stairs to the room, just in time to fall asleep on the deepest bed in Brittany.

∞

I woke up early, the room was just becoming grey. I felt the familiar depression of being in a strange place. I knew no one. My academically acquired French was not likely to sound intelligible in these parts. I had no maps, no guidebook. I wanted to stay in bed. I got up.

In jeans and a cotton sweater, I left the room and then the building. Once outside, I noticed that the grey light of the room was everywhere, a high foggy overcast with no particular directionality to the light. The sound of my boat shoes on the stones of the walk was soft, muted, slowed in the air.

I knew from the trip out here that the ocean was vaguely on the other side of the road from *La Ruche*. And I knew from the only research I had done before coming here—finding block D-6 in Plate 70 of the Times Atlas—that I was on a peninsula about ten miles long and between one half and two miles wide. Therefore, if I walked away from where I knew the ocean to be until I came to the shore on the other side, then turned right and followed the ocean, it should lead me back here.

I set off out the back of the inn toward a wide-branching, oak-looking tree about three-fourths of the way up the meadow. From there I could see a line of evergreens along the top of the next hill. The evergreens proved to be growing in front of a ledge of loose, rocky outcrops, which I walked about a quarter of a mile to skirt. Coming around, the land fell away from me, the salt wind touched my face, and I saw the Atlantic blending greyly into the sky, folded under the land. Below me there was a road paralleling the edge of the high ground above the shore.

The road made easier going, and gates and trails on either side showed recent use. Though most were unmarked, one ungated path to the left had an arrow carved of wood, nailed faded and split-grained to a post, pointing vaguely downward.

The path led through a slippery rock gully between large fractured blocks of hard, smooth stone. The sea sounds came up and the air grew wetter, then the trail ended at a small table of rock on which stood a statue carved in the local granite of a tall, straight, sturdy woman looking out to sea. With both hands she was holding on her right shoulder a young child reaching with both its arms toward the grey, empty air and the water before us.

I could feel the sea licking at the land with its ever-hungry tongue.

There was no plaque, marking nor inscription. These people did not share the American need to explain, brag, catalog, list, codify, direct, organize and interpret which clutters up most sublime (and every ridiculous) piece of public art in our country. This was private, inscrutable, disturbing and simply itself. I leaned for awhile against a nearby rock about twice as tall as the statue, trying to make out the expression on their faces. The child was clearly happy; does it see a familiar sail? He or she seems too young to be so discerning. The woman's face shows nothing; she stares stonily out to sea.

I climbed back to the high road and followed a line of low evergreens that edged the road. Their rhomboid tops tilted away from the sea and the North Wind.

Huge chunks of earth broken off the firmament trailed like a broken necklace into the curve of the sea. The Bretons only work the land next to the sea; they don't live too near it. The houses are on the lee side on ground well back from the headlands. Only the thin, strong lines of fences dare to touch the edge.

∞

In the distance where the track I was walking met a fence at the next rise, a large black dog jumped up and stood, then sat outlined against the sky and looked my way. I saw, then heard him bark once and turn to look behind him. He jumped back down and disappeared.

About five minutes later, as I approached the fence, I saw there was a serpentine stile built into the stone-work just there, and from the other side I could hear a horn—a high alto, piping something that sounded syncopated in a wailing minor key.

The wall was only about four and a half feet high, but I could see nothing of the other side. As I stepped through the turning, the earth dropped away in front of me and I looked out on the North Atlantic and down at a set of steps carved from the cliff face leading to a flat platform of stone, 60 yards along the cliff to my left and jutting out 20 yards into the ocean at my feet, fitted like 90° or 100° of an arc into the rough, broken cliff space.

The sound of the water on the rocks was a strong sibilant rush which muted as I gingerly picked my way down the steps, not daring to look out at the great expanse that lifted and fell with endless power ever nearer my feet.

At the bottom of the steps, I heard the horn again, this time I recognized the tune and saw at the same time the man playing. He was now above me in a slight concavity—about a third of the way up the large mainland wall sitting on a slab of rock that slanted down to the platform.

The song I knew from an old Fred Neil album called "Sessions." It was one of a repertoire of music etched on my DNA by experimental efforts in the late sixties. I began whistling with the piper at the third line, bending the notes as I walked closer. The dog was sitting beside the man, his head cocked, looking at the sea and nonchalantly at me. When I got to the bottom of the slab, which angled up at a nearly 45° incline, we came to the end of the song I remembered, but the piper went on to a chorus which took the longing and despair of the bluesy piece I knew and spun them up into a swirl of something higher, deeper and older and infinitely sadder, that slid into the deeper basements of the blues than even Mr. Neil's extraordinary basso ever took me. When he returned to the verse, I stood quietly and listened again to the tune of the pipe and the sea.

Then the song ended and only the sea spoke.

The piper stared out at the sea and I came back to my senses enough to begin noting his appearance. He was dressed in loose blue denim and chambray and wore a kind of cloth cap I saw many farmers on the road from Responden to Morbihan wearing. The dog barked again, once; I noticed how large it was and saw the sea-bleached, curly auburn cast to its short hairs.

The man turned his head towards me. I looked up at him. His eyes were clouded and he looked old for rock climbing.

"Hello," I called, "*Bonjour.*"

"Hellor," he said. "I foorgot you war here. Oor maybe I thought I dreamed you. Come up if you car to visit." His English was good, but strongly inflected with a hard accent.

I reminded myself of the basic rules of roofs and friction slabs: shoes flat, weight low and over the feet; a few seconds short of a minute later I came up even with a thin-faced man of some advanced, but indeterminate age who looked through me with pale blue, sightless eyes.

"How is it you only know half the song?" he asked, not turning his head from the sea.

"Well, that's all I ever heard. What was the chorus?" I whistled the first five notes and he spun them off briefly again.

"What do you call it where you are from?"

"Well, I heard it was a traditional Appalachian folk song, which means it probably came from England and the title is the first four words: The Water is Wide."

"Ay, the water is wide, but that is only part of the song and only the part where someone put words to it. The music was first, long before the words. Like much of the things in the world, new laid on top of old, sometimes the new covers the old completely. I do not know the true, old name for the song, but now it is called "Carrickfergus," which is a place in Ireland."

"Can you play me other old songs?"

He reached into a canvas bag I had not noticed and picked up a metal flute. To a marching beat, he played a sweet air of happy steps that escalated to higher tempo and a more desperate flight of tone and then resolved with a modal shift to a lonely minor restatement of the theme and tapered off into an eerie trill.

"What was that?"

"Here they call it 'Ainga's Song.' The Irish called it something else and claim it was written by one of theirs. There's a story about it I'll tell you tomorrow if you come back. And bring something to drink. Now leave me. You set off something with your whistling. I need to go back to it."

He turned back to the sea and picked up the old horn he had been playing as I arrived. I started down the slab and as I reached the bottom, the horn began again calling its soul to the sea.

∞

At the top of the stone steps I re-entered the field and looked around at the normal, safe, green grassy hills knit together with miles of the grey stone fences. Rather than go back the way I came, I set my course uphill to the highest point in view, intending to find a return route on the other side.

The day was warming as the clouds blew or were burnt off, but the overcast, mist or the spray in the air fogged the outlines of the coastal lands and fields I left behind while the lines of the hill in front of me grew clearer.

At the high point I could see directly back behind me down to the last cliff line leading over to the sea, but in front of me the slopes were more gradual and I could only see the next fence line. When I got to the fence, I looked down into a shallow bowl where a giant rock circle of upright stones stood surrounded by a serried array of other, not quite equally large stones.

I remembered my dream, but glancing quickly around, I could see no forest, nor for that matter, no mystery lady in green. Reality check. There was also no central stone as in the dream. Considerably relieved, I walked among them, touching their chill, lichened sides, looking up, spanning their width with my arms.

Reading about these megaliths was no preparation for walking among them. Like the whale that once sounded next to my boat off Block Island, casually misting us with fishy spume, then rolling like a train endlessly past, revealing a tail twice as wide as our length, I felt dwarfed, diminished, and frightened as on the return of the dream; anxiously unsettled. I walked around the circle again, clockwise. I wondered if there was a danger to going widdershins. I touched each stone and a weight seemed to grow on me.

The distance I had walked and the unknown distance I had to go pulled at me. I should have brought food or water or a map. I should have stayed in bed. I should have exercised more. I should drink less. I sat on a fallen stone and reviewed my major and minor failings and the hollowness that was at the center of everything. So what. I was going nowhere; had nothing to show of my life but a bunch of hi-tech toys that nobody even wanted to steal. I was pushing Clio away from me as effectively as I had blown off any other intimate and I had just let myself be ridden like a street hustler by someone I didn't know, didn't trust, and did not even consciously choose.

I had nothing much to go back to Boston for, but even less reason to go anyplace else.

It was a grim summary and in fairness to all points of view, I thought about suicide. It still looked like the right answer to the wrong question. As the old sailor said to Lord Jim before his fall, strictly speaking the question is not how to live, but how to make the sea which wants to drown you, bear you up.

That topic neatly covered, I decided that I needed a drink, which proved to be enough motive power to lift me from the stones and head me on a contour cross through the forest of risen and fallen stones, over another series of fences and fields and onto another country lane that emerged from the turf at a place where three fields met.

I walked along the lane vaguely downhill past other gates until I came to an unpaved but obviously more traveled road. I turned right and walked on.

After about an hour, there was a settlement where the road I was on met a paved road. The buildings were stone. The common walls of one framed courtyards or small paddocks for the next. About a half dozen buildings clustered on each side of the paved road. In front of the one across from me hung a sign carved with the word *Armorica* which I could not translate. The intent was promising and, as I approached the door, I heard voices talking over each other in the friendly layering of barroom discourse worldwide.

The door opened to a push, scraping lightly across

the stone floor of a surprisingly bright and warm room which became immediately silent while I was reviewed as a new species.

I took a table removed from the hometown crowd by as much as the division of the room would allow. It did not evidently afford the other patrons sufficient privacy to resume their previous conversations.

A young boy left one of the tables, picked a *carte* off a dark, primitive breakfront, and brought it over.

I greeted him with my best academic Parisian, nasalized "*Bonjour*" and he replied with a slurred "*Bujur*," but a pleasant smile.

"Eenglish?" he asked, indicating I had not quite passed as a Parisian.

"*American—les Etats-Unis.*"

"*Ah, les Etats-Unis*—Rambo? Eh?"

"*Oui*—Rambo," I said resignedly, taking the menu.

I ordered bread and cheese and a bottle of red and sat quietly after he disappeared through a doorway hung with a blanket. The conversation around me resumed, subdued and in a dialect I could not follow but for a few words such as "Mitterand," "Thatcher," and "*merde*"—evidently a gathering of contemporary political philosophers.

When the boy brought back my lunch, I asked if this road led back to Morbihan. I was able to learn that a left turn out the door would get me there in two or three kilometers. I attacked the coarse bread, sharp cheese and dark wine with enthusiasm. My spirits improved considerably and the room seemed a fine and solid place.

I began to think again about what I expected to do here. In Duxbury, it seemed a simple question with a yes or no answer. But how was I going to learn anything from people I could not communicate with beyond hand signals and an unconstructed cheese sandwich?

I tried asking the Sylvester Stallone fan if he knew where someone named Ashbrook or Clark had lived but between pronunciation and the present perfect tense, we lost the thread.

One of the greybeards from a table against the far wall watched silently. I realized that everyone in the village would know my question after I left and I would probably never know the answer.

I gave up; paid up; went out the door and turned left.

I got back to the inn around two; washed my face in the corner sink in the room, pulled off my clothes and burrowed into the high, soft bed. I was asleep without thinking and slept without dreams.

∞

A couple of hours later, the dinnertime noise climbed the walls of the kitchen garden and woke me. I put on a decent pair of slacks, a knit shirt and a blazer—traveling uniform, tourist disguise—and walked into the village looking for a bookstore, apothecary, someplace where I could find local information. It occurred to me I was not sure what day it was; on reflection, it figured to be Thursday.

About a half mile along, I saw, up a street merging obliquely from the left, what looked like a small park with a number of cars, more, in fact, than I had seen in the village square, pulled onto the sidewalks. The small park was actually plantings around a neatly painted white building housing an art museum representing the work of a colony of impressionists who once flourished here.

The gallery was still open and, for 10F, I wandered among several dozen lovely beach and picnic scenes all beautifully rendered if somewhat romantically conceived. Then, in another room, I was drawn into the work of an earlier local artist, more representational, genre scenes of the fishing life, net menders, the sail loft, the fish wives. The largest painting in the room looked to be eight feet wide and six feet tall. There was a bench before it and, as I took in the picture, I sank to the bench.

The canvas revealed a crowded room of plain white walls and wood-beamed ceiling like my room at the inn. There was one window on the right which let in the only light on the people, mostly men, in dark leathery, oiled canvas clothes who stared from their side of the room toward the only points of color in the room under the window: the muddy mustard-yellow of the shawl on the woman who bent over the still, white-faced body of a man in a bright yellow slicker laid out on the table. The faces around reflected the tragedy and my breath escaped with a shudder. I wanted to cry.

For a long time, I sat and looked at each face, the resolve on some, wonder on others, the rage, the horror, the loss.

When I could look no more, I got up and paid little attention to anything until I found the museum shop. I bought a postcard-size print of "The Drowned One," a pamphlet on the local school of painting, and a blessed map of the peninsula.

Retracing my steps, I got back on the main road, reached the village square and, off a side street half a block from my first stop in town, I picked up three bottles of wine, two unknown locals and one prestigious burgundy, along with a thin book in French titled *Menhir, Dolmen, Cromlech*, which had a drawing of a solitary, leaning, finger-shaped stone on the cover. "*Le Mystère de Morbihan*" was the subtitle.

Feeling competent, if still a little rattled from viewing "The Drowned One," I returned to the inn for a more leisurely dinner than the night before.

Madame Mulon was wearing an elaborate starched white cap and equally brilliant white blouse over a full skirt of the same bright blue she wore the day before. As I enjoyed the scallop dish she recommended, I puzzled through the mystery of Morbihan. It became readily apparent that a dolmen was a single finger of upright stone, a menhir was a line of dolmens, and a cromlech was a circle of them. This did not tax my French too much, as the second page of the booklet had three drawings appropriately labeled. Following the introductory text was a simple outline map of the peninsula with a smallish piece of the mainland attached and one island I had yet to see from the shore laying off to the Southeast. Numbered symbols scattered about the land showed the location of dolmens, menhirs and cromlechs as dots, parallel lines and circles. There were thirty-two sites on the map, a busy little spot, it seemed.

I found what I thought was the circle—cromlech—I had visited this morning. It was site 12 and the guide referred to it as *Les Bonnes*, which I could not translate. There seemed to be a story about young girls—*jeunes filles*—who danced "*ne jamais plus*"—nevermore.

As I was stumbling over the phrase, Madame Mulon stopped at my table to inquire about my stay and saw the book.

"Do you look for the stones?"

"I was not looking for them, but now that I have found them, they seem to be everywhere—*de partout sur le plan.*" I showed her the little map.

She glanced at it. "The Bretons and their rocks. They have no idea about them. They build around them, plow wheat around them, graze animals among them. But what are they? Who knows, who cares?"

"So you are not from Brittany."

"*S'il vous plaît*," she drew herself back, "*je suis Parisienne.* I only wear this costume for make believe ... I make believe I belong here. I make believe I still have a reason to live here. I make believe I am not an old widow. My husband was Breton. He brought me back here with the strength of his love of this land. Now he is gone and I have not the strength to leave. This was my life, so now I stay here.

"My husband once thought he was *un explorateur* of those old stones. On a warm day in the spring before the war, he and two hundred other fools pulled one of the fallen stones ten meters then put it upright. It took all day and it made no more sense than the rest of the stones. Just there." She pointed at a spot just inland.

"How old are they, *combien d'annés?*"

"Oh, three thousand or five thousand years, I think. Nobody knows. Maybe my husband knew, but I don't think so. I think nobody knows. He never talked about how old. He used to talk about how they would do it; how many people it would take and then how many more it would take to feed them and how many to keep them all in order and working together. For awhile it was a great interest but then, he said, he grew up. He was a beekeeper, maybe he talked about it with the bees but never with me. They had all his secrets. So, if you are not looking for rocks, what do you look for?"

"Is there a business in town that you know of called *Agence Privée de Bretagne*?"

"No, but this could be an agency for property to rent?"

"Is there a telephone directory?"

"Maybe there is an old one in my office," she said, "behind the stairs." She nodded to the front. "Come by in the morning and knock. Now I must go see to my other guests."

∞

It was about dark when I got back to the room and thought since this was going to be home for a few more nights, I should unpack my other piece of luggage. During the process I came across the torc in its small, black velvet, drawstring bag.

In the dim light of the room, it seemed darker and it felt heavier than I had remembered. A broken circle, a symbol of life, she said. I put it on my left wrist, with the open side in. It was a bit of a tight fit, but once on felt comfortable, solid, like it grew there, as a lost friend used to say.

He had been my best man at the wedding; another broken circle. I still had my ring, somewhere. The friendships survived no better than the marriage, or, I guess more correctly, the friendships did not survive the demise of the marriage. Half a couple socializing was awkward as a three-legged race and there were the inevitable gender-based sympathies and alliances. If I sent Christmas cards, that would probably be all that was left.

The metal band around my left wrist had been around through two thousand years of stupid human tricks. I wondered about wearing it. It was certainly valuable, but did not seem particularly fragile; quite the opposite.

The metal certainly couldn't be softer than 18 karat gold. I looked at the plain signet ring I had worn since my teens, through the Army and the war games and everything since. There was not much left of the florentine that I remember was there when my mother showed it to me the day we buried her father. The florentine was still sharp when I got possession the day I turned sixteen. I have worn it ever since. There is Michael's family crest in fairly deep relief with edges still sharp and crisp. Michael was a gentle man who lived a peaceful life. In his years the ring never saw the abrasions I had put it through. I remember cleaning red Khe Sahn mud off with my rifle brush.

My mind kept circling around the torc. Had it been a sign of office, a mark of nobility, an emblem of wealth when it was made?

Looking more closely, it appeared the semi-circular shaft was a solid cast piece with the two terminal bosses separate parts fitted on and hammered tight. There was really no decoration, there was just the thing itself.

I wondered what it was worth and whether there were antiquities laws I should be aware of before my next pass through customs.

"I want you to have this from me," she had said. It was an outrageous gift, flagrantly generous, rare and valuable. It had changed how I felt about her. I was fascinated when I met her, then physically overwhelmed, then frightened; wary at the Dolder, I had been charmed by her beauty and attention to me. With this gift I felt a thrilling sort of happiness overlaying physical desire with neither canceling out a fluttery anxiety that rose and fell, but never left. Did she still frighten me or was I only frightened of what might happen next because I had no control over it? Whatever she wanted from me, I was sure she would have it.

I took off the torc and put it back in the drawstring, tucked the velvet pouch inside a pair of socks, and turned in.

∞

The next morning after breakfast, we were unable to find a listing for *Agence Privée de Bretagne* in a phone booklet no thicker than my local art history tract. With my two bottles of *vin ordinaire*, a half loaf of the Madame's bread, a pair of borrowed cups commemorating a forgotten event, four apples, my Nikon binoculars, the guide and the map in my small backpack, I set off directly for the cave of the old musician.

The black dog was waiting for me and led me through the stile, down the stairs and up the slab to where the man sat adjusting or assembling a small set of bagpipes. Today he was wearing a red cap and red socks with a bright blue vest under his jacket.

"Hello, *Bonjour, bonne matinée*," I called a little breathlessly as I got closer to him. The dog had set a sharp pace.

"*Bonjour, monsieur, comment ça va?*"

"Ça va, ça va bien, et vous?"

He ignored my *politesse.*

"Do you find your friend the Ashbrook yet?"

"So you know the people at Armorica, is it?"

"Maybe I was there."

I thought back. I hadn't seen him there, but I was in no way certain he hadn't been there or could not have gotten there before me.

"Maybe you were, but I didn't see you."

"Maybe there are many things you don't see that are there."

I couldn't think of anything kind to say on this point to a blind man.

"Are those Irish bagpipes? They're smaller than regular ones."

"This is *le biniou.* It is smaller than Scottish pipes, but it is not Irish, it is Breton."

"What is this place, bagpipes, Irish music, miniature Stonehenges everywhere, a language I can barely understand. Was this part of France once British? I don't remember anything about that."

"The name means 'little Britain'. The music and the words are Celtic or, as these people were called in the Kingdom of the Franks, Gauls—Gallic, Gaelic. The stones are much older."

"In this book," I pulled it from my bag, but then realized he would not be much help with word for word translation, "it does not say anything I can translate about when the stones were put up. In Denmark, I have seen upright stones that are a thousand years in place, but the Druids built the stone circles in England, I thought, and Caesar writes about them. So this is really a frontier remnant of Celtic society like Wales, Cornwall and Ireland."

"You are wrong on several points, but it is true that Bretons, like the Welsh, the Cornish, the Basque and the Irish are the remains of people pushed out to the limits of their land by more heavily armed societies well before the Romans or the Saxons."

"And this is the music you played that I had heard as hill country folk music in America?"

"Hill country and seashore, hiding and escape, the hunter and the sailor; outsiders with a careful eye on the horizon."

"What about the stones? Where do the stones fit?" I thought again of the brooding enervation that held me in that circle of rocks on the hill.

"The stones were here long before the Celts and the music. I once heard ..."

"What?"

"Maybe later. What did you bring to drink? I promised you a story about that song yesterday in return." As I extricated the bottle and extracted the cork, he filled the little black embroidered airbag and settling the trailing pipes, began playing the first quick-stepping notes.

"Muscadet?"

He ignored me and went off with the rest of the tune. On the pipes, the dancing notes turned more formally, perhaps ominously, or sadly, and the first chorus was unaccountably sad.

When he finished, I said, "It begins like a light-hearted dance, then becomes a madder dance, then a march, then a funeral."

He turned his blank eyes in my direction.

"You hear music well. Now, give me the wine."

I gave him one of the nickel-plated commemorative cups I had borrowed from the Madame and helped myself with the other.

"The story of the song here is of a beautiful young maiden named Ainga who danced by herself in a circle. Other girls her age tried to dance with her, but all fell away, so perfect were her steps, so intricate and precise her timing. A young man sees her and is drawn, first to watch her, then to love her. She invites him into the dance and they turn one perfect circle. But he is called away, perhaps to war, and does not return alive and she dances alone."

"And it's called 'Ainga's Song' here? There's a poem I learned once by an Irish poet called 'The Song of Wandering Aengus.' The Aengus is a nature spirit, isn't it?"

"Your information is again as inexact as it is superficial. Yeats made up new myths to suit his mad visions of mystic Erin. Aengus was the son of the Good God Dagda on whose living harp the seasons were played. Aengus was an eternal youth, a god of love and beauty."

"But that's not so far from the song where Ainga is now a girl—maybe even a 'glimmering girl with apple blossoms in her hair who called me by my name and ran ...'"

"'And faded through the brightening air... '" he finished, "No, it is not so far and all these songs and poems, like streams, all proceed from a very small number of springs and wells."

"You said yesterday that the Irish have another name for the song."

"Yes. A man named Turlough O'Carolan, also blind" he nodded, "is credited with a harp version he called 'Megan Morgan.' But he was the last of the medieval bards, so it was part of a memory tradition of unknown origin, not a composition. It could have come from here or maybe both versions came from someplace else. Look around these coasts from Spain to Scotland and you find endless common features, place names, saints, music, the stones. I was going to tell you before, the oldest story I know is only one line: 'We came to this land in ships'."

I was sitting still, hearing every word and the world turned around me and I saw myself from a great distance alone with a blind man and a large, black dog at the edge of the ocean at the end of the land.

Megan Morgan.

I was glad to say nothing while we emptied our cups and the dog and I watched the sea birds.

Megan Morgan. Ana Megan Morgan.

As I poured our second cups, I asked, "May I know your name?"

He turned to me levelly, and I realized he had not been born blind.

"I am Paul Languedoc."

"Phillip Gardiner."

"Where are you from, Phillip Gardiner?"

"The United States. America."

"Were you born there?"

I laughed. "I was born in my father's kingdom. As soon as I could, I left for the United States."

"What does this mean?"

"My father's family mostly lives, usually dies, and, in the case of the first-born male, is buried on a piece of family property. I hated the place. It's about twelve miles in from the end of Long Island. It's technically in the United States, but it's my father's land and laws."

"What makes you come here? You are looking for this Ashbrook? This is a woman?"

"No. It was just a name of someone I heard once lived around here, used to live down the road from me in Massachusetts. Is there much of an English or American group or colony or resort here?"

"Not at all. The only people who usually visit here are French, for the big *pardons* sometimes people come from Cornwall or Scotland. But I rarely have the chance to practice my English in Brittany. How far are you staying from here?"

I guessed at five to seven kilometers. "Just at the edge of town," I said. "The Beehive of the Wheat."

"I knew him that ran it. We grew up together."

"Do you know where I'll find this place," I asked,

pulling Ana's card from my wallet. "*Folgoât, St. Chèldré, La Forêt.*"

His face lost its thoughtful expression, became as blank as his eyes.

"Yes. Oh, yes. I know it. I visited it when I was younger, often. It was Anne of Brittany's summer place. Strange you go from Mulon's place."

"Why strange?"

"Nothing, it is a memory of that place. It's privately owned, though; it's not open."

"I am invited there tomorrow. Is it far from here?"

He was silent and immobile.

"As far as yesterday," he said.

"So you were there? What was it like when you were there?"

"Oh, it was a great weathered pile with moats and towers, a drawbridge. It had a wide stone terrace across the front. The evenings I was there, the dining room and both parlors—*les salons, le petit salon, le grand salon*—were opened onto the terrace and the party flowed in and out of the light, into the night and back, like a day's rhythm."

"Were you playing music?"

"Maybe I was there because of my music, but not to play it. *La Mademoiselle de ma jeunesse y demeurait*"

"I'm sorry. The young lady of your youth did what?"

"*Y demeurait.* She would stay there. For three summers, she came to stay with her aunt. I was a student at the music school in Nantes. She heard me play at a local fair."

"What happened to her?"

" After the summer of 1933, I never saw her again. But then, after that summer of 1933, I never saw anything else again, either."

"What happened to your sight?"

"I lost it one night. In the darkness I fell, they tell

me, and my head struck a stone just right, they said. Just wrong or just so, but so I can never see again. Mulon was there that summer, too. And it was he who found me they said."

"What did he say happened?"

"Mulon never spoke to me again. He left for Paris the same day and only came back when he inherited the *notaire...* "

"What is a *notaire*?"

"The *notaire* is a local way. It is a member of one family who keeps local records. In tradition it passes from father to son. But Mulon had no son. Now it is with another family.

"So I lost a young woman, a friend and my sight and the blindness is the easiest."

"I can't imagine that." We were about finished with the first bottle and the wine was as light as sea air.

"Certainly you can. Just close your eyes. After a while, that's what it looks like. What you can't imagine is what the world looks like. Without your eyes to renew it. Close your eyes and imagine any other place and time; all you can call up are pieces and parts. Now suppose you were there, but all you could imagine were your pieces of memories. Without your vision, the continuity and the whole is fractured, lost, for a while. Then you find another way to live within the world and there are other ways to the whole. Music is mine, now. It is everything."

"And you never heard from the mademoiselle?"

"No, and she seemed to ... we seemed ... I was very young and it was the last best year of my life and I do not wish to say anymore."

"He was there that summer, the beekeeper where you stay. And he was who found me I was told. But he never visited or spoke to me again.

"Would you like more muscadet? I could open the other bottle."

"It will take two hours of playing here to get free

of what you've poured me already. A drunken blind man on these rocks is a brief joke."

"I can help you."

"I prefer to navigate with no help but the dog and I would prefer to play for the hours first. But you have been good to visit with me. Here is the tune that brought you here yesterday."

He inflated the air bladder, set the pipes and played a shrill lament that brought tears to my eyes and great sorrow to my throat. It was the perfect meeting of colors—the song and the instrument's voice.

When it ended, I managed to ask, "Is there a story to that song?"

"There are several, and many versions of the words. But the music came first. The words were something added later to try to make sense of the feelings."

The blind man turned back to the pipes and after another song, without another word, I left him there with his black dog, the great green sea and his soaring music.

∞

At the road, I pulled out the map again. Not wanting to retrace my steps from yesterday and having no desire to descend again into the cromlech called *Les Bonnes* and think about suicide, I set a cross-country course toward what seemed to be the highest point on the peninsula. It took about an hour and change.

The air was much clearer than the day before and I could see back to the mainland on the windward side. On the lee side, the islands were visible out to the largest and most remote *Belle île-en-mer*, not very imaginatively named, but at least I could translate it. I located a smaller but still substantial piece of real estate which the map identified as *Er Lannic*. I could not translate the name, which did not even look to be French, but the map showed two interlocking cromlechs, one on the island, the other apparently in the water. With the binoculars, I could verify this figure of eight, one leg on land, the other completely flooded by the ocean. The guidebook section on Er Lannic allowed me to understand there was a boat landing—*quai*—on the opposite side, *de l'autre côte de l'île*. I could assume that " *subsidense*" meant what I thought. There was another paragraph about something else on the island that was *très unique*, but untranslatable and *décoré d'un style inconnu hors New Grange en l'Irlande.*

I opened the second bottle of muscadet and sat and thought about this land and all that brought me here.

I did not care about the spooky operation that was using the *Agence Privée* , etc. cover. I did not want to get involved in whatever swindle or operation S, B was managing. I was flat out of it.

The old songs and Ana and her name spun around me.

I imagined the 21 spies' identity dancing in a circle, recycling their houses, names. Ainga Megan Morgan.

Dancing around the stones to the tune of bagpipes? Madness. Too bizarre.

However the world works, music has no power beyond the personal. Music may reflect the metaphysical, but it does not have the handle. Look how poorly it pays, on the average.

The stones had to be a form of calendar. I knew about the speculations on Stonehenge and could read solstice and equinox in the guidebook. The likely theory is that knowing the seasons of the sun improved the efficiency of agriculture, but these ten- and twenty- and thirty-ton objects in the hundreds were way beyond function. The determination of the solstice can be managed with two sticks, one if you are pressed.

Maybe it was some kind of civic pride run amok. Less destructive than war and not quite as dumb as professional football and just a touch more ambitious than the Jaycee's Fall Festival.

I remembered watching the sun and planets whipping around within that narrow band from East to West in the Hayden planetarium one summer when the subway cars still had wicker seats. The sun would accelerate through the equinoxes but slow to near glacial progress until it finally and truly stood for a moment; then, its movement at first indiscernible, it would do its slingshot pendulum return to the other pole. The rigorous precision and absolutely limited range utterly fascinated me as a child.

A narrow figure of eight is the course the sun will trace in a year on your ceiling or wall if you set a small mirror just right in your window. It is called an analemma. The first year with Jayne, we moved into a house on my birthday in the spring, and I set such a mirror on the western sash of a north window and marked at odd intervals my proof with pushpins on the east wall.

Without a mirror, a keyhole or needle eye or even the end of a pole will serve.

When the sun approaches its two extremes, there are days—about a week and a half total—when it is rounding the turn and shows no noticeable north or south displacement. But with the keyhole or eye or pole far enough away from the focal plane of the light or shadow, there would be a precise polar limit which, marked once, would be invariant.

The solstice is a fairly subtle event, but the annular procession of the sun through the ecliptic now seems obvious. Marking days on notched sticks would work once you figured out which notch meant rains came, which meant plant, harvest. Someone would have to be responsible for moving the day marker every turn of the earth. Anybody could, every one or every household, could keep track, compare notes, self-adjust, reach consensus.

Not the human way. Suppose the people who figured it out first kept quiet about the precision. Like a card counter at a casino, they'd have a little edge, maybe pass on tips—don't let the rams in with the ewes until thirty days after the sun marks the wall in grandfather's tomb just there. More of the spring lambs live. The tribe increases.

Through nutrition, strength, economic power, force of arms, the sun-counter becomes the source of order. But how do you get from there to all this high tonnage construction?

There had to be more going on than I could figure out here. I was too close to the subject and it made no sense.

I had another pull on the bottle, tore a piece of bread off the baguette and hacked up one of the apples with my Swiss Army knife.

Forget the stones, what about the 21 people? In truth, I had no information. Maybe there was property finagling going on at S, B. Maybe old Ralph was churning the accounts somehow or, more likely, someone much smarter who worked for him saw the opportunities Ralph's dull pomposity allowed. The pattern I found was due to carelessness on the finagler's part.

There were no spies.

Ana was simply a different kind of woman than I was used to: European, independent, mature, strong. So her name was a common old name around her hometown; so was mine. Besides, she seemed to truly like me; the night at the Dolder, the gift, the invitation, the night I arrived. I spent a time with memories and feelings.

I thought back on all the chaos and collapse of the last two years in Boston. It seemed like one headlong rush, out of control, downhill, over the cliff, careening off mini-disasters along the way. Infidelity. Separation. Divorce. Petra. The business all the time playing companion tunes of hope, greed, anxiety and despair.

Maybe things were different than they seemed back in Boston. Maybe I needed a little perspective. Maybe I needed a vacation.

Sitting on the hilltop watching almost 360° of water throw light and sound everywhere with no electronic, mechanical or human intrusion, I exhaled a sigh as big as the sky and fell back on the ground, spread my arms and legs and stretched. My shoulders and legs cracked dramatically.

Sometime later—I think I even napped, I know I finished the wine—I put my odds and ends and empties back in the pack and walked slowly and without recourse to the map several hours along the spine of the land to the hillside behind the inn. It was a lovely walk. I was more relaxed than I had been in years. I looked at the way the stones in the fences fit together and the mosses and grasses grew between them. The contrast and arrangement of sheep in a field was endlessly fascinating as viewed from multiple perspectives. In my mind I took dozens of pictures with the camera I had left at the inn.

At the inn, I found it was just six o'clock and a long shower and a disorganized change of clothes put me in the dining room before seven. It was unfashionably early by city standards but none too soon to get Madame Mulon's attention before the restaurant began to fill for Friday night.

After giving her back the cups I had borrowed, I said, "I have to go somewhere tomorrow at noon—can you help me get a car or taxi?"

"Taxi," she laughed, "in Morbihan?"

"I know. I know. *D'accord, mais une voiture avec un chauffeur, c'est possible?"*

"A quelle heure?"

"*A midi*, I want to go here at noon." I showed her Ana's card.

She paused for a beat and then asked: "How is it that you go to visit this place?"

"You don't know? *Savez vous comment on va là-bas?*"

"No. No. I know how one goes to *Folgoât*. How is it you go there?"

"This person invited me. *Je suis invité.* Can you help me get there at noon? *Je suis invité pour midi.*"

"Yes, I think I can do this. But wait and talk to me after dinner. Then I will know."

For dinner I passed on the terrine of eel, had a smoked salmon appetizer and rabbit with red peppers in a local sauce I forget how to spell. There was a salad of sharp-flavored greens, then cheese, bread, salt butter. Red wine from Burgundy; this close, I would be a fool to drink any other red. I was still hungry, so uncharacteristically I had dessert—a *crème brulée* that was pure heaven with a tart wild lingonberry sauce. As I was thinking about giving the spoon another lick, I noticed that the room was emptying out and that I must have taken close to two hours to eat.

Madame Mulon came to the table with a bottle of Calvados and two glasses. She filled one and gave it to me. "On the house, as you say. I will be back in a few minutes and join you."

"I have your way to *Folgoât* tomorrow," she said later, sitting down. I poured her a glassful and refilled mine. It had a sharp, spiky taste, but I could not detect the apples. I kept trying.

"He will be here at ten, outside; à *dix heures, dehors.* You will pay him 50 francs. How do you get back?"

"I don't know. Maybe I will stay a night."

"This person you go to see, does she live there?"

"I think she just visits there."

"Everybody just visits there. There is no family; just visitors."

"My friend's aunt lives there."

"Oh, yes, the visitors are always nieces and aunts and cousins and brothers and stepsons, but where is the family? The mother and father, the son and the grandparents. These old families have nothing left but their names anymore. No vitality. Only the property gives them the illusion."

"So you know this place?"

"No, I know these old families with their noble claims and the rundown lands whose rents they live on while they dream about the days when the servants knelt."

Madam and I discussed distributive justice and the persistence of property and privilege. She was evidently in favor of another revolution as long as it stopped redistributing things before it got to hers.

I was at the end of my third glass of the surprisingly potent Calvados. She had just finished her second.

"Your husband was some kind of local official recordkeeper, is this not so?"

"He was *notaire* for this place."

"What does this word mean, *notaire* ?"

She reiterated Paul's explanation. A hereditary office. A clerk of records. He maintained official birth, death and property transfer records for the countryside.

I was thrilled.

"Tell me, where did your husband keep his office as notaire?"

She looked at me in silence for a second.

"Just there," she said gesturing towards the cubbyhole under the stairs where we had gotten the phone book."

"All the records for this *campagne* in there?" I asked smiling. "*C'est impossible, non ?*"

She did not smile in return.

"The files and ledgers, all the paper was in the old man's room. The room of his father."

"Who was *notaire* before him?"

"Yes."

"And now?"

"I have no son if that is what you ask. No children. None. Never."

"I am sorry. I mean who now keeps these records?"

"It is a man in *La Forêt.* His name is something like Gilliou."

"Would you help me get his address?"

She was quiet again and then appeared to agree, getting up to leave.

"One thing I do hear about *Folgoât.* I hear they—what is the English word?—they consume—*comment le dire?*—they use up their guests." She got up.

"What do you mean?" I asked, rising with her. "What are you saying?"

"I say only what I hear. Maybe it is too much. But people who 'visit' there—the parents of the countryside will not let their daughters go near, and they worry about their sons."

Five

I was finally into the rhythm of time off by Saturday morning. I asked to be served at a table in the garden. In fact, I insisted, but politely. I had toasted French bread, a connoisseur's array of honeys and an infinite succession of pots of *café au lait*. The insects hummed and buzzed around me; a scatter of cosmos and bachelor buttons lit up a corner behind a stone bird bath, never patronized in my presence. I could hear the birds in the pines behind the wall. I had given up on getting anything more out of *Le Mystère de Morbihan* and was left with nothing but the *Pelican Book of Middle Eastern Mythology* which was still fairly dry chewing. I had already plowed through Mesopotamia in the SwissAir departure lounge and was now catching up on Gilgamesh, as seen by the Akkadians.

> "Gilgamesh, whither rovest thou?
> The life thou pursuest, thou shalt not find.
> When the gods created mankind,
> Death for mankind they set aside.
> Life in their own hands retaining.
> Then Gilgamesh, let full be thy belly
> Make thee merry by day and by night.

Of each day make thou a feast of rejoicing
Day and night dance thou and play.
Let thy garments be sparkling and fresh,
Thy head be washed, bathe thou in water
Pay heed to the little one that holds thy hand,
Let thy spouse delight in thy bosom.
For this is the task of mankind."

Why, indeed, not? The task of mankind; eat, drink and be as merry as you can under the circumstances. My sympathies were all with Gilgamesh, but despite being two-thirds divine, the narratives all turn out poorly for him. The next story was about a guy named Adapa who played "Let's Make a Deal" for eternal life and, on the advice of his father, turned down the deal of a lifetime for what was behind the curtain. His consolation prize for mankind was "misfortune and disease... allayed, however, by the ministrates of Ninkarrak, the Goddess of Healing."

I threw the book down. This was not helping the vacation spirit. I tried just sitting there enjoying the day in the full sobriety of my sense—"of each day make thou a feast of rejoicing."

A church bell rang somewhere in town and then another. Peals and rounds of peals then rose and overlapped and went on and on. I was on the verge of going to find someone to tell me if the Martians had landed, the Germans surrendered or France won the World Cup. Madame Mulon called out through the top of the split door into the kitchen.

"*Monsieur Gardiner, votre voiture est ici.*"

My *voiture* was barely *ici*. It was a canvas-sided and plastic-windowed *deux chevaux* —the two-horse people's car that gave legs to the French transportation revolution as Dr. Porsche and his *führer* thought the VW would do for their *volken*. The passenger's seat was an instrument of torture draped in a blanket no longer useful for the horse. The driver was my old friend, *Lui*, from arrival day.

He was voluminously more voluble than the Swiss chauffeur, André. Unfortunately the distance between how and how fast he pronounced words and which and at what speed I could translate them left us at about the same place. His friendly spirit, however, encouraged a great deal more effort and we got along famously.

It took us a half a mile to establish that the sound was "*les cloches sonnent*". I was only certain when we passed a peeling bell tower and both of us grinned and pointed. Further points of meaning were puzzled out through Abbott and Costello exchanges that left us both laughing.

The reason for the bells sounding was *la fête de Sainte Amury, une grande fête* and I readily agreed to a detour to *voyez* the *spectacle.*

We took the left turn off the main road that had led me to the gallery and, passing through the square, shortly began climbing a hill out of town on which there was a substantial volume of traffic, including a goodly number on foot.

The road meandered gradually up to a point where the ocean appeared immediately adjacent to, but far below, my right elbow and then we turned inland up a more gradual incline to the crest of the mainland. A large valley opened perhaps eight miles square, something less than four miles long and maybe more than two miles wide. The vegetation was drawn from the same palette of green and purple and gold, the roadside fences were the familiar bright stone. But the valley was full of people. I am no good at estimating crowds. I got permanently confused by the discrepant counts reported by opposing sides of the few serious crowds I have seen. So let us say that church authorities would claim there were fifty thousand people and the atheists would call it fifteen; by any reckoning, lots of people, flowing and massing together.

There is a curious vitality to crowds. Not only do they energize their members, the crowd has a clumsy lumbering life of its own. A crowd is frightening if you are in it, but fascinating on the periphery. One graduate school professor who specialized in mass and collective behavior had pointed me to the dynamism of the edge, where individuals decide to join, give up their individuality for the draw of the center, visibly alter their rhythms of movement and expressions. I have had a chance to check out a few humdingers including one that turned into a riot with looting, etc. and while I probably never got as much useful knowledge from the experience as Professor Q, I am able to report that the edge is strikingly safer. There are many more escape options and you generally get advance warning about such things as tear gas, dogs and water cannons.

The strategy did backfire on me once. I had a suit job with the Dean of the Graduate School I was attending and was returning from lunch when I came upon a group forming in the middle of the Oval. Their sound quality was awful and the turnout was light and already committed, so it was not that dynamic a group. I circled around and headed on towards the Administration Building. When I was about twenty-five or thirty feet along my way, the leader/speaker broke over their voices and I heard "Follow me! Shut it down! Shut it down! Shut it down!" and I looked over my shoulder to see him walking backward, following me. He and they followed me—or I led them—all the way to the Admin Building where several of my co-workers doubtless got to ask themselves and each other even more questions about my character.

This crowd was not chanting, or marching, or even milling. The mass of people was forming into six blocks arrayed star fashion, radiating from a central stage on which, as we got closer, I saw six altars with gold crosses.

"*Le grand pardon*," Lui explained. As best I was able to understand, all the local congregations, and all their family and friends out to the sixth generation, it looked like, gathered to celebrate the feast of Ste. Amury here every year.

As we got nearer to the valley floor, of course, traffic slowed and the crowd dissolved into individuals, less awesome, more human, but less interesting—although the women's starched headdresses were fascinating, medieval as a nun's habit before Vatican II.

As we climbed the other side of the valley, I twisted in my seat to watch the mass grow more coherent and finally static, all joined in the ritual, to kneel as the bells ring, stand as the priests speak, listen and come forward when called.

I wondered how many thousands of people the late M. Mulon had calculated those megaliths required. The constructions no longer seemed so improbable, but feeling the human dimension I now realized must be involved put another side to my thinking about the stones. What would it take to get thousands to work together, hundreds and thousands at once; how do you harness and direct the physical force? The stonework seemed both much more proximate and much more improbable.

We turned left onto a wider, faster road which took us west until just past a sign saying: "*La Forêt 6.*" There we turned to the right up a broad, paved single lane. The lane passed briefly through a well-tended forest, between large cultivated fields into another, older, even better tended forest manicured like a manor's deer park. On the other side, a hedgerow of evergreens that looked to be spruce sprang up close to the lane, closed in, trimmed flush with the drive over twenty feet high seemed to funnel us into a large, white stone-walled driveway and carpark.

Lui apparently did not like the looks of the place. He offered all manner of help in getting me and my pack out of the car in short order. He also missed the shift to second on his way back down the drive.

∞

Before I could get seriously concerned about spending the night on the stones or walking back to Morbihan, a man in a sturdy, handmade black suit, white shirt and striped tie greeted me by name and offered in English reminiscent of Paul Languedoc to show me to my room. He reached for my bag before he quite saw what it was and awkwardly caught hold of the top lifting loop, so valuable in hauling such bags up thousand foot rock faces. Any embarrassment I felt was evaporated by following him through the halls, watching him trying to hold the knapsack at some distance from his body with as few fingers as possible. As a result, I missed a good deal of the decoration on the way in, but what little I saw was grand on a scale only possible in a private home of centuries-old wealth.

The room he led me to was a spacious and thoroughly modern one. The furniture was the best quality contemporary reproductions of French Provincial. The prints on the walls were signed but undistinguished to my eye. There was a television in one of the cabinets, I discovered. It was more than anything else like a hotel room. There was even a phone.

It rang.

"You are here," I heard Ana observe after I answered.

"*Oui, je suis ici.*"

"Your pronunciation is very good," she said, "but the accent is most confusing. I would not know where this person is from, but I think his teacher studied in Paris."

"There were several teachers, but I mostly like the sound of the French words that slide together, the vowel blends and diphthongs. One teacher did claim to have done time at the Sorbonne, but another was a hillbilly absolutely unconcerned with how they said it in Pair-ee.

Prhet-A un mor-so do poppy-yA," I pushed poor Miss-What's-Her-Name's Ohio-River-Valley accent deep into West Virginia.

"Stop," Ana cried, laughing, "That was horrible. Do not do that any more."

She had a happy smile in her voice that I had never heard, much less seen. I felt more comfortable with her than I had ever been. The phone was a big help. It was just a conversation. She wasn't really there.

"Are you ready to go for a ride?"

She was really there.

"Sure," I said, hoping I sounded sure. The small current that had been running through me all morning became audible, tangible. I began pacing within the narrow limits of the phone cord. I picked up the base unit in my left hand.

"Where do we meet? How do I get out of here? I forgot my bread crumbs and thread when I packed."

"You are funny today," her voice smiled at me again. "From your room go either right or left; either way leads to a branch of the front staircase. I'll wait for you downstairs."

She was right and I found her quickly. And she was as fine as anything in the house. She pulled my hand to her and kissed my right temple as we met.

I felt the electricity pass well beyond house current. I also noticed she was wearing riding boots and jodhpurs. Uh oh, horses.

∞

It's not that I don't like horses, it's really more a matter of plain distrust. And, of course, there is the issue of size. They are big, mostly stupid and have generations of reasons for considering humans, at best, a nuisance. My encounters with them have been largely unsuccessful from the start.

My father, as something-or-other of the Lawn and Polo Club outside Bridgehampton, had arranged for my personal introduction to the species as a hot walker at the age of ten. It was not a prestige position, as most of my colleagues were about three times my age and looked to have no fixed addresses. In response to some physiological requirement or superstition of the turf, our job was to walk horses which had just come off the field until they had cooled down. The first one stepped on my right foot and broke everything but the bones in my three largest toes. Three decades later, my right foot looks like one of Dr. Frankenstein's early failures.

In my teens, a girlfriend's number two hunter-jumper ran—and I mean whatever speed is just below a gallop—ran right at and under a low-hanging branch on the only tree in the field. I did duck in time.

There was another unfortunate event at French Lick involving an unplanned dismount at a fork in the bridle path.

Ana led me out a side door across a ten-acre expanse of clipped and nitrogen-rich grass. She asked about my travels to and around Brittany. I recounted how I had arrived, where I was staying, said I had been walking around the peninsula mostly.

"How do you find this country?"

"Very different in so many ways. The age of things, the simple and immediate presence of the land and sea; I am beginning to get a sense of the community."

"What is that?"

"Very conservative. Not politically, but culturally and very close, and probably pretty closed to outsiders. But I did meet one or two friendly people: the Madame at the inn and a musician named Paul Languedoc."

"He is blind, yes?"

"Yes."

"He is wonderfully good. He plays all over the world. How did you meet him?"

"I heard him practicing outdoors one day. We talked about music. He invited me back and played some songs for me." I left it at that.

We arrived at a three-story wood and stone building about the size of the public library in any town of a couple hundred thousand people. There was the fine, strong odor of horse and hay and oiled leather. In the paddock, two of the stable's residents were being saddled: a shiny, sleek Arabian-looking grey with a black forelock and a larger, wider bay with a nervous, twitching air and sea-green eyes. No bets on which one I get.

My khaki pants and boat shoes were the subject of substantial concern between Ana and the head groom. Apparently nothing could be done in the riding pants department—*rien à faire*—but a pair of polished, but well-used workboots were produced resembling what J. M. Barrie calls the Wellington style and Sear's and the Hell's Angels call an engineer's boot. Miraculously, they fit.

Ana, on board her horse, identified the animals as "Helené" and "Marcel" as I, with the help of a small stool and the backing of two grooms under the supervision of the head man, successfully mounted Marcel.

"Okay, Marcel, *où sont les neiges d'antan?*"

Ana laughed her lovely soprano laugh again and steered Helené through a gate onto a wide meadow. Marcel released the breath he'd been holding with a snort, shook his back to see how much slack he had in the girth and whether I was going to come off easily. I gave him a harder pull to the right on the reins than intended and as he lurched, my heels dug into his side. He came around smoothly and, trying to regain my balance, I reined him in tight so we followed Ana and Helené like I knew what I was doing.

We walked the horses side by side for about a quarter of a mile. Helené was a thing of beauty to watch. I was never aware of how fragile a horse could look and still be so obviously powerful. Marcel was twitching and given to stamping a hoof at odd pauses in his gait.

"What is wrong with Marcel?" I asked. "Why is he so unsettled?"

"It is not his fault, partly it is because he likes to run and partly it is because of Helené. It is near her time."

Uh oh.

"But it is not a worry, Marcel is a gelding."

"Well," I heard, with disbelief, myself say, "if running is all the fun he has left, why don't we race to, say, that tree line off to the right?"

She looked at me with the first expression of surprise I had ever seen on her face, then the intense determination returned and the smile.

"Yes. Let us go now," she said as she spurred Helené into a jumping start that gave her a ten- or fifteen-yard lead before I could get Marcel oriented and motivated. The first half-mile her lead expanded as Marcel and I tested and negotiated various travel arrangements. Some saurian part of my medulla realized sheer survival required that I exert more effort than I thought humanly possible and, with the help of adrenaline, I did. The stirrups were high and I finally got into old Marcel's rhythm. It may not have been a pretty sight, but we started eating up the field and soon his strength brought us up on a diagonal toward Ana and Helené.

If I have known a thrilling moment in my life, this was it. We rode side by side twelve or fifteen feet apart, however fast those horses could go for five or ten or fifteen minutes. I can shiver anytime at the memory of Ana and Helené fitted together like nothing I have ever seen: Ana floating, determined, staring straight ahead; Helené, her nose open, great bunches of muscles exploding from her shoulders to her hips, and on and on—the golden sunlight on the glimmering girl in the saddle and the superhuman power she controlled. Helené flowed across ground, the efforts of her extension gracefully blended to a smooth pace of amazing power.

Marcel and I kept up in spite of each other or perhaps because of what we were witnessing. As the tree line drew halfway near, Marcel tried to increase his speed, but I was no help and just as clearly as if she had downshifted or found another heart, Helené and Ana pulled away.

We reached them after Ana had dismounted and she was walking Helené around in the shade.

Marcel ran straight toward them and as he picked up Helené's scent again, he whinnied and threw his forelegs up in the air. Fortunately, I had annealed myself to the reins and stirrups and rode him up, but I saw his lunge had taken him right up to Ana, who now stood against Helené beneath his hooves. With a full choke on the reins and my arms nearly around his throat, I threw the weight of my body and all the strength and leverage of my legs and back to pull his head and shoulders to the left.

With a shock I found myself rolling on the ground ten feet away, while Marcel was getting his legs back under himself between me and Helené. Ana was there to grab his reins and she tied him to a low branch away from where Helené stood, ground tethered. She was running towards me as I got up, apparently undamaged and wondering what causes those sparks you see sometimes after exertion—short circuits in the optic nerve, adrenal cortex overload, dying brain cells?

"Are you all right?" The fear and worry on her face was clear. She hugged me strongly, tenderly, her body was trembling.

We did not say another word, but pulled at each other's clothes until we found the places and relations we sought. This time it was my turn and she was quiet, then generous and then most eager. We were both wet with sweat and the insects were noisy when she spoke again, lying by my side staring at the sky, her face so relaxed I would not have known it.

"That was most dangerous."

"Which part?" I laughed.

She turned to me, her face's tension returning, then she laughed, too, and pulled me to herself again.

∞

Marcel was favoring his left foreleg on the trip back and I was discovering exactly which parts of my body had taken the force of the gymnastic dismount. Ana was full of spirit and talked more than she ever had. She told me about Helené's bloodlines back several generations and the personalities of her dams and sires. I asked about Marcel, but his family was less distinguished and, although promising as a two-year-old, he had grown too big, she said. I asked why, if he was a gelding, he was so affected by Helené's pending estrus.

"Well, you see, the operation was just recently."

"How recently?"

"In April."

"Always was the cruelest month, Marcel." I patted his head as he plodded us quietly back to his remaining pleasures.

It was so fine to be with her so happy and both of us far from anything else but each other. To keep up the conversation, I asked about the place.

"I heard there was an old Castle here, but the building seemed newer."

"There is a chateau, what you would call a castle. But it is a piece of history that is difficult to live in. To modernize would have been a crime, so we built a new dwelling inside the shell of one of the more recent buildings, actually the old stable. It was built in 1730 and had offices for the overseer and a school room. Now it is the best place to live. My aunt sometimes entertains in the chateau and a few guests like to stay there, but the kitchen is in the new building and there are no servants in the chateau."

"I would like to see it."

"My aunt has invited us to join her for dinner. We will dine in the council chamber where Duchess Anne agreed to bring Brittany under the French crown in 1491."

"*A quelle heure?*"

"*Huit heures et demi, mais rencontrez-moi une heure avant et je vous guiderai.*"

"Meet you an hour before and you'll show me around, right?"

"You are a good student. I think you are very curious."

I was wondering how she meant that.

"Claude-Philippe says you are deeply interested in many things."

"That is probably true, but how does he know this after two brief conversations?"

"Oh, he will know much more about you than what you told him."

I remembered the old resumé he had obviously gotten from S, B.

"He has mountains of electronic data, but I doubt if I am anywhere in there."

"He has many other sources of information, contacts, acquaintances, old friends. Claude-Philippe gets information from many people."

"Yes. He asked me to consider working with him managing academic and contract research."

"He told me he would do this. He will make you very busy. Do you like this?"

"I am not sure what I will do. But I think graduate school was where I was happiest in my life. I didn't realize it at the time, because I was looking for something better which never came along."

"The research projects Claude-Philippe has done are not graduate school papers and books. They are directly practical."

"What do you mean?"

"You should talk to Claude-Philippe about this. I do not know what he intends. Besides, this is your holiday and our weekend; let us not talk of business."

So we did not talk of business and got poor, limping, newly gelded Marcel and sleek, glowing Helené back to their grooms. I got my boat shoes back and discovered despite the high boots that I had a couple of hot spots on my inner ankles from the stirrups.

We walked back to the new building in the fine glow of the day under clouds that looked as near as the sheep on the hills, a hundred times whiter and a thousand times as large.

She directed me to my room and I left her at the bottom of the stairs, her hair a mess and one cheek smudged and all her clothing wrinkled. She never looked lovelier.

∞

Back at the room, I showered until the stiffness in my left shoulder had melted. I envied Marcel his grooms and liniment, but, on reflection, little else. No wonder he was so feisty; they may have removed the plumbing, but the wiring was still intact.

A somewhat baroque and vaguely antique-looking marble clock, which on closer inspection hummed rather than ticked, told me the time was just past five.

I lay on the bed wrapped in a large, dark green, terrycloth robe reconstructing each moment of the afternoon until my feet got chilly. I got up, got dressed and got antsy. I turned on the TV, but European television is awful. There was a panel discussion which seemed to be about whether existentialism was still relevant to modern literature. I heard one man, who had to be the worst-dressed adult I had ever seen, say that existentialism had never been relevant to literature. He was interrupted by another panelist who insisted that all literature was existentialist. The other channel had a soccer match that was almost indecipherably fuzzy with a white vertical band sweeping regularly across the screen every four seconds.

I still had my Middle Eastern Mythology as a last recourse, but I was not yet that bored. There were no bookshelves in the room. I looked in the night table drawer, no Gideon Bible. I began to look in all the drawers. In the dresser, I found a white box of matches with no trademark and a piece of graph paper with a pencil sketch of what could have been a machine part or an unusually unlivable building. In the credenza, I found nothing.

The desk that held the telephone was a gold mine, though. The top drawer had shallow dividers holding square paper clips, plain lead pencils, a blue BIC fineline accountant pen with a bent pocket clip, and a pile of stationery. The top sheet was embossed with the name and address of the estate, the same green ink and print as Ana's card. I folded the sheet to take as a souvenir and the second sheet on the pile jumped up at me.

Same paper with blue and red ink and a Germanic sort of Times font.

"*Agence Privée de Bretagne*" read the headline, but the address was the same.

"Folgoât, St. Chèldré

La Forêt, Basse Bretagne"

I sat at the desk and listened to the clock hum on the other side of the room which seemed to have gotten much smaller.

Six

I looked again at the clock. Time had not advanced. The paper was blank except for the letterhead. The room got intolerably smaller. Without an idea of why, I walked out the door. The hallway was as vacant, unremarkable and quiet as before, but I felt like an intruder at a private club and I was certain I was being watched.

Nonetheless, the prime lesson of adulthood is the importance and facility of acting plausible despite all evidence to the contrary. So I turned right and walked slowly down the hall, paying scrupulously curious attention to the walls (high gloss, only slightly shaped wooden wainscoting in a cherry wood and dark silky-feeling paper), the furniture (virtually non-existent), and the light fixtures (shell-shaped alabaster glass wall sconces). Since the sconces, walls and furniture were all alike, my plausibility was feeling a little thin by the time I reached the stairs, but there I could switch to the banister and balustrades (same wood as the wainscoting, also lightly worked) and runner (a richly detailed, hand-knotted oriental held down by brass rods). I have always wanted to live in a house with a stair runner held down by brass rods. So I was genuinely curious about how they were fitted. The angled retaining blocks on either end had knobs that screwed into the rods. The retaining blocks themselves were only attached to the riser, so the tread edge could swing away when the rod was released. It occurred to me that all the places I had lived with stairs belonged to some-one else; life on the single-floor plan.

At the bottom of the stairs where I had met Ana, I saw the phone nook from which she must have called me. It had a heavy, glass-windowed French door, the phone was the same as the one in my room. In the oppo-site wall was a double wooden door into a coat closet with several dozen heavy brass and wood hangers and one inevitable umbrella which I imagined would have at least one missing or broken rib and an unreliable catch.

Opposite the large, glass-paneled front door was an equally large, solid, wooden one which opened to re-veal another hall with another glass-paneled door show-ing daylight at its farther end. Midway down, on each side, there were two sets of the double, glass French doors. On the right I looked into a largish dining room with a Queen Anne style pedestal table about twenty feet long surrounded by an even number of dark-looking Duncan Phyfe chairs and the requisite sideboards, china, and linen chests in the same style as the table. There was a large oil of something darkly rural that could even have been a Millet or Corot, but the empty, institutional flavor of the room discouraged me from even entering to check.

Besides, the other room was much more interest-ing. It was on the southwest side of the building and so was deeply lit by the late day sun. The room was a warmly comfortable library living room with a bay window at the left end and three more windows set into bookshelves along the wall I faced. The right end of the room had an office set up with a four to five foot globe next to the door and a large, double-sided partners' desk in the cor-ner—surrounded by bookshelves on top of paneled cabi-nets, each with its own neat, shiny, brass key hole.

I turned immediately away from the desk and strolled ruminatively down the room to the bay window, then slowly examined book titles with infinitely more interest than I felt as I moved back towards it. I paid enough attention to every item in the room to write a separate volume thereon, but there was really nothing of note except that the furnishings, books, and prints of this room differed from everything else in the building by virtue of appearing personally chosen, comfortable, and well-used. The room felt as if it had been transplanted. The prints were engravings, three or four were tinted, mostly common subjects; there was a small Dürer of two loaves of bread I had never seen reproduced. The book titles were fiction—lots of eighteenth and nineteenth century authors in finely bound editions.

I lined my eye down the expanse of the Waverly novels and thought about how differently time stretched then. It was inconceivable to me that any balanced person outside of a school would ever read such books today. The average reader expects the writer to get the job done in a three or four hundred pages, even the most dedicated get impatient with all but the masters over five hundred. Mailer is the only author I will stay with up to a thousand and then only for the admittedly forlorn but persistent hope that he will one day yet deliver. During the divorce, I read that interminable *...And the Ladies of the Club* memoir and as an adolescent *Atlas Shrugged*, but I stand by my statement about balanced minds.

The books nearer the desk were references, dictionaries, atlases, general and several specialized encyclopedias. Then it struck me that these books, all the books in this room were in English. It seemed bizarre. Anyone living here would have to be at least bilingual; why were there no books in French, again so personal, so idiosyncratic.

I walked around behind the desk.

Paying scrupulously close attention to the shelf above, I slid my left hand down and tried one of the cabinets below, locked; the top desk drawer, ditto. The cabinet doors behind the desk to the left swung open with the pull of one finger. Nonchalant as a street thief I glanced in: a pile of ledgers on the right; a set of narrow drawers on the left. Reaching down as though to adjust my pants cuff, I looked in more closely and softly pushed the doors shut as I straightened up. The drawers were labeled I-V, VI-X, XI-XV, and XVI-XX. The top ledger had *Agence Privée de Bretagne* embossed in the lower center of the cover. I could have lifted it, but there was nowhere to conceal its size on my person.

I continued my inspection of the fine writing surface on the desk top and the beautiful solidity of the burly wood.

Behind the globe next to the door by which I had entered was a suit of armor I had not noticed. It was Renaissance style, highly detailed, ceremonial, no match for the old broad ax, but beautiful like a finely crafted man of metal, the joints scalloped, the body mass closely fitted. The body was smaller than mine but of the same proportions—an athlete's bones with a starveling's muscle.

I wondered how much it would weigh, I lifted the arm. It was surprising light, but I remembered how the basic field pack didn't feel too heavy either at first. Anyway, this was some pretty boy quattrocento courtier suit not built for Uther Pendragon or Roland. It was a shimmeringly detailed construction and I must have spent several minutes noting how the fabrication allowed for the various articulations and movements of the human body. Range of motion and rotation were somewhat limited, but it looked like a masterpiece. I began to feel the shape incarnate, so completely realized was the human contour.

I looked through the narrow visors. Nobody home.

I was examining the grand globe by the door when the voiceless valet who had received me earlier appeared in the doorway.

I smiled briefly at him and resumed my study of sub-Saharan Africa trying to remember which countries were now called what, radiating nonchalance and plausibility. The globe was about fifteen or twenty years out of date. I had plenty to work on: Rhodesia, that's now Zimbabwe; what was Botswana called…? Plausible or not, I did not hold his interest long. Was his passage a coincidence? Was something wired?

It seemed like a good time to inspect the outdoors, so I went out the back door and found myself at the foot of a path that sloped up and over an embankment. At the top of the bank, I realized I was standing on the outer defensive perimeter of the large castle I finally saw about three hundred yards away.

It was slightly backlit by the sunlight now turning a dusty yellow. I remembered Paul's description of "a great old pile with a moat." Yes, there was the moat and a drawbridge. The light obscured the front of the building and made it seem less distinct yet more massive.

I did not want to go exploring anymore. It was enough to sit on the bank and watch the light change on the trees and the earth and the building itself. There were birds, a small, sonorous black species preferred the high branches; a flock of chattering sparrows passed through.

It was engrossing to study this place built first of all for defensive safety. The earth had been recontoured to form the outer perimeter I sat on and to divert a river into the moat; the castle ground itself was the high point. In a less secure age, the trees inside the perimeter would be cleared and the forest that now touched the embankment on several sides burned. The embankment would probably be topped with a wooden stockade wall. I imagined the defenses pulling back into the castle, then under siege. The attackers are unable to get close to the walls due to quickly focused massed fire from the castle's archers. Attempts to build siege machines are broken up by skirmishers on horseback dashing across the drawbridge with lances and long swords; flaming arrows from above. At night, perhaps, a messenger leaves by the postern gate, a spy arrives. I tried to remember where the postern gate would be located.

I had about given up and decided it was my fantasy and I could put the damned postern gate anywhere I wanted when two figures walked across the drawbridge. Even at the distance, I was quite sure one was Ana.

Without standing up, I got below the crest of the bank and headed back to the room where I dressed quickly for dinner in the ten minutes I discovered I had before she called.

∞

She was alone at the foot of the stairs dressed in a short black party dress showing superlative legs I had somehow failed to notice before. Around her shoulders she had a large grey wool scarf or shawl that hid her shoulders and most of her arms.

"It is never really warm in the old place." She watched me look at her and watched me walk down the steps with that same intense open face which had captured me from the first.

Now what happens? Here comes the night.

She complimented my suit; I, her dress. We walked through the wooden door down the hall and out the back as I had earlier, but without the library inspection detour.

The sun was now setting behind the old castle and shadows were forming in the hollows of the trees and the banks. She told me the current structure was fifteenth century but was built on an eleventh century foundation. Compared to what the Medici were throwing up at the same time in Italy, *Folgoât Surmont*, as Ana called it, was heavy and brooding. But there was true grace to the stonework arches and walls and I would certainly prefer this to the Pitti Palace when bad company was expected.

"Anne kept Brittany as her personal duchy when she was forced to marry first Charles VII and then his son Louis XII," she said. "But Louis required Anne's daughter Claude to marry his heir, François. Within twenty years of Anne's death, Claude died and Brittany became part of the Frankish Kingdom. Anne must have known it was inevitable. After eleven hundred years, there was neither the economic nor the military strength in rocky, rural Brittany to resist."

Across the bridge inside the walls was a small open lawn split by the stone path leading to the main building with the terraces Paul had described. The effect was of a fine chateau that just happened to be built inside eighty-foot stone walls. It was friendly as long as one did not look to either side where the arms of the walls wrapped and loosely clasped around behind us. The air had the ever-chill moist breath of the earth and deep canyons.

"Was this place ever attacked?" She looked at me before answering.

"It was occupied by the Nazis when they were here. The Jacobin and Republican mobs of the same sort have raided in other centuries. The Normans and the Franks destroyed the old buildings in the thirteenth and fourteenth centuries. Before that construction, this was always the high ground. People have lived here forever. It has been attacked many, many times."

"It seems so commanding and impregnable."

"Commanding, perhaps, but it has been captured often. You think it is a place of safety. A castle is a trap."

"It seems to me, given the technology of the times, that a castle is a logistical necessity for common human survival. When the bigger gang comes along, you need a place for everybody on your side. You need stockpiles of food, weapons and specialists to use them, support services like religion. That's a big group of people; protecting and sustaining them takes a massive amount of stonework. Outside and on the run a few might survive—the fleet, the strong; but in here, the group will survive, the community, the aged, the wise, the skilled."

"When the gate is down and the mob is within—and they will always get in—the castle is a trap. And now when the mob masquerades as the rule of law, the castle has no defenses."

I had never heard her speak so darkly nor of such strong ideas.

To lighten the subject, I asked if there was a postern door. It seemed to work and she pulled me through a studded plank door with great black strap iron hinges in the side wall. We passed along a stone corridor with high narrow windows and an occasional ancient trunk or table. At the second turning we went through another solid door into a circular stone staircase that spiraled counter-clockwise, Ana said for the benefit of defending swords-men. We went down past one door and, at the bottom, stood in a largish, vaulted, bell-shaped room with doors on either side and two 100-watt bulbs failing to reveal much of anything else.

"Help me with this, please. It is heavy."

Together we pulled back the door in the outer wall. It had a center plate of iron or steel and double-crossed plank layers on either face. It must have weighed a quarter of a ton.

Iron rings studded the wall on either side of the door for further reinforcement. Looking out, we faced a mossy great wall forty or more feet across from us and the scummy green depth of the moat. I remembered a few of the reasons why people liked to stay out of the moat. Today's moat gets its excess nitrogen from soil run-off. In olden days, the nutrients were doubtless more varied including household wastes and the odd late resident of the lower chambers.

Ana took hold of one of the rings and leaned out over the moat.

"Look at this," she invited. I grabbed the next ring up and swung out beside and behind her.

We were facing to the right, looking at a right-angle turn in the water and the walls beyond and above. The moat had a yeasty sour smell. The far walls looked cruel and high.

"Now look up," she said, and lay her head back on my chest. I inhaled her hair deeply before following her eyes to look above us at an out-thrust of the upper wall.

"With a rope from that turret, it is said one can swing from here to the top of the moat wall opposite the corner."

I looked at the angles and arcs.

"I'll take your word for it, but one would need to be highly motivated."

"This is the only back door." She swung herself back inside and I followed. After we pulled the door into place, she led us back up the staircase several turns and floor levels to what I judged to be the second level above where we came in. The door opened into a museum room.

"This was Anne of Brittany's council chamber." I followed her absently under flags, past tables, paintings and tapestries I could only admire without identifying.

"And this is my aunt, Madame Vera Eliane Charlotte."

She stepped aside to present me to a small, white-haired person who did not rise nor extend a hand to greet me. Impossible to tell her age, her skin was so finely wrinkled; in the light it looked smooth. I wondered if she even had fingerprints. Her eyes were dark and steady and she had not the slack, nervous, uncertain manner of the very old, although she was clearly frail and slight. It seemed merely a final attenuation; the body no longer being necessary, only the spirit and intelligence that shone from her eyes remained.

"Please sit down, Mr. Gardiner," she said in a bright, strong voice, "you will be more comfortable and I will not have to strain my neck looking up." She had a pronounced British accent.

A heretofore invisible factotum held a tray next to my right hand as I sat down on the edge of a brocade hassock nearby. The glass was heavy, held ice and Jack Daniel's; apparently I was expected. I was surprised and pleased that Ana had been so observant and considerate. I glanced over at her and smiled.

Aunt Vera spoke again. "You look much better now."

I felt much better now. I had another sip. I felt better again.

"Thank you." I finally got the synapses back on line in the courtesy circuits, "*Merci*, it is a pleasure to meet you and a rare experience to visit this lovely old place."

"This is a midden of rotting stones where crude, overbuilt antiques are moldering and I am a contrary old lady who can see clear through your airy persiflage."

Airy persiflage!?!

I broke up in a bark of laughter while Aunt Vera smiled placidly in my face and Ana's face changed not a bit. I quickly clamped down, but saw Aunt Vera all differently then. What had looked so slight and frail now seemed to be vibrating like a tightly wound harp string.

"I am pleased to meet you too, Mr. Gardiner. I know Ana has shown you around. Tell me, what would you do with a white elephant of this magnitude?"

"I hope I would be able to preserve it."

"Why? And how? And at what expense? It has long outlived its use. Preservation would require the same labor of legions and treasuries of kings that it took to construct; neither commodity is available any longer. It should rot and crumble."

"Surely the historical value warrants preservation."

"A footnote; four hundred years ago this was a minor queen's place in the country reconstructed on a Templar ruin, built over a Roman hill fort, constructed on top of a Breton barrow; centuries of rubbish. Commonplace. In its present form, it is a nothing. It has never kept out an attacker, because no army ever attacked it. The Jacobins and the Nazis walked in, no one else cared."

"Then just as a monument to itself, it should endure."

"Well, it will not endure. It will decay. No reasonable expenditure can save it. But you could purchase it and try."

"Would you take a 750 square-foot condo in Boston as a down payment?"

"You mistake my standing. This place is not mine. It is owned by a corporation. I am simply living my last days here and I try to avoid this old building because it is too much like my body, inconvenient, uncomfortable, and falling apart."

"It was so good of you to make an exception for this encounter."

"Ana is behind this. She wanted me to meet you and she wanted to remind me of other nights in this room when we were both younger."

I glanced at Ana , who was giving all her attention to her aunt.

Vera continued, "You are a charming young man, but Ana has to know that I do not care to think of the past. It holds no appeal. There is no meaning there."

She looked at me as she finished and I felt Ana's eyes on us both.

The factotum returned and, catching his eye, Aunt Vera rose strongly to her feet with the briefest reliance on a beautifully knotted wooden cane. I stepped toward her and offered my arm which she looked at long enough to let me know she was thinking about it and then accepted with a smile.

"Very well, Mr. Gardiner. We shall proceed together. And since it will take us a while to get to the table at my speed, please tell me what is left of Boston. Is the Athenaeum now surrounded by rude commercial buildings? And what has happened to Locke-Ober?

I assured her both were relatively untouched and recounted our first annual corporate Christmas dinner at Locke-Ober in one of the private rooms that I fantasized once fed Howells, Hawthorne, Melville, the whole Atlantic crowd. I got her to laugh as I drew a series of unflattering parallels between the two sets of diners.

Ana walked on her other side and smiled at the right places but said nothing. As we got Aunt Vera seated, Ana met my eyes and mouthed the words, 'thank you.'

We began dinner with a jellied consommé of some sort, lamb perhaps. Aunt Vera and I talked about Boston, its successes and its conceits. She was delighted to hear that the city still calls itself the Hub of the Universe.

She asked how it was today. She knew about Southie. I told her about Dorchester and Somerville—Dorchester with trees, bankrupt Chelsea; the Navy Yard going yuppie; the pretension floating like a scum over the dirty-neck reality of the city, held in place by the *Globe*, the Red Sox, and the Democratic Party. I quoted Durrell's description of Cairo, "...ill planned, ill built and ill drained."

"Tell me, is the Isabel Stewart Gardner house still intact?"

"There is a museum. I've never been there. Do you know it?"

"Yes, a perfectly beautiful accomplishment. It was one of the finest period homes in the world. A museum, now? Well, that is just right. Collectors and librarians are seeking complete perfection and order and no one can live like that."

∞

The dinner was of a kind you can best enjoy, indeed cherish, by traveling. In one's native culture, the predictable banality of social exchange makes time petrify, sounds take on a machine shop quality and the IQ drops like a bomb. But there in that great old room of stone, the chill of the vault and the fool behind my lips were swept away by the physical pleasure of the meal, the grace of the space, the force of Aunt Vera's spirit, Ana's beauty and my delight-filled presence.

Aunt Vera and I hit it off wonderfully. She had a dry, direct caustic humor and seemed to enjoy my stories of the eastern United States.

"When were you last in the U.S., Madame?"

"1934."

"And what brought you?"

She looked at me the quick, funny way all primates seem unable to avoid in moments of uncertainty. Her face immediately sharpened with resolve, the polished marble strength showed through.

"I could say business... business... and a young man like you," she said, and stared placidly back at me.

"In 1934, what was I like?"

She looked at me askance.

"Physically, the young man was probably a few years younger than yourself, Mr. Gardiner; personally he was not your equal in wit, although I think just a shade your better in charm."

I smiled. This was fun.

"And where is this witty charming fellow today?"

"He is dead in Boston, Mr. Gardiner."

I stopped smiling.

"I am sorry."

"So am I, Mr. Gardiner, but I have not seen him for close to fifty years."

"Oh."

"It was a brief relationship. But he came to my mind; all this talk of Boston."

"Was he from Boston?"

"Oh yes, ever so."

"Would I know his name?"

"Ralph Stonington Adams Baxter."

"Which Ralph Stonington Adams Baxter?"

"The last one, I believe. At some point he began calling himself 'the third', although technically he never ranked higher than a junior."

"But I know him. He's alive. At least he was the day before I left."

"I have learned he is recently deceased."

As my ideas of what to say next all died before being spoken, I looked at Aunt Vera and she looked at Ana. When I glanced at her, Ana was staring at me.

Baxter! A shade my better in charm? I was horrified. Dead?

"I see," I said, seeing nothing.

Not wishing to speak ill of the etc., I also had nothing further to say.

Ana broke the pause, "We received the news over the wire in Zurich the day after you left. He was not in good health, I understand."

I agreed that had certainly been my impression.

Another one bites the dust.

"How did you meet, if I may ask?"

"We met at an auction in Köln."

"And you both bid on the same antique…"

She smiled.

"In a sense. We were both there to buy the same thing—a hundred square kilometer coke and steel operation. His firm had syndicated the financing for one group of bidders. I was with a competing interest."

"Who got the steel plant?"

"It became a joint purchase. In many ways, he was responsible for your being here tonight."

Ana said, "Vera was active in business before the last war. She was quite a successful investment manager."

"Europe was littered with bargains—the States, too, for that matter. All that was missing was cash, confidence and patience."

"How was he responsible for my being here?"

"Discussions that led to the joint purchase revealed an array of complementary interests between his firm and our bank. You are aware of the result."

"And did you and he arrange the partnership?"

"I was involved. He was not, directly."

She made a brief, rueful smile and nodded.

"At least not on their side. He was extremely helpful to us."

"How?

"He liked to talk and he said more than he realized on most topics. After returning to the States, he went to work for a Senator determined to change the banking laws in your country. I am sure someone at his firm arranged it, thinking he would be a good source of inside information. And he probably was for them. But since they had, quite reasonably, not thought him clever enough to be used as an active spy, he was not aware of how significant the new laws were for his father's firm. So he told me, too.

"He was so proud. The Senator was protecting 'the little guy.' 1929 would never happen again. The money trusts would be broken up. He could be most boring on the subject ... and most informative.

"When the right time came in the negotiations, we delivered to our soon-to-be partners a report on the impact of the legislation on their business and a vote count of committed Senators that proved to be exactly correct.

"Agreement on terms was most expeditious after that.

"Baxter was highly favored over here as a result. But I shouldn't wonder if he was less popular in Boston. We insisted he be put in charge of part of the new business we provided, to protect him."

How kind, I thought; most people would just leave him hanging in the tree.

∞

I asked if she knew of Paul Languedoc.

"Yes, his family fled one or another late medieval persecution in southern France and settled here; tried to start a vineyard, the fools; did better in town. He is a fine musician; he plays all over Europe, although I am sure to small audiences. I heard him first at a Harvest Fair in 1932. He made the most delightful music; he was a spirited young man."

"He played here," Ana surprised me by interjecting. She was smiling at Vera.

"Yes," replied Aunt Vera without a smile, "in a sense."

"Was that the summer he fell among the stones and lost his eyesight?"

They both looked at me.

Aunt Vera spoke first, nodding sadly, "He was lucky he was not killed. He should not have been there."

"Phillip has met Paul," Ana said, still looking at me.

Aunt Vera seemed to smile a bit.

"Have you heard him play," she asked.

"Yes, several things, one a Breton tune with Ana's name, Megan Morgan, and another called Carrickfergus in Gaelic."

"The Rock of Fergus," Aunt Vera said.

And who will go with Fergus then, I thought.

"Are these local rocks the property of heroes and gods?" I asked, instead, still looking at Vera's thoughtful face.

Ana replied, "They all have fanciful names and legends, you can believe anything you want of them. There are post cards and souvenirs in the villages."

"Are there megaliths near this place?"

This time Vera responded. "There is a circle about three or four kilometers northeast, but they are everywhere. It is a nuisance, it attracts flocks of dull, earnest people with books, all wearing ghastly clothes. They leave the gates open and scatter film boxes and cigarette packs in their wake."

I smiled at Aunt Vera; she smiled back.

"Phillip and I went riding today," Ana said lightly, but looking at Vera.

"You would have loved it. We raced to the oak tree where you told me you met with Paul. It was very exciting."

I felt the implication was embarrassingly clear.

"Riding and its excitements are of no further interest to me. Such physical pleasures are a well-lost addiction of youth."

"I would never believe I'd hear Vera Eliane tell me physical pleasure is well lost."

"And I say as I have before to you, Ana, there is a truth in life that is greater than the life of the body. It comes with age and I believe it is called wisdom."

"What you call wisdom seems to be a denial of life."

This was obviously a deeper topic with a longer history than I could know, but Ana seemed so cruel to her great aunt, practically mocking her years.

Without considering, I said, "But aren't they both phases of life in which we learn from our physical experience the wisdom to deal with our physical limits?"

"Ana does not believe in physical limits, Mr. Gardiner, only in herself and what she can take of life. She is particularly opposed to wisdom which might suggest otherwise. One could say she strenuously avoids it."

"As did you," Ana interjected.

"As did I," Vera nodded, "but no more. And I wish I had been wiser sooner, but the avoidance of wisdom is likewise an addiction of youth."

"And your wisdom is foolishness. It is childish to turn your mind from the physical."

"Perhaps," I said not thinking, "it is just a matter of your differing years."

Ana looked at me with narrowed eyes and I saw how high her feelings had become.

"You do not know what you are talking about."

"I know enough to think you are being unreasonable."

"You both infuriate me." Ana stared hotly, first at me, then Vera.

"And you deserve each other's company." Looking at me she went on, "I am going back to the New Building. You may escort Aunt Vera back."

Turning to Vera, Ana said, "I leave tomorrow at first light. Good-bye."

She walked from the room without another word or glance to either of us.

Vera Eliane relaxed back into her chair, seeming once more her advanced age, tired for it and drained by Ana's anger.

"Was it something I said?"

She resurrected a weak smile.

"No, Mr. Gardiner. It was simply the last words in a long, long argument. We were once so close ..."

"I'm sorry."

She seemed to think her own thoughts for a bit, then looked at me.

"Thank you. I can see you are. Ana has a more desperate view of life than I do. She has come closer to dying than I am."

"Really," I asked.

"Quite."

When nothing further was forthcoming, I lobbed the conversational ball back to center court.

"I liked what you said about there being a truth in

life that is greater than the life of the body, but it strikes me as a dangerous proposition. Religions, governments and other assorted maniacs claiming to have that truth have wasted millions of physical lives that were arguably much more valuable."

"Quite true," Vera replied, "but I had in mind a simpler, perhaps more immediate, or personal truth."

"Camus wrote that there are truths, but no Truth."

"Yes, more of an existential truth. But if we are going to talk French philosophy, we should start walking back to the New Building. French philosophy always puts me to sleep."

"Well," I said, standing attentively as she got to her feet, "What do you think of modern Latin-American novelists?"

Without giving her a chance to answer I said that I thought magical realism wore better in shorter novels and stories and mentioned a friend who called Marquez's work One Hundred Years of Boredom.

"Your friend is too impatient."

"It is a modern human trait."

"Yes it is. Essentially, eminently human; worse in modern times."

By this time, we had passed from the castle keep and across the courtyard, technically the donjon, if I remembered right from Ana's tour. I wondered whether Ana had been saying good-bye to Vera for good. Was she that cold-hearted to turn her back on someone she might never again see alive over a comparatively simple argument about philosophy? And what about me? Was she quit of me; was I free of her? It was queasy situation.

We walked across the drawbridge onto the path through the park-like woody plain. There was moonlight but more shadow and the spacing of the trees was randomly balanced. I realized it must have been planned.

"This is a beautiful landscape," I said.

"Yes, you are right, but I have only begun to see it

so lately. There is beauty in the world. As I have gotten closer to death, I have begun to see it again."

I said, "Perhaps that is another of the truths we were speaking of. Doesn't mortality drive every human act: love; creation; procreation; acquisition of wealth, power, knowledge."

"Yes, again you are right. But there is more."

"More to life or more to that truth?"

"Both, of course; but I was thinking of what you said to us about physical experience giving wisdom to transcend physical limits."

I did not remember putting it that intelligently.

"Ana troubles you," Vera asked, "does she not?"

"Well," I began.

"She should. She has been through extremes and she lives by extreme values. You should be careful."

We were at the back entrance to the New Building. Inside the entry, Vera Eliane turned to a door to the left of the hall door. I had assumed it led to the kitchen.

"I shall leave you here for the night, but I must say how good it was to meet you. You have revitalized me in ways Ana did not intend. I now see how something might be possible on which I had given up. I will see you before you leave, I'm sure."

She held out her hand and I nearly kissed it, so grand was her presence. If I had thought I could do it right, I probably would have. Instead, I returned her brief gentle pressure, smiled into her lovely, lively aging eyes and said, "*Merci, madame, bonsoir.*"

After she went through the door, I heard elevator doors open and close and then a deep electrical hum.

∞

Back in my own room, the lamps were bright and I regretted leaving the flask of Jack at the inn. I did actually get undressed and get into bed. Lying on one side, my thoughts would jumble along, reliving the day, the evening, the argument, trying to make sense of Ana's anger. I realized I had no idea of how to find her in this building or reach her once we left. Turning on the other side produced a video montage of more dramatic emotional effect but no clearer conclusions. On this spit I turned until the bed bore the thoroughly unsleepable funk any insomniac knows much too well. Giving up on sleep I rolled onto my back and stared up toward the invisible ceiling.

∞

I could not sleep like that, but at least my mind settled down and I realized that, everything else aside, if there were answers to the questions that drew me to Brittany, they were downstairs in that library cupboard and tonight was my only chance to find them.

Once I had that thought, the fear of what I was about to do made it somehow impossible not to do it. The tension could only be relieved by action. From the knapsack, I got the brass mini-maglite I've carried since I saw how dark it gets at night in a airplane when the power fails. I must confess I got it from the Sharper Image catalog, but it was before they went public, if that counts.

Backing off the threaded lantern head turns it on. The beam illuminated my toes. I turned it off and got dressed in my last pair of fresh slacks, dark grey, and a black knit shirt. I wondered if I looked like Roger Moore; on reflection it did not seem likely.

With the maglite off, I leaned against the door, heard nothing and, with my weight still against it, turned the door latch slowly. There was no sound.

I thought about plausibility. I am going to get a book. I opened the door normally and stepped out. The hall was dimly illuminated by the sconces, turned down another two or three stops since I came in. I slid the flashlight into my pocket and walked directly down to the library which was dark.

With the flashlight on I went in to the room and across to the bookshelves. Examining titles, I selected for this evening's bedtime alibi a gorgeous red leather bound volume of Shelley.

Right, face; forward, march. I pinched the beam down to a pin light and moved around the desk. The polished cupboard door reflected my light to the floor and I saw my fingers shake as I reached for the handle and, at that moment, had the simultaneous awareness of something behind me, a blind rush of fear and ...

"I felt sure I would see you before you left, Mr. Gardiner." Vera Eliane's voice froze me in place.

I turned slowly, aiming the beam at the ceiling. It gave back little light, but I saw her in a wheelchair next to the globe and armor. The Ph in my stomach had gone to zero and the blood roared in my head.

"You have the manners of a career criminal, Mr. Gardiner. But I am glad to see you here."

"I..."

"Don't bother."

I was rigid with fright.

"We both know what you were doing and I believe I know why. And, contrary to any reasonable fears you might have, I can help.

"Now sit down and turn off that little light before someone sees it. Let us talk. You presumably were intending to examine records of *Agence Privée de Bretagne* that are normally kept in that cabinet. They are not there. That fact coupled with your heading straight for it indicates that you had come across them during previous snooping and activated the alarm."

I sank down in the desk chair. When I pulled my legs under me, my right foot went into a "sewing machine" spasm familiar to fatigued rock climbers and the survivors of auto accidents.

With the light off, the vague bulk of the globe and armor overshadowed Vera Eliane and, in the conversation that followed, I could only locate her by sound and occasional sense of movement.

She continued, "To help you understand the situation, let me tell you why you're here.

"In Boston, you made someone nervous. At his reckless initiative, your apartment was investigated and you were thought to have a too curious mind. The investigators reported '...a ton of books...' and the photo survey documented a fairly impressive range of titles and a good deal of outdoor equipment. Although the investigation was a mistake, it was concluded you might be dangerous.

"You know something of Claude-Philippe and Ana's ambitions and have had access to more information than they would like.

"Since you were working at the firm that manages individual assets and something has called your attention to the *Agence Privée de Bretagne*, I can conclude you have researched the life histories and found something that persuaded you to pursue a reckless investigation of your own.

"Now, I don't want to know what you have learned, because I have no intention of ever having to lie about it.

"I merely warn you that anything you do further will cost you either your life or your soul."

"My soul?"

"No... not a vague, religious conceit. Your spirit, your imagination, your emotions, your human dignity and pride; that which lets you hear beauty in music and see it in the sky."

"Or my life... ?"

"Death is preferable, believe me."

"Life is all we get, isn't it? I don't understand preferring to give it up."

"It is a matter of perspective. I have lived much longer than you. I am tired of the endless, 'awful knowing and knowing' as one of your poets wrote."

"I guess I can understand, watching over forty years of human history and reading about the rest gets pretty depressing."

"Mr. Gardiner, I am over five thousand years old."

I could think of nothing to say. Of all the things I had imagined, this was at the same time the most familiar and the most remote, the most entrancing and the most unfathomable; immediate and impossible.

I wanted more than anything to see her face, to look in her eyes, to know if she told the truth, was deluded, senile, joking. Five thousand-year-old eyes, I tried to recall; they were grey and clear.

"It is an unnatural and evil condition and I wish to end it; but we don't die easily and are awfully hard to kill."

"You have tried to kill yourself?"

"Others have tried to kill themselves; with heroic effort, a few have succeeded, but I conclude suicide is equally unnatural and evil. Besides, I have a great curiosity about the human process of dying. It is the only thing I have never done."

"I can agree suicide is evil and perhaps unnatural, but living—an extended human life—how can that be wrong?"

"Not just extended, Mr. Gardiner—forever."

Forever.

"How?"

"That I will most definitely not tell you, help you learn, nor encourage you to pursue. It is a great wrong."

"Wrong to live forever ... ?"

"Why do you want to live forever, human? Is there something you want to do that will take that long?"

"I am nothing but experience, am I not? Why should I want that experience to end?"

"Endless, pointless experience, human; is that what you seek?"

I tried to think about what she was saying, but I kept coming back to: How? How? How?

"Earlier tonight, Mr. Gardiner, you said that death lies behind all beauty. You were close, but it is the awareness of death that is the mechanism; the perception of the transient uniqueness of the experience is what makes you cherish it. The first kiss or the last. The newborn child. The moment of sunset. Love. Even the most stable beauties of music, art and architecture a human perceives uniquely each time, because a human changes.

"We do not change. And human life goes on around us desperately engaged in emotions of joy and grief long lost, to us. And we feed upon them, on you."

"Is that how? Are you cannibals?"

She laughed at me as she had when we first met.

"No, Mr. Gardiner, I will not tell you how it is done. But would you eat another human to live forever; would you murder?"

"Murder... no, ... "

"But cannibalism, maybe? And then later, whatever was required. It is an evil. Those who do not die can see no value in mortal human life beyond the utilitarian."

"Like with Baxter?"

"Yes, precisely. Very good. But he lived longer than he ever would have had he been as curious as you."

"And he was not blinded like Paul."

"Correct. And so you may gauge the danger you face. You should be aware that only amnesia saved Paul's life."

"Why were you waiting for me here?"

"To warn you against pursuing any further investigation."

"Okay. Thanks for the warning. What if I won't stop?"

"Yes, I assumed you would not. I want to tell you enough to help you destroy the others."

"Destroy? Personally, I would rather try to join."

"You are not welcome. No human is welcome."

"Are you another species?"

"Oh, no, more like a small cult from an ancient tribe, superstitious, xenophobic and savagely dangerous."

"How many?"

A long pause.

"More than you know about."

"And they live all over the place, but come here twice in their lives. For what?"

"No, Mr. Gardiner; dead end."

"So you won't tell me how it's done, only that you want me to destroy the others. Assuming I accept, then, why? How?"

"Expose them! Prove these unnatural things exist. Human society will take care of the rest."

"You expect they would be killed if they were known?"

"Not deliberately, perhaps, at least not initially, but, yes, eventually. Humans have destroyed three-quarters of us so far. Up until recent times, anyone ever widely suspected of immortality has been killed. I told you that Ana had been closer to death than I. In twelfth century England, she was beaten, stabbed, and thrown bound into the ocean. Modern society has spared us, allowed us mobility and places to hide that were impossible before the eighteenth century."

"This is what Claude-Philippe and Ana manage? The mechanism for evading human society... and law?"

"Yes, and your only hope for surviving your encounter is to stop your impulsive investigating, act completely incurious, and cooperate with their plans for you. If you are patient and cautious, you should be able to document enough of the identities to prove to the world these monsters exist."

"If what you say is true, that sounds more than a touch risky."

"Mr. Gardiner, you are already in what I believe is called a highly leveraged situation. If you do not stop investigating, they will have you killed to prevent your learning too much. If you refuse to cooperate, they will assume you already know too much, with the same result for you. Your only viable tactic is to avoid further suspicions, cooperate and develop the documentation carefully, slowly, over time."

"And what do you think it would take?"

"Simply proof that the same faces and bodies have been living lives over and over again, time after time. Although this century has allowed the group greatly increased mobility and privacy, images are captured now as never before. Identity cards, passports, news photos; the evidence will be there now.

"Claude-Philippe and Ana have a plan to create an autonomous country which would centralize most of the documents and images and make them even more susceptible to exposure by someone like you inside."

"An autonomous country, where?"

"There are several current candidates, but after an initial failure, they are proceeding more slowly."

"Wait, let me get this right. They intend to set up a new country—a new nation—and they've already tried it once—and you advise I join this venture as a mole?"

"I believe you have no other choice."

"And if I follow this advice, and develop this information, you want me to expose them? Why do you want them destroyed and, more to the point, why should I do it?"

"I think I have judged you right and you will see, as you think on what we have said, that you must destroy them and the secret. But if you do not follow my advice, you will soon be dead."

"Five thousand years," I said, "What have you

seen, what can you tell me about life, about your life? Where were you born?"

"In a land long flooded, between Denmark and England. For centuries, we lived on ships, only coming to shore occasionally, as needed. We waited for the water to stop rising. It took two thousand years. Then we began building places two to three days from the shore for storage and retreat. In the times of travel, we traded with farmers along the shores. Sometimes we took what we wanted. We stayed to ourselves because of our differences, but had ways to make those on shore do work for us. We told them stories, which they believed; and we showed them advantages to cooperating and dangers to resistance.

"We settled in different locations, separate groups. There were probably groups that did not survive. There may be survivors today we don't know about, but I doubt that."

"And all of you can reverse aging at will?"

"Under certain circumstances."

"Certain circumstances?"

"Yes." Her voice smiled ironically and the strength of her character drew a tide of admiration from me.

"Why did Ana want you to meet me? You made it clear it was not your idea."

"My last chance for life is soon. If I do not take it, I will surely die, before the next. If I take it, I will be Ana's age again or, perhaps, a bit younger. Do I make myself clear?"

I was embarrassed, challenged and charmed.

"Then I will take it personally if you don't take the chance."

"That is sweet, Mr. Gardiner. I take back what I said about the late Baxter."

"How did he die?"

"He was not in good health."

"Ana said that."

"He had lunch with Ana."

"Oh."

"These are desperate and dangerous beings and you are nothing to them but a casual tool, at best; a brief irritation easily eliminated, otherwise. No human restriction will stand in their way."

"Have you always looked at us this way?"

"Yes," she sighed, "and I find it to be the essential evil. Only our lives matter. Our endless, singular, selfish lives—endlessly extended, repeated cycles of energy, ambition and eager appetent desire; with no time for thought or the wisdom that experience gives, if allowed to mature."

"And in your maturity, you conclude that life is evil."

"No, not life; life forever is wrong. There must be death. There can be no nobility in will and choice if consequences can be reversed. There is no art if the moment is not fleeting; no love, if beauty does not fade. That is why we have no physical interest in each other; and, of course, we are infertile. And in our constant drive to ensure our extended life, we devalue and destroy the truly noble, artful, loving beings—mortal humans. We should be destroyed. Perhaps my own sins in this area became too much; perhaps the process is an anodyne for conscience.

"You have met Paul," she said then.

"Paul, yes, but..."

"How is he now? Does he seem content, does he seem wise?"

"Wise, yes, I guess; but, content..." I remembered his firm corrections of my musical and literary histories.

"Content, I'm not sure—wisdom and contentment?"

"I would wish that for him in return for the damage he was done and things he will not know and what he thinks he lost that year."

"You mean when he was blinded?"

"I mean when I sent him away. He wrote for years afterwards, at first in words that spoke such aching truths, but soon the writing became illegible and then there was music that was more painful. Wire recordings, then tape; who knows how a blind man finds his way? Of course, I got them all and, of course, I never replied. But it was too much pain and loneliness to walk away from or maybe it was simply the last measure for me. But when the time approached for me to … do what we do, I did not. And then I did not again. And then the arguments with Ana began. She sees my choice of death as a repudiation of her. And it is. For Paul, I tried to do... good. Perhaps for the first time in… forever.

"I put the recordings in the hands of both record companies and musical scholars. Paul has become well known and though he lives simply near here, he is widely successful in academic and classical circles as a musician and musicologist.

"It changed me finally—that small, small kindness did—and now I am letting the rolled back years return and the hardy mechanism of this body is finally running down. If Paul could have wisdom and find contentment, then there would be a satisfaction for me that I had not been totally evil.

"Now I am going to leave you. And I expect I will not see you again, but I hope you will remember me and understand that I have considered these things for centuries; and you will see I am right."

"Wait. I want to know more."

But the only answer was the hum of the chair and a small thump as it went over the tread of the doorway to the hall.

I sat there at the desk until the windows began to lighten. About the time I could read the title but still not see the color of the volume of Shelley on the desk, I heard a small helicopter land and then take off on the other side of the chateau. I presumed it was Ana's departure.

In the time after Vera left, I sat listless, depressed. I had learned everything and nothing; there was forever, but there was no door, maybe only a dangerous window. If I were lucky, I would live a sinecure like Baxter, but the wrong move either way and my life was forfeit. And if I learned enough to prove it was all true, I was expected to be wise enough to destroy it.

I thought of blind Paul and dead Baxter. A mole in Claude-Philippe's operation, someone for Ana to play with or not; frightening. The answers might be there, but I saw little hope.

Oh, yes, and if I were a good little human, incurious and cooperative, I might live; otherwise I was dead.

I could make out the details of the armor suit and shapes on the globe, but the room had a glassy grey light that made everything look like it was made of smoke.

I watched the light change and the substances of the room solidify and particularize into hard edged virtual reality, then got up, left Percy Bysshe on the desk and went quietly back to the room.

When I got there, the phone was ringing. It was Ian.

"How is your holiday, Phillip?"

I said it was fine.

"Hope we're not waking you." The line sang with a hollow echo. Was it just international relays firing paranoid circuits in my skull?

What was that line from Ian Fleming, I don't mean this as a threat, but if I were you, I'd take it as one. Or was that John D. MacDonald? What would my paperback heroes do now: something bold and direct.

I thought about running away. Get back home. Do not pass Zurich. Do not collect... whatever is waiting there.

To avoid the long arm of Claude-Philippe's suspicion, indirection seemed in order; incurious, cooperative indirection.

No, I thought, better to keep the appointment. Act nonchalant. What made him call *per alium*? On Sunday. Could he know what Vera told me? Was the library bugged? No. If it had been, there would be no doubt. There would be no call. Something from Boston? Have they found the birth and death cert copies and the disks? If they could have my place broken into by "investigators" professional enough to leave no sign of entry, they could certainly ransack Clio ... I think that was the first thought I had given her since the dinner at the inn right before Madame brought by the Calvados. Dear Clio, how would I ever ... I began to see how I might have placed her in some very heavy traffic.

Could they find her? Would they know to look? Maybe not. I tried to talk myself into being sure we were not known to be connected. I was fairly persuasive, but not entirely persuaded.

My time in Boston with her now seemed idyllic, the things we had grown comfortable doing together. Riding for miles in the car with the radio on, she would slide her left hand under my right leg. It was friendly and familiar. Half asleep, touching toes in the morning. Reading for hours on Sundays, saying nothing. I could see a quality of contentment I had not realized we had. Could I ever get back to it?

Seven

Picking up the phone again, I saw it had no dial or buttons. I held my breath and listened to it ring thirty or forty seconds to the edge of my patience.

"*Oui? Qu'est-ce que c'est?*"

"*Je désire un petit déjeuner—café au lait, deux croissants, jus d'orange ou pamplemousse. S'il vous plaît.*"

I held my breath.

"*Oui, café au lait, deux croissants, jus d'orange ou pamplemousse. Lequel désirez-vous?*"

Oh, well, I get a choice.

"*De pamplemousse, s'il vous plaît; un grand verre.*"

"*D'accord.*"

"*Autre chose?*"

"*Oui.*"

"*A huit heures et demi, un taxi ou une voiture pour me remener à mon hôtel.*"

Pause.

"*Oui, monsieur huit heures et demi.*"

Exhale!

As I changed clothes and packed, I wondered how the French got *pamplemousse* for grapefruit. Orange must have a Latin root, since the Spanish have it as *naranja* where the French have *l'orange*. But maybe the grapefruit came along after the fall of Rome. The Spanish word is *pamelo*, what is the Italian? I realized I was walking around the room aimlessly, all packed, thinking about the Italian word for grapefruit, when breakfast was served.

I opened the door to another aging beige face in a suit off the same rack as the rest of the help, pushing a tinkling, wheeled tea cart.

The face and suit departed before the cart stopped jiggling it seemed. I looked at my breakfast, and dinner seemed so recent. But I knew if I didn't give my body essential nutrients like sugar and caffeine, I was in for an uncomfortable ride back to *mon hôtel* and a maddeningly slow-witted brain for figuring out what to do next.

My departure from the chateau was a simple, lightly attended affair. At eight thirty, I let myself out the door, walked down the hall and stairs, admired the brass rods again. Should I take one for self-defense? Am I crazy? Can I just walk out?

I could. I did.

In a few minutes, as I was noticing that the day had not gotten much brighter than it had been at seven, a 300SD wagon pulled up next to me.

As I said, it was a lightly attended affair, just me and André. He sat behind the wheel and waited silently.

I got in.

To my continual surprise at each turn, he chose the way back to the inn and did not pull off into a field and murder me.

Needless to say, I got no useful thinking done on the trip. Nor can I remember anything I saw.

I can remember our conversation, though. Word for word.

As always, nothing was said.

At the inn, I nearly fainted when I got out of the car too quickly. I had been so tense, mouth-breathing and locked joints, the sudden release was like that trick you learn in school where you end up biting your thumbs passed out on the floor with everyone standing around in a circle laughing. Their voices come from the top of a well a hundred feet deep. I heard the Mercedes pull away at a great distance and the walls of the inn distorted briefly, then my head buzzed as everything came back into focus. Clearly something wrong in my tuning circuits; must be in a fringe area; may need a larger antenna.

Inside the doors, normalcy blessedly prevailed. The Madame bustled into the dining room with a bread-basket such as I had had—what, two days ago?—outside in the garden. I looked out, the foggy, grey light flattened all the colors, the garden looked like a pen, the walls like a prison. I went into the dining room with the rest of the guests where there was the mid-morning clatter of life and even a small fire on the hearth.

Maybe another breakfast would help, certainly more coffee.

After the second pot, sitting still became a physical impossibility and I vibrated up to my room.

It looked like a museum preservation where everything is recreated as though someone resided there But even without the velvet rope, you can tell no human has lived there for decades or even centuries. Nathaniel Hawthorne's writing chamber, the last room of Edith Cavell, a side corridor of Schoenburn, a backstairs at Versailles.

Making a conscious attempt to pull my thoughts under control, I got the timetables and maps from my suitcase. In the afternoon, there was a three o'clock train going east and three minutes later a train going west.

With Madame's help, I arranged for a car to take me all the way back to Responden, packed up a half kilo each of cheese and bread, a bottle of wine and fruit, and prepared to depart. I insisted on paying for the whole week I had agreed to for the room. I asked her to tell Paul Languedoc *merci encore* from me if she saw him.

"Do you know him?" I asked her.

"His music, but not him."

"He said your husband was once his friend."

"That may be. My husband only mentioned him once, but it may be."

I asked her about the man who was now the *notaire*, had she found his name? I got the clear sense from her guttural *non*, that there was nothing further about the topic she wanted to know

"Did your husband ever say anything about the records he kept. Was there anything he was uncomfortable about?"

"Ha. That is a bad joke. Being *notaire* made him a miserable man. He should have stayed in Paris. We should have stayed in Paris. The Nazis would have been easier to live with.

"Did he talk about why?"

"He complained about the people, bare-footed, superstitious farmers, piggish shopkeepers, the arrogant ones... of... the... Château."

"What did he say about them?"

"No. Nothing. Never."

"Yes. Something. When? What?"

She looked at me the same way I look at window envelopes from the IRS; anxiety and mistrust and dread washed her features.

"It is my life," I said, "If you know anything about those people that can help me... "

"And it was my life. And in any case I have promised."

"What ?"

"To give something to someone only if he asks."

"Something about the people at the Chateau?"

"I do not know and do not care to know. It is a record book like he kept."

"Will you give it to me; will you let me see it?"

"No, only to one and only if he asks."

"Who?"

She nodded her head several times in silence.

"That is the last bad joke. To someone to whom it would be of no use. What good are written words to a blind man?"

"Paul? Languedoc?"

But she would say no more.

"Will you come back?" she asked.

"I don't know. I would like to, I think, but maybe not."

"*Je ne vous comprends pas.*"

"I know, me either."

"What happened to you at the castle?"

"Nothing," I said. "I went for a horseback ride, had dinner. Stayed up late talking. I'm just tired. *Je suis très fatigué*".

I didn't think she believed that either.

∞

My faithful Breton companion, Lui, finally showed up with generous demonstrations of his horn and much gesturing and grinning, apparently pleased to see me again, eager to go on another outing. I wondered if he was the village something-or-other, he was so much more demonstrative than the rest of these quiet, dour folk.

Under Madame Mulon's gimlet eye, Lui and I took off, honking and scattering goose feathers, Laurel and Hardy, Quixote and Sancho—more misadventures.

Even his spirits, though, were no match for the day and the road held no quasi-pagan pageants or dramatic vistas. We did spend about fifteen minutes while a large fold of sheep massed and flowed upstream around us. They filled the space from bank to bank along the road and their dirty grey-brown backs rippled like shallow flooded, muddy water. I wondered if it was possible to get a later train, but I still had not decided which way to go.

Eventually we arrived with twenty minutes to spare before the first departure. I bought two liters of water. Always take water on trains. I once did what was called the overnight train from Singapore to Bangkok; second class. The kitchen car had not been available for this run; we were held at the border sixteen hours. On the second night, there was an unscheduled stop at a station labeled Kentosoto. I had had nothing to drink in twenty-six hours. There were two light bulbs on the platform. Under one sat a small boy at a table with a pile of oranges. My car stopped sixty yards past him in the dark. When we didn't move, I picked up my bag and went to the door. He looked a long way back and the ground in between was dark and inscrutable.

For inscrutable Asian reasons, we had stopped beyond the station. To get to him, I would have to go back past the end of the train. If the train started without me I had a very real chance of seeing a great deal of Kentosoto. I looked and thought and calculated and ran for it. I bought all the oranges I could fit into my pack and pockets in a breathless, no-questions-asked, money-is-no-object spree that left him giggling. I got half his supply—eight or ten—and ran clumsily back over the rails and ties to the door.

Someone had taken my seat, but I found another, less desirable one over the rear wheel trucks of the last car. I sat and began to eat my juicy oranges. I ate three and resolved to save the rest for later. The train, by the way, did not move for another hour. There is probably an important and subtle lesson to this story, but it's never been entirely clear to me beyond the need to carry water.

I found the two trains on the schedule, and the tracks listed on the board, adjacent to each other. Train 322 departed for Quimperle, Vannes, Nantes and points east at 15:00 from Track 2 and train 436 departed from Track 3 at 15:03 for Quimper and Brest, the end of the line west.

Now what does the incurious, cooperative human nonchalantly do?

I got in the ticket line, but still had not decided which way to go when I got to the front. The agent asked a second time.

"*Destination?*"

"*Brest.*" May as well go all the way to the end.

"*Aller? Aller-retour?*"

"*Aller.*"

As I was tucking my ticket and paper change in various pockets, I thought I saw a familiar form from behind a newspaper standing against the far doorway to the tracks. It looked like André.

I went through the nearest doorway and crossed to the platform between Tracks 2 and 3.

At seven minutes to three on the big clock, the eastbound 322 screeched, groaned and sighed to a halt and people began moving out of, around and into it. I walked toward the most forward car. At four minutes to three, the Brest-bound 436 pulled in; activity doubled. I reached the forward door of 322 and the unmistakable André appeared at the other end of the platform.

I got on the first car of the train. There was only one way this could work. I started working my way back down the train through the center aisle. When halfway through the second car, I took a seat on the right side away from the platform where I had last seen André. Pretending to read a paper blessedly left behind by a thoughtless, sloppy, littering benefactor, I watched the crowd until I saw him walk past my car heading for the door he saw me enter. This could work.

I got up, left the paper for the next fugitive and headed down the car as fast as my luggage and my fellow travelers would allow, more than occasionally faster than they would have preferred.

I was in the next-to-last car when I heard two

things: a strong ruckus behind me suggesting the progress of another larger and physically determined presence headed my way; and the call: "*En voiture, s'il vous plaît*".

Immediately in front of me a hydra-headed family of sari-clad women, small pear-shaped men in white shirts and a chattering, active mass of colorfully dressed children was distributing and redistributing itself in four seats and a good deal of the aisle while several of their number struggled to hoist a piece of luggage approximately the size of a small closet into the overhead rack.

With great gestures of politeness and paying no mind to the sounds of André's advance, I offered to help with my greater height.

They stepped back, I passed my two larger bags—the blue Boyt and the brown Land's End hanging bag—to the rear and got my hands beneath the closet. With the myrmidons on either side, we raised the object just to the lip of the rail. I held it just until I saw André enter the car. And then I overbalanced it just slightly to the right so it slowly wheeled and tumbled and crashed into the vacant aisle on the other side of the family and sprang open, throwing several cubic yards of the family's possessions towards the front.

The men looked stunned and then at me as the women and children screamed and began climbing over the suitcase jammed open and upright between two seats.

"Very sorry," I said. I bowed, grabbed my bags and did not look back as first the men and then, from the opposite direction, André joined the muddle.

I ran unchecked through the last car and jumped off just as the 322 began moving. I walked diagonally across the platform to the nearest car of the 436 train, got on and sat down. Less than three minutes later, we left. I wondered if André had a ticket. I was pretty sure he would be meeting a conductor.

On the way to Brest, the land opened up, flattened and then became more settled, more developed.

Eight

After action assessment: André was there to either watch or follow or grab me. Maybe he was supposed to have dropped me in front of the train. What would be the response to his failure?

There would be virtually no way he could get to Brest before the train, so at most, a local agent might be hired, given my description. I folded the blazer into the suitcase and got out levi's, boat shoes, dark crew socks and a rough blue Chambray work shirt I had bought in Morbihan. I wished I had gotten a cap. Before the train made its first stop, I was changed and back in the seat. As an afterthought, I got up and wrapped the too-bright-blue Boyt bag in my dun-colored parka. It even zipped closed. With a little finagling, I tucked in the sleeves and collar for a neat, invisibly beige, snug package.

I sat back down, wishing again I had bought a cap. Most of the men on the train wore something. I slouched down in the seat and turned my face to the window which occasionally reflected it back to me; stared unfocused, thinking.

The incurious, cooperative human act was going to need serious shoring up in Brest.

It occurred to me that André had probably not come to kidnap or kill me. If that was his mission, once he found me his best move would have been the most direct, which would be his instinct if I correctly gauged his unsubtle nature. He hung back, so he was probably only there to watch or follow. No one would expect André to go unnoticed for long, so if he was to follow me, I was to know I was followed.

But now what?

By evading him on my own instincts, I now had to decide whether my best move was to keep running. All the adrenaline was washing out of my system and the fact that I had not slept for over thirty hours announced itself in aches and stupidity. I could still feel where I had near-blisters on my ankles from the stirrups of horny old Marcel.

The train brought us through increasingly heavy industry and then through railyards into a surprisingly modern center of town. I had next to no information on Brest. The Frommer's guide did not mention it. At the station, the number of blue uniforms reminded me that it was a major naval port. Excellent.

I carried my parka-wrapped suitcase on one shoulder the way I saw several sailors carry their denim sea bags. The other bag I slung under my arm like laundry. Next stop: transient hotel.

Outside the station, I kept in step with the crowd and moved purposefully onto the main street looking for what city planners call the adult entertainment center. I followed the sailors. It was three blocks away.

In the middle of a street between two bars advertising "*danseurs*" and "*danseuses nues*" was a doorway and stairs to *La Lune Bleue, salle à louer.* The coincidence was worth a look. The stairs were well enough lit to at least encourage me to go up and the second floor lobby, though sparse, was clean and smelled only of today's cigarettes.

A ring of the desk bell brought a completely uninterested middle-aged man whose face kept changing hallucinatorily into an ant's head as I blearily stumbled through the arrangements for a room. I paid cash; he asked for no verification that I was indeed Sydney Carton of London and Paris as I signed the register.

The room was up three flights of a smoky-smelling, narrow, skylit spiral staircase and down a spare, narrow hallway. It was a sailor's quarters, scarcely bigger than a Pullman berth. But it was in the mansard and had one tall window that opened and looked onto other roofs and windows and just a patch of the harbor. Street noise and gulls' cries were the last things I heard until sometime deep into the night.

I woke up thirsty, hungry and frightened. No dreams this time; this was on the natch, as Lord Buckley would say. I was safe in this room. I was invisible. I calmed down. But I was still hungry and thirsty with an emphasis on the latter.

From the window I could see a few people walking on the street and one of the bars still had lights on. A man with a reasonably steady gait came out of the door.

A few minutes later, trying not to look like I had slept in my clothes, I walked in. On the left was an unlit stage with a man asleep in a straight-back chair. On the right was the bar; in back, three brightly dressed women shared a table. There was no one else in the place. I went to the front of the bar and looked over the industrial-quality furnishings and decor.

Eventually a bartender materialized and I was able to buy a pernod and water and learn the time: 4:30 a.m.

I still did not have a clue.

I had another pernod.

I avoided looking at the women, having a fairly clear idea of what would be inferred if I did. I was fascinated by the guy sleeping in the chair on the stage, Andy Warhol performance art.

I decided not to have a third drink and, on the short walk back to the hotel, it hit me. I had been torn between running away and continuing my schedule. I could do both. At least until Friday. I could possibly buy three days of lead time.

It was getting light when I got back to the room. I cleaned up, changed, went back out, had a workman's breakfast at a busy place across from the train station. When the post office in the same block opened at 8:00, I sent a telegram to Ian confirming that I would be at the scheduled meeting on Friday at 11:00 "as discussed."

∞

Outside the station, I hired a cab and had it wait while I checked out of *La Lune Bleue*. I was at the airport by nine and, just after ten, took off on a twelve-passenger, twin-engine rattle trap deHavilland that was overdue to be sold to the third world.

I got the port side Cuisinart seat. It happens often and I don't appreciate it. Seats 2A and B on these commuter planes are directly adjacent and only about two and a half feet inboard of the propeller blades. There is a substantial amount of noise and physical vibration associated with these seats, but I have always been more disturbed by the speed of the blades' rotation so close to and in approximately the same vertical plane as my torso.

It happens often because as a solo, healthy-looking individual, not to say obviously Western male, one fits the profile gate attendants use to assign these seats at the head of the cabin, next to the door and emergency equipment. I also get exit row seating frequently on the larger, in-country commercial flights, which I do appreciate because those rows have about two more inches in what the industry mysteriously calls scope. Scope translates into English as room for your limbs.

Knee and elbow room you get plenty of in the port cuisinart seat because there is no seat in front as on starboard, only the retracted doorsteps and cables. The only drawback was that to enjoy my scope and stretch my legs I had to intertwine them with the lines and cables by which the door was raised and lowered.

Oh, well.

We landed at Plymouth, England and cleared customs and passport control before noon. Three days, twenty-three hours left.

The only thing that could have changed Claude-Philippe's strategy toward me since we parted in Zurich was his learning something new about me. It could have been my afternoon snooping in the chateau library; but maybe something I had done before we met was just called to his attention? I remembered the scrapbook. And Clio, again Clio.

The ticket lobby of the Plymouth Airport was a mix of mid-fifties British, commercial-grade design and eighties-bright point-of-purchase displays. The papers and the magazine rack had the usual lurid tabloids and a selection of poorly printed, soft-core skin magazines that rivaled any I encountered while in uniform.

I looked around for a few minutes as though lost to see if anyone seemed interested in me. A police officer began to stroll in my direction. I headed for the British Airways desk where I booked through Heathrow to Kennedy.

I bought a blue and white travel bag to carry the backpack a bit more surreptitiously, but figured I was probably in the clear.

The airport was quiet as such things go and I caught up on English language news. Various senior British officials were quoted in assuring tones about events in an Eastern European city with an unpronounceable amalgam of consonants for a name.

The dollar was or was not stronger; Wall Street and Washington haggled. The Japanese circled overhead. A large number of people were injured and/or arrested at a soccer match; no one was killed. A ferry sank in Indonesia; no one survived.

Art Buchwald was still not funny. The serial cartoons had not advanced their story lines more than a few minutes. The Word Jumble was easy.

EFRVE

THADE

SECRES

MEFROR

WHAT THE FOREMAN'S GIRLFRIEND WANTED HIM TO BE:

HER "_ _ _ _ _ _ _ _" MAN

I know these letters because I saved the puzzle. I used the square of paper as a bookmark for the travel-reading successor of Middle Eastern Mythology.

It was a Missionary Society edition of the Revised Standard King James Bible sold to me at the Plymouth Airport for a five pound donation to the Society by an apple-cheeked, high-breasted, country-looking young woman in a Salvation Army blue serge uniform that must have been intolerably hot. She was obviously warm and "glowing," as my mother would say, since females never sweat (only horses) nor perspire (only men).

I had not found anything at the book stand for serious ballast, although I did get a paperback about a character named Wilt which turned out to be a sort of ribald marriage of Benny Hill and Thomas Berger. I got another book which was thrown away after three chapters. I probably bought several magazines, but the Bible I still have. And the Word Jumble is now on page 700. And for all that has passed since then, I am still enjoying the rich gumbo of human longing and torment and turmoil and joy; the vengeful God; the burdens of the Covenant. And, through it all shines the hope; not the hope for eternal life that got grafted on by the Hellenes and the Christians, but the stolid Old Testament hope that the Covenant would turn out to be worth something, the next city hospitable, the next day clement. The simple act of getting up and going into the fields and vineyards; the privations of travel in the wilderness. All for a hope that emerges as insentient, instinctive, unarticulated except in metaphor, and always at work.

Beginning with Genesis in the waiting "lounge" of the airport on a molded fiberglass chair, a Formica table, plastic glass of Bushmills and slushy, machine-made ice, I read of the events that doggedly literalistic, seventeenth century Archbishop Ussher calculated were begun at nine a.m. on October 23 in 4004 BC.

I got well into the fates of Sodom and Gomorrah (insufficient details) and Lot's wife (unclear sin, weird punishment, clear lesson: do as you're told) before the London plane was called. The disjunctures and repetition of the verses gave the sense of a jumbled collection of oft-told tales, but obedience and retribution seemed the strongest theme; the pillar of salt, the plagues of Egypt, forty years in the desert for a party that got out of hand while Moses was rock climbing; heavy dues.

Lately, re-reading Genesis, trying to understand the original sin, I discovered that there never was a proscription against noshing from the tree of life.

The plane to London was a 300 Series Airbus: surprisingly, a fairly comfortable plane. I had two seats to myself. A meat pie was served at one point, but I evaded it. I ordered another Bushmills and went through the magazines, started the Wilt book.

In London, I had two and a half hours between planes, but with baggage checks, duty-free shopping (a Murphy clan wool scarf for Clio and two liters of a

Bushmills Reserve label I had never seen in the States), money exchanging, security checks, passport control, ticket checks, and more security checks, there was really only about twenty minutes of slack time in the departure lounge to size up the rest of the cattle. There were two groups identifiable.

About thirty silver-headed citizens made up one group, all with a common rainbow-striped baggage tag attached to their hand-carried items—camera bags, purses, video camcorder cases. Some looked so dazed and clueless that I would have put tags on them, too, were I the organizer. I could see them being whipped through the tightly planned sequence of "Seven Days in England." More active than many had been in decades, they went up the tower stairs, through the Sackville-West gardens, the Abbey, one or two palaces, an afternoon at Harrod's, day tour of the moors, another castle; amazing you don't hear about more tour group heart attacks. Maybe a cover up? A government plan for euthanasia, senior citizen centers deeply involved.

The other group was more ominous. They all wore tee-shirts or sweatshirts of the same runny brown color with a large, simple geometric logo invoking trees and birds and flames. They looked capable of bursting into group songs, clustered together like a self-aware flock of starlings, appearing almost physically coterminous. The intense togetherness must have been intoxicating; they looked beatifically stoned. I prayed to whatever they believed in that we be seated apart.

Apparently it worked.

I got the seniors.

Booked as a block and mostly coupled, they were placed so every couple had one member on the aisle; this filled both the two's on the sides and four of the five center row seats in the 747: 2:5:2 main cabin.

When I saw my aisle seat was next to one of the silver tags, I expected a conflict. His wife would be sitting there, she would be right back. He just smiled and I settled myself in for the next six hours.

"You going back home?" he asked, before I could get the belt buckled.

I half-nodded a bland, smiled assent.

"Me, too. Boy, I'll be glad to get home."

I managed to be completely involved with my seat belt, expecting the Dodsworth version of Europe. Life imitating Sinclair Lewis. Six hours at a used car lot.

"These old people are crazy. I'll be glad to get away from them."

I looked over at him. He seemed the same age as the rest: early to mid-seventies.

"All they do is complain."

"*No hablo Ingles.*"

"*¿Habla Español? ¿Como esta usted? ¿Eres d'España, de México?*" He shot off in animated, lispy Castillian that I could not follow except for the "*nombre*"—name—*Juan*—John.

"Uh ... John ... I am not a conversationalist," I said, "Let me know if you need to get out."

"You do speak English?!"

"Not after this. Let me know if you need to get out."

I know. It was cruel and misanthropic, but there is nothing more tiresome than bad conversation. I read a behavioral science analysis of boring people—it concluded that the label of boring is really just a prolonged conversational style characterized by a concentration on detailed, negative, personal experience generally delivered in monotone.

But even if John had been half his age, three times as bright, and female, I was still in no mood for people.

We managed to get through the next hours in a pained and pointed silence that eventually faded into unconsciousness somewhere over the North Atlantic after his second Heineken.

I resolved to relax as much as possible, get as much rest as I could. I reluctantly concluded that was not compatible with the planned double martini.

There was a dinner service which I refused for both of us.

He snored, but only intermittently.

∞

For some reason, I remembered back to the beginning of things in Boston. In the middle of the computer confusions and the Baxter gavotte, charming Harry surprised me with an act of generosity which he yet managed to turn into an insult.

He stopped me in the hall one day and said, "I've got two tickets to a benefit tonight that my wife made me buy. I just got an excuse to get out of it, but maybe you'd like to go? It's some kind of dance thing, some feminist cause. You want them, I'll give them to you."

"All right, Harry. Yes, I would. Thank you."

"I thought you would. You are the first person I thought of when I saw the tickets. Here."

Later, on opening the envelope I learned that the feminist cause was the League of Women Voters, and the dance thing was the renowned Pilobolus troupe. The ticket envelope was decorated with the image of one of the group's movements where the elbows of five or six people are linked. They appeared to constitute a star or flower petal body composed of all legs and bottoms. It looked like a human walking flower star; I wondered what besides assholes and elbows Harry had seen of me.

What a sweetheart. I noticed at our second or third meeting that he wore his watch inside his wrist like pilots and rally drivers. I could not feature him in either role. It was a well worn steel Rolex bracelet and I found he made a point of never revealing the face. It was either fake, broken or both. He was just the type to have bought one for a grand with two hundred extra for the papers from the brother of a Tuk-Tuk driver; then flashed around the office for eleven days before it died and the jeweler told him what he had. Whenever I asked the time, he always looked for a clock.

I called Clio at her work number and somebody patched me through.

She had said she did not want to stay out late.

I assured her that the League of Women Voters was not a heavy party-hearty group, as a rule. We agreed on where to meet, the Mexican place in the alley off Chestnut, and when, six thirty. I was early and did not have a frozen Margarita, no salt, while waiting.

Clio came into the room like a breeze, waving the host away and at me, gusts and eddies of people's awareness of her spreading subtly as she passed. She had a way of walking into any place as though she knew it intimately, but had been gone a long time. It was an expression of confident enjoyment that anticipated further pleasure, the return of old friends, comfort and kindness.

It gave me such a feeling to see her see me and advance, saying my name.

"What do you think of this?" Clio dropped into the booth across from me, letting the leaves of a pebbled leather portfolio slap the table as she fanned it in front of me. She had shamed me into giving her the disorganized notes and newspaper rippings that constituted my file on our Boston Necropolis project. Now what she showed me was a complete layout. The historical notes were in Times; the texts of each stone, back and front, were in a script font or italic style. There was lots of gorgeous white space and Clio's photos were arranged in odd, but pleasing patterns. A thin art deco line on every page led nicely through the book. The cropmarked prints were sleeved in the back.

"I'm blown away," I said, blown away. "Where did you get the typography done?"

"I tacked it onto a catalog order the agency was printing. The plates only cost you a hundred dollars which you owe me. We need to discuss a printing schedule."

So, we did.

After dinner in a fast crosstown cab, she told me about a project she was working on at the PR/Ad firm. They had been hired by the Commonwealth to develop a marketing campaign including print ads and direct materials for the sale of a list of public property, primarily long vacant state institutions. Among them were an old Tuberculosis Hospital and a Mental Health complex adjacent to Franklin Park, across from the Arboretum. The buildings had been vacated gradually over the last thirty years as the wars on TB and mental illness had been declared victories. She was going to be allowed to go in with a camera on the shoot, but not as a part of the regular photo crew. The Art Director had encouraged Clio to bring whatever she got to him.

We talked about technical choices in cameras and films. The nice thing about buildings as subjects, they will stand still for long exposures. She was planning to use an ultra low speed trick film I had never heard of. I got to say, "reciprocity effect failure". She said, "gamma". I offered to loan her my heavy duty tripod. The way I said it, she laughed.

"Not tonight."

The performance was in a weird round building on Columbus called the Cyclorama. The program said that it had been built shortly after the Civil War to house a large historical mural of the war. That mural was to have been followed by other new and equally majestic murals as the first one moved on to other similar, circular venues in other cities. I could imagine the stock certificates. Evidently, it did not catch on. The high vaulted brick and timber construction defined a perfectly majestic Industrial Revolution cathedral. There were seats for maybe two hundred people. I checked the ticket stubs again, but there was no price. This could not have been cheap. My ticket said we were invited to a reception afterwards with Boston culture magus Robert J. Lurtsema.

The dance program was just three pieces and I cannot begin to describe them, but they were fluid, amusing, graceful, occasionally vulgar, endlessly fascinating, constantly revelatory - a thing to experience, or only just to see. They were set to, first, a Coltrane number; then, a Mozart piece; and finally, a commissioned modern work for an instrument made by Kurzweil.

The last piece ended in one long, heroically intricate move. The group resolved an athletic set of rhythms and positions by the choreographic equivalent of an interminable coda sequence parody. I found myself, unaware, turned to and holding hands with Clio, both of us laughing at each strange new note in the arrangement of bodies.

At the end of the show, after a brief, but highly leveraged pyramid encore, we all milled slowly out of our seats. On the way through black curtains to the lobby, posters indicated that the next use of the space would be the premier performance of Isaac Asimov's "Nightfall"; coming soon was "Jump Camp".

A braided and worn maroon plush rope funneled us departees along a wall and then into the lighted entry area. Halfway along, an unfortunate young man, boy, really, watched a gate. He wore a tuxedo and had a port wine stain over virtually all of his face. He tried not to look at me seeing him. I was sorry he was not successful.

Behind me, Clio thanked him and I turned and saw her wink at him.

A group of eight followed us and we all headed for a larger gathering about a third of the way around the building, near the back of the stage.

I was determined to have one drink. There was a single bartender and it looked like a third of the audience had the same exclusive tickets as we. While I was reconnoitering, Clio began talking to a man in a chalk-stripe suit and a competition-style, hot-wheels, Everest & Jennings chair. I swam into the crowd using the firmer parts of knee and hip and elbow, pretending to try to cut across the mass rather than into the line. Far too many people in the crowd were wearing the men's perfume du mode, it smelled like a magazine in places.

The drinks were not serious. I got Clio a wine spritzer and myself a gin on the rocks. I thought about Matt Helm on the way back, then Dean Martin, then Jerry Lewis. I was thinking about Jerry Lewis and watching his oleaginous telethon, sunburned, in a sand-fouled bed on the Jersey Shore at the end of a too long ago summer, when I caught sight of Clio.

She was an animated part of a group conversation which included at least two people signing. Then I saw her speak with her hands. I took a drink. Bad gin.

As I got near, the guy in the E&J dragster was completing some chain of logic. As he spoke, one of the other signers made a complex hand movement that caused Clio to smile as she listened.

I was introduced to a collection of Green Line intellectuals and members of the Rainbow Coalition. There was so much sincerity in the room you could smell it over the brick dust and pigeon guano. I had another sip of bad gin.

Clio sipped her wine soda and handed it back to me, speaking and signing simultaneously. I saw her in the midst of everyone, all these strangers raptly focused, all their senses on her. She looked at them, ignoring me and I think I saw her as they did. Her participation in the signing world of the silent was a revelation that let me see her as a universe in which I had known but one planet.

The host issued from the Dressing Room, an ursine tuxedo searching perhaps for his motorcycle ride back to the *Pensione Grilpratzer*, surrounded by the causally clad, limber dancers. The principals slowly dissipated into the crowd, losing their coherence, slipping into individuality, becoming a lesser part of a larger group. Mr. Lurtsema or, as everyone called him, Robert J. was soon surrounded by the worshipful converted.

Our group broke up in the gravitational pull of celebrity.

"School night," I reminded Clio, finishing the gin with a chill juniper rush, "ready to go?"

On the way out, I asked about the signing. She said she learned it growing up at the Library her mother now directed. Later she did a children's story hour in finger spelling and what she called Amslan. She explained the difference.

"What were you talking about?"

"Mark," she nodded to her left, where the man in the chair had been, "and I started talking about the dance performance, then his sister and her friend came up and the tall man who talked a lot knew one of them. He was talking about non-traditional expressive forms, but Mark's sister made a lot of jokes in sign."

"So you and she and her friend were having a separate conversation?"

"More like a commentary."

A silent gestural commentary on a discussion of non-traditional expressive forms.

All this and freckles, too.

But not that night.

∞

I rarely sleep without drinking and no one except infants really sleeps on airplanes. But I was able to drift through a hypnagogic state which at least let my body rest.

I dreamed I was in Amagansett, back on the Beach Road past Montauk in the dark of the August moon. I walked over through dunes to the ocean side and lay down facing the southeast, looking up at Cassiopeia.

As I dreamed I lay there watching the Perseids and it occurred to me that although it is the body that dies, it is time which kills it. And I saw time as the consequent spin, the directionality imparted by the great mass of the universe upon little earth and tiny men warping through their changes. The moon pulls the tides and our own salty blood, the planets pull each other, the sun pulls us along its arc of procession. All the windings and turnings weaving a shroud of mortality, pulling time in one direction only, pulling us to death, entropy, and the final event horizon.

And like that dark night on the beach, I seemed to fall into the sky. And it was cold.

At the solstices—summer and winter—the sun stands still at its furthest southern advance and northern retreat. Around these moments, the children of the earth dance their lives. They have learned the coming and recession of the floods, the changes in the heat and fertility of the land.

For those along the Equator, the sun's retreat is a blessing, bringing the rain, the monsoon, the water from the sky that gives life back to the earth, ravaged and parched by the sun.

In the north, the sun runs from its fragile children every year and they survive for its return. They wait upon it and watch. They watch its pitiless retreat and mark the days by the lengthening shadows at noon, the more southerly and lower, shortened arc of its path. They mark the day it pauses and once again begins to return to them like a lover that changes her mind.

I saw you. I saw you. I saw you, coming back to me.

∞

I woke up.

It was freezing in the cabin and the small, thin blue monogrammed blanket never went far enough in any stable arrangement to keep one part or another of my body from getting cold.

I looked around, no one else seemed to be so affected. Did I have a fever? No, just the opposite, my forehead felt cold, then my hand felt cold on my forehead. Then I shivered again; heat death of the sun, as if I didn't have enough to worry about.

The airplane began to lose altitude as we flew over the Maritimes. My seatmate continued to snooze. As gently as possible I dislodged myself, aching in most major muscle groups and joints. In the galley, a stewardess was willing to give me a cup of hot water for one of my last Twinings tea bags, which was as wrinkled and bent as I felt. I stood by the exit door and looked out through the porthole at the moonlit cloud bank into which we slowly sank.

In all this travel time, I had done no useful thinking, maybe I was wrong about not drinking. The tea seemed to ease my muscle aches and the returning alertness reminded me that I had finite resources of time in which to consolidate my position. I had until Thursday, if I was going to get back to Zurich for the meeting with Claude-Philippe. In any case time was up Friday at 11:00, if I was going to blow it off.

Vera had said there would be proof: "The evidence will be there now ... identity cards, passports, news photos." News photos reminded me of the scrapbook. Was it Ana in the photo with Baxter? This next time I looked I would be sure. I knew her. I felt I knew her physically so well I could find her face, her eyes, her spirit in a thousand generations of descendants. I would know her.

I tiptoed back to the seat among the slumbering, stirring and awakening lives and, as silently as possible, slipped the catch and lowered the overhead compartment.

Unzipping first the flight bag, then the backpack, I wormed my hand inside until I found the velvet bag with the torc. I palmed it into my pants pocket and went back to the galley again. I asked for another cup of tea, deciding to save my ultimate Twinings bag and hoping for the best from BOAC. It was Lipton's. Sticks and seeds. But it worked.

My brain finally ignited the other three, five or seven cylinders and I started working things out. The next trick would be getting me and the torc back into the U. S. preferably without official notice.

I put the torc on my left wrist and covered the velvet bag with a napkin in the empty paper tea cup, which I stuffed in the galley trash hamper. By the time I got back to my seat, the main cabin lights were coming up, the stews were passing out customs declaration cards and John was returning to alert status. Be a lert. America needs lerts.

When he saw me next to the seat, he recoiled slightly and pulled himself more upright.

"Look," I said, "I'm sorry about last night. I was very tired, not feeling well. I'm probably a little afraid of flying. I just didn't want to talk. Okay?"

John, bless his heart, believed me.

I helped him fill out his customs form. I declared my excess liter of Bushmills. After he had listed sixteen items totaling about $45.00, I read him the part about the $200 allowance. He told me who he got each of the items for, described them both, the gifts and recipients, in great detail. I was wrong about his being boring according to the text. He was not at all negative or personally annoying. He was only just extremely attentive to detail and, lacking any narrative sense or line, his recitation was like having someone read to you from a catalog and a telephone book simultaneously.

I paid attention. I asked questions, established relationships, several with long, deep histories. There was the widow of a deceased brother in whom his interest seemed more than academic.

The plane landed and taxied long enough to get to New Jersey if not Connecticut. We stopped in the middle of nowhere and everyone shuffled out the exits onto a blue and grey scissor-lift bus which settled back down on its chassis with a bump and a sigh and then drove us over the field to the profound embarrassment which is JFK.

Our feisty, colorful, chaotic neighbors to the south can enter through smooth, polished, spacious, secure Miami; the crowded, jumped up, veterans of the neon-lit Ginza arrive from Japan at calm, bland SEATAC; LAX processes millions of arrivals with the clean, familiar, commercial smiles of Mickey and Donald and Disney-like efficiency. JFK, our gateway to Europe, is a shame. It has all the charm of a welfare office, the architectural grace of a jail, and the noise, chaos and cleanliness of a third world bazaar.

I imagine some refined, solitary European or Middle Eastern aristocrat's son raised on America's exported image of Norman Rockwell towns, Doris Day romances, John Wayne heroes, Beach Boy dune buggies, Top 40 songs, TV glitz, and magazine glamour. He walks through flimsy, soiled, urine-colored, ill-lit hallways, shuffles through an hour's worth of lines to be inspected and distrusted by a none-too-clean, semi-uniformed functionary or two. The final half-opaque, scratched, bulletproof door screeches open on its warped hinge, his feet grit on the dirty marble floor and he faces a jumbled polyglot mob of awaiting families, friends, cops, thieves, porters, hustlers and other lost souls. If he is lucky and careful, he keeps his bags and wallet. He is escorted to a cab by someone who charges him $10. The cab has no shock absorbers and the front seat bows into the back from the weight of the 350-plus pound driver. The cab cuts out in front of the traffic, causing a shuttle bus to veer into another cab. The driver screams a curse, shakes his middle finger out the window and accelerates out onto the awesome potholes and jarring pavement joints of the Van Wyck Expressway.

Welcome to Cyprus, goats and monkeys.

While I was imagining this Pilgrim's Progress, I shuffled alongside John and the rest of the silver-tag gang. Their luggage was being segregated by a lean, sharp-edged, chain-smoking woman of middle years, great energy, and a fast tipping hand. I asked John to watch my flight bag which, added to his own ambitious interpretation of the concept of carry-on luggage, effectively immobilized him.

With the flash and pass of a ten dollar bill and my luggage claim tag, I got a young man with a blond rat tail and an earring, wearing blue coveralls to hand over my suitcase and bag. I rejoined John, who was beginning to look nervous as his group began moving, making toward an exit.

"Here, John, I'll trade you. Let me take your carry-on and you carry my little blue bag. It's lighter."

"Oh. Well, if you don't mind."

"Not at all."

I herded him in front of me and transferred his carry-on bag's silver tag to the Boyt. In the next room, as I expected, were the tour leader, a customs agent and a rectangular arrangement of the group's luggage. While the tour leader and the agent completed the details of the negotiations, I slid my bags, the Boyt's prominently displayed silver tag nicely setting off the royal blue cordura nylon fabric, in between a grey Samsonite and a red plaid American Tourister near the back of the rectangle.

The customs agent swept his hand through an arc in the general direction of the luggage. The tour leader nodded her head several times sharply and took a drag on her cigarette. They shook hands and we all followed her through another set of double doors; behind us, sky caps began to pile the luggage on several carts.

"You know," said John, "I am really glad to be home."

We missed the aforementioned polyglot mob by coming out into the arrivals corridor behind them. The other passengers from our flight were nowhere in sight.

"Where's home, John?"

It was of more than idle curiosity since my luggage was doubtless soon to be on its way there.

"Woodbury."

Having gotten me through passport control and customs without official record or any questions about the antiquity on my left wrist, John had been a good traveling companion. Helpful; one could also certainly say, forgiving; but I was not going to Woodbury with him if I could help it. Unfortunately, I had no plan for extricating my luggage from the group or explaining the silver tag. But when we all came up to the two rumbling diesel monsters that were to take everyone home, it appeared there was to be a parting of the ways among the group with the two buses going to separate towns. There were hugs and kisses and there were all the bags being lined up at the curb.

As John headed for his, I got out the little Swiss army knife which I really only carry for the corkscrew. For maybe the third time since I got it, I opened the shorter knife blade. With the handle butted into my palm, I covered the back of the blade with my index finger and followed John closely.

"See yours, John?"

"Yes, yes. There it is. The one with yellow yarn on the handle."

"Okay, you stay here with our carry-on bags. I'll go get it."

"Okay. Thanks."

On the way, I spotted my bag nearer. I reached

down as though checking the silver name tag and cut it with the knife. I pushed the tag into the open outside pocket of the bag and walked down to the yellow ribboned handle.

The grey woman looked up at me quickly, alert and feral in her suspicion as I approached.

"I'm just helping my friend."

I held up John's bag and called to him, "Is this it?"

He smiled and nodded vigorously, waved at the grey woman who turned away without waving back and focused on whatever it was she was doing that was much more important than me. On the way back, my two bags were no longer so surrounded by other bags and I picked them up. With John's luggage and my own I had to be carrying close to seventy-five pounds. I can't say I made it look easy.

I got back to John, got him on his bus, apologized again about "*no hablo Ingles*," heard him say at least twice more that he was glad to be home before I was left in an oily cloud of exhaust in the noisy, noisome, grim concrete cavern looking for a cab stand.

∞

Fortunately, it was not far and I found a licensed yellow cab with a North African driver who agreed to take me solo to Penn Station with two stops of no more than five minutes for $50, half in advance.

We got to Penn at about one in the morning and I booked a first class compartment on the overnight to Boston. The train pulled in from Washington at about one thirty and, by two, I was in the compartment with the bed made up, my shoes, socks, shirt, and pants off, sitting on the bed in my underwear drinking wine from the bottle. In a little bit, I got out the cheese and crackers and then, after another little bit, I put them away. To show some restraint, I put the cork back in the bottle before it was empty, but only just before. I was asleep when the train pulled out and slept in long, dreamless reaches as we climbed the Connecticut coast.

It was full daylight when we reached the construction mess that was Providence's latest urban renewal project. This time in order to enlarge the downtown, the train station and the Northeast Corridor Mainline were being moved. I wondered what "highest and best use" would supplant the warm, dark, funky old small town station that had always made Providence seem so comfortable and welcoming a stop: the rural expanse of open land on the side sloping up to the great old Bullfinch Capitol—easily the grandest in New England, nothing like building on a hill—the Biltmore welcoming on the other. Now the Biltmore had a modern exterior elevator that was as aesthetically compatible as an anatomically correct vibrator in your spinster aunt's Victorian parlor.

As we left Providence, I got dressed and thought about coming into Boston. The schedule I picked up at the Penn Station ticket counter showed a stop before Boston in something-boro. I was waiting at the front end of the car when the trainman stepped into the vestibule from the car just ahead. If he was surprised to see someone leave the sleeper before Boston, he kept it to himself. We stopped and he dropped the steps, climbed down, and walked back around the last car.

I followed.

The Amtrak station was a purply clay brick and tile shadow on my left, the train a humming steel form on my right. Presently the train pulled out leaving me standing alone on the left-hand side of the tracks. On the other side were about twenty or thirty commuters. Bingo.

I got off the commuter train in Milton and caught a cab to the apartment.

It was unlikely anyone was looking for me and even less likely anyone knew I was in Boston. If I kept a low profile, it looked like a safe base of operations.

The place smelled stale and stuffy like closet dust. Opening a window at each end lightened the atmosphere. Furniture, books, possessions looked foreign and out of place, but a quick tour showed no apparent disturbance, no destruction, no further inspection.

"Your apartment was investigated and you were thought to have a too curious mind."

I felt like an insect under a magnifying glass. I remembered how kids incinerate ants on a sunny day.

I looked outside. It was a sunny day.

Enough!

A cup of hot Prince of Wales tea, a shower, my big old Drake Hotel robe, then clean white wool socks, clean Levi's, a fresh shirt and sweater; it was nine a.m., time to go to work.

Ready or not.

I called the agency Clio worked for, Bartlett and something or other; the receptionist transferred me.

"Traffic. Murphy."

"Hi. It's Phillip, Clio. I just got back."

"Oh. I didn't expect you until next week."

"Yeah. I came back early. I need to see you. Can you have lunch?"

"Today? Ah, no; today is weekly staff lunch. I have to present a summary of current bookings."

"Dinner?"

"I am having dinner with my father tonight, but you could probably come. I could call and check."

No lunch; dinner only a maybe.

"Okay. I guess I'll have to call you back, then. But, please, yes. I would like to. Listen, Clio, did you get that package?"

"Yes, what was that? You told me you might get a package, then when it came, it was from you. And you wanted me to hide it. That was a lot weird. Now you're back and in a hurry to see me. What are you involved in?

What was in that package?"

"Honest, just a scrapbook and some accounting information. I was spooky after the break-in. I'm sorry I left so abruptly; it was an abrupt assignment and I came back early to see you."

"Really?" Hard to read nuances on the telephone; any note of sarcasm was lost in the electrons.

"Look, let me call you back after you check with your father, okay? What did you do with the package?"

"Well, I wasn't going to do anything with it. Then I thought I'd just mail it back to you, but then when I thought about how weird you acted, I was afraid it was something stolen or drugs and I decided to get rid of it."

"Where did you get rid of it?"

She actually giggled.

"Well, I didn't like get-rid-of-it get rid of it. I put it someplace. Like you said. Remote but accessible, right?"

"Right. Where is it?"

"In the library. The one you went to that day in Duxbury. I stopped at my apartment for lunch the day it arrived, on my way to Plymouth on business. There's a regional chain. We do a lot of placements for suburban retailers with them. Anyway, there was a billing problem."

"In the Duxbury Library. Where in the Duxbury Library?"

"What's in it, really?"

"Just as I told you, a scrapbook and accounting data. I'll prove it to you. I'll show you tonight, okay? Now please tell me where in the Duxbury Library you put it."

"You told me about that locked room. I got the key. It's in the file cabinets. Under G. Remote. But accessible."

"You're very clever and very nice to have done that for me. Thank you."

"I still want to see what's in it. And don't thank me. The way I felt at the time, I just wanted it out of my house."

"I'll call you back."

"Okay." She hung up.

Do women always know when you've been with someone else? Even over the phone and beyond Clio's peeve about my precipitous leave-taking, I felt a physical reluctance to allow me near.

Maybe the act of sex aligns vital currents of the body and polarity is altered; the alignment is unique to each couple. Something at the ethereal, prototypic vibration level says, "Muddy Waters, another mule been kickin' 'round your stall."

The Duxbury Library opened at ten. I listened for the last chaotic five minutes of Charles Laquidera's Big Mattress Mishigas in the parking lot.

"And if the good Lord's willing and if the creek don't rise and no one pushes that little red button, we'll do it all over again tomorrow between six and ten right here on...

"... The B i i i i i i i i i i i i i i g Mattress!!"

Noises, cheers, rattles, applause. I shut the power off and pulled the key. The library door was unlocked by a young man who disappeared from sight before I could get it open. The reference librarian was in her office and remembered me.

"More research," I said. "May I get into the local history room again, please?"

She passed me the form and, after I completed it, the key.

"Look," I said. "I'm bringing in an old family scrapbook to compare some pictures with some in the old newspapers. I don't want to have a problem when I go to leave." I showed her the big envelope I had sticking out of my shoulder bag."

"Let me see it."

Having no choice, I pulled the envelope open and exposed the family scrapbook I had brought.

"Open it, please."

I showed her a page of my Long Island ancestors.

"That's not around here, is it?"

"No, but they visited."

"All right, but check with me before you leave."

"Sure, will do. Should be pretty quick today."

I let myself into the room and turned on the lights. There were the files and, among the G's between "Gander" and "Great Barrington," was the envelope addressed to me at Clio's. I opened it, took out the disks and separately distributed them in coat and bag pockets so they would not rattle. I tucked the birth and death cert copies into the S, B book and put them both into my bag with address faced in. I put my family scrapbook and envelope into the file. Now the tricky part; getting out.

I walked over to the windows. The room had been added as a low dormer extension over an existing roof. The windows were narrow, but opened. I looked down below the window; the roof resumed briefly before ending in a gutter.

I got a copy of "Graves of Revolutionary War Patriots" from one of the shelves and leaning out, squirming and stretching and half hanging, I was able to set it on the roof where it slid slowly into the gutter and stood a few degrees short of upright.

Leaving a small patch of skin behind, I got my upper torso back inside and slid the window closed.

I left the light on, but pulled the door locked behind me.

The reference librarian was still at her desk.

"I think someone is trying to steal a book," I said. It got instant attention.

"Who? Where?"

"You have to come outside to see it. It's a theft in progress."

"Where?"

"Follow me. I'll show you."

At a good clip, we exited her office, past the main desk, out the doors.

"Around this way."

In the back, from the ground, the red covered book stood like a solitary soldier on the precipice.

"I couldn't reach it from the window. I bet they're planning to come by at night with a ladder—or even a long stick."

"I must get Mr. Dawson and... and a ladder. Mr. Dawson will know what to do."

She took off back towards the main entrance. I followed, letting her get further ahead of me. Before she got through the door, I called from the end of the walk.

"I'll be right there. Just put my bag in the car."

She waved vaguely over her right shoulder.

With the scrapbook safely in the car, I started for the front door, only to meet the librarian coming out.

"Mr. Dawson is bringing a ladder."

I followed her once again to the back where we held an agitated conversation about whether "they" had gotten away with other "reference materials" already. I said I hoped the book wasn't damaged by sitting in the gutter—standing water, rotten leaves. She gave a small shriek, which made me think I had overdone it, but it turned out to be a greeting for Mr. Dawson who was a great slow-moving bear of a man carrying a twenty-foot ladder like it was a yardstick.

I volunteered to climb it and, with the solid anchoring hold of Mr. Dawson and the direction, advice, supervision, oversight and commentary of the librarian, I was able to climb up and retrieve the volume in less than a minute.

She turned and patted and inspected and cooed over the book, finding nothing damaged while Mr. D. folded his ladder and lumbered away.

"I left the light on," I said, pointing up at the windows. Once again we proceeded to the entrance. This time I followed her in up to the room, where she began an intimate inspection of the shelves. Might she actually be able to tell if something is missing from memory? While she was at the far end, I pulled my family scrapbook out of the file and, to cover the sound, I cleared my throat.

"Well. Uh. I'll be leaving."

She came back to the world and thanked me; glanced at the scrapbook and asked if I wanted some coffee. I said I preferred tea. She said that was available, too, and invited me to the kitchen, which we found in the basement.

She had gotten me a styrofoam cup of hot water for the tea bag I pulled out of my pocket to her amusement and was just stirring something from a pink envelope into her coffee when she dropped the spoon.

"Why, I have to report this. I must tell the Director. And the police!"

She started for the door.

"Just stay here and enjoy your tea. I'll tell the police where to find you when they come."

I smiled and waved her away.

As soon as I heard the hall door close, I got up and quickly left the kitchen, heading the opposite way down the hall. A marked exit door opened onto a single flight of stairs that took me up a level. I edged the door at the top open. I was looking into what had probably been the foyer of the old building. It was the room between the modern section's main desk and the old sitting room where I had passed the rainstorm.

The room was vacant and I swung the door open casually, to be nailed to my stance by Ana staring out at me from the portrait on the wall.

Nine

That was why she had captured me so at our first meeting. Déjà vu, for real. I felt her hold me as though her hand had me now cuffed by the heavy torc I still wore; deep in my gut I felt her presence—a hollowness that reached my throat—her easy control of me all along. I was thoroughly frightened. More than in the car with André. Then I was only expecting a murderous attack, an action I could confront. Now I was staring at the face I feared to see in my dream.

And, just maybe, at proof.

Stealing the painting with the police on the way, however, was clearly not a good strategy. So I did what I do best; I split.

The main desk was unattended, the other patrons absorbed. I was the smoke, I was the wind. I was scared witless. Ana behind me, with me, on me, in me, the local law on the way. I remembered Robert Schekley writing: "It is axiomatic throughout the civilized galaxy that when you call the police, your troubles really begin."

I got out of the parking lot with no patrol car screaming into sight. Even in sleepy Deluxebury, the constabulary must have higher priorities than an attempted theft at the library. I drove back towards Boston, planning what to do next. It struck me that I should equip myself for mobility for the foreseeable future.

At the Newton branch of my bank, I arranged for my checking account to make automatic payments on the credit cards and got the limit doubled on both VISA and Mastercard to five thousand dollars. In Cambridge at a computer store, I bought the most powerful laptop they had. It was a Toshiba with enough RAM to run the Data Base Management System—and lots of ROM for the accounting MATCHUP files. If there was hard evidence in my grasp, it simply had to be in those files.

∞

While in Cambridge, I also picked up Camille at the kennel. She started bawling me out when she heard my voice at the reception desk.

"Does she do that at home, too," the receptionist asked.

"Uh. Not usually. Sometimes at night if she's seriously on the wrong side of a door. But, not usually. Was she talking a lot here?"

"Just like that. Every hour or so. It upset everyone. We're glad you're back. Sixty-five dollars."

Camille quieted when I picked her up out of the cage. The shirt I had left her was matted with fur and wadded into a corner.

"You can throw that out," I said, and slung Camille over my shoulders, forepaws in left hand, rear in my right. She began to purr and laid her head down.

In the car, however, once the door was closed and the engine on, she went into pace and howl mode again. There is a note cats can hit that must be the same as the essential prime tone in the cry of a gravely hurt human. Dogs barking, no matter how naggingly interminable, are at worst annoying, but a howling cat really touches something emotional. Intermittently yelling at her to shut up and dodging the wildly unpredictable menace of cross-town Boston traffic, I got back to my block, parked, and carried Camille into the apartment through the back door.

It smelled fresher than this morning and I got the cat and myself some food, then went back to the car for the new computer and my bag of goodies.

I worked all afternoon, interrupted only by a phone call to Clio to learn that I was invited to dinner at her father's and to convince her to meet me first at a decent bar on the Cambridge/Somerville line that had good chips and Mexican salsa. When facing a dinner of dubious digestibility, I like to gas up first. Makes it easier not to be tempted to eat something fresh from the microwave with more ingredients than a Gilbert chemistry set. Home cooking in the convenience age is a horror show.

By five-thirty, I had nothing to show for my efforts. The Toshiba ran fine; the display was tolerable, though annoyingly sensitive to the angle of view and any sources of glare. I sorted and arranged and looked up the MATCHUP files every which way – inside out, upside down, backwards and sideways. Twenty-one lives and only five things I could find in common.

1. All clients of S, B and all customers of Boehrkopf Frères
2. All unmarried
3. All allegedly inherited their money from unmarried relatives—aunts for the women and uncles for the men
4. No payments to doctors, dentists or hospitals
5. All accounts started with initial payments to *Agence Privée de Bretagne*. In late March or September.

∞

The investments showed no pattern other than prudence, intelligence and occasional good luck. I printed the dates of each initial payment or set of payments to *Agence Privée de Bretagne* and shut the machine down.

Camille was sleeping on top of my unpacked suitcase when I left to meet Clio. The Toshiba and the scrapbook just fit into the bookbag with the expansion fold unzipped. It was a bulky and somewhat heavy package, but readily carried under one arm. I put it in the trunk of the car, wrapped in two furniture pads that can double as a bedroll on desperate occasions, and drove to Cambridge.

Nobody drives to Cambridge. It's as bad as Beacon Hill for parking places and tickets. Everything reserved for residents. I know Back Bay is the same and there is a resident sticker on the Volvo, but Cambridge somehow makes it seem like the non-resident is not morally advanced or intellectually elevated enough to deserve parking. Come on the T or be born here is the attitude.

That's why I drive to Cambridge. Usually find free parking, too. It is a matter of attitude.

The Alewife station had just been finished, but the neighborhood was not yet commercially devolved into the inevitable industrial-grade food, beverage, parking and sundry services center that the passage of five or ten thousand people twice a day would support. There was still a one-story strip mall with open parking between two of the intersecting streets.

I found a legal place on the street half a car length past the front of the bar, just over the Cambridge line. There was time on the meter. It was just six o'clock. I felt better than I had all day. Free parking and a drink in sight.

Clio was not inside, so I took the stool at the corner of the bar just next to the door and tried to look out the windows. Between the curtains, the neon beer signs and the dirt, it was impossible to see anything right or left. I gave up and ordered.

I was counting my change when the door opened behind me and Clio came in. I saw her in the mirror. I saw her see me. I saw her see I saw her. She did not move.

I turned and went over to her.

"I am glad to see you again," I said, "I missed you." I looked at her still green eyes. Ana had green eyes. I broke the contact.

"Would you like a drink?" I led us without touching her to the bar.

"No."

"Soda?"

"Okay."

I got her a soda with lime. She sat up on the stool and turned towards me. The window light loved her. She was wearing a navy blue pleated wool skirt and a light grey fuzzy sweater. Her lively skin and hair blazed in contrast. Sitting at a bar with a good-looking woman is one of my favorite things in life—even if I have been doing it overlong. Instead of comfortable, I felt like I was on stage; the walls were flats ready to fly away, revealing bare proscenium and empty house. There was no solidity; confidence in any dimension was impossible.

"I'm sorry," I said. I realized that was how we had started this relationship—me, apologizing, in a bar. "I had seven hour's notice to make my plane. "

"Did you?"

"Oh, yeah. And then it was late." I told her the story of the flight; made the other passengers funnier, the delay a bigger trial.

"What was the trip about?"

"The people I worked for here in Boston wanted me to evaluate a computer-to-computer linkup with an associated firm in Switzerland."

"How did it go?"

"It went well."

I felt like I was being interviewed. I did not know what she was going to ask. Her questions opened pools of freely-associated, anxiety-ridden topics I did not want to get into. I had forgotten to bring the scarf I bought her. I felt the evening slipping.

"Where did you get that bracelet?"

"Um. This … I found it. In Brittany."

"Can I see it?"

I pulled the torc off and passed it to her.

She held it in the palm of her left hand and lifted it two or three times, then set it down on the bar. She pulled her hands away from it.

"You found that? It looks awfully clean and polished. Did you find it in a store?"

"Yes. I mean, no. I found it in a field, but I had it cleaned and polished in a jewelry store. One of those ultrasonic baths."

"In Brittany?"

"Yeah," I said lamely and got my hand around my drink finally. I took a small sip. Heaven.

"I don't like it, but it's peculiar. I guess, it is interesting. Are you going to wear it every day?"

"No. If you don't like it, I'll put it away. Tomorrow, I'll put it in my safe deposit box."

"Is it valuable?"

"I think so. It's old."

"How old?"

"About two thousand years." My voice sounded echo-like in my ears.

"Is it legal? I mean, you just found it and took it with you?"

"Uh. I don't know what the law would say, but it is rightfully mine. I'm sure of that." I looked her in the eyes again, telling the whole truth for the first time since I said I was sorry.

I put the torc in my coat pocket where it bumped my hip and settled in.

"What was Brittany like?"

"Neat. Rugged. Old. Lots of stoneworks. Great food."

"You look tired."

"I just got in this morning at eight. I called you first thing. I really did miss you." I remembered how distant the good, quiet times with Clio had seemed from Brittany. They felt equally distant this evening.

She smiled. I felt further away from her as memories of Ana washed through me like a low, funky tide. Her smile faded.

"I met a blind musician in Brittany. He played me some beautiful local music. I want to find recordings of the music so I can play it for you."

"Did you meet many people?"

"Oh, the lady who ran the inn. A guy who drove me around. No one else really."

I chased that lie with the rest of my drink.

"Did something happen to you on this trip? You seem nervous."

I tried to avoid imitating Don Knotts.

(Are you nervous? "***Nope!!!***")

"I'm just tired. It was a long trip. I tried to do too much. What time does your father expect us?

"Seven or so."

"You want another soda?" I asked, signaling for a reprise of Jack Daniel's, rocks.

"Uh. Sure."

We managed a semi-awkward accommodation between our history and a current awareness that the situation was changed.

"Tell me again what was in the envelope," she said a few minutes later.

"A scrapbook. And some computer disks with some accounting files. They're out in the car. I'll show you on the way to dinner. Are you ready to go now?"

"Sure. Okay."

We left a small glass of Jack Daniel's-flavored ice, a half of a soda and lime, and a twenty dollar bill on the bar. I wondered if I would ever be back.

At the curb, I got the bookbag out of the trunk, turned the scrapbook upside down. When I handed her the S, B scrapbook, I let the certificate copies slide back into the bookbag. She leafed through it as we drove down Mass. Ave. toward Harvard Square, then off at an angle to her father's street.

"See, I checked it out of the S, B library when I got summoned to this thing in Switzerland. I wanted to research the Swiss associate firm and the librarian gave me this. I sent it to you because I was afraid of another break-in. Because it isn't mine."

"And the accounting data?"

Reaching into the backseat one-handed, I dropped one of the MATCHUP disks on the open page in front of her.

"Just my bank account records. Stuff like that."

Clio looked at the 3.5-inch square diskette with its jaunty blue label neatly reading "M3" as flatly, as opaquely as she had the torc.

∞

Professor Murphy now resided in a substantial late Federal, painted yellow with Greek Revival touches to the trim. It had a one and a half car length driveway leading to a one-car garage which I pulled up to, my car blocking the garage but still visible and close to the street. Clio handed me back the diskette, but kept the scrapbook under her right arm.

"I'll finish looking at it inside. Okay?"

"Okay."

She let us in a side door which formed a halfway landing between the basement and first floor. I noticed the high front porches across the street. The neighborhood was probably based on fill and once prone to flooding.

"Dad. Where are you?"

"In the kitchen. Come back and join me."

We walked through a dining room of bare wood floors, plain white walls, and Shaker furniture. The effect was monastic, peaceful, and austere.

The kitchen was the antithesis. Someone had pushed out the back wall, opened the ceiling, and added a greenhouse. From the second floor ceiling were suspended polished wooden tools—a hay rake, a scythe, a spinning wheel—while baskets and plants hung from the exposed beams and joists. The greenhouse plants threw off a dense, earthy perfume, like mossy ground after a rain. On the right, moving between a butcher block island and a six-burner stove, Professor Murphy was concocting dinner.

Clip dropped the scrapbook down on a table under a skylight to the left.

Professor Murphy came around the island that separated the sink and stove counters from the rest of the room and hugged Clio for a friendly length. She was smiling.

I handed him a gift bottle of Grande Echeveaux and we shook hands. He was smiling.

I smiled.

"So, Phillip, you have been traveling in Europe. Where did you go? May I get you a drink first? Clio?"

He turned to her, leaving me smiling, about to say either "yes" or "France" or both.

"No, but I'm sure Phillip will."

"No, thank you, sir. I'll wait."

"Well, I shall open this fine wine of Phillip's to let it breathe and have a glass of sherry. Sure you won't join me, Phillip; it's Amontillado?"

For the love of God. Sherry with the professor, Montessor.

But it was a lovely, dry round drink that went sparklingly well with the plate of smoked Appenzell cheese and tart Granny Smith slices he brought us.

"Now, where were you traveling, Phillip?"

"France. Brittany."

"What took you there?"

"Curiosity. And the fact that I could find little or nothing in guidebooks or local libraries. Then I saw in the atlas that there was a province called Finisterre opposite Land's End in Britain. Both places are much closer to each other than to Paris or London. I wondered if they would have much else in common."

"What did you find?"

"I think I found another country. Old and pretty basic. Very old. Primitive, in a way. In Brittany, I saw a huge outdoor mass—six altars and people in ranks around them in the thousands. And rocks, stones, big stones, upright, stacked, in rows, in circles. The stone works were everywhere."

"You were in Morbihan?" He asked so matter-of-factly, I was not shocked.

"Yes, how did you know?"

"Along the Breton coast it is the most concentrated site for the megaliths. Did you see the great stone in pieces?"

"No. What was that?"

"It was either the tallest stone ever set upright by ancient builders or a project that was beyond their ability. Five pieces of a 340 ton stone 70 feet long lie on a high field at Locmariaquer on the peninsula. Erected, it would have cast a shadow on the mainland at sunset."

"Have you been there, Professor Murphy?"

"Just once on a driving holiday. Interesting cult. Not much science on them, I gather. Local lore was syncretic and heavily Christianized. What did you learn?"

"Nothing, really. I got a book in French, but it was just like you said, local lore. What do you think made people build those great stone arrangements? What is your animist theory here?" I asked.

"Oh, I imagine... uhm... a ritual that would tie generations of neophyte farmers to some understanding of the earth and the cycles of the sun."

Clio opened the front page of the scrapbook, .

"Okay. So," I said, "some understanding of the earth, however defined; but the sun cycles—that would be a big learning jump. That would be a useful thing to be clear on."

He said, "There was a big jump up the human learning curve between thirty and ten thousand years ago. Hunter-gatherers, at least in Europe and Asia, found all their large meat mammals dying off or migrating north following the retreat of the glacier as the climate warmed and the forests took over. Yet these people had enough leisure time to develop a surprisingly expressive though curiously limited form of art and to keep count of things which may have included the annual cycles of the moon.

"By around 10,000 BC, they had adapted to the protein loss in their traditional environment by developing vegeculture and boats that could take them out to the seas.

"Physical improvements in the land start to show up then. A road in southwestern England was built in 9000 BC, earthwork walls in India and China soon after. A few thousand years later, funeral barrows—mounds of earth requiring years of labor often surmounting a stone chamber, occasionally penetrated by stone-lined passages. The form is homologous, it must spring from a deep symbolic understanding of death and impermanence."

"Homologous," I asked, " same form, different roots? These barrows show up independently in lots of societies?"

"Oh, yes, the Inca passage graves, your pre-Celtic megaliths, Egyptian ziggurats and pyramids; North American moundbuilders."

"So your implication is these earthworks are a funerary tradition that developed a solar or celestial orientation at some point. How?"

"Obviously, no record exists of the rituals, but funerary objects suggest a belief in after-life—the food, the favorite objects, the warrior buried with his sword in hand, the wealthy and powerful man with his chariot, a child on a swan's wing. The wheel clearly symbolized rebirth in Iron Age LaTene and Hallstadt cultures"

"Is this the place you went to in Switzerland?" Clio broke in, holding the scrapbook open to the reception invitation from 1934.

"What is that, Clio?" Professor Murphy asked.

"Yes," I said.

"Phillip borrowed this scrapbook from his employer before going to Europe."

"May I look at it, too?"

"Help yourself," I said, feeling the conversation slip away from me and head for muddy, troubled water.

"What is Boehrkopf Frères, if I may ask?"

"An investment bank—the proverbial Swiss bank. Old money, numbered accounts."

"And getting a computer system?"

"No, they already had one. It was a question of compatibility and security in connection with the Boston firm."

"Look at this. Why is this here? This news clipping. The Glass-Steagall Act was one of the biggest setbacks to the big Eastern money establishment in this country's history. Why would anyone in this circle memorialize that?"

"I think, because someone knew that the reason the Boston firm was taken over— eaten by the Swiss group, Boehrkopf—they are now little more than agent rather than a partner—someone knew that this Act was the reason they were vulnerable—and maybe someone knew that the way it happened was due to this person here." I pointed to poor old Baxter. "In fact, he may have done the scrapbook himself and included his highest and lowest hour for some unpalatable stew of reasons."

"Who is the woman in this picture?" Clio asked unnervingly.

We all looked at the picture and I said, "I don't know. It doesn't say."

Clio turned the page to a menu from a luncheon a few years further along and that reminded Dr. Murphy of the dinner work. He went back to the food arena, Clio went on in the scrapbook, and I returned to my Jerez and silence.

∞

We moved into the dining room carrying plates and glasses as directed by Clio's father. She said something to him I did not hear and he laughed.

He went back to the kitchen and returned directly with a bowl of spinach salad tossed in an herb vinegar dressing and a larger bowl of steaming noodles exhaling basil and garlic.

Clio served the salad, he passed the pasta, I poured the wine.

"You were saying that the funerary earthworks got oriented to the sun at some point and when I asked how, you started talking about the belief in an afterlife. What's the connection?"

"The earth and the sky are the connection; death is in the earth while eternity and the continuation of life are in the sky. The mounds, the patterns, the figures of earth and chalk and stone—the serpent mound in this country, the virile man and the Uffington horse in Britain, the Nazca lines in Peru—suggest a reflection back to the sky of the patterns and figures seen in the stars. By moving and working the earth below, the primitive connects with the eternity beyond. I read a quote from a

Native American in the 1840s that the mounds were letters written to the sky."

Professor Murphy took off.

"How heavy must the weight of the sky have been when men knew so little of the earth and had done nothing to remake it? Now we ignore the sky in ceilinged cities covering miles of continents, blot it out with industrial haze or wash it out with sodium-vapor light scatter. But for the first three quarters of a million years of our evolution as a genus, there was only the narrow path of the earth one walked and the distance one could see—eight or twelve miles in most habitable terrain, less in forests, more from hills, while the uncivilized sky was circumambient.

"If man looked into the sky and could see pictures, and man has never failed to, how logical that man should make pictures on the earth to reflect an image back.

"The serpent, the horse and the man, the creatures, have been more the subject of popular rather than scientific interest because they can be easily placed in a known context.

"The rocks and circles and processions Phillip has seen are more enigmatic, because except for the funeral barrows with which they are associated, there is no social or cultural history, no context for this pattern of moving stone and earth.

"About eight to five thousand years ago, a large number of similar stone-based constructions were laid down from the Mediterranean to the Baltic around the coast of Europe and the British Isles. There are insufficient data to place any but the funeral barrows in any cultural setting.

"At many of the stone circle and oval 'race track' arrangements are found remains of earlier wooden post patterns. But that only moves the dates further into the mists of pre-history.

"The same such post patterns have been found in

this country at Cahokia across the river from St. Louis and in Georgia. Perched rocks and funeral barrows are common on both continents. But the discrepancy of the dates again indicates either an independent genesis or a dispersal pattern that is more extended in history than any known culture.

"Of the European megalithic culture, nothing is known except the dates and the rough techniques used—no miracles of Merlin or chariots of the gods."

"Yes." I put in, "A woman I met, the innkeeper in Morbihan, said her husband and a hundred or so other men moved and set a stone in a day."

"Well, and then went home, had a warm dinner and an early bed.

"The original earth builders and stone movers were twenty to thirty pounds and several inches smaller. They were less nourished, much less comfortably provisioned and housed, less strong, less healthy, shorter lived - most did not see thirty years. It was not a day in the country for them. It must have been large pieces of their lives. And then consider the size of the population that had to work to support this work with food, ropes, tallow, whatever.

"If we follow Jaynes," he continued, "was it the result of some common vision, a cult that spread? Or if we believe, as I think we must, the findings of astronomy, was it a form of solar calendar?

"Of all the arrangements, standing solo, forming corridors or long ovals, the one which most admits of inference is the circle. The corridors could have provided definition or security between two sacred or safe sites, although nothing substantiates this. The long ovals which look so much like racetracks may very well have been, but there is no evidence one way or another. A cross-section excavation would be interesting. To my knowledge, none has been done on an oval.

"But the circles, being a geometric regularity, have

been studied and many have been conclusively shown to have a celestial orientation. Extended inferences are weakened by the imprecisions wrought by time—the wear and shifting of the stones—complexity of the calculations of historical alignments, and the extremely large numbers of possibilities. Given enough computer time, some graduate student could prove a given circle was built to mark the moon's transit of Cassiopeia. And maybe it was. But why?"

"Yeah. The only thing that would make sense would be some 'human' reason."

"Maybe everybody dreamed of circles when the moon transited Cassiopeia," Clio said.

"Or maybe somebody," I said, "one person, convinced everybody else to share a common vision. Or follow his. You said these stoneworks were found from the Mediterranean to the Baltic. Did they start in the Mediterranean? Five to eight thousand years ago would be towards the end of dynastic Egypt, right?"

"More confusion, I am afraid, Phillip. For a while the proximity to Egyptian civilization and the refined, finished style of the Mediterranean stoneworks suggested that Egypt was the source; all those stone pyramids. Chariots of the gods, I'm afraid. More accurate dating shows the Mediterranean works are much later than the North Atlantic or Baltic ones. The culture or cult or practice of stoneworks spread from Northern Europe; Brittany and Denmark are the two best guesses for the oldest. The dispersal pattern and locations, all within 100 miles of the coasts suggests a seaborne life."

"We came to this land in ships," I said. "A musician I met told me that was all that remained of the oldest known lyric in his tradition."

"The ships may have been the agent for this culture's dispersal, but the early development of agriculture is the most likely precursor of megalithic culture.

"Remember: when the last glacier pulled back

20,000 to 10,000 years ago, it moved a half a mile a year. Within seasons, a location would go from rich and hospitable to impoverished as the cold-adapted vegetation died before harvest and the large furry, animals migrated. The human population survived with technology: agriculture—the first social attempt to alter the land, where the more regular measurement of time was rewarded—and by exploitation of the sea where precise location is essential."

He paused and nodded.

"Celestial navigation might have much to teach a farmer; especially in seasonal precision. The celestial year is regular. Paleolithic evidence suggests that the first timekeeping calculus was lunar and the lunar year has a very long cycle of inaccuracies, clumsy at best. Contact with sailors might help guide the local farmers who had been in the thrall of the obvious but misleading moon."

"Where do the stones come in?"

"Hmmmm...," he paused. "Symbols of power, domain; site of ritual. Or taxation. Or agriculture fairs. Or a deeply embedded blend of all these things commonly known as one."

"You said ritual. What kind of ritual?"

I felt the evening turn cold like a breath had withdrawn the final, fugitive warmth of the day.

"Unknowable. No written record. No artifacts with any pictorial context or use indicated. As a matter of alignment, it may simply have been the ritual of watching a shadow cast by one stone on another."

"Or maybe it was more occult." I said, "Maybe the alignment was only observed by a single person whose knowledge of what to align and what it meant gave him leadership and authority over the rest."

"Isn't that a rather specialized role, a highly differentiated individual in primitive community?"

"There have always been highly differentiated individuals. I don't believe humans were ever fused in consciousness as a community. There are always alphas, leaders, people with higher energy, driven to move things, to be in control, get more for themselves, do exactly what they want. It must be deeply genetic; every social mammal must show it."

"What does this all mean about the stones?" Clio asked, I realized speaking for only the second time at the table.

Trying to summarize for myself I said, "In a period of time four or five times as long as written history, it is possible that a tribe of ocean-going adventurers passed along or imposed on agrarian groups first along the coast of Northern Europe—then maybe elsewhere—the practice of building celestially oriented earthworks. I think that's fascinating."

Professor Murphy frowned. "That sounds a bit like Prince Valiant, Phillip. I believe an organic community development is more probable."

"Based on your animist theory of primitive thinking?"

"Yes."

"It's too static and benign," I asserted. "Change and development only come from outside influences. Stable, closed societies are afraid of change. Besides, this archeo-astronomical evidence requires a level of intellectual attainment that is orders of magnitude higher than a primitive farming community. Your conclusion fits your theory, my theory fits human history."

Prince Valiant, indeed.

Clio spoke again, "Well, so once these solar alignments were built, how were they used?"

Professor Murphy and I glanced at each other and I nodded to him.

"Probably as the site of regular celebrations such as we find in syncretic or decadent forms today celebrating solstice and equinox—rebirth at winter solstice, fertility at the vernal equinox, death and harvest at the autumnal. Like Aboriginal songlines and the Nazca clan traditions, a form of communion with the unknown powers of life; turnings around the circles of stones, processions and parades."

"When?" I was surprised to find myself asking.

"I beg your pardon?"

"When were these communions, these celebrations?" What are the celestial orientations? The Solstice, the equinox? Where do the stones point?"

"Many are solar, some are arguably lunar, some don't seem to align with anything, some are aligned to others nearby. East-West alignments show up in both solar and lunar orientations as well as a few others so it's the most common."

"The equinox line," I said.

"Well," the Professor conceded, "the sun's apparent motion, its speed and energy, are the greatest at the equinox. It moves North or South more than its diameter from sunrise to sunrise. And then at that one time, the rising sun from true East throws a shadow point-to-point that is returned as it sets true West. The natural symbolism of death and rebirth at these seasonal points is clear."

"You said 'turnings around a circle'. Which way do you think they would dance? Clockwise or counterclockwise?"

"Hmm. Odd question. Well, of course, impossible to know. But ... hmm."

"There is the Christian prohibition or superstition about walking around churches counterclockwise," I ventured.

"Yes, widdershins; but the Moslem on the Haj marches widdershins around Qom. No, there's something else. Something about ... wait a minute. I'll be right back. I was just reading this."

Professor Murphy left the table and his nearly untouched plate.

Clio said, "I'm glad you're getting along so well with Dad, but this is a colossally boring conversation and, if it keeps up, I'm leaving."

I was looking flatly and, I'm afraid, bleakly at Clio when Professor Murphy galloped back into the room.

"Here," he said, "listen to this, 'The kings and priests all obey the laws of the land, but the source of all life is the sun and it obeys the law of the sky.'"

He went on to read a fairly detailed ritual requiring the King of Ireland to circumambulate his realm in the direction of the sun from east to south to west, clockwise.

"But," I said, "the sun's actual apparent motion relative to a point on the earth is retrograde. Or, as it is called, 'Counter Clockwise'. Any close observation of its relative declination would pick that up. But all persistent European tradition would say the 'clockwise' direction is the sacred way."

"And the reverse is the devil's way, evil, bad luck," Professor Murphy added.

"Just so."

"I have to leave now," said Clio. "You two stay and talk all night. I'll take the T."

"No. Wait."

She was already halfway to her father, kissing the top of his head, patting his shoulder. I followed her out of the room, down the stairs to the landing, inside the back door.

She turned the door handle and then looked at me in the low light.

"Phillip, you are so selfish, I don't want to be around you just now. You are completely self-absorbed. You have paid no attention to me; you have barely answered my questions; you have asked me nothing about the book project. Watching the two of you there so self-absorbed, ignoring me, lecturing to each other. I'm not going to make the same mistake my mother briefly did.

Your attention is wonderful when you want something, but . . ."

She opened the door, turning away quickly.

"Clio. Please. Let me talk to you. What..."

"Not now!" She shut the door behind her.

I jumped to open it. She was up the driveway, past my car.

"I'll call you. Can, may I call you?" I thought I saw her hand wave.

Her back said nothing except away.

I went inside.

Ten

Professor Murphy had cleared Clio's place when I came back; there was coffee for just the two of us and a plate of butter cookies.

"That happen often?" I asked.

"Has it happened to you before?"

I looked at him for a bit.

"Truthfully, yes. And you?"

He laughed. "All the time. Clio has never forgiven me for the divorce and precipitous departures are her revenge. She doesn't appreciate having it pointed out. I imagine she blames my absence for many of her problems."

His affectless dissection of his daughter turned me cold, the emotional baggage they shared was only a source of cruel humor. How was I like this? She was wrong. I had to tell her.

I drank the coffee in three strong jolts while it was still much too hot. My tongue and palate stung with pain. The caffeine kicked the mainspring of my body clock, though, which was still operating on something closer to European than local time.

"Well, I really have to go, too. Can I help you with these things?"

"No. No. Go on. See if you can catch her. But I'd advise you to give her some time."

"Thanks. Maybe I'll do that."

I had to see her now.

He seemed to know.

I left.

∞

Back in the car, scrapbook and computer repacked, I drove to Back Bay over the Mass. Ave. bridge, enjoying the downtown sky and a near-full moon. Nearly the equinox, I realized. Saturday was the twenty-third.

That was when I saw it whole; Epiphany on the Charles. The equinox and the stones were the engine of eternal life. Aging was unwound, the clock of life turned back, by walking around the stones. I remembered the feeling of the megaliths next to me, the binding of space they defined, their mass and extent. At night they would reach to the stars. I recalled the Amagansett dream.

The human life-form has evolved in a gravitational field no less pervasive and powerful than the field of visible light. And our bodies, as with other life, manifest the adaptations, the tropisms, the resonances to the other correlative bodies: our circadian rhythms, lunar cycles, annular flux, time, aging, death.

The critical flicker frequency of our vision is just slightly above the wave frequency of visible light. That is only reasonable, but it is also evidence of how closely patterned the body is to the physical energies in which it lives. Science is now beginning to understand the electrical fields which surround, permeate and are generated by life: electroform patterns of the cell, heart, blood and brain. Just as air and water and food are essential components, static, alternating and magnetic currents are elements of life -- a medium of physical exchange and influence between life and its context, its matrix, the flux of existence.

"Time, Professor Murphy had said, "is the dimension in which we experience existence. Living, we experience a progression of time that cannot be expressed scientifically. Like all transpersonal reality, categorically difficult to prove."

"A collective hunch."

"Very good."

"Lily Tomlin," I had credited. "So, time could be a mass delusion?"

"Not a delusion. Horses cannot see strobe lights. You cannot hear a dog-whistle. Snakes sense heat. Every creature lives in its own sensorium and that is its reality."

"And we have a sense of time."

"I think a sense of time is inherent in our models of causality. It is not inherently physical and mathematically it need not be asymmetric."

"Meaning it could be reversed?"

"Meaning it could be anything, coextensive, circular, infundibulated, parallel, omnidirectional."

I thought of time shooting off in all directions like a star shell in the night, phosphors fading into distant stars.

I saw a gravity of time imposed by the spiral courses of heavenly bodies that hurtle massively around our small places on this spinning mortal plane. It was a pervasive and determinant network or web of something I could call chrono-gravitation and it was the heart of time and entropy and death.

So perhaps there are places on the planet where these forces are or can be focused; intersection and nexus, where focused amplitude is matched to the force of the entropic; and the asymmetric valence and polarity of time is reversed or reversible.

The payments on the equinox, tribute to the clock keepers. A safe place to rejuvenate, away from prying, superstitious local peasant eyes. Like Paul's.

I recalled another thing Professor Murphy had said earlier when I asked for his summary take on creation myths. "Looking at everything from Norse to Hindu to the various Aboriginal and the pre-Judaic Middle Eastern myths there emerges a strong consensus on the existence of a super race of highly combative and appetently sexual beings prior to a great flood."

"In those days" I had quoted Genesis, "there were giants in the earth."

∞

Just after I caught sight of the Commonwealth Avenue sign, there was a rare opportunity in traffic to make an illegal left that would let me pull behind the apartment without the usual six rights. Done. A cab's horn crowed indignantly after me. I stopped on the only good investment I had made in Boston, my $5,000 parking space. It measures about two hundred square feet, lined in yellow, stained concrete for which I had paid fifteen hundred extra with the apartment condo. And for some perverse reason, while the demand and price for living space was down, parking space was a seller's market. One of my neighbors had offered me the five large just after I started at S, B.

The sodium light made my hands look grey; dark shadows, high contrasts, strong relief.

When I got inside, I found Camille dead.

The terror that had stalked me in Europe opened itself and swallowed my heart, my lungs, my guts. I staggered, nearly vomited and fell to one knee.

When I came up, I was enraged.

I swore with all my vulgar, hate-filled, inarticulate primal strength. And she still was dead. Lying on her right side, extended, head up, tail out, looking like a show animal displayed for conformation, rotated ninety degrees, side view, recumbent.

Just so there was no ambiguity for me, she was placed on a fan of two dozen white calla lilies.

Western Union could not have been clearer.

She was dead.

The bastards.

In the silence, I listened for other sounds. Was I alone?

Following Sergeant Coleman's pattern, I looked. I thought about a weapon. There was a Buck knife in my tool box under the kitchen sink; a punji stake somewhere on my desk, dulled by long use as a letter opener, and an unsharpened shirken paperweight. Fortunately, I found no one. Where would I get any kind of weapon I could use and carry?

With the laws in Massachusetts, I was probably not going to be able to re-equip myself with an M-79 and a sidearm tonight.

No lights. No sound. In the kitchen closet, I got out a folded entrenching tool and a towel. And a brown paper grocery sack. As I was picking up the third item, I realized my left arm had been clutching the shoulder bag with the computer and scrapbook, etc. tightly enough to whiten the knuckles.

Just the basics. What do I need? Items in hand, money, checks and cards. I changed shoes and put on a 1967 London Fog trench coat with a distinctly downscale urban patina of stains.

I laid Camille on the towel and curled her little body into her sleeping position. As threatened tears again boiled off in rage, I folded the towel over her and placed her wrapped body in the bottom of the brown paper bag.

The entrenching tool was a problem, but with a web belt around my neck, I slung it under my right arm inside the coat.

I went out the back door, aware I might not be back and did not look anywhere but casually ahead. Nothing shaking. I left the shadow of the back door, moved toward the fence, past my car, to the alley. Mass. Ave. rumbled to the right. I waited until a step van with a bad headlight came up from the left and then crossed the alley behind it. Behind me I heard a car start. But I reached Mass. Ave. with no other traffic coming up the alley.

On the sidewalk, I kept my head down. Need to get a hat. Too many people on Newbury Street. Why is there a universal human urge to wear expensive clothes, eat and drink in public? By the Presbyterian Church of the Covenant, the artists and the beggars were discussing cocktails, specifically the beggars' consumption of same in the artists' "gallery." Camille's body bumped my leg in a slack rhythm. The tool bruised my rib. The computer bag was heavy. I began to sweat. Coming past the Ritz, a man getting out of a cab saw me and got back in until I passed.

I jaywalked across Arlington to the Garden, down a walk lined with dark flowers, past a statue, to the right, under a big willow tree, between two roots on a little knoll, where the swan boats go by. I buried her and then slid the tool into the water.

I stood up alone. A light-headed rush made the leaves stand out and sounds were amplified. There was someone crossing the bridge. In a fast turn I ducked around a branch and headed towards the Commons under the elms. A breeze was coming up and the moon was high; rustles and shadows.

I fought down panic.

The best place to cross Charles would be in the worst light with the most people. There was a mass of construction with steel plates and temporary lights at Boylston. I took off the flasher coat, slung it through the shoulder strap of the bookbag; slipped through a gate and joined the crowd; stayed in the middle, peripherally checked out the cars and people. Nothing familiar. No information. Why kill my cat? The finality of her death came again. Then rage. I left the crowd and cut into the Commons. No one followed.

I sat on a bench looking up at the Massacre monument for two hours, alternately resting and panicking; waiting for something to approach, thinking of what to do next.

∞

It was a safe place. I could see 360° around me, mostly downhill. I was in shadow. What next?

I had no weapon, but I could see anyone who might approach. They had to come to me. I was in a fury. I wanted to kill. It is a feeling beyond hatred. You find yourself acted by another person who is utterly fearless, competent, brutal and apparently charmed. After action, I would feel at perfect peace or horrified, depending on personal damage or unit losses. Troops tend to get giddy after, they need to be kept focused.

I waited; nothing; kept focus.

Everything I knew was useless. With a grenade launcher, a .45 and a rifle platoon, I could secure any ground in the park. This skill was as irrelevant to my current situation as it had been for the last eighteen years of my life.

Only the fear was the same, as it came seeping in when nothing happened.

It was not cold yet, but it was dark and the dark is not friendly.

In a fugue state, my thoughts flew around in circles.

Brittany. André. Ana. Clio. Vera Eliane. Claude-Philippe. Ana. Camille. Switzerland. Side trips to the MATCHUP files. Paul. Ralph. Me.

To calm myself, I did eight-count breathing exercises. The clamor would subside and panic decrease as I concentrated on counting up and down. Then someone would come down a walk and I was back at full adrenaline, Bravo-11 alert, then waiting, then nothing. And waiting, then dread.

It occurred to me that I was comparatively safer without the scrapbook, disks, and copies on my person.

At that point, I must confess, I thought about Clio. I had said I would call her. It was late.

The Park Street Station area was bright, but from the shadows of the Commons to the entrance was less than fifty feet. I caught an Ashmont train to Washington, exited at Downtown Crossing, walked up Washington as the street people took on the night. At State, I took a Blue Line Wonderland train to the Airport with an unscheduled but memorable pause for power outage under the Inner Harbor; ozone, stale, damp air. We stewed for five or ten minutes in intimate darkness, no one moving. Then a shot of sparks lit up the tunnel and the train lurched and stopped, sparked again, lurched and crawled, then rolled smoothly upgrade and into East Boston station.

At the Airport stop, I let one round of buses go by. No one stayed with me. The first bus to come by a second time took me to Terminal C Departures. Between a live lobster vendor, closed for the night, and a loud, dark, smoky bar obviously open, was a souvenir shop and a bank of lockers. For most of twenty dollars, I bought a zippered canvas purse with something advertised on it. For three quarters, I rented a snug little room for the purse to keep the scrapbook, copies and disks for twenty-four hours.

My shoulder bag felt ten pounds lighter, but was only slightly less bulky. For another twenty dollars, I got a blue canvas sport sack that had screened on it I HEART MA. The top coat and shoulder bag fit nicely into it. The only clothing available was in the hat department. Is there a fate worse than death? I bought a Red Sox cap.

There was a phone bank; it was 11:30.

She answered on the third ring as I was just thinking of hanging up.

"Yes."

"Hello, Clio, it's Phillip. Are you awake? Are you okay to talk to me?"

"Yes. I guess. I mean, what time is it?"

"It's late. I'm sorry. Should I call back tomorrow or what?"

"No. I don't know. What time is it? Oh. It's only 11:30. I just laid down. Hmm."

"Look. Please. I'm sorry. If this is... I woke you up. Tomorrow. I'll..."

"No, it's okay. I wasn't asleep. Just kind of drifting. I was thinking I was talking to you but you were in a tube and couldn't hear me. And then you call. I just called you before, did you get my message?"

"No. What was it?"

"Oh, just to call me. I wanted to say I was sorry I lost my temper. You two are insufferable, but I was not polite."

"I'm sorry I'm insufferable. I am. I get so wrapped up in one thing I forget everything and anyone else."

"That's the wicked truth."

"I don't want to be like that, but it seems to be hard-wired."

"Hmph." She said nothing.

I said nothing.

"Well."

"I want to get back to how we were. I want to do anything I can to be different. I feel like I've lost touch with you. And it's wrong. I miss you," I said, as I looked at hollow corridors and people around me.

"I feel like I've lost touch with you," she said.

" Ah... I've had a... a complicated and unpleasant day and night. Could I see you?"

"Tonight? Phillip, I'm tired. I *was* asleep. Thank you, though, for what you've said. Let's see each other tomorrow."

"Tomorrow? Okay. I'll call you. Okay?"

"Okay, Phillip, good night."

"Good night, Clio."

Needing a place to sleep and work for the next 18 to 20 hours, wanting to keep out of official registers and electronic records, and having already debased myself with the Red Sox hat, the next step was easy.

"Ackley, here."

"Ackley, it's Gardiner."

"Gar-di-ner, foul beast, black fly bearded Lion."

"Ackley, you're drunk."

" 'Course I'm drunk; it's nearly midnight."

"Yes. I see your point. Listen, Ackley, you offered to help when I didn't have a fire in my apartment, but now there is a gas leak and I need a place to crash."

"Crash and burn. Smash and grab."

"What's the apartment number?"

"17E for Eagle."

"Is it okay, Ackley?"

"Call me Eagle."

"We've been through this before. I won't call you Eagle."

"Call me Eagle, old Lion, and I'll say yes."

"Come on, Ackley, Eagle, whaleshit!"

Nothing.

"Ackley?"

"Did you call me Eagle?"

"Yes, I just did."

"I thought so. When are you coming over?"

"In a few minutes."

"Oh, good. We can have a drink."

A fast cab slid through the still-crowded Sumner Tunnel, made an illegal left onto Atlantic and dropped me at the Aquarium in twenty minutes. I watched the street traffic for a few minutes, the activity around the **christy's**, young urban professionals mixing with mature urban failures. The wine selection running from thirty dollar Chianti to Richard's Wild Irish Rose at a dollar ninety-nine. Radar food and raunchy magazines, fluorescent lit.

In a few minutes, I walked to the nearest tower and Ackley buzzed me in.

The corridors had fuzzy red carpet overbrightly lit with blue/green-shift neon behind white waffle web diffusers. Hospital corridors are lit the same way; that's why everyone looks so good. Too many mirrors, slow elevator. E was on the left. I knocked.

"Knock. Knock. Knock," came muffled from within. The door did not open. I knocked again.

"Knock. Knock. Here's a man ..."

"Can the Shakespeare, Ackley; go to hell with the rest of the English majors and open the door."

"You're supposed to say... " he said, opening the door.

"Thank you, Ackley. May I have a drink?"

"Drink—the great persuader and the great dissuader."

"I don't want to hear it, Ackley. Where's the bar?"

"Conveniently located at elbow height, here adjacent to the sitting area." He led me around the entry way and the city gaped at me through a bank of windows, crouching a couple hundred feet down. It looked slickly beautiful in a malevolent way, like a medical illustration.

"What's it to be then, eh?"

I winced. "Whiskey, preferably bourbon."

Wild Turkey.

Wilderness is paradise enow.

Ackley was in a mood one could best call expansive. I was fried. His logorrheaic idiocies made me giddy with relief. I was safe, surrounded by insanity.

I had another drink, told a few expedient lies. He complained about my handling of an incident thirty years previous. In the process, he managed to quote the Gita, Aristophanes, Thomas Jefferson, and David Bowie. It was, even for him, a performance.

"Ackley," I broke in, "What do you do during the day? You are ballistic."

"I push buttons, tap keys; money moves around. We keep some of it."

"Sounds easy; why doesn't everybody do it?"

"Many are called, but few are chosen."

"And you, one of the chosen people, Ackley; a poor toiler in the vineyard of the money machine? A simple manual laborer, helping stamp out the vintage where the grapes of worth are stored."

"You need another drink; that almost made sense."

He was way ahead of me.

"Ackley, dear fountain of wit, I just got back from Europe at eight this morning. Nothing makes sense. Where can I sleep without interrupting your continued debauch?"

Deflated, he showed me a small office with just enough floor space in which to open a convertible couch. There was a double window overlooking Inner Harbor and the airport. He brought me two sheets, a towel, two pillows. We shook hands.

"Ackley, really, thanks. I'm sorry I'm not better company. Tomorrow. Maybe we can sit up late tomorrow."

He is a good person, but his speed freak 110% in the face act is difficult at any time; and tonight, after two drinks, impossible.

Life had kindly conspired to allow Ackley to encounter a few people who can see his unique wit and sad beauty through his often bizarre flights of imagination. He had always been like this. The only chemicals at work were his own production.

Masters and boys alike shunned him, his family evidently thought him a freak. At heart, he really was a prince, kind and generous, intensely interested in ideas and cultural history. But lacking a conventional social personality, he lacked any regular society. On a good tear, I can keep up with him for three or four laps of Robin-Williams-goes-to-Oxford. But then, as it persists, it feels like he's pushing away any human contact and most people get annoyed and leave. I know this is all he has for social discourse, and I can usually ricochet around him with weird tangents and non sequiturs. It is a form of acceptance that seems to please him. And he is the only person in my life who has made a sustained effort to keep in touch with me.

∞

The foldout mattress had the usual two steely lateral breaks at the hinges and, being so fatigued, I slept with little movement all night. I woke up with the sun on my face like the breath of a dog and intense pains in my back and legs as I tried to turn away. I imagined being two dimensional and gate-folded; stapled. Plaything of the month. I remembered Ana and the rest of my situation came rolling back over me. I fell back into the sun with a groan and squinted and rubbed my eyes open. They seemed grainy and the sun hurt. I got up, creakingly, my left knee popping a reminder of its less than perfect fit. My feet look awful. In addition to the two right toes squashed by some crypto-socialite's polo pony, two on the left remain misshapen from a later porch-climbing accident.

My clothes looked bad, too; dirt on the pants, shirt visibly wrinkled, jacket a little of both. I put on the shirt and pants without underwear and went looking for a clock and a kitchen.

∞

I found them both, the former reading 8:43.

The latter faced the harbor and, with the sun still in my eyes, I half blindly pawed through several cabinets until a collection of cups materialized. Boston tap water in a microwave probably generates some new life form.

With a bag of black Prince of Wales soaking in a brown Morning Pro Musica cup, I went back to the little bedroom office.

Friday morning at nine o'clock, she is far away. But it was Thursday and when I called she was not in yet.

I needed clothes. My apartment was not safe. The threat was real, but still, measured. No one could know where I was now. What next? My eye caught the computer screens across from me on Ackley's white particle board office furniture. Heavy-duty set-up. I did not even have to leave the foldout mattress to boot it up. While it was beeping and prompting and responding, I folded up the bed and pulled out the only chair-like device in the room, apparently designed for an ergonomically correct kneeling posture. The idea of kneeling before a CRT work station is industrial-strength unconscious western irony in peak form. I found a way to sit on it backwards with my feet on the kneeling pad. It worked, but it was a little high and slightly unstable.

Ackley had a DOS-based system with file servers A through G. Three were locked and I would not dream of trying to guess what Ackley might use for a password. Besides, if he wanted me out, I would stay out. All I needed was the basic utilities. The communication stuff was in F.

CompuServ is in Westerville, Ohio. I was actually once in the building where it was started as a tally service for corporate balloting and university research. Now, however, it connects me to another dimension or space. CompuServ is still finite, but through the internet, it has an almost infinitely high degree of connectedness. And the internet is not entropic. It grows; new connections, new dimensions, a little grey window into something else, greater or lesser, still basically electro-mechanical but hugely transpersonal; vast libraries of data, cavernous rooms full of people, endless potential, the door into tomorrow, elsewhere, anyone, anytime, infinitely interconnected.

An astronomical almanac from one of the encyclopedias was able to tell me that, in fact, the payment dates for the *Agence Privée* transfers coincided with the dates of equinox and that the Autumnal event this year would occur at 11:52 p.m. Eastern Standard Time the day after tomorrow.

I checked on flights to Zurich; SwissAir overnight, if on time, would land at 9:00 a.m. I would not do what they wanted. I was right to be in the U.S. It was more than marginally safer and mobility was my refuge. I printed out the SwissAir schedule. Then, thinking a little indirection could still be helpful, I booked myself for tonight, business class, open return.

I printed out all the shuttle schedules for the Y Corridor, the Eastern United States airspace, an amazing 3-D juggling act by a few hundred people separately plugged into headsets and screens directing large metal alloy tubes full of humans hurtling around each other at hundreds of miles an hour. I also printed AMTRAK's schedule.

Logged off at 0914 EST.

I thought about stashing a copy of the Toshiba's hard disk files in Ackley's system. But until I knew what the MATCHUP files could prove, I wanted to keep them to myself. Besides, this was clearly dangerous. He should not be involved.

I patched the Toshiba into Ackley's big screen and, for the next several hours, worked over the MATCHUP data. The sorts got more farfetched, the logic extended, the run times longer. "Dumb" time, it is not "down" time, the computer is up and running; you are just sitting there dumbly watching the prompt or the icon blink.

In such a period, I came upon the idea of trying a hack on the S, B system to see what was new in the files.

Number Q?

Entered.

Dialing.

Connect.

Bingo!

There was the familiar initial screen with 18 point shadowed Tiffany font letters announcing the front door of the S, B network and requesting a password. I had fifteen seconds. My old one, PILGRIM, was not worth trying. Peggy Crandall was a middle-aged, i.e., -just-over-mine, office manager who really took on the changeover project. She helped me immensely breaking down office forms and procedures to data fields. Crandall was a greying redhead whose password had been REDTOP. It still was.

MAIN MENU

1. HELP

2. INDEX

3. I CATEGORY

4. II CATEGORY

I.N.D.E.X. ENTER

The screen began scrolling. I stopped it by entering 1.7.3. Trusts and Estates Accounts Payable.

II CATEGORY ACCESS CODE Q?

Shit.

Pushed **PAGE DOWN** and the scroll resumed.

E.1.9 FINANCIAL SUMMARY CURRENT

II CATEGORY ACCESS CODE Q?

REDTOP was not at the top of the food chain.

HELP

HELP

1. INDEX

2. NEXT

3. PREVIOUS

4. RETURN
INDEX
INDEX
1. ABOUT HELP
2. ACCESS
3. I CATEGORY
4. II CATEGORY
I CATEGORY
I CATEGORY
1. PERSONNEL
2. PURCHASING
3. LIBRARY
4. CORRESPONDENCE
1. PERSONNEL
1. PERSONNEL
1. RECORDS
1. RECORDS
ENTER NAME Q?
BAXTER, RALPH STONINGTON ADAMS.
DECEASED.

Back to the main menu to **LIBRARY**, searched for SCRAPBOOK, no listing. Scrolling through the S, B listings, I found **"Sedgwick, Baxter — THE FIRST 100 YEARS." 999.99** ENTER.

VOLUME MISSING.

Feeling less comfortable, I went back through the main menu to **CORRESPONDENCE.**

ADDRESSEE NAME Q?

CLAUDE-PHILIPPE.

The prompt blinked. I stared, drenching my face in extremely low frequency radiation, needing another cup of tea.

Beep.

A list appeared on the screen. I opened the first file. It was a witless, small-print summation of previous year-end pending actions and transactions. The prose was as thick as sludge with abbreviations, obscure references, and terms of art. The second letter was no better.

It took over an hour to get to June, whereat Harry Shell's rabbi wrote in response to C-P's recent inquiry that the computer project would be completed on schedule. Harry's pencil neck really was on the line.

In late July, Ken wrote a casual letter to Zurich that apparently accompanied a report titled: "Third Quarter Returns" according to the enclosure notation. He described the returns as "Satisfactory." In his closing, he asked if "all required information is in your hands, or do you wish further research?" ending with, "Our colleague's regrettable initiative was not without useful result?" There was no reference in the letter to anything that made sense of either question. It was clearly another topic, but what?

And then, on August 24, I found a surprise. Baxter wrote to Claude-Philippe an extravagant litany of complaints and warnings about the continued efforts of one Phillip L. Gardiner and their effect on "the sacred fiduciary trust" (awesome, the holiness of money) vested in S, B. Less than two weeks later, I was on my way to Zurich and Baxter was, as the screen put it, DECEASED.

The last letter affirmed the receipt, the day before yesterday, of the "Centurion" security protocols for the system and stipulated that they were being immediately installed. I logged off at 1215 EST and called Clio again.

"Murfry."

She had something in her mouth. It was the first graceless thing I'd known her to do. I was charmed and remembered her casual friendship in our times together and smiled.

"What's for lunch?"

She gulped.

"Oh, I'm glad it's you. Everyone's gone out and I was starving and as soon as I took a bite, the phone rang.

"Are you okay? You sounded funny last night."

"I was just very tired and couldn't sleep. I am still a little jet lagged, my body clock is only half back across the Atlantic."

She laughed.

I did love her. Was there any way back?

"Can we get together tonight? I want to see you. I want to talk and just not be alone and without you ... Can we go on?"

"Let's talk about it," she said, "Tonight. Where?"

"The Copley?"

"I can't talk in there, it's like a church. Let's go to Peaches on Joy Street."

"Say a time and I'll be there."

"A little after six. I'll just come from work."

"Great, I'll see you then, okay? "

"Okay."

"Clio. I really have missed you."

"Thank you, Phillip. I think I have missed you, too. I'll see you tonight. Okay?"

"Okay."

∞

A little before one, I left to get clothes and toiletries. I thought about going to Bromfield Street and buying a few disguises, then I remembered how naked I felt in the Commons at night unarmed. There was no way I could get a gun in Boston in any kind of time. I could drive to New Hampshire. I have never owned a weapon. The only ones I've ever used were property of the U.S. Army. What good would a gun do in this situation? There was no one to shoot at, only rumors and fears and, somewhere, the person or persons who killed my cat. I thought of poor, dear, dead Camille and saw her there again and felt her limp weight as it bumped my leg for the last times down Newbury Street in a shopping bag. And the rage returned and I did want a weapon.

Thus deranged, I got to the Coop and bought a black blazer; one blue and two white shirts; two pair of ready-made trousers—one dark, one light-grey; three ties and three pair of underwear and four of socks; one belt; one pair of deck shoes. It all fit into a large brown cordura bag which looked nowhere as sturdy as the Boyt bag and was cluttered with cute compartments, internal divisions and external pockets.

Instead of Bromfield Street, I went to the Zone.

At night, the area can scare up a reasonably dirty, dangerous atmosphere and you can buy some serious trouble for yourself in lots of doors and alleys. In the day, it was a sad, tattered remnant of a slum surrounded by hungry neighbors. Two blocks of early seventies urban decay preserved in smut. It was after two when I walked into the adult magazine-Kung Fu-biker-bondage boutique. The decor was starkly utilitarian: display cases of objects shining and sharp, black and leathery, mean and knowing; racks of cellophane-bound, bright yellow and red bordered close ups of human flesh; all the wood painted black along with the walls, floor and ceiling.

A balding, bearded hulk dressed in guess-what color completed the little tableau: every parent's vision of the big, ugly world.

The hulk scanned me and my new bag and used clothing. He said nothing.

I went to the Kung Fu display. The kendo stick was appealing, but at a yard long, a little cumbersome. Nunchuks were more portable, but my only exposure to their use was at a Bruce Lee film festival about fifteen years previously. Shirkens—the little throwing stars like my paperweight—are not serious weapons. But, there in the corner of the cabinet, next to a pair of elaborate trident-shaped knives, was a boxed item labeled "Thunder Power".

Nested in Styrofoam was a six-inch fly-belly,

green-black, symmetrical hand grip with two stubby horns sticking out. On the top of each horn, about three inches apart, were two chrome metal studs. There was a thumb switch on one side of the grip. It looked like a TV remote unit with a terminally bad attitude. A black braided strap and silvery belt clip were separately wrapped in slots next to the green-black thing. There was an insectile mandibularity to it, a mean nightmare beetle or maybe a mutant, bifurcate scorpion.

"Excuse me. May I see this?"

The hulk lowered his graphic novel, I could not read the title, but doubted it was *Maus*.

"May I see this, please?"

He came around the counter with the wary swagger of experience.

"You goin' into a heavy neighborhood?"

"Just curious."

"We don't get many casual shoppers in here. What do you want?"

"What is it?"

"Thunder? Ol' Thunder is what you get after the lightenin' hits." He laughed at his joke, revealing the surest sign of inescapable lower class poverty in America, ruined teeth.

"What does it do?"

"Knocks ya on yer ass and makes you stupid for a few minutes, no permanent damage. 85 bucks. Plus tax. You want it?"

"Is it legal?"

"You doin' a research project here, Stanley, or ya wanna buy the fuckin' thing?"

"How does it work?"

He walked back to the cash register and got something from a drawer.

"It takes a 9-volt battery," he said, coming back, holding up a key chain. He unlocked the cabinet and got out the box. As I reached for the box, he pulled my arm towards him and shoved a duplicate Thunder Power into my solar plexus.

I heard a sharp electrical snap and felt a blow to my lungs and heart; I collapsed like a marionette with cut strings. My head seemed to explode with a sensation that rang through my fingers and toes. On the floor, my arms and legs twitched and jerked. All I could see was silver and black; and black and black.

Slowly my vision returned and I was staring at a pinched, yellow-brown cigarette filter a half inch away from my face on the gritty floor. It took a little concentration and patience to sit up. Standing was slightly more involved and less stable. I considered sitting back down.

The clerk was back at the register with his comic book.

"You're quite a smooth salesman," I managed, "I'll take it. Got any batteries?"

He claimed to have no batteries but recommended rechargeable ni-cads. He was also careful to keep a counter between us at all times. He was in no danger from me, especially if there was any chance the stun gun held two charges. Jesus, it was mean!

On the way back to Ackley's, I hoovered a bunch of toiletries and several nine-volt rechargeable batteries from a CVS. By 5:00, I was clean and freshly clothed with a slight residual numbness about the extremities and two small welts three inches apart on my chest. According to the instruction sheet, I had been the lucky recipient of 120,000 volts. The instruction sheet advised against "directing the unit to the face or thorax." Perhaps the sales clerk had not read the directions. I imagined an international graphic symbol of crossed red circles superimposed on someone getting a shot to the nose. "Don't try this at home, boys and girls." Jesus, it was mean. I clipped mine to my belt at the small of my back, making sure both safety switches were on.

I left the Toshiba, extra batteries and charger, new

clothes, toiletries and suitcase loosely organized in the bedroom office and was out the side lobby door by twenty after. The previous days' clothes I dropped at a Sarni storefront cleaners the other way from the all-night **christy's.**

Traffic was godawful, the Central Artery and all the on-ramps were parking lots. The surface streets had big gaps around manhole covers, wheel-size potholes. Cars banged and bounced and sat and fumed and honked. Times like this, it's good to be a pedestrian.

I walked up State, past Maison Robert restaurant in the Old City Hall on Court, went into a two-story bookstore that fronted on Cambridge and browsed my way slowly up to Pemberton Square level, then climbed Ashburton to Bowdoin, past Joe and John and Robert and ultimately Teddy and Joe, Jr.'s. pied-a-terre at 122, through the State House porte-cochére onto Mt. Vernon and left on Joy.

I was early and, sticking my head inside briefly to be sure Clio had not beaten me there, returned to the street to watch. The sun was shining on a wall across the corner, so I crossed and stood where I could see in three directions and lean against warm stone.

The Thunder Thing dug into my back. I can't say I felt any more secure, but the whole way over was spent without any thought of my essential problem which now returned with real solidity.

I was out of time. SwissAir Flight 16 would be leaving without me in a few hours.

Suffolk students, rooming house rummies, political yuppies and occasional DBs (displaced Brahmins) edged and flowed around me, each other and the corner.

The rush and pattern and apparent substance of a city are made of millions of tiny hidden lives buzzing with immediate concerns. The physical forms whose energy and effort embody this substance are individually overwhelmed by the extent and otherness of it all.

A well-dressed, notably older woman wearing white gloves struggled in frustration with a shopping cart against a sagging granite curb. Two young men carrying books, walking side by side, separated and passed on either side of her. A livid-faced street person lost his balance yelling unintelligibly at the two as they passed him. The woman crossed to the other side of the street. A pretty mother and daughter walked past, eating ice cream; both in slacks with great athletic strides. Where was Clio?

I began to get impatient, wished I had bought a book, touched the Thunder Thing. If she did not show, should I get the stuff out of the locker next? Where was she?

∞

I tired of leaning against the wall with arms behind my back, the aches and anxieties of inactivity forced me to move. I went back to Peaches and asked the hostess if anyone had called for me. If they had a bar, maybe I would have stayed inside. Clio had called. The message was lightly transcribed: "Her father. The hospital. Call her at home."

They let me use a phone in a cubbyhole office with a desk piled to the low ceiling with cookbooks and catalogs. It felt like sitting below a hanging glacier. Her machine picked up with her same greeting. I recorded the fact that I had received the message and hoped her father was going to be all right. Said I would call back in an hour. I got Professor Murphy's number and called there: no answer. I called home and entered the remote access code:

"Hello. You have two messages."

Whirr.

Deedle, deedle, deet.

"Phillip, it's Jonathan Parker. Give me a call, if you would. I had an inquiry that might be an opportunity for you. Thanks. Bye."

"Wednesday. 10:20 a.m."

Beeps.

"Phillip, this is Clio. Everything is okay, but my dad had a heart scare and they took him to Mt. Auburn and called me at work. He's okay. I'm at the hospital now while they finish up tests. I'll call you back at your apartment when I get home."

"Wednesday. 6:20 p.m."

"That was your last message. You may hang up and I will save your messages ... or enter remote code now to replay your messages ..."

I hung up before we got into the remainder of my dandy options. I called Clio back and left a second message saying I was not going to be at my apartment and would call her hourly beginning at seven.

In front of the State House, the first cab in line was a Red and White. With a shrug, the driver agreed to take me to Rowe's Wharf. He turned right down Park Street and joined the snarl at Sumner and then onto Atlantic. It took about five changes of lights for the first, three on the latter; $4.50.

The water taxi was loading and I stood on deck, watching the modest, but impressive harbor skyline backlit by a gold-blue sunset recede as we crossed past the derelict East Boston waterfront to the Logan dock. A white van dropped me at the C Terminal.

The stun gun had found a comfortable adjustment to my back and I kept one hand in a hip pocket as I approached the locker. The key clicked, the door swung and no one moved with me as I removed the canvas purse with the scrapbook, copies and rattling diskettes. No one followed me out to Arrivals Ground Transportation.

I reversed the procedure from last night. Rode the shuttle bus around twice because one guy stayed on for one full circuit, but then got off. At the T-station, I went down the Wonderland side and watched an Inbound across the tracks fill and leave an empty platform. I crossed back over. A group of students joined me on the next Inbound boarding.

At Government Center, I surfaced under the giant neo-fascistic cave and walked towards the 1812 Oyster House sign, then down Congress to South Station. Signs led me through construction constricted hallways around a corner. The man at the baggage office checked the purse.

"I'll pick it up in a few days," I said.

"Up to thirty, it ain't going nowhere; after that, it's out. Printed on the ticket. Have a nice day."

"It's too late."

He had turned away, then called, "What?" turning back.

"It's too late to have a nice day. It's after dark." I smiled.

He looked at me for a second, then nodded his head, considering. "Fuck you," he said and turned away with the bag.

I wondered if the purse was going to see 30 days. And, by the same token, what were my chances of seeing it again. From the temporary waiting room filled with milling people only yards from the track, I called Clio's number.

The machine answered, I left a brief message and walked slowly back up Atlantic in the thinning crowds to the Towers.

∞

The apartment was quiet and getting dark. The refrigerator compressor engaged as I closed the door.

"Ackley, you home?"

He was, but he wasn't answering. I found him in the office on the floor with an awful sunken dent in his head and a great amount of blood for his pillow.

Eleven

My scream seemed to reach my ears before it left my lungs. It preceded any awareness of fear. But as I clamped down on the scream, the fear and horror flooded my body like the visceral pain of an awful, low blow.

I scrambled frantically under my jacket for the stun gun and swung my head left to right to quarter left to quarter right so quickly a pinched nerve shot an electric tingle up my skull.

With my ears still ringing from the scream, bowels threatening to unloose, neck tingling and waves of revulsion flooding my mind, I stepped closer to the ruins of my friend.

∞

How can the dead smile? I had never seen this before. He was no longer familiar. The features were those of a stranger, a still, pale stranger with a small, sweet smile. I began to cry, great wrenching sobs.

In my life, he was the one person who had known me since childhood who still wanted to be in touch, to help. And though he was difficult, metaphorically impossible, it mattered to me that he cared. And I knew how limited his human connections were and it had pleased me to be rare enough to be one of them.

To have been. Past perfect tense. Just perfect. Just so. The phrase reminded me of Paul Languedoc just as I spotted, through my tears, the murder weapon.

It was the Toshiba lap-top. With a brown-red clump of hair on one cracked corner, it lay in two pieces on the far side of his body.

The heaves of my sobbing slowed and I wiped tears and mucus from my face on my coat sleeves. To hell with Lord Cardigan. The buttons raked my nose and cheeks. The fear returned.

With the Thunder thing—all safeties off—extended in front of me like a short-nosed pistol, I walked to the kitchen. On the other side of the living room was the door to Ackley's bedroom. It was closed. I considered how much I wanted to know who or what was in there. I backed into the kitchen where I could see both bedroom and entry doors, out of line of both, and reached for the phone.

9.1.1.

"Nine, one, one. What is the problem," a clear, young male voice asked. The recording warning beeped.

"There's been a murder. Harbor Towers, Apartment 17-E."

"What is your name?"

I could not immediately answer. I could not, it seemed, think of any of the words. The warning beeped again.

"What is your name, please?"

"Gardiner, Phillip L. Gardiner."

Beep.

"Are you at the address?"

"Yes."

"Do you know the victim?"

"Yes."

Beep.

"What is the victim's name?"

"Ackley," I sighed, "William Eagleton Ackley."

Beep.

"Do you live at that address?"

"No. Just visiting."

Beep.

"What is your address?"

I gave it to him and the beep. When he asked for my phone number, I realized he was instructed to keep me on the line. I hung up.

I heard a siren in the street. In the city, you always hear sirens in the street. It stopped abruptly, nearby. I kept my watch on both doors.

The loud knock came shortly and I walked towards the front door, only realizing, as I reached for the knob, that I still held the stun gun fully armed in my right hand. I locked the safety switches and slipped it into my jacket pocket.

The doorway fairly blossomed with energy. Two, large uniformed men quickly moved to either side of me.

"You the one called?"

I looked left at the sharp dark eyes and strong, inexpressive features of one J. Lobosco. It was like facing a live TV camera, all intake and no feedback.

"You the one called?" he repeated.

"Yes. Gardiner, Phillip L."

"Spell it."

I did. A rustle of paper and a click to my right suggested his partner, whose name I had not seen, was recording my answers. I did not, could not break eye contact with Lobosco.

"Address."

I gave it again. The partner wrote again.

"What happened?"

"I don't know. I came in. I found him."

"Where?"

"In there." I pointed to the right rear of the room.

"Show us."

"Do I have to?"

"Yes."

∞

Behind me, a radio squelched and I heard the other cop call in some alphanumeric sequence and then a "code something." The radio squelched again.

"Roger. Out."

Squelch.

In the room, Ackley lay as before, the blood and something else throwing up a hollow, coppery tasting smell with a finishing note of rot. The blood looked flatter, darker. The sun was just down. I reached for the light switch and the cop grabbed my wrist with about twenty or forty pounds more pressure than required.

"Don't touch."

We both stared at Ackley's still form, posed like a figure study, one arm out, legs loosely crossed; the fan of blood around his head like a Mummer's crown.

My stomach convulsed and I ran to the john holding back vomit in my mouth, spewing it in the sink and commode. I was on my knees, hanging onto the bowl and tank when Officer Lobosco walked in and shined a flashlight in my eyes.

"You have a big dinner?"

"No, I haven't eaten. Why?"

"Then you should be done. Let's go."

"Can I wash my hands?"

"No. Let's go."

He took hold of a clean spot on my jacket and led me at an arm's length back to the living room.

"Where the fuck's Homicide? This faggot just did the big spit and his boyfriend in there's in no condition to clean it up."

"Central said they're rolling."

"What do we do with him?"

"All we do is secure the scene; detain witnesses or suspects."

Noises in the hall announced the next team, a very black man in a blue-grey striped suit and two white-uniformed Southie types with an accordion-folded gurney-thing on wheels.

Idly, J. Lobosco and the black man talked quitely with repeated glances at me. I have no idea what they saw, but it would not have been good. The black man spoke into Lobosco's radio; the radio squawked back. The two policemen continued the conversation, the glances. Lobosco said something he evidently thought was funnier than the detective did, but they both looked at me again and I felt the full focus of the plainclothes man hold me.

Another group of people came in the door. There were now more people in the room than ever visited Ackley on an annual basis. Nothing so unbecame his life as the leaving.

The guys in white stayed inside the door, Lobosco and his partner went out. I heard them knock on the next apartment door. The black man walked towards me and the new group in coveralls went past him to the room where Ackley patiently waited.

"I'm Lieutenant Davis," he said and showed me a gold badge and a picture I.D. "What happened?"

"I don't know. I came in. I found him."

"You live here?"

"No. I told Officer Lobosco and 911, I live on Commonwealth, 224B."

His irises were as dark as the pupils, the vitreous humor clear white. He was broad of nose and mahogany dark in skin color. A hundred thousand years of genetic drift was the smallest thing that separated us.

"You do it?"

"No," I fairly shouted. The blond twosome in hospital whites looked over and quickly away.

"He your lover?"

"No. A friend. He was my friend." I looked him in the eyes and showed him my grief. "He was my friend and I found him dead."

"How did you get in?"

"With ... uh ... key."

"You have a key." It was not a question, but I answered it anyway.

"Yes. I was ... I stayed here last night. I was just visiting."

Lt. Davis had a cordovan leather notecase and a slim black and gold Cross pen.

As he wrote, he continued the questions.

"You were visiting from your apartment on Commonwealth? In the 200 block, that's less than two miles away. I don't get it."

"He was a friend. I was visiting him."

"Lieutenant Davis!" One of the coveralls leaned around the doorway, "M. E. wants to show you something."

I slumped down onto the couch, the Thunder Power thing slapped my leg. Oh shit. I was considering stuffing it under the cushion when Davis returned, clicking his pen.

"Would you come back here with me please, Mr. Gardiner?"

I did not ask if I had to.

∞

The body was mercifully covered and the pieces of the gory Toshiba were in a thick, clear plastic bag with colored tape and writing on the edge. It looked like there was a part missing. My new clothes, toiletries, and suitcase dominated the room with their out-of-placeness.

"These things yours or his?"

"My things."

"New clothes and new suitcase, new shaving kit?"

I nodded.

"And the lap top?

A breath and a sigh.

"Yes, that's mine, too."

"New model, isn't it," Davis asked casually.

"Yes, I just bought it ."

"What's the clock speed?"

I told him cautiously not sure of what this meant, but he seemed only to have been curious. He nodded at one of the men wearing a plastic apron who picked up a yellow case and followed us as Davis led me back to the front room.

Davis spoke to the angels by the front door, "Go ahead, M. E.'s done with him."

They rolled their condensed stretcher around us and toward the other room.

"You mind we take your prints, Mr. Gardiner?"

They would not be hard to find, being all over the Toshiba, the office and the kitchen, to say nothing of relics I have left in several federal files beginning with the Army.

"No. Go ahead."

Lt. Davis looked closely at my hands and face as I was being printed, then turned his attention to the rest of the apartment, getting down on the floor in the kitchen and spending considerable time in Ackley's room. I limply allowed a technician to ink and firmly roll each of my fingers and thumbs onto the space provided. When all were filled, he gave me a foil packet with a solvent-impregnated cloth and a large sheet of dry handi-wipe paper.

While I was vainly rubbing the greasy ink around on my fingers, Davis went out to the hallway and I heard him call for Officer Lobosco.

The two men in white were bumping and trundling Ackley's shrouded remains out the door when Davis returned.

"What time did you find the body?"

"I don't know. I don't have a watch. About 7:30, I think."

"Where were you before that?"

"I was waiting for someone outside a restaurant. Then I walked back here."

"Anyone see you? Anyone with you?"

"No. Yes. The people at the restaurant. They let me make a bunch of calls."

"What time?"

"I don't know, 6:30, a quarter of."

"Then you came here?"

"Yes."

"What was the restaurant?"

"It's called Peaches, on Joy Street."

"Distances a problem for you?"

"What do you mean?"

"You visit a friend a mile and a half away, you sleep over. Takes you better part of an hour to get from Beacon Hill to the harbor. What were the clothes and suitcase for, you planning a trip to Cambridge?"

"I needed some new clothes."

We looked at each other for an uncomfortably long time, but I held his eyes.

"I don't like any of this. But the security chain is broken off the door frame while you got a key and the people next door heard a scream just after the weather ending the seven o'clock news. They called 911 ninty seconds after you. The medical examiner puts the time of death at least an hour earlier. I'm not going to hold you. But I want you to go home and stay there. Don't take any big trips like to Allston or Brighton until I tell you. Understand? You are only legally not a suspect."

He opened the door, "Sergeant Lobosco, deliver

Mr. Gardiner here to his address and see that he goes inside."

"Come on, tutti fruiti," Lobosco said to me. Turning to his partner, he said, "You handle him, he smells like shit and probably has that AIDS thing."

In this warmly sympathetic company, I returned to the next to last place I wanted to be.

∞

I went inside without turning on any lights. Street and headlights threw rhomboid shadows and illuminated stray corners and places.

The calla lilies were still sprayed on the table and their decay filled the rooms with a cloying funeral air. I remembered the Chanel Number 5 I first smelled as my mother left for her father's funeral. She almost never wore scent, so it may have been the first time I smelled a perfume. For a long time, I could not stand perfumes and even now that lily note is uncomfortable. Only an enthusiastic college-era lover with a taste for musky Estee Lauder ever got me to accept the practice. I still prefer the unscented.

Staring at the lilies, I began to shake, in shock, horrified beyond fright. Fright was only the pale foreshadow of reality.

Hag-ridden with all my existential dread. I had really only seen death's human face twice before. The grandfather I found and the day in August, 1968 when the jungle lit up. I felt no fear either time, the first due to incomprehension and confusion: why does he lie there like that? What are these fluids?

The second experience was instantaneously immediate. On a chicken-shit patrol, we encountered a company-sized unit of completely camouflaged sappers. Our movement and noise discipline had been excellent. We got in deep before we saw each other.

I believe I screamed the whole time it went on which may have been no more than ninety seconds. We killed everyone behind us getting out. I ran over a man with a tiger-striped bush hat and shot him in the face as he tried to swing his rifle around. My one grenade shot blew up a loose conglomerate of body parts and weapon pieces. There was more.

One of my guys froze after the first kill. A new troop. I tackled him, but he came down without a head. I dragged and carried the rest of him as we withdrew.

We secured a position a half click back and above the way we came in on them, waited for a counter-strike, called in for air and artillery support, and extrication. We got all four. There was more.

I bundled Camille's flowers in the trash bag and was carrying the bag back to the kitchen when the phone began to ring. I tossed the bag towards the middle of the kitchen floor and walked quickly to the answering machine in the front room.

On the fourth ring, the machine picked up and I listened to my voice.

"Hello. This is Phillip Gardiner. I'm sorry I missed your call. Please leave a message after the tone. Thank you."

Beep.

"Phillip. It's Clio. Where are you?"

∞

I picked up the handset.

"I'm here, Clio. I just came in. How is your father?"

"Oh. He's all right, very philosophical, lots of Heidegger on the way home."

I laughed at the thought and the casual way she accepted him and knew him and cared for him. I felt hysteria gulpingly near, it would have been easy to scream and babble. I missed her utterly. I could feel how real and valuable every moment of living was for her. "It's a gift," she once told me in the midst of one of my long, speculative lectures on life.

"Are you okay? I'm sorry about the restaurant, but your first message said you'd call again at 8:00 and it's almost 9:00. So I thought I'd try calling you."

"Thank you. I'm sorry, too. Wanna try again?"

"Uh. Sure. When?"

"Now?"

Pause.

Wait to breathe.

"OK. Yes. I'd like to see you tonight, Phillip."

"All right. I'll meet you where we met the first night. The Church, OK?"

"OK," she laughed.

"I'll leave now. Come as soon as you can. I'm desperate to see you, Clio, please hurry."

"OK."

"One more thing. Please bring the message tape from your answering machine."

"What?"

"Please, Clio, just bring the tape. I'll explain. Good-bye."

I hung up on her and ran to the bath, shedding clothes like they were burning. Buttons flew and chattered across the floor. I was out the back door in twelve minutes wearing my best tailored blue blazer, white shirt, rep tie, khakis and boat shoes, a total reversion to childhood. I carried the Thunder Stick inside the jacket.

Quick-stepping up the alley to Mass. Ave. there were no vehicles or noise behind me, but I felt cross hairs on my cervical vertebrae. I caught a northbound Red and White cab.

"Quincy Market."

We rattled out onto Storrow, got off at the rotary on Cambridge to Court to Congress.

"This is fine," I told the cabby, giving him a five in front of Brannigan's.

"Sheriff or husband," he asked.

"Huh?"

He just laughed and I left, heading for the still-crowded consumer theme park. I went into a building on the left, up two stories, over, down, one story back to where I started and out the door. As I walked, I felt sure someone moved with me about 30 yards back on the other side. I went into the Durgin Park Fishhouse, the crowded picnic table noise and brick wall echoes thickened the air, already dense with cigarette smoke and fish and Mel-Fry. Quickly downstairs and by the vacant "wait here" stand, I went directly down the hall towards, then past, the Men's and Women's to the Fire Exit with the big red bar that said: "Alarm will sound."

It did; but the City Cab I caught on Clinton took me out of earshot quickly. It was driven by a young woman whose hair reminded me of Clio, a Polish name though, playing a Bonnie Raitt tape. She let me off at Park Street Station where the Green Line took me to Copley.

Clio was getting out of a cab as I walked up.

She looked lovely in a green knit dress that showed her strong and full body a little lasciviously, or was it just me?

"Tie," she smiled as she watched me walk towards her.

"Dear Clio," I touched her hand and held it lightly as I kissed her cheek, "Dear Clio."

She moved back slowly and took my hand as she looked into my face. I seemed to fall into her as in my dream of falling. It took all my strength to hold back tears.

"I have missed you so," I said with all my heart.

She looked down, then back up to my face.

"I've missed you, too. C'mon," she tugged my hand towards the door the brown-uniformed man held open for us, "I've been hungry all day."

At an over-linened table in gorgeous creamy light, with excellent food and invisible, efficient service, we were back together again and my words poured out. As I sat down, she asked if I was feeling all right.

"Why?"

"You look, I don't know, not tired, but pale or something."

"I'm sorry, I'm not all right. Not all right at all. I've stumbled into something big, real big, and I'm scared."

"Is it the Swiss thing you did?"

"Yeah, kinda. It's real confused and I can't prove anything, but there's lots of money involved—a billion dollars—and some real scary people."

"What is it? What's the story?"

"Clio, I promise I'll tell you the entire story when we are both safe."

We looked at each for a while.

"You will be safer," I said, "believe me."

"Okay," she finally agreed, not smiling, "but you promise, the entire story."

"I promise."

Still unsmiling, she held out her hand and I shook it and then I held it to my cheek and nearly cried.

She pulled back her hand a little slowly and saw how deeply I was feeling, but said nothing.

"Clio," I began, "I'm not very good about feelings. I'm out of touch with a lot of things about myself. Most of my life has been a flight from any kind of intimacy. You are only the second woman with whom I've ever had an emotional argument. I never cared enough to get mad. You. You engage me so much in life the way you enjoy your moments, your earnest and complete self.

"I have been told that I put myself first, but it's not true. I never put anything first. For all my life, as far as I can tell, I have not cared about anything or any person or any city or any situation for any significant amount of time. I took what came, did what was around, went where there was to go. And left. Always left.

"In the last few days, I have seen how the world could be completely taken away from me and how it might be given.

"Whatever happens, it only matters to me from now on whether or not I can come back to you.

"I have lied to you and I have been... worse. I deeply apologize for all of it. I am at the bottom of my life right now. And I can end up here or you can help me construct a reasonable human being out of this mess.

"I am going to have to go away again. For... our common good. But I will come back and I will tell you the entire story. May I come back?"

"Yes," she said in her green-eyed way, "you may."

I nearly sobbed aloud with relief, but the flood of pleasure and happiness, her smile, the dinner, the wine brought me around.

At one point, she stopped me by taking my hand.

"I can figure that you lied about the scrapbook and computer disks."

"I... "

She stopped me again with her hand.

"I don't like that and you haven't said you're sorry."

"I am sorry! But the whole idea was so preposterous when I left and so dangerous when I came back. I'm very sorry. It was, you'll see, I don't know, but I apologize."

"I accept. Do you want me to do anything this time?"

My God, what a feeling.

"No, I want you as far away from this as can be. I won't see you again until it's safe."

"What about tonight?"

"If my phone is tapped, your apartment could be watched by now. When I heard your voice, I wanted to get you off the line and warn you face to face. No one followed me and we never said the Copley, just the Church, remember? So, to keep absolutely safe, after we split up here, you should go stay somewhere anonymously for a few weeks. I had in mind a visit to Colorado"

"Colorado?"

I explained an intermodal route I had planned to Crested Butte and gave her the name of a restaurant to check for mail. I gave her all but three hundred of my cash and one of my bank cards.

"Just to be safe," I said.

"Scary people?" she asked.

"Very scary. But call this number." I wrote Petra's from memory. "When it's clear, I'll leave a message there for you."

There was another reason to stay alive, preventing Clio from hearing Petra's polymorphous perverse take on my personality, but after Clio, Petra was the closest thing to an acquaintance I had left.

"Is this your friend Ackley you told me about?"

"No, she, her name's Petra. It means rock, she's Danish. I tried to live with her once, but it didn't work. She was the first woman I ever argued with. When I left, she told me that she had done all the hard work on me, and the next time I might be able to get it right. I hope she was right."

"Do you trust her?"

"In a sense, but not emotionally."

"Not emotionally, like what?"

"I mean, with my feelings. I couldn't dare care for her, she's too good at hurting. I could not tolerate her anger. I never knew where it came from. She was very incisive and threw things."

"Yeeks. Threw things. What did you do?"

"Ducked."

We both laughed and I was the happiest I had ever been in my life.

At the end of the meal, I said, "I'm lost without you, Clio. I have no idea what I've been doing before you or why. I've been alone all my life, more so when I've tried to be with people. But being with you is like going through a door to a place where I'm someone else. Thank you."

"Phillip...," she started to say, but I held up my hand.

"Please, let me say one other thing. I have done a lot of stupid and unkind things, but I promise I will do everything I can to change. I want to get back to where we were in the days before I left."

She leaned forward on the table and looked at me with such compassion. Our awareness of each other seemed to grow. She leaned closer and her breasts shifted freely under the dress.

"What about the nights?" She smiled slightly.

"Have you ever slept at the Copley?" I asked, looking straight back with, no doubt, a smile of my own.

"Not yet."

"Check, please!" I mouthed the words and mimed the universal signing gesture to our waiter.

Twelve

At the registration desk, I showed my passport and gave the clerk four fifties plus a story about lost luggage. He gave me the key and promised to send up courtesy packages for us both. I embroidered on the story with Clio nodding and thanking the clerk for his sympathy and help. When he asked where we were arriving from, she was faster than I.

"Ireland. We were visiting my great aunt in Bantry. She's eighty-three and walks three miles a day."

The clerk turned his gape to her and must have seen the same glow I felt in her presence. He never noticed how egregiously I misspelled my own name nor how illegibly I signed it.

He was telling her how much he wanted to visit the old country when I passed back the registration card and turned her gently away. She waved over her shoulder at him.

"Do you really have a real aunt in Bantry?" I asked as the elevator doors opened.

She pulled me into the car and we stepped together in an embrace that started at the knees and ended at the hips and deepened and softened and arms and legs and there and then the bell pinged and the doors sighed open.

We slowly came unglued and I got a hand on the rubber safety strip before the doors reclosed completely. She hung languidly back against the elevator wall and I pulled her, arm fluidly extended, with me out the door. She came along slowly, rolling her movements, looking right in my eyes.

"This way," I said, breaking contact briefly to glance at the number plaques, "to the right."

We managed the walk down the hall with sufficient decorum. I put the key in the door and opened it a few feet, then turned and lifted her in my arms to her surprise and to a kiss that was just soft and kind.

As we separated and opened our eyes, I carried her in. The only place to go was the bed covered in eyelet cotton. We kissed again, deeper this time.

"Wait," she said, putting her hand on my chest. "I'll have to wear this dress out in the morning, let me at least hang it up."

She stood up and pointed behind her neck under her hair.

"Help me with this clasp." She held her hair up and stray wisps and freckles dusted the skin there. I bent my mouth to the place just exposed below the hairline. She shivered and hummed a little and backed into my front, her hips rubbed my erection and she made another throaty noise.

"The clasp."

I did as asked and the two sides of the dress fell away from her spine to the beginning of a dark slip.

Holding the dress up with one hand at her throat, she went to the closet and got a hanger. One true sign of a luxury hotel, the hangers have real hooks. She took this one to the bathroom and I hung my blazer and tie on another; kicked off shoes, pulled off socks. I was sitting on the bed, wiggling my toes in the rug, when she came through the doorway of the bath with the light behind her; her hips and legs and the spaces in between showed through the thin slip which seemed to be all she now wore.

She turned the light off and walked towards me with that utterly delightful directness I had seen from the first, smiling a bit, but also a little uncertain. Bathroom lights will do that.

"Shy one," I recited, "Shy one.

Shy one of my heart.

She walks in the firelight.

Pensively apart."

The only light in the room now came through the curtains behind me.

"Is there a view?" she asked, going to the side of the curtains and pulling the cord.

Was there ever; the Square far below us, the dark twinkling mass of the Garden and Commons, the blaze of the State house and downtown to the right. She stood looking out and I stepped up, looking over her shoulder. The slip had spaghetti straps and was a dark, dark emerald in silk with a panel of sheer lace across her breasts and at the hem. Her skin seemed lunar pale and milky in the light from the city.

Lightly, touching one shoulder, I lifted her hair and kissed again the back of her neck. She gave a small laugh and then moved into me again, lifting her right arm to hug my head. I slid both arms around her waist and pulled her to me all along our hungry lengths and reached up to cup her breasts as I straightened up. Her head went back and she stretched her neck, arching against me and my hands, face to the ceiling, eyes closed, mouth so slightly open.

I saw our reflection in the window and held us there as she relaxed and opened her eyes.

"Someone could see us," she said, after I saw her focus on the reflection.

"Not even with the MIT telescope," I said, "and besides, they will never think of looking for us here."

She shivered a laugh and snuggled into me, turning around.

"I'm tired of backward kissing," she explained, "let's do it this way awhile."

And so, for awhile, we did.

We were both breathing fairly deeply when I broke.

"I need to, uh, wash my hands."

"If you're going for a contraceptive, I have been taking the pill again since thirty days before you left. I was going to tell you before you ran off. That's one reason I got mad at you. The next time, I had wanted to say, you don't need to, that I trusted you and know you would not hurt me."

"And now," I asked, needing so very much to hear it.

"I trust you, Phillip. I know you would not do anything to hurt me."

I just held her and cried. All the remorse and pain of the last days of Ackley and Camille, all my guilt and fear of Ana and the rest flowed out of me in deep, chesty sobs, but it was a healing grief and it washed out of me; and she held us together.

As I quieted, she asked, "Will you be okay, now," and went into the bath, returning with a warm, wet wash cloth and soft towel. She washed and dried my face and smoothed my hair with her hands and then kissed me.

"Now," she said, "let me show you something."

She stood up from where I sat at the desk chair and stepped back from me and the window light. With her right hand, she lowered the slip off her left shoulder and off her breast. She looked down and then at me and, leaning down, just slightly caught the hem in thumb and forefinger of each hand and slowly lifted, looking into my eyes.

I was intoxicated.

Reds and greens, and arms and legs and lips and

kisses and grasping and deeply holding. And on the bed she swelled against me, raising us both with the power of her climax, her muscles squeezed, rippled, and I surged into her, my head snapping with each wave. And we rode on great wings in broad reaches through the wind, with the surf sounding below us.

When the present returned, we were breathing together, sharing the job of holding me up, still together.

"I saw the ocean," she said.

"We were soaring."

"Yes."

∞

In a bit, we began moving. I retrieved clothing discarded in mid-sentence, she took a shower and came out in a monogrammed, golden-yellow terry robe. It looked like a good idea, and was.

She was under the covers with her robe at the foot of the bed and I was halfway towards her when someone knocked and called something at the door.

The fish eye revealed an anamorphically distorted megacephalic in a brown uniform carrying two parcels.

"Who is it?"

"Bellhop."

Well, maybe.

I opened the door the chain distance and looked in person.

It was a doughy kind of face of any years from twenty to thirty.

"Courtesy packs." He held up two white-wrapped bundles.

I shut the door, reopened it, thanked and tipped him after getting the packages. On the way back to the bed, I read the contents.

"You get a nail file, but I get deodorant. Let me know if you want to trade."

I took off my robe and turned out the light, getting in with her.

Our hands reached together and we slept facing each other, touching.

∞

I awoke a little before 5:30 as the sky brightened slowly, cloudy, and watched the light change in the room, hearing her breathe and move beside me. Memories of the night before stirred me and I slid next to her and she snuggled warmly into me. I began to stroke the backs of her thighs. Her breathing changed and her eyes, still closed, twitched. She rolled over as she liked to sleep, and her legs opened and I moved first my hands, then myself between them.

Soon she stopped pretending to be asleep and we moved together gently, kissing as we came together.

"I love you, Clio" I said to her.

"I love you, Phillip," she replied.

∞

"What time is it?"

"Just seven, I think."

"Am I really going to Colorado in an evening dress without seeing you again?"

"I think it's the best thing you could do."

And she did.

I looked out the window, trying to see her in the street, but only saw us again at the window last night. The day was darkening instead of getting lighter; a storm. In the climate-controlled room, I had not noticed a thing, pressurized.

I called Lieutenant Davis just to make sure he wasn't looking for me. He was out.

I called my machine. It rang, clicked, spoke.

"Phillip, this has now gone far enough," Claude-Philippe's unmistakable voice said. "Take the next available TWA flight to Paris. There is an envelope at the Logan desk for you under the name Sydney Carton. It is vitally important to you. And to Miss Murphy."

Beep.

∞

So I did.

From the airport, I called Davis again debating what to tell him. He was out. I left the message I had had to leave town. Family emergency. Tell the lab to check the Quadram clock. I spelled it. I said I would call again.

I wondered. If not, it would not matter what the Toshiba's internal clock card read.

I tried to imagine asking Lt. Davis to put Clio and me in protective custody while he looked for an eight-thousand-year-old cult in western France.

The tickets were coach, and the flight was full. We left at 11:00 a.m. There was no time to do anything but ditch the Thunder Stick and mail the South Station claim check and Clio's message tape to Davis.

At Logan, I bought a pair of clean socks. I was tracked from the ticket desk. The envelope I picked up was a bright royal blue. Two medium-sized men, one in grey, one in brown, took up positions about 10 meters back of me on opposite sides of the corridor and went at exactly my pace to the gate. They left me at Security.

International Departures is relatively clean at Logan. I bought a bottle of Jack Daniel's at the duty-free shop, a couple of bars of luxury-priced chocolate, and got on the silver bird like a good tourist. I had gotten the exit row aisle again, so it was not too bad. A long-faced woman with a long-faced child sat next to me. The child colored and listened to a headset. The mother read and slept.

I tried to prepare myself for the next step, whatever it was going to be. From the looks of things back at Logan, I was apparently not going to have much choice in the matter.

There was a meal. I ate the fruit. Drank juices. Thought about the fifth of Jack, tried to relax.

For hours I wrangled with my situation, but my thoughts were like a cage full of hyperactive mice.

The plain fact was that I was not in control of the play. If I hid successfully, they would look for and might very well find Clio. If I was unsuccessful at hiding, they could readily have us both. If I gave myself up, Clio had a much better chance and I was burning with a rage over the deaths of Ackley and Camille and a terror for dear Clio. It was the purest fire. I wanted to engage this threat; I wanted the confrontation. And I knew what I wanted from it.

I thought of the night of the Pilobolus dance benefit and the plain stupidity of my character there made me feel like low tide in a dirty harbor. At that point, I had been thinking of Clio as simply young, semi-exotic, suburban ethnic, a wised-up child of a broken marriage, two thirds my years. Yet she could talk about dance with a crippled stranger, make jokes with the deaf, wink at the marked for life and do it with such honest good spirit that all were charmed. And I, with all my generations of advantages, too much education, white glove etiquette lessons, dance classes, un-air-conditioned summer afternoons balancing crustless cucumber sandwiches and the desire to scream, endless funereal family dinners with lectures on what was expected of one, I was an outcast, headed for the bar, a watcher from afar, carefully disengaged, endlessly cynical, just waiting for the flaw to be revealed, the ugly words spoken, the meanness and banality to show through.

I longed for her, grieved for her absence, feared for her safety, wanted to cry with the misery of separation; my precious loneliness, how small my life had been before, how little it would be without her. How soul-expandingly much it might be possible for me to love her. Claude-Philippe I could face; I felt there was no power as strong as these feelings.

There was also no way to prepare. There was no value to thinking about steps and strategies. I pushed all thoughts about next steps away. They wanted me to come to them; I wanted to get us out. The clearest way out was through. I thought about Clio. And coming back. And I held to that.

∞

We landed at de Gaulle, eleven p.m. local time. It looked like a "Barbarella" set. After the last official station, you make a right and go through a set of opaque painted glass doors to the public area. As soon as I stepped through the doors, two dark-haired men with strong, closed Romany faces converged on me, throwing their arms around me as though I were a comrade, roaring in drunken, garlic-laden French and showing me a silenced small caliber automatic in a tasteful matte-black finish.

Les amis pulled me through another set of doors and the camaraderie faded to a pair of high-bicep holds. I tried to look into their faces, but they kept their eyes averted, heads turned, watching opposite sides, like halves of a split-brain creature.

The next door led outside to the parking area. They accompanied me to a van and sat us down on a bench in the unlighted back. One tapped on the partition to the driver's compartment and the van pulled out.

Many turns and maybe two miles of driving later, we stopped. And waited. And waited. I tried to talk to my escorts, but they made it immediately and painfully clear I was to be quiet.

After about twenty minutes as the pain was receding, two quick knocks came at the back door. The nearer of my companions knocked once and the other pulled a lined ski mask over my head, backwards. Two more knocks and I heard the door open and was handed out. Something was thrown over my shoulders that could have been a blanket and I was quick-marched thirty yards to a set of springy pull-down steps of what could only be a small plane.

They led me to the left and cross-strapped me into a backward-facing seat. The engine vibration made the compartment rattle and I thought I could smell coffee. We took off and flew for somewhere over an hour, but less than three hours.

The straps were locked.

After landing, I heard several people pass through the compartment and exit the plane, but I stayed seated.

A few minutes later, I heard a turbo-jet helicopter rev up and take off; it sounded large and nearby.

Another few minutes and I was back on my feet, in motion, still seeing nothing, smelling humid wool and JP exhaust, then diesel.

A car, this time, and a short ride to a destination I had already guessed. I wondered if André was driving. I had mercifully forgotten about him until then. My death was a real outcome of this if nothing went right. I thought of him doing it. He would not use a gun. He would use his hands.

I was led across gravel to a hall, up a stair to a room in the old castle and sat down in a chair, straight backed, large, hard and wooden. The hood was pulled off by someone from behind. I heard a door close.

The lights flared and sparkled in my eyes, my vision blurry. I rubbed them.

∞

"Mr. Gardiner, you have caused us exceptional

concern. Before I decide whether to have both you and Ms. Murphy eliminated, I want to know the whereabouts of the data base you stole."

My eyes focused on Claude-Philippe and I saw the tapestry behind him. I looked to his right and saw Ana watching me without expression, the original blank and pitiless gaze. The Sphinx who slew all who could not solve the riddle of man's life.

"And the scrapbook, we should like that back, too."

I turned to her right, stunned to hear and see Ken Sedgwick. The fiber seemed to melt in my body, I felt goosy-liquid, transparent, insubstantial, overwhelmed.

Ana continued, "Not that there could be anything useful in poor Baxter's pathetic memento. It was such an embarrassment, it should have been burned in front of him. But he was an object of pity."

The three of them faced me across a substantial table from which my chair was set back.

Claude-Philippe spoke. "Your response, Mr. Gardiner."

"First of all, Clio knows nothing, has nothing. She is not involved."

"On the contrary. If you do not cooperate, you will see her dead and then you will be disposed of."

"And if I cooperate?"

"When these things are back in our hands, we will discuss your future."

I imagined it would be a short discussion.

"You're too late. I packed everything up; in three days it goes to the State Attorney General's office, unless I stop it."

"Goes as what, Phillip, science fiction?" Ana sneered. "He has done nothing. He thinks he is the cowboy," she said to the others.

Claude-Philippe spoke again, "You have the rest of the night to think about it."

"Take him," he said to André, who proceeded to.

"No. Wait," I shouted.

Miraculously, André did; but he kept me facing out the room.

"What is it?" Ana asked my back.

"Prove to me Clio is safe, and I'll give you everything. I just want to know how you found me. In Brest as Sydney Carton; in Boston, at Ackley's."

"The torc. It was a transmitter."

"And Ackley's death?"

"It was a mistake."

"A mistake?"

"He was thought to be you; there was a struggle. Your friend was outraged by the intruder and defended the computer quite violently. Our directions were very clear. We wanted to see what information you had. You were on the verge of being dangerous to us."

"And Clio," I said, "prove to me she's safe and I'll give you everything."

"Really, Mr. Gardiner, you disappoint me," said Claude-Philippe. "That is not at all how it plays. You give us the items, Clio lives. Beyond that, we promise you nothing."

"Clio knows nothing."

"And the diskettes and the scrapbook?"

"Now you disappoint me. I will tell you that I have arranged for them to be sent, along with copies of twenty one interesting birth and death records, to some professionally curious and persistent people if I have trouble returning from this trip. Beyond that I can promise you nothing."

"If we were to believe you, this would be an impasse."

"An impasse! Do you expect to get away with cold-blooded murder? Ackley and Baxter count for nothing in your scheme?"

"Phillip, now, once again, you are the disappointment. How can someone as cynical as you be so naive?

We gave them the best we could at the time."

"Death was the best you could do?"

"Because of your meddling, it was the only thing possible. But do not expect we shall have any problem with the police; it is usually simple to kill a total stranger with impunity. The police need a connection they can understand. You, for example, are the obvious link between the late Messrs. Ackley and Baxter. And as you have now left the country without police permission and on a false passport, your position on this matter is somewhat precarious."

"I imagine Mr. Gardiner is tired from his long trip and may need time to think over his choices," Ken said.

André did a little of the Tighten-up. At the door I yelled back, "And Vera Eliane? Where is she?"

"Aunt Vera is gone where she wished to be. Should you see her before I do, ask her if she is happy now." Ana's laugh followed me down the hall in André's grip.

∞

André led me out through the stairway door by which I had first entered the chamber with Ana. He handled me like a clumsy piece of luggage, down past the bell chamber of the postern door through a large iron grated cage door and down again below ground water level to the dungeon. On the way, I felt the crumbly damp, rotten texture of the age-old stone wall in the wet of the earth and wondered what they planned to do with my body. André deposited me in a doorless cell with a straw mattress and a single candle; he lit the candle and then went back up the stone stairs and out of the dungeon, locking the large iron grate at the top with a substantial clang. It echoed. Something dripped. Something rustled.

I stared at the burning candle blankly for several minutes; a side melted, evaporated in smoke, dripped a long tongue of wax that curled a piece of straw. I picked up the straw, held it in the flame and watched it burn. The candle got smaller.

I pulled a straw from the mattress and marked the candle in the middle, then at the approximate top and bottom quarters. I stared into the flame and considered the choices and actions available as the candle burnt down to the first mark. When the flame consumed the mark, I got up with the candle in my left hand and began exploring the dungeon, keeping a solid wall to my right, a rational search pattern. I found other stairs ending in walled doorways. As the candle burnt down, I moved faster, keeping my right hand on the wall, watching the footing ahead. At the steps André brought me down, the gate, shaken, seemed solidly locked. I explored past the gate until the candle burnt out and then found the way back to the gate by touch in the dark.

It has been my clear experience that the lowest point is the easiest place from which to set direction. The situation reduced to the basics enforces clear thinking. When you're all the way down, up is easy to find.

As far as I could tell, there was only one way in. I began to slowly shake the barred, locked gate. It moved a little for me. It was huge; strap iron, two to three inches wide, one-quarter to one-half inch thick on six to eight inch centers. The metallic tone as the door's weight shifted was deep and broad. There was serious gravity involved.

Working steadily, I tried to rock the gate's mass against the bottom hinge, working the bottom hinge anchor in the old masonry and the wetted rock.

The legs are the strongest muscles of the human body. Biceps are showy but no curler can beat a dead lift or squat for tonnage. I began by finding secure footing on the step, just below the lock. With my back straight against the gate, legs one quarter bent, I took a good reverse grip and a deep breath and released it. And strained; and lifted, maybe just slightly; and relaxed. A sixteenth of an inch or less, but it dropped. I took another deep breath.

I did three sets of ten and was sweating in the cool air. My legs were getting pumped and the hinge was giving more, working a half inch up and down and pulling free of the wall, leaving a diligent little pile of masonry dust, just visible from the two bulb unit outside that painted such penitential patterns on me. It was cold. I got back to work, loosening the bottom hinge ten lifts at a time; sissy squats the steriod boys would call the exercise. I thought of Officer Lobosco and did the next set to twelve.

The gate began to flex with it own life, balance, movement, inertia, mass.

With the leverage of the gate's mass, I slowly loosened the second and then, cautiously, the third hinge. The huge gate's balance shifted, reached an extreme, then held. The lower bolt sagged outward but still held. Then the lock broke apart scattering shrapnel which slugged my right arm numb. The edge of the gate near me dropped to the step below, the upper and middle bolts flying out like spent shells, and the great thing slid to the side, tilting toward me. With the greatest effort, I pushed and held its balance. Re-settled, the gate's corner was dug into the stone three inches from my foot and holding.

I backed off the pressure I was using against the gate, one muscle at a time, slowly, slowly. It was quite, quite big. It could fall forward at any point, but it now rested stably on the corner and the final lower bolt. Whenever the final bottom bolt dropped, the gate would tumble, slide, chop, slice, dice, blend, and puree its way down the steps.

But, there were now openings at the top and bottom where the gate sagged sideways out of the doorway. The opening near the top hinge looked human size, but would require climbing the gate. The larger opening on the bottom was about the size of a case of wine, a dog-sized rat could crawl even beneath the gate's fingers nearest the sagging lower bolt.

Assuming the worst would happen, I decided I would rather be reaching for the top of the gate than trying to get out from under it.

I looked up and touched the bands of iron. The gate moved lightly as I reached for it, flexing. The straps seemed alive to my touch. I began to climb right above the point that dug into the stone step and followed a line up from there to the gap, ready to let go and do what, I had no idea, at any moment.

As my right hand reached for the top edge, the bottom bolt dropped and the gate revolved against the top stair edge and the hinge side of the doorway. I dove for the floor beyond as the great iron mass revolved, scraped through the door and slid down the stone stairs, clattering and banging like a train wreck. I raced away from the still-echoing noise and rounded on the postern gate, then up to the ground level. The hardwood courtyard door was barlocked. Up the next flight. The council chamber door was solid modern steel. I went back to the postern door, opened it and looked at the moat bright by the moonlight. Smelled it. Looked again.

The primordial stew, a protein soup. Do the funky chicken. I jumped in.

Knees bent. Eyes closed. Legs crossed. Grabbed what I was taught to grab.

The water belched me greenly to the surface. It smelled like mud. And vegetable rot.

I could taste the smell.

The risen moon now lit the moat, lit the far wall where a part of the upper rock had fallen into the water. Cautiously, I paddled to the wall, recoiling from the touch of various soft slippery things in the water, finally reaching mossy stones.

These were all the worst conditions for climbing,

I thought, taking off left shoe and sock with right hand, tucking under left arm, taking off right shoe and sock, socks inside of shoes, shoestrings tied together, around the neck over the back, all the while looking for The Line, estimating distances—twenty meters maybe less. Vertical distance is hard to estimate in the dark. It was, after all, only one step at a time. The wonderful thing I learned on my first climb took over: complete concentration, no thought of before or afterward, only the choices and holds of the present. Colorado sandstone or New Hampshire granite: no thought. My hands and toes pulled chunks of moss loose digging for solid rock, soon the toes bled, then a hand, but The Line was going and I made the top.

∞

There was a warm breeze like a breath of summer with cut grass and fresh hay. I recalled the sound of the gate falling and ran for the shadows of a tree line.

There was no alarm nor new lights in the old building. I fell back to the earthwork, the old circle. Vera had said, "...a Templar ruin built over a Roman hill fort constructed on top of a Breton barrow..." Was this the clockwork, the antidote, eternity's analemma unwound; mounded? The top of this mound, though, was overgrown with dense shrubs and young trees at the place I struck it and only became at first cleared and then manicured as it approached the new building near the spot where I had watched Ana and Vera leave the Chateau. There was another circle of stones, Vera had said, northeast of here a few kilometers.

If there were anything to my theory—I calculated the time difference. Five fifty-two a.m. would be the equinox—I looked at the sky. It is possible to tell the hours by the stars. I hadn't a clue. My body felt like it should be yesterday at noon or tomorrow at five. Here it was still dark which meant that, as far as I could tell, it was not yet dawn.

In a wide, cautious circle, I walked around the new building to the barn, thinking about how handy one of those brass stairway runner rods would be and feeling a blister form on each foot from my still-squelching shoes. As the water evaporated, shivers ran through my long muscles and my calves and arches felt crampy.

The big center barn doors were opened to the night and I stepped in from the shadowed side. The horse in the near stall snickered and then was still. Finally dilated, I walked at high stealth up the center, slide step, rebalance, slide step, quarter the area.

Marcel was stabled just inside the moonlit entrance. There was a bridle next to his door, but it was little more than a hemp rope lead. There was no bit.

"Marcel," I whispered as I walked towards the dutch-cut half door, "hey, Marcel. Remember me?"

Not particularly. But he did not spook and pull a hi-ho Silver in the stall.

I made a clicking noise and he nodded his head down and up as he walked over.

"Want to go for a walk in the moonlight?"

∞

He took the bridle well. The animal in the next stall snorted and clattered when I swung the door open, but then was quiet. Mercifully there was a saddle blanket on a work table next to the open door. I led Marcel there, threw on the blanket, and using the table and his mane, climbed aboard.

He was tall. I had forgotten or maybe the insecurity of my unsaddled seat made it look further to fall.

The band of light that cut into the darkness where we stood made the outside look utterly open. I thought about going out the back, but Marcel and I would not be as quiet, or as unnoticed by the other tenants, going out as I was, alone, on the way in. I did not want a ruckus.

We rode out into the eerie no longer night, every sensitivity on high. The fading moon saw us head for the far trees, angling at forty-five degrees from where I fleetingly aligned Polaris. The fields rose and the predawn sky brightened. We found our way through two fences.

About a half an hour later, at the top of a saddle back between two large hills, I looked into a down-sloping valley. To the right there appeared to be a dark mass. Or masses. On a round, flattened mound.

I stayed at the contour of the gap and closed on the site from above.

It was a circle of upright stones. There were no henged top stones. Inside the circle appeared to be a number of other low and high stones. We circled. Saw no one.

The sky began to lighten silver yellow in the East.

We stopped. Marcel exhaled and I considered getting off. As much as I wanted a relief from what parts of his body were doing to parts of mine, I could not figure how I could get back on.

At least down at the stones, there would be a step. I rode to them. Saw no one.

From horseback, they were still large, but not as overpowering. Marcel whinnied as one of his shoes skidded on a flat stone laid in the ground, part of a path, I saw, around the outside of the circle. With urging, he took us between two stones into the center. The area was forty or fifty feet in diameter, less than half a football field. The interior stones, lumped and humped, stood in no order I could see.

I stepped off the horse at a convenient, low-fallen upright.

André stood up from behind the next rock.

Nemesis smiled at me with a closed mouth and brought up to his shoulder a long shard of stone, a club really, in his big hands. I dropped the halter.

He moved out from the rock. I backed around another one. Marcel moved away and began to graze.

I ran to another, wider stone, caught my toe on a low one and, stumbling, found myself now facing André and his weapon. We moved around in a circle, but he closed the distance smoothly.

The rage and anger that I had felt from him from the first was gone. He was happy and relaxed now. He smiled at me again.

And swung the stone shaft past my face then reversed to bring it down on my skull. I pulled away, but the club crunched into my left shoulder and the whole arm went dead. I looked and it hung forward. The club then struck my head.

I fell most slowly to the left to land on the arm I thought had no more feeling. The pain shot through my dreamy vision. And André stood above me.

It seemed to happen forever. He raises the club above his head. I see he is up on his toes. I reach for his cuff and pull. I hear a dog bark in my left ear and a high cry from the horse which towers above us both. And André falls away.

I rolled, and scuttled to the right to a nearby rock, shocky cold, long muscle tremors, my hands too weak to grip for shaking. A strange noise, throaty and rattling. Was that me? Then nothing.

The horse was far away, the angles canted, space swooped. A dog? No dog.

In the moonlight, I saw that my left arm was covered with blood and the blood was flowing. It seemed to purr and shimmer.

I reached to my head where I could feel nothing but found a soft hole and touched something softer within it. I smelled dry sage and saw the Rocky Mountains on a July day in the distance, Middle Brush Creek below. There was our car. By the stream.

I heard a scream.

There was a feeling of finality and remorse, but acceptance.

And then I remembered all that brought me here and I tried to crawl out to the stone path, but now I could not move and I watched the sky spin under me as I fell finally, sickeningly, up.

∞

Noise.

A noise.

Voice.

A voice.

The voice had an echo that attenuated and rang with a beat that synchronized with the waving of the shapes and proportions before me.

"*Qu'y a-t-il?*"

It came again and rang and beat and beats and waves. I tried to raise myself, but lost my balance and fell to the left on one knee and then on my back.

A black dog towered above me and was gone.

"*Qu'y a-t-il?*"

I could not recall a word of French.

"Here," I tried to call from a hollow cold place far away. I heard a croak.

I was looking up at Paul Languedoc.

"*Qu'est-ce que c'est?*"

I could whistle.

One note. Two notes. Four notes. The Wa-ter's Wide.

"Phillip? From *les Etats-Unis? Où est-il?*"

Five more notes.

And I Can-not Cross.

As he bent down to me, I rolled my intact right side towards him and his outstretched arm. He grabbed for my hand as it touched him and I clung to him.

Up.

He was asking something I could no longer hear and I leaned on his left side, steering us to the outer circle.

At the first step, we seemed to fall against a current that wanted to push us backwards and each step seemed composed of smaller increments of movement. I held us into this current and like a boat against the wind, we beat on.

Shards of what appeared to occur can be described, many things simply cannot. The sky would wheel and another fate would be before me. Some new voice would speak. In clearest vision, all manner of being.

At length, the voices resolved to my own.

It was bellowing.

"No."

"No."

"No."

∞

I looked at Paul. He could not hear me.

Each stone, each step was passed in strange dimension and great emotion. I saw not my own life, but life and self and every other.

I saw Ana in greedy eagerness and I saw myself in her. To live forever. To have anything.

I saw Clio and saw her as Ana saw me.

And the screaming.

At mid-point in vast, unconscious dreamwork, I noticed Paul's dog. It was in the center of the circle of stones, standing upright, but bent almost double as though chasing its tail. It appeared to be watching us intently standing frozen and twisted on two legs.

There were circles of light in the sky.

I saw a chain of life that was an organic beauty of great accomplishment, refinement, and power and a heavy burden, a great distraction and a foul deceiver, avaricious, unevolving, ultimately conservative, permanently infertile.

What is the being that is all these things? Is it human? Is this life? Or something else?

I saw life's values reverse like the negative of a favorite picture. It could all be different. I felt the great power.

The last consciousness I have of that state is an experience like the dream of the hooded figure reaching for my hand and, as I am searching for the face to see if I should accept the touch, it turns to me.

And it is myself.

∞

And we came back to the bloody smear where we began. Stepping onto that stone, I heard the dog bark as it streaked to us and we turned to each other.

"Phillip. You are Phillip. What have you done? What have you taken us through?"

My own screams still echoed in my head. No. No to what? To life? To death?

I stared in wonder at my left arm's implausible, uninjured normalcy as it reached to touch my dry, dirty, undamaged skull.

The dog reached us and slowed warily.

Paul turned to her and whistled and she quieted and came closer, but still kept an eye on me while she sniffed him.

"Paul," I said, looking at the stones and the brightening sky. "*C'est une bonne idée, allons-y.*"

I picked up Marcel's lead and tried to walk away.

"What has happened?"

I tried to explain. "I think we have taken back a year of our lives. I think we are now a year younger. For every time you do this—walking around such a circle like this, at the equinox, you unwind a year."

Paul was agitated, shaking.

"That is... but...."

I could see the experience had touched him, too. But his response surprised me.

"And does this mean I lose everything I learned this last year?" he asked. "Things I may relearn less well or not get the chance to learn at all? Experiences I can never have again, memories questionable? Have you stolen a year from my life? And the idea of what you say is awful. No one should know if this is true. What evil must be at the heart of an engine for the perpetuation of the flesh."

"Paul," I asked, "Why were you here?"

"This night I had the accident, those years ago. Always on this night I am restless, usually I walk. This time I remembered how to come here. This was where I was coming that night. I know this. *La mademoiselle passera me prendre ici.*"

"She led you here. Was this Vera Eliane?"

He stared blindly at me under the lightening sky.

"What do you know of her?"

"I have met her. She remembered you."

"Where do you meet her? Is she near?"

"I don't know, Paul. But I met her several days ago at the Chateau."

The dog barked again. He was nosing something in the dirt and barking sharply, insistent. It was André, lying on his back, knees and lower legs over the stone that tripped him, his own club buried deep, obliterating his forehead. The eyes bulged, bloody and dark. The tongue protruded. There was more.

"Someone is dead here, Paul, and I must tell you something.

"I think you were here thirty-something years ago for the same reason I am tonight. And I think someone like this dead man thought he did to you what this one tried to do to me. They're guarding a secret and I have learned it. There is a way to reverse age, erase the effects of injury. I have just shown you. If you walk around these stones once for every year, you will grow younger, you could see again."

He was quiet for several minutes.

"This seems unlikely, but you are so sure and just now... it sounds so... but, no. Even if this is true, I would not take back my life, erase my experience. Things I understand now, peace I know, music I can make. These came from injury and age. They are worth more than youth or vision and the opportunity to make less good choices or become someone else I do not want."

"But you, you have done this," he said louder in grieving awareness and shock.

"Yes, to both of us. And, yes, it worked."

"I feel this is an evil thing."

"Let's talk about it somewhere else."

∞

We set off in the direction of his house about fifteen kilometers, ten miles away.

"Don't you see? What I have told you is what you were looking for the night you were injured."

"I do not want to know this thing you cannot take back. Not to age irreversibly. Not to die. No life should have this temptation. If people did not die, they would have to be killed. Death is the balance.

"Monstrous," he called it, "*Monstrueux*".

"Remember Vera Eliane? She remembered you."

"Yes."

He visibly forced himself to stop at that.

"I met her a week ago. At the Castle."

"Yes, how is she?"

"She is dead."

"What? When? You said a week."

"Since then. She wanted to die. She was very old."

"She was old? She was … "

"She was over five thousand years old."

"*Monstrueuse*".

"She was sorry about you. It may have been you, or what happened to you, how she felt about you, that brought her to embrace death."

"What did she say?

"Why should you care for the words of a monster?"

He said nothing more. In a failed attempt at prompting him, I relayed some not altogether verbatim remarks of Vera's. I did not tell him what she had done for him.

We walked through long green grasses in the brightening air and energy and perspective were new. My body seemed to vibrate between awareness of the particularity and novelty and beauty of the moment and the next towering challenge of the situation. In a way, it was a great excitement and joy; but still, with the freedom, fear. And in the face of great fear, greater confidence.

In time, we crossed fields and pastures, the day rising in a glorious North Atlantic High sunrise with clouds that broke into dozens and dozens of low marshmallow shapes grazing the sky like a fat, rich herd of sheep. Marcel accepted it all philosophically. Paul's dog led the way.

As the land began to flatten in a broad alluvial plain, Paul let us through a gate to a dwarf pear orchard drooping with fruit and into his back dooryard. A series of low, lightly-dressed stone buildings half circled us. Three black-faced sheep bleeted and baa-ed behind their fence. The dog barked. Paul went inside briefly and came out with water for the two of us. I found a curry comb and a good-sized roofing nail and went over Marcel tooth, hide and shoes. He was in great shape; one small stone in the left rear; no cuts. Ready to do it again. I patted his neck and turned him in with the sheep. Paul came out with breakfast and let the sheep into the orchard. I got Marcel a half bucket of water and a couple of cups of oats from Paul's kitchen.

In the dooryard, I rinsed the mud and strangely dessicated blood off my hands and head, wadded up the ruins of a jacket and was surprised to find my pen still clipped to the inside left pocket. I felt my scalp and peered at my shoulder where the blows had fallen. Seamless. Good as new. Just like it grew there.

For breakfast, we had an unsweetened thick oat porridge, milk that tasted of onion or garlic, boiled coffee.

In Paul's house, in my stocking feet, I noted the unornamented appearance of a blind man's rooms. Paper seemed unlikely, but I found a large gilt-edged Bible. On the second to the last blank page, I wrote: "Circle the stones counter-clockwise at the equinox."

Paul was visibly distracted and clumsy. Both of us were most physically fatigued by then, but emotionally charged and energetic. There was an amphetamine zing to colors and sound to go with the bone-deep weariness. I felt there were particles of sand in my eyes.

I said nothing more to Paul of what we had left of André in the circle, only that there had been an accident. I did not think either of us was safe company for the other.

"Paul ," I said, "you have not lost a year of your memories. We both remember we met within the last year. You can prove it to yourself. Go to the inn where I stayed and ask how long ago I was there. And while you are there ask Madame Mulon for the book she says her husband left for you. Ask her to read it you."

"*La Ruche d'epi,*" he exclaimed, "*Mulon?*"

"I think he left you an explanation of what happened to you. Maybe more. What happened to him. It may have answers for both of us." I knew it was an unwarranted extrapolation, but I was pulling out all the stops.

"And what about the dead man?"

"I'm leaving now; if you do too, there's no proof we were here together."

Finally, he said, "I think I will do this. For the first time in years my life has been refilled with the unexpected and the long forgotten, perhaps there is some greater strength for me in holding the answers no matter how frightening. Perhaps I am just full of the feeling of this day on me and what you say has happened."

He left.

If I was wanted officially, I could not expect to get away; and if I wasn't, running would only expose me to the others.

The police could follow the trail easily, if they were alerted. Was I safer going to them myself? Or waiting to see who came? No action seemed right. But doing nothing was worse. Not to decide is to decide. I never was good at waiting, but forced myself to hide until dark in the loft of an outbuilding.

I had made three postcards from the flyleaf of an old book of sheet music. On each I wrote my sevenword summary of the secret of the stones and addressed them to Ken, Ana and Claude-Philippe in Boston, Folgoât, and Zurich respectively. Paul had agreed to post them from Morbihan.

At dark that night, in countryman's clothes, I left. Traveling cross-country, it took three nights to reach the outskirts of Rennes.

I walked at night to the waning moon, which, rising later and later, made me stumble in the dark for the early part of each leg when I was still stiff. I ate at coarse *cafés*, slept in insect-ridden piles of chaff and grain and straw, washed in streams.

This was the first time in my life I had traveled a country in a true linear way. I had gone for walks, hikes, climbs and patrols, but they all started and ended with being dropped off and picked up by car, bus or chopper.

I seemed to sink into the land and be absorbed by an impress of the life of the people. I remembered hearing from one of his descendants about the chronicler who accompanied Coronado on his exploration up from Old Mexico, through the El Paso del Norte, across the great Southwestern plains, looking for Quivara and the Mississippi Valley. He refused a horse and walked the way, saying, "If I am to write of this country, I must know it with my feet." Since this probably got him out of wearing armor and sitting a late medieval, Castilian wooden army saddle, it was probably good strategy as well as good philosophy.

What I felt or found was a sense of the joinery of the land and the care and craft of the lives that made it, that passed it on, that lived within it. The fields in fruited harvest fullness were walled by stones and fed by streams set and channelled by long centuries labor, a thousand years and more.

No brook was clotted by debris nor flowed an untended way. The water moved through the land in great smooth sweeps losing grade only slowly, hoarding its water from the sea, sharing it with the land. There were no roadside turnouts with discarded appliances, rotting sofas, trash bags, newspapers and tree stumps. Thomas Jefferson wrote that one only held land rights in usufruct; the right of any generation to the use of the land being conditional on its passing this birthright to the next, improved.

"The earth," he went on, "belongs to the living not the dead."

Neat, narrow gardens and backyard compost; crops already harvested and winter crops sprouting; mustard and kale, bitter rich greens and cruciforms, cabbages and cauliflower.

Since I traveled by dark, I saw few people; what I

rather saw were the artifacts and remnants and spoor of their lives. Each encounter had an apparent significance and the features and small touches of them could move me deeply. The bicycle leaning against the stone dooryard wall where a kitchen window breathed garlic and apples and burgundy and mushrooms spoke volumes of the life within.

The gorgeous curve of handlaid stonework and natural landscape reaching to a distant set of glowing buildings would swell like a cello note in me. In fact the whole walk was as voluptuous as the most seductive music: Brandenburg #2, Toccata and Fugue in D, Rhapsody on a Theme by Paginini, the Moonlight Sonata.

The regularity of the country, its evenness began to hold my eye. Features flowed into each other with gradual smooth fullness as well maintained streams drained fields and lowlands, found larger streams, then rivers; fences became walls, walls became buildings, buildings became villages which swelled and then receded and resolved to buildings, then walls, then fences, then fields and streams.

I saw that humans had done this, had cared for the earth for so long, for each other, for those who will come after them. I saw there was a generative caring force that sustained and gave to the future life which the present knew it must give up. I began to think that sacrifice and kindness were not the anomalies I had always considered them; Paul's instinctive helping hand, Clio's offer, Professor Murphy's willingness to search and answer, Ackley's ultimate gift.

The simple physical experience of walking, eating, walking, sleeping awoke in me, completely isolated from all humans, but aware of them anew in the light of my experience, a great love. A school teacher with whom I walked for five kilometers one night nearly filled my eyes with tears each time he asked a question. "Why are you alone?" "Do you need a place to rest?" His questions sprang from such sympathy, such caring.

One dawning I watched a field of big strangely aligned boulders become a herd of cows.

Another morning just at sunrise when the grasses were still wet and a haze lay on the low shadows, I walked past yet another stone-walled pasture holding several black and white cows. Movement caught my eye as a rabbit hopped along a trail the cows had worn in midfield. The hare stopped and twitched. At the far wall, uphill about fifty yards, a fox was sitting, watching. Frozen, the hare twitched again. The fox raised its head and seemed to look at me. He yawned and retreated over the wall behind him. The hare, still frozen and twitching, now looked at me. The cows looked at me. I looked again and the hare was gone and the cows had turned away.

A young boy and a long-haired dog walked past on the road after sunrise, alone and complete.

At night, as I walked through villages into suburbs and into the larger town, I saw the lives within the buildings as though they were transparent. I imagined seeing into each life, the hopes and cares and love.

To love the love that loves the love that loves to love.

From Rennes I took a train to Paris. I wrote this account in Paris and this is the end of it.

Thirteen

I want to tell one last part of the story. I learned several things about my rejuvenated body on the way to Paris. It seemed to heal astonishingly faster than the standard issue; took less sleep, less drink, less food; was capable of extended concentration and energy. The manuscript was finished in five days, averaging about twenty thousand words a day. I stayed among the students on *rue Descartes* over a *café*, ate or shopped when the students did. Otherwise, I stayed in a clean little room with a dark wood table and a gable window that looked out on roof lines that could only be Paris and flocks and flocks of pigeons.

I used an earlier model of the Toshiba that killed Ackley. Purchasing it without a passport required a chat with the American Express operator - What was my most recent purchase? Copley Plaza. Two charges.

The machine itself was readily familiar. The French language Microsoft Word took an hour or so to get used to. There were lots of idioms I was unsure of in the command structure.

But it was just typing. All there is to tell is what happened.

As to why.

Forever Man

∞

When I was growing up, the evanescence of life seemed to pluck at me at every turn. The day after he turned and snapped at my teasing, the spaniel I grew up with disappeared behind a story about his taking a vacation with an aunt. My grandmother went to the hospital and the next week there was a large, quiet family gathering where people brought lots of desserts. I ate most of a spice cake and had exceptionally acid indigestion. I never saw her again, either. I do not remember what I was told.

Were the adults trying to protect me with silence and misdirection? It was way too late for that. I knew death was an Eater, hidden and eager. The TV cartoons and Saturday adventure films made it look so dramatic, simple and clean; I could see they were false in most other respects, too.

The next year there was a stillbirth in the family, no funeral. There was never a burial in the walled plot on the property while I lived there.

As I grew, in my own time, I tried to scale the walls around the burying ground. There was an iron gate, locked, that would have been easier to climb but it was in view of the main house. One afternoon when both my parents were in the city, I tried it anyway and dislodged a hornets' nest. I was stung over twenty times on the back, legs and arms before I got to the back door and the gardener turned the hose on me – frantic, twisting and screaming. When I recovered, I concentrated on the back wall, furthest both from observation and the horneted gate.

The walls were rough-dressed, ruddy granite blocks in a regular mortared construction. The first challenge was finding a way to climb on the wall's surface. My Buster Browns were a disaster and afterwards looked it; bare feet were equally ineffective and much more painful; tennis and boat shoes were also flops. Success came with an engineered system based on Converse High Tops liberally coated with carpenter's glue. I think I got the idea from a Batman comic. It left a hell of a mess on the wall and may only have been successful because it was coincident with my actually learning basic hand and foot placement and route finding techniques.

Inside the walls was a quiet, always cool courtyard overhung with grey-barked, deciduous giants in dark red-purple leaf. The mausoleum was set along the West wall, made of the same granite stone in a higher state of finish and polish, names and dates on six of the five foot squares, more blank.

I sat there the afternoon my mother died. I was thirteen. I do not even remember her going away or being told she was sick. She was just not there and then I was told. She would not be buried here; burial would be in Pennsylvania. My father said he would "represent us." This meant I was not to go. Only later, did this seem wrong. My father's reaction had nothing in common with mine. He tried to act stoic and brave, but I could see he was for the first time in his life profoundly confused and uncertain, and afraid. Of course, he expressed nothing to me; and, of course, he did not cry.

Of course, I did.

What I saw was not the particularity of the loss, or the loss of her; but rather it was the loss of the loss - the finality of the separation, the end and the empty center of all hope. And I did not cry for her, please forgive me; I cried for all the loss to come, all that stretched before me, all that I did not know would be and my implicit own, not as a particular tragedy or even sorrow, but as another embodiment of the continuing losses. The awful impermanence now revealed; I cried inconsolably for the enormity of it.

A Gardiner's grave I looked up in Hartford, one adulterous, arrantly dissipated weekend with Petra, read: "Well, sick, dead in one hour's space. Engrave the remembrance of death on thine heart." But I had gotten that message long before. Not for me, Ivan Ilyich's misprision of ontology that let him think he was exempt.

And for years, maybe all my years, I have cringed from hope; prepared to fall through the trap at any time; trusting no one not to leave, leaving before anyone else could.

Of course, all the death songs were mine; the TB-haunted romantics, lugubrious mold lover Poe, World War I poet-casualties, Hemingway, bleak junkie prose of the beats, James Douglas Morrison; ultimately I found the spirit of *nada* everywhere. My senior English thesis proved that the Beatles (pre-Sergeant Pepper, mind you) were nihilists. She loves you, yah, yah yah. So what.

The saddest things I have known all proceed from the instinctive way life persists in hope. When Jayne found the final proof that Petra and I were, well, what we were, she turned to me for comfort and hugging and tears that scoured and etched my soul as I held her and tried to say how I was sorry. A journalist, still among the missing, whom I met at a floating opium den and restaurant in Saigon told me about the time he had to kill two kittens and how the second one sniffed the gun barrel, and then rubbed against it.

Now with what I had been given, found, stumbled onto, there was something new about life that was at once beautiful, awful and commonplace. I saw all human effort—the constant doing and trying, the inability to sit quietly in one's room, the need to act, the explicit assumption of futurity—as a massive act of bravery and a tragic driven instinct: like the Chosen People through reversal and plague and diaspora keeping up the belief that the Covenant was somehow worth the candle. There was the sad grace and dumb beauty of an animal trying to please a viciously cruel and inconstant master.

The figure and ground of my philosophy had reversed. Death did not negate life, life persisted in the face of death. Life believed and loved and tried and helped and nurtured and grew. Death stole and took and frightened and hurt. And people everyday wake up and step forward and try and act and believe and love and nurture and grow, in spite of death.

There seemed to be such heroism in the unstoppable instinct to live.

Life is too good for death.

Ho megas Thanatos tethnakai.

∞

And I kept coming back to the feeling I had for life and humanity on the walk to Rennes. It returned like the golden light that persists when a perfect poem glows again as you touch its memory.

While walking I had seen the land being tended and improved over centuries, millennia for the good of the future, life in usufruct. If the future were open to all, if all would live there, a serious general and individual responsibility is given to all. The future is no longer the frontier, the margin, the edge over which we can throw the garbage, the place where the debts come due for the next generation, somebody else's problem. Would a race of Immortals clean and nurture this planet, limit their numbers to sustain all, or learn enough to leap into space, or evolve beyond the physical to other unknowable, noospheric dimensions?

As I was writing this chronicle, or more correctly in the times when I was not, my mind worried at the question of what I might be about to do. To give the human race what I had learned might be passing along the last item in Pandora's box.

I once read an interview with a man who was Dinetah, which we call Navaho. He had gone to Washington DC on tribal business and a taxi driver had been cruelly rude to him. This man concluded that the heart of the city was bad because a stranger could be cruel to another stranger knowing they would not know anyone in common nor ever see each other again. In his land this would not be possible for they were all the People, descended from the same beginnings, related by family and clan, responsible to themselves and each other forever.

So I teach the Superman.
Man was made to be surpassed.
Now we must all love one another or die.

∞

I never went to the same restaurant or store twice.

The issues that stayed with me as I wrote were the real positive moral function of death. It put a limit to human errors. The worst of men would always die. But perhaps all vicious greedy urges are propelled by flight from death. Would we rape and plunder the planet and each other if we knew we all had to live here together, forever?

I thought about how working dog breeds have been infantilized to emphasize fetching or other youthful behaviors. Would the immortal world lack maturity, everyone about the same age, or younger.

Death was an essential in population control. But Vera said immortals did not breed. Would this mean the end of evolution? Or a new form?

At 10:30 on a Wednesday night, I went down to a print shop at Georges Cuvier Place and stood around with other younger, paler, pimply people. Watched while a black-haired woman in a smock, who had made it clear she did not think I spoke French, loaded in a disk file I gave her titled *Forever Man*. The text fit easily on one High Density disk.

The printing company had a new, German-made, digital high-speed printer. For twenty-five hundred U.S.

dollars hard currency advanced on my VISA card, they imageset, mastered, offset-printed, collated, bound and packaged around three thousand copies. We shipped nine hundred each to Ken, Ana, and Claude-Philippe. Nine hundred bulked out to be a nice, four by four by four, pallet-sized load. Wrapped and banded, it would make a significant logistical impression upon arrival at anyone's home or office.

Finished with the physically engaging task of writing, repressed concerns returned. What was my leverage here? Vera had said they were "awfully hard to kill." How much more was there to learn? What could I prove?

I posted up the whole story to sections of several Minitel Chat Line Bulletin Boards and on CompuServ.

The French government gave the Minitel keyboard-with-screen terminals away in order to create an electronic network. No one gets a telephone directory, dial a Minitel; plane and train schedules and tickets, consumer goods, services, financial transactions, encyclopedias, games, chat lines and bulletin boards for every interest—many delightfully continental. Most would not let me post files larger than 125K, so it tends to be found in groups of four. I remember I used Clea, Justine, Balthazar, and Mount Olive on one adult dateline. I did Oberon, Titania, Puck, and Bottom on a gay bulletin board. Through CompuServ I arranged for a service in California to set up a Web page with the whole file available as Forever Man. Posted a notice that the manuscript was available free to a couple of newsgroups and the CompuServ LITFORUM. Then, while still connected through CompuServ, I posted to the Boston Computer Society BBS.

I had thought about placing an ad in the IHT, maybe something to Ana and Claude-Philippe. *Vera is happy. Are you? Reply: Box XXX.*

No. This was either going to work or not on the straight bluff. Nothing they would say would be trustworthy. I was going to be free or dead. My bet was that as long as I lived, my story was just a story.

I had sent a telecopy of a handwritten note to Claude-Philippe's office. "Hope you enjoyed excess galleys. Hardcover edition follows. Watch Book-of-the-Month Club Selection. Maybe Alternate."

A day later, in the IHT personals, I read "Science fiction. Ana."

The first review was in.

I called Petra from a *Poste* at *Place Madeleine*; calculating the time right, I got her machine.

"Petra. It's Phillip. I'm calling from, um Europe. Please tell Clio it's OK. She can come back to Boston. I'll be in touch. Thanks. Tell her I will see her again, in church."

After I hung up, I remembered that it was her birthday that day. Anniversary of my last sight of her.

I stopped at Richard's *Savannah Café* on my last night. Further caution seemed irrelevant. He let me store the remaining three hundred or so copies in his cooler room. Wrapped in black plastic, they filled a corner between two shelves.

∞

From *l'Université Poste* across from the métro stop, next to the horsemeat shop, I mailed three copies to myself, General Delivery, Crested Butte and one to Lt. Davis of the Boston PD. I carried a boxed copy back to the U.S. with me. I traveled on the fake passport and the TWA return ticket and there was no trouble. I got in just after noon.

At Logan, I went into the Ambassador Club and joined with my last hundred dollar bill. I called Petra, got her machine, left the club number. I shuttled to the Holiday Inn and checked into a $120 dollar room that should have cost thirty-five. Location, location, location.

I slept for four hours and went back to the club. Petra had called. I called her. She was in.

"What is going on, Phillip? Who is this child calling me?"

"She's a friend," I said, strangely unaffected by Petra's jibe. "Would you give her this number when she calls again?"

"That will probably be within the hour. She's very regular, your friend. Very reliable."

"That's nice."

"What is going on?"

"May I tell you later? I don't want to tie up your line."

"Your way or the highway, still."

"Please, can we talk later? Just give her this number. Please."

"Very well, Phillip, once again."

I made another call.

"Homicide. Adams."

"Lieutenant Davis, please."

"He's on nights."

"Tell him Phillip Gardiner called." I spelled it. Tell him I'm back. Do you know if he wants to talk to me?"

"I ain't his wife, his secretary or his partner. So how am I gonna know? What about?"

Shit.

"Just tell him I called and if he has any questions to call me. He has the number."

∞

I stayed in the Club with the other Ambassadors and counted the minutes on the brass Sessions mantel clock set above the nonfunctional marble hearth. Twenty-two.

"Mr. Gardiner. Mr. Phillip Gardiner," an electronic voice paged me.

I took her call in an empty conference room.

"Clio."

"Phillip."

"Everything's okay."

"Are you all right?"

"I'm fine. Have you had any problems?"

"No. Nothing. Where are you?"

"Logan. I believe that everything is clear. I believe there is no more danger. I came back as I said. Where are you? Can I see you?"

She said she was at a friend's in Cambridge.

We arranged to meet at the back gate at Mt. Auburn.

A cab let me off and there were no cars in the lot. Then I saw her off to the left, next to the stone with the door cut in it. She saw me and came half-running towards me.

We met and hugged and felt so good together, so much like coming home. She drew me towards the stone with the opening door.

The sunlight shown through the opening to cast a perfect square of light on the ground despite the extreme angle of the sun; the oblique cut of the door.

"I bet it was better yesterday. The actual date."

I looked at the words and the numbers etched in the metal . The date of death was yesterday, twenty eight years ago.

"Clio," I said as she brought a camera out and began circling the stone and its shadows.

"Here's the story I promised you when I came back."

I laid the boxed copy on the next stone

"Before you read it... I want to ask... would you like to go to Brittany with me in the spring? It might be a little crowded, but I know an out of the way place."

The End

A Note on the Type

The text is set in digitized Janson which admirers of Virginia Tan know was actually the work of a Hungarian named Kis; "an influential and sturdy" Dutch type popular in seventeenth century England.

Books printed and bound by Rose Printing Company.

Next

Vera's Chronicles

Pennycorner Press
Post Box 8
Gilman, CT 06336
Phone (203) 873-3545
Fax (203) 873-1311